THE GUILTY HEART

JULIE PARSONS

THE GUILTY HEART

MACMILLAN

First published 2003 by Macmillan
an imprint of Pan Macmillan Ltd
Pan Macmillan, 20 New Wharf Road, London N1 9RR
Basingstoke and Oxford
Associated companies throughout the world
www.panmacmillan.com

ISBN 0 333 90701 9 (HB)
ISBN 0 333 90704 3 (TPB)

1 3 5 7 9 8 6 4 2

A CIP catalogue record for this book is available from
the British Library.

Typeset by SetSystems Ltd, Saffron Walden, Essex
Printed and bound in Great Britain by
Mackays of Chatham plc, Chatham, Kent

For Liz, my mother,
the best story teller of them all

Acknowledgements

My special thanks to the members of An Garda Siochána who spoke to me about their jobs and their lives; Gemma Holland of the COPINE project; P. J. Lynch and Ursula Mattenburger, who enthused me with their knowledge of paper, brushes, pens and inks; Dave Wall for his knowledge of the urban fox; Selma Harrington and Nasiha Hravçic, who spoke to me about Bosnia before and after the war; Paula O'Riordan and Renée English for their interesting conversations about children; Alison Dye for her faith, hope and unfailing sense of humour; Phil McCarthy, Cecilia McGovern, Renate Ahrens-Kramer, Sheila Barrett and Joan O'Neill for the comments, criticism and fun; Maria Rejt for her insights and Chantal Noel for her support; my husband John Caden for his love.

Grief for sin,
Rends the guilty heart within.

J. S. Bach, St Matthew Passion

The children are always out there. They number in the hundreds of thousands. They are as many and as beautiful as the stars of the Milky Way. Their small faces peep from the brightness of computer screens. They open their mouths and their white teeth shine. Their hair is dark like the night sky. Their hair is fair and golden like the flowers of spring. They are plump and round, well fed and cosseted, with dimples like the imprint of a finger in their cheeks and elbows. They are thin and bony, neglected, half starved, their shoulder blades like stubby angels' wings protruding from their skinny little backs. They stand and sit. They squat and lie down. They offer no resistance. They show little pain. They wait in silence, in the darkness, for the moment when the keyboard is stroked, the mouse is caressed, the comforting purr of the machine brings them to life. They are always there, always waiting, always willing. Always yours.

One

Midsummer, no time to be in New Orleans. Sweat dripping down between Nick's shoulder blades each time he moved away from the cold blast of the air conditioner, and thunderheads building into black towers that loomed over the city every afternoon before crashing to the ground in huge swollen raindrops.

He should have left after Mardi Gras, maybe gone west again to California, back to San Francisco to the woman with the bead shop. She had told him there'd always be a place for him at her table. There would be work for him, designing and illustrating the brochures she sent out to her mail-order customers. She was setting up her own website and he could work on it if he liked. But she was getting too close for his comfort. So he left her and her dark-eyed daughter and came south to the city on the crescent-shaped bend of the Mississippi River.

He should have left after Mardi Gras, but he stayed on. The work was good. He got a job teaching life drawing in the art school at Tulane University. And, from a card on the noticeboard in the college, a room in a dilapidated wooden shotgun house on Esplanade, just outside the French Quarter. He could make his home here, he thought. At last an American city where he could walk with comfort and ease. Down the straight streets of the Quarter, catching glimpses through latticed gates of courtyards cool with heavy green foliage. Along the river bank, the levees ten feet or more above the city's red-tiled roofs. Wandering through the tree-lined avenues of the Garden District, the huge, decorated facades of the houses at one and the same time welcoming and forbidding. Or catching the streetcar to ride down St Charles Avenue, a gaggle of tourists, videos clamped to their eye sockets, oohing and aahing at the huge evergreen oaks which hung over the track, grey-green Spanish moss trailing from their branches, as far as the university, across from Audubon Park, its elegant Romanesque buildings laid out among green lawns and gardens.

An art school on classical lines, he had thought, as he greeted his class of freshman students that first day. None of this conceptual shit or performance carry on. Behind him in the high-ceilinged studio the model had taken her place on the platform, dropping her robe. There was an intake of breath as the kids gazed at her. Not because she was beautiful. She wasn't, but she *was* naked. He had turned to look too. A real woman. White breasts, with large brown nipples, which hung towards her belly and splayed out to rest on her ribcage. Dark hair in her armpits. A stomach that was round and soft with stretch marks like luminous snail trails across her skin. A delicate bloom of varicose veins around the backs of her knees. Feet with calluses on the heels and toes that were distorted and ugly. She would do a good job, he remembered he had thought. Show these kids that not every female body comes airbrushed to perfection, packaged and sanitized ready for their gaze.

'Change,' he had called out to her every two minutes, 'Change' and 'Change' and 'Change'. Like a ringmaster in a circus. Or a ballet master in a Russian studio. And she had obliged him, twisting and turning her torso, lifting her arms and lowering them, leaning first on one leg, then the other. Raising her chin, throwing back her head, crouching, squatting, finally lying curled in a ball, her hands over her face, her knees pulled into her chest, until he had called a halt. Told her to take a rest, while he walked around and looked at the work that the students had done.

They were fun, those classes. Every day of that first semester the experience had changed for them all. He had watched how they developed their tentative scratchings with pencil or charcoal on huge sheets of cartridge paper. Some of those kids really knew how to draw. He was fascinated by their work, the way they saw through the surface of the model's mottled skin, and imbued her with a personality, a character, a nature that was individual and unique to her alone. They had reminded him of the drawings he had done of Susan, his wife, or former wife he supposed she was, years ago, when they were both students. A sunny day in Stephen's Green, exam time. She, with a pile of medical textbooks, showing him drawings of musculature, ligaments, bones, her fingers grasping the pages as if she wanted to dig beneath the surface and take hold of what lay beneath. He, gripping his pencil and glancing quickly at her from time to time, as he transferred her image onto paper. The heavy fall of pale hair, the smooth fair skin of her face, neck and arms. The roundness of her body beneath her long dress, patterned with blue and white daisies. Her feet, bare, the toes flexing and curling, animated by a life of their own, as she talked.

Her feet that were Owen's feet. Nick had cupped them in the palm of his hand that first morning when his son came into the world. He had pressed the ridged sole to his mouth, then slipped his index finger beneath the toes, watching them curl around it and grip tightly: as tightly as the child's fingers, like tiny starfishes, gripped his thumb. Then he had walked around the hospital room, while Susan slept, her body slack and empty against the white pillows, whispering to the child, making him promises and pledging his love and loyalty.

There was a series of drawings of Owen's feet somewhere in a cardboard box, probably still in the basement of their home, where he had left them, unless Susan had done what she had threatened. To destroy everything and anything that might remind her of Nick and how he had betrayed her and their child.

Now, late summer, the students still on vacation, he was teaching a class of mature beginners, middle-aged ladies mostly, who had enrolled for a six-week course, mornings only. They had packed up their fancy paints and cleaned their expensive brushes, taken off their flower-print smocks and gone off to lunch, their drawling southern accents echoing down the hall, leaving behind in the studio the faintest hint of perfume and cigarette smoke. Nick stood at his easel, the air conditioner rattling in the window frame and the afternoon sun slanting through the wooden blinds, and began to draw again, this time from memory. The feet, the long skinny legs, the slender torso, the head with its cockscomb of thick short hair. But where was the face? Why no eyes, no mouth, nose, chin, cheeks, forehead? Nothing to fill in the blank space, to form his child once again. To bring him back from wherever it was that he had gone. Nick's hand grasped the stick of charcoal, hesitated, then came to rest on the paper. He pressed down hard. The stick snapped in half, leaving a splattering of black, deep and intense at its centre, across the white surface. He gazed at it then reached out and smoothed it with his fingertip. But still the dark centre remained. Like a hole, an indentation, with around it a halo, a splintering of skin, of tissue, of bone.

He would get drunk tonight. Even now as he stood and tore the paper into four quarters he could taste the beer on the back of his tongue. Jax was the local brand, bitter and strong, the way he liked it. He would take the Freret Street bus to Canal Street, then wander through the Quarter, watching the tourists and stopping off at every bar he came to. He'd go to Bourbon Street, pretend he was there for the first time ever. Ogle the half-naked girls in the windows of the strip clubs. Buy a bunch of carnations from the flower seller on the corner of Iberville Street, and hand them to the first pretty out-of-towner who came his way. Maybe he'd go to Pat O'Brien's and get himself a Hurricane in a tall glass, which he'd carry around for the rest of the night in its protective cardboard box. Or maybe he'd find himself a woman. Not care whether he paid her hard cash or just bought her drink for the night. And end up wrecked, out of his head, in her bed, with a hangover so spectacular that for days afterwards he would think of nothing except how to get rid of it.

It was hot now, mid-afternoon, as he pushed his way from the bus into the crowds on the street. He stopped to buy a bottle of Barq's root beer from a street vendor, tilting back his head to take a long swallow, wiping the dribbles from his chin with the back of his hand. Around him the sun flashed and glittered from shop windows and the roofs and bonnets of the crawling downtown traffic. He stepped from the glare into the shade of an overhanging awning and stood still for a while, taking refuge from the brightness. And saw the sudden flash of lightning, and heard, seconds later, the roll of thunder as a long shadow began to move across the street, and rain poured as if from an upturned bucket. Again and again the thunder sounded, drowning out the noise of the cars, of the heavy bass beat of dance music, of the human sounds of footsteps and chatter. The rivulets of water in the gutter rose above the edge of the footpath, flooding over the road and in towards the shopfront where he sheltered. They swirled around his feet, a stream of foam and debris – paper, cigarette butts, empty cans of Coke, even a half-eaten burger still in its polystyrene box. He stepped back and away. Then, as the deluge began to ease, he moved tentatively out into the open and turned the corner into Bourbon Street.

Two

It was one of those cases that wouldn't go away. No matter how many years passed, still people remembered. The boy who went missing. The distraught parents. The appeals on television. The news reports of the search, the most intensive and thorough ever conducted by the guards in a non-terrorist case. The sightings. Seen in Donegal, seen in Wexford, seen in Belfast, seen in Cork. Seen in Grafton Street eating a McDonald's in the company of a middle-aged man and woman. Seen here, there and everywhere, but never seen. Never seen again.

People still remembered his name. Even ten years afterwards. Owen Cassidy, aged eight. Thick fair hair cut short. Bright blue eyes. Thin build. Wearing a blue anorak, black cords, a red hand-knitted sweater and trainers. Last seen by his best friend Luke Reynolds, crossing the grass in front of Victoria Square, Dun Laoghaire, sometime between two and three on the afternoon of Halloween, 1991.

And what was he doing that day? What every other kid of his age always did at Halloween. Preparing for the bonfire. Gathering firewood, swapping bangers, putting the finishing touches to his costume. Plotting the amount of sweets, money, treats he was going to acquire in his trek from house to house around the local streets and squares that night.

And why was he on his own? Why wasn't he supervised? Why did it take until six-thirty that evening for anyone to notice that he wasn't around and that no one knew where he might be? Well now, that was where it got interesting. Serves them right, people said, nodding their heads sagely over their pints. What can you expect, if you don't know where your kids are? I blame the parents. They seemed like such a lovely couple. But you know, did you hear, what a thing to do, having it off with one of the neighbours while your wife's at work and your kid's gone missing. What a chancer.

Seemed like such a lovely couple. Professionals. She, Susan, a doctor, a cancer specialist in the best children's hospital in the country. He, Nicholas, Nick to his friends, a writer, an illustrator of children's books. 'Award winning' the newspaper articles all called him. And so attractive, both of them. She with her fair hair in a neat coil at the nape of her neck, her skin unlined and her son's blue eyes. And he with his dark hair to his shoulders and fashionably dishevelled, 'rock star good looks' the tabloids said, with his son's thin face and long legs and arms, wearing jeans and a leather jacket and looking half his age.

And then there was the kid's minder. Where was she that afternoon? Well, she was a sad case. Her name was Marianne O'Neill. She was nineteen, nearly twenty. Delicate and pretty. She'd lived with the family for the last two years, but she'd known them for much, much longer. She'd been one of Susan Cassidy's patients, had leukaemia in her early teens, had been treated and cured. Her family had kept in touch with their doctor, and when Marianne wanted to come to Dublin from Galway, she had moved in with the Cassidys as their au pair. It was an arrangement that suited everyone. The O'Neills were happy that their daughter was safe in the big city. The Cassidys were delighted to have someone to take responsibility for their son. So they could get on with their busy lives. She with her sixty-hour working week in the hospital; he with his books and his drawings and his dalliances. A perfect arrangement.

So why was it that, instead of looking after the child as she was paid to do, she spent that afternoon with her boyfriend, Chris Goulding, who lived next door and his sister Róisín and Róisín's boyfriend, Eddie? All hanging out in the Gouldings' basement, getting stoned and drunk and up to all sorts of mischief. While the kid and his friend had gone off, money in their pockets, 'Buy yourself some sweets, go look for firewood, go anywhere, but don't come back until later, do you hear me now, Owen?' Stopping his protestations, his whining, his insistence that he be included, with her words. 'Go away, Owen, I've told you already. I don't want you around this afternoon.'

That afternoon, Halloween, 31 October 1991. When the whole perfect, cosy, neatly constructed edifice came tumbling down. And nothing was ever the same for any of them. Ever again.

Owen Cassidy, the name and the face. What on earth ever happened to him? He couldn't just have disappeared, could he? But he had. Indeed he had.

Three

The bunch of keys was with Nick always. Clipped to his belt when he went out. Lying on the table beside his bed when he was inside. First thing he reached for every morning. Last thing he touched before he rolled over on his side to sleep. The key to the front door of the house he had shared with his wife and son. The key to the basement where he once had his studio. The heavy iron key to the gate in the garden wall. Keys to the garage door and to his and his wife's cars. Often he would hold them up and swing them on their ring from side to side. Then lay them out in front of him and check them off. Call out their name and function. Remind himself again and again of what he had left behind.

Until eventually the women he met and got to know, sometimes grew to love during those long years of being away, eventually they got around to asking him.

'Tell me, Nick, why, what, where?'

Sometimes he would and sometimes he wouldn't. It all depended. On the way they felt, the way they smelt, the way they used their hands, their eyes, and the nature of their smiles. The ones he told would fold him in their arms, cradle him to their breasts, smooth the hair back from his forehead, kiss him gently. Try to make him feel better, not so responsible, assuage his guilt. Until he would push them away, with anger, shouting that they couldn't take it from him, the knowledge, the certainty, the dreadful sense of responsibility. Couldn't make him better with their words and gestures. Most of all couldn't bring his son back to him.

And then they knew that he had said too much. Left himself bare and helpless. And that nothing would ever be the same again. And that now the relationship was over.

And he would move on. To the next town, job, room. The next bedside table on which to lay the keys at night. The next woman who would take pity on him, befriend him, fall in love with him. The next set of questions. Tell me about the keys. What are they for? Tell me, tell me.

Well, you see, years ago I was married and I had a lovely house in a nice street, in a small town. I had a son. His name was Owen. He was small and skinny. He had thick fair hair and bright blue eyes. His front teeth had a gap between them and he had a small scar on his chin from when he fell off his first bicycle and cut himself on the stone pavement. And one day I left him and I went out to see someone. A woman, not my wife. And I thought he would be fine. He was with his friends. He was with his minder. And I didn't care. I wanted to be with her. I didn't even say goodbye. I can't remember what my last words to him were. Except that they were my last words. Because I never saw him again. No one ever saw him again. He disappeared. Something happened. I don't know what it was. But I know it was bad. And now all I have to remind me are the keys to my house. To our house. The house we lived in, Owen and his mother and me. Except that I couldn't live there any longer. So I left. I brought nothing with me but the keys.

Lock the door, Daddy, don't forget.
Lock the door, Daddy, keep out the baddies.
Lock the door, Daddy, we'll be safe, won't we?

The bunch of keys was with him always. The day that Owen went missing it was lying where he had dumped it, along with his loose change and his watch, on the dressing table in Gina Harkin's bedroom. What time had he meant to leave her and go home? Sometime between four and five that afternoon. But he had fallen asleep, his head buried in her pillow, and when he woke he couldn't work out what time it was. Was it the middle of the night, was it the morning? He wanted to stay there, not move, breathing in her warmth, but she roused him with a cup of tea. Told him it was time to go. Handed him his keys, his watch, dribbled the coins from her small hand into his broad palm. Waved at him from behind the dirty glass in her front window. Watched him as he fiddled with the keys, looking for the right one to slip into the lock of his front door. And saw how, before he could, the door was opened. By Susan, home early from work. Earlier than they had expected. Saw how as he stepped over the threshold he held out one hand back towards her, the keys dangling between his fingers, and waved them up and down. Then turned his thumb up, his arm outstretched, the last thing she saw as he disappeared inside. Making her laugh at his daring, his heady foolishness. And thought no more about it, until the police knocked on her door, early the next morning, to ask her.

What had she seen, what did she know, what could she tell them?

About what?

About Owen Cassidy, aged eight. Who had not been seen since early afternoon the day before.

And some days later questioned her, said:

Tell us about Owen Cassidy's father, Nick. Tell us again, Mrs Harkin, can we call you Gina? Tell us. What time did he come here? What time did he leave here? And what, Gina – you don't mind if we call you Gina, do you? – what was he doing for all those hours he was here with you? What exactly was he doing? You're an artist like him, aren't you? Was it business he was taking care of here, or was it pleasure? Which was it, Gina?

And she could not answer them. And neither could he. Could say nothing which would explain, mitigate, defend, excuse.

Could say nothing at all.

Four

How drunk was Nick when he saw the girl first? He wasn't falling down drunk. He was still capable of standing, of getting on and off a bar stool. Of walking as far as the men's toilets. Still able to judge the arc of his cascading pale yellow urine onto the stained tiles of the urinal, his eyes meeting the gaze of the man standing next to him in the smeared mirror that ran the length of the graffiti-scarred wall. Still capable of zipping up his fly, washing his hands, walking back to the bar to order again.

'A pitcher of beer, for my friends here, barman, please, if you would be so good,' with a wave of his hand, indicating the guys who were lined up on either side of him. Drunk enough to focus and to speak, and drunk enough to feel numb and almost happy. As if the world was about to become a good and beautiful place again. If only for a few short moments.

And then he saw the girl. She was up on the rectangular stage that ran along the front of the bar. There'd been girls dancing there all evening. He'd hardly paid any attention to them. The beer was more interesting. A much more potent drug than the bare flesh that was on show. Most of the girls were nothing special. As plain or as pretty as any cross section of the population. Some were small, some tall, some plump, some downright scrawny. Some had breasts that drooped, others had pumped-up silicone with lives of their own. Most gazed over the heads of their audience, jaws rhythmically chewing gum to the beat of the music, half-heartedly fingering their nipples or running a hand down their crotch with nothing more on their mind, he was sure, than what to cook for dinner, or what time the babysitter was leaving.

But it was getting late now. The clientele in the bar had changed. Gone were the out-of-towners with their bulging wallets and their wives waiting for them back at the tour bus. These men who huddled in small groups, their hands constantly busy, fiddling with keys, with cigarettes, with money, were from a different world. As was the girl who now was standing above them on the stage. Nick stepped back to get a better look. Her body was exquisite. Her dancing was expert. His eyes slid up her long legs, across her smooth, round stomach, over her small, dainty, up-turned breasts. Her skin was white. She looked untouched, almost childlike as if she was on the cusp between puberty and adulthood. He raised his glass and took a deep swallow. And looked at her face. A mask covered her features. It was in the shape of some kind of animal. Small ears jutted from the top of her head. Triangular slits framed her eyes, and a pointed snout gave her an air of danger and deceit at odds with the delicate beauty of her body. Nick felt suddenly light-headed as he gazed up at her. His blood sounded in his ears as he watched the way she moved up and down the stage in front of him. A strange kind of silence had fallen over the room. All conversation had ceased. Everyone was watching the girl in the mask. He looked around him, at the other men, their faces upturned. What were they feeling? he wondered.

And then stopped wondering. The girl's masked face loomed down at him. It was at once familiar and strange. In one hand he saw that she now held a whip. A riding crop made of stiff, oiled leather. She dangled it over the crowd, flicking it closer and closer, and then with a sudden movement that made him jerk back with surprise she brought it down hard on her right thigh. Then again on the left one, and turning around she struck herself on her buttocks and lower back. He wanted to leap up beside her and snatch the whip from her hand. But all around him the men had begun to cheer and whoop. Again and again she used the riding crop, sometimes so hard that it made him wince and draw back, other times gently, drawing it across her skin so it left no mark at all. The men pressed forward, barely able to contain their excitement, Nick with them now, calling out for more and more. She leaned towards him, reaching down, holding out the whip, flicking it across his head. He felt the sting on his scalp through his hair and he winced.

And then suddenly, with no warning, the music stopped and she stepped forward and, bending one knee, curtsied formally and with a flourish pulled off her mask, and held it away from her face, dangling it by a strap so it twisted from side to side, a severed head, held up for the delight of the crowd by the executioner. He gazed at it and saw what it was. The face of a fox, its jaws half open, its small pointed teeth in a grin. He raised his eyes from the mask to the girl. Her hair, dyed white blonde, was slicked to her small skull with sweat. She was gasping for breath, a look of elation and triumph on her delicate features. She curtsied again, her back flat and parallel to the stage, one foot pointed forward. The gesture of a ballet dancer not a stripper, he thought, as her head sank almost to the floor and the fox mask dangled within inches of his face. And then he looked at her as she raised her upper body, stretched up to her full height, pushing herself onto the tips of her toes, then turned, jumped down from the stage and disappeared through the throng towards a door at the back of the bar.

'Jesus.' The guy standing next to Nick lifted his drink. 'What do you make of that? A helluva piece of pussy.' He swallowed the rest of his drink and gestured to Nick's glass. 'How about it, bud? Same again?'

But Nick didn't answer. He could taste the sour tang of beer and bile on the back of his throat, his stomach heaving with nausea, and a slick sweat of self-disgust filling his nostrils with its stench. The girl's face was suddenly so clear to him now in the gloom of the crowded smoky bar. It was Róisín Goulding, the girl from next door. Sister of Chris, daughter of Brian and Hilary. Much older than Owen, she and her brother. He was twenty-one, she was nineteen. Friends with Marianne O'Neill, Owen's minder. Always in and out of the house. And Owen was always with them too. Tagging along in their wake. Listening to their music. Coming home full of stories. What they'd done, where they'd gone, who they'd met. Begging to be allowed to stay out with them, late at night when they hid in the Gouldings' garden shed to watch the fox, the vixen, that came into the garden. With her new cubs. Creeping out onto the lawn in the moonlight. 'Go on, Owen, you're the smallest, she won't mind you. Go on, Owen, see if she'd feed from your hand, give her a biscuit, a piece of bread.'

As Nick stood at an upstairs window, the light falling in blocks of silvery blue across the roofs and trees, and below him on the fair hair of his one and only, his son.

The girl's white-blonde head bobbed past him in the crowd. He began to push through in her wake, shoving people out of his way, stepping on toes, ignoring the protests as glasses of beer slopped. But the door behind which he had seen her disappear was locked. And as he struggled with the handle, twisting it and turning it, then putting his shoulder to the wooden jamb, a security guard with a T-shirt stretched tightly across his barrel chest and swelling biceps, grabbed hold of him, pulling him away, his grip rough and forceful.

'No way, man, no way you get to go in there. Not unless you've paid upfront and the little lady says so. And tonight she said nothing. So you just calm down, go back to your friends, have another beer, or else.' He jabbed at Nick's chest and grinned as Nick staggered backwards, struggling to keep his balance.

'Fuck off, leave me alone, don't you fucking touch me,' Nick said, pulling himself upright, conscious suddenly of the slur in his voice. 'I know her, it's OK. She'll want to see me. I know she will. I'm telling you, just let me in. Hey,' he stepped forward again, squaring up his shoulders, 'Aren't you listening to me, arsehole?' Then stepped back again quickly as the bouncer held a warning finger to his lips, then hefted a heavy black cosh from one hand to the other.

'Now, now, we don't wanna hear talk like that in a nice place like this, sir. She doesn't want to see you, she don't want to see anyone who hasn't paid. I asked you nicely first time, fella. If I have to ask you again, second time won't be so nice. So just take yourself off, go back to the bar, get yourself a drink, then go home. Or I'll put it to you like this. The Charity Hospital is just a couple of blocks away on Tulane Avenue. They treat people real nice in there. Even arseholes like you.'

Iberville, Bienville, Conti, St Louis, Toulouse, St Ann, Dumaine, St Philip. He counted off the names of the cross streets as he followed the girl from the back door of the bar. She moved quickly and without fear through the late-night revellers who milled around the streets, drinking from bottles in brown bags, shouting out to each other and any woman who happened to pass by. But, without her mask and dressed in a pair of jeans and a nondescript T-shirt, she looked like nothing out of the ordinary as she walked quickly ahead of him. At the corner of Ursulines and Bourbon she turned left towards Royal Street and he turned too, hearing in the sudden quiet the sound of the soles of her sandals clicking on the cobbled paving. She turned again, fumbling in her pocket as she stopped outside a door beside a shop window advertising herbal remedies and health food. As she raised her hand, a bunch of keys catching the light from a neon sign, he called out her name.

'Hey, Róisín, it is you, isn't it? Róisín Goulding, from Dublin.'

She turned slowly towards him, her face suddenly anxious.

'Róisín.' He stepped closer. 'Hi, how are you? Remember me?'

In the ten years since he had last seen her, she had hardly

aged at all. Her small pale face still looked as he had remembered it. The kid from next door. The one who barely spoke a word when he bumped into her in her school uniform, or when she came to visit Marianne, and sat in their kitchen drinking coffee or lolling on her bed, reading magazines. They had babysat Owen, she and her older brother, in the days before Marianne. Chris and Róisín, who might have been twins but for the two years between them. The same slight bodies and light brown hair. The same way of staring at the floor as they spoke. Of deflecting the curiosity of others, of keeping outsiders at bay. In fact, if he remembered correctly, Róisín never spoke if she could avoid it. Chris always spoke for her. Answering any questions that might be directed towards her. Anticipating any questions she might want to ask. A real show of big brotherly control.

'Róisín, hey, remember me? Nick Cassidy. From Dublin. Remember?'

But her hand had already shoved the key into the lock and turned it, opened the door and, before he could stop her, slammed it shut, leaving him outside on the street, pressing his face to the grille set into the heavy wood, calling after the figure who disappeared quickly down the dark passage towards the bright light at the far end. As he banged on the door with the flat of his hand, then randomly pushed the row of bells above the line of mailboxes on the wall outside. Waiting for the buzz of the door lock. But there was no response.

He stepped backwards off the pavement and into the middle of the road. It was quiet here now, no traffic. Lights filtered down through blinds and curtains onto the street. He looked up at the long windows and wrought-iron balcony, which jutted out over the footpath. Saw a figure there, standing looking down at him, silhouetted against a beam of buttery yellow. Then saw nothing more as heavy curtains were closed over and all was dark again.

Five

Outside, the moon hung in the black sky. From time to time dark clouds put out its brightness. Inside, Nick lay on his back, his eyes open, watching the glow from the street lights pattern the ceiling. When he had woken first he hadn't been sure where he was. He had been dreaming about home. There was no form or narrative to the dream. He could remember nothing of what had happened or not happened. But he had been there, in that house that once had been his, and now as his eyes flicked around this darkened room its shape was unfamiliar and strange. The windows were in the wrong places. The ceiling was too low. There was no full-length mirror on the wall in front of the bed. And where was Susan? In his dream he knew she had been lying curled up beside him. He could still feel her thighs pressing against his, her breasts and stomach soft against his spine, her hand holding onto his.

He lay still, listening for the sounds of the world outside. What would he hear? The early morning call of a thrush or blue tit? The slow toll of the first bell of the day and the hollow thump of Mrs Morrissey's front door as she banged out of the house two doors down on her way to early morning Mass?

Somewhere out on the river a tugboat hooted. It was a low and mournful sound. He lay still, waiting for an answering call, and heard it in the tone of a second boat a note or two higher. He listened to the two boats' voices across the river's rippled black water. And remembered the foghorn which sounded every winter in Dublin Bay. An insistent lowing, an ugly sound. November weather. Mist in the morning and evening. Stillness and silence, blackness in the dead of night and barely any sun at all, even at midday. The fires of Halloween burning to keep the dark away. The day that Owen had gone missing. Mist in the afternoon and a cold northerly wind. And that night and every other night of that long month of November, lying without sleep, Susan flat on her back beside him, both with their eyes open, watching the clock, listening for the phone and hearing only the sound of the foghorn, bellowing out its ugly cry, regularly, reliably, every twenty seconds. Feeling the cold on their faces, wondering. Where was he? Was he hungry, thirsty, frightened, injured? Was he calling out for them? Was he waiting for them to find him? Reaching out to take Susan's hand, realizing that at last she had fallen asleep, the tears wet on her pillow. Knowing that no sooner had she woken than it would be his turn to sleep. So they would avoid yet again the words that had to be said.

How could you?
How could you leave him like that?
Why didn't you check where he was?
Why didn't you make sure that Marianne was with him?
What were you doing all afternoon, anyway?
Why won't you tell me the truth?

Knowing that the truth would end it for them.

Do you love me?
If you love me, as you say you do, how could you do it?
Don't you want me still?
You don't, do you?

As they lay side by side, not touching, listening to the sound of each other's breath and the moan of the foghorn. Each one crying in turn as the hours passed by.

Now he sat up and switched on the light, unable to bear any longer the images which pressed in upon his eyelids. This room took shape. Small and square. Unadorned white walls and dark wooden floor. A bed, a chair, a wardrobe. A ceiling fan that whirred slowly above. He got up and opened the bag which was lying half packed in the corner. He rummaged inside it and pulled out a large plastic wallet. He reached into it. His hands were filled with photographs. Owen's face stared up at him, newborn, cradled in his mother's arms, his skin so perfect and untouched. He flicked through them, watching as Owen grew and took shape before his eyes. Crawling, standing, taking his first tentative steps. Running, kicking a football, riding his bike, playing with his friend Luke from across the square. His first day at school. Learning to swim, on holidays in their favourite village in Crete, wearing a snorkel and a mask, standing on the edge of the swimming pool, poised to dive, while in the background Susan looked up from her book, the sunlight glancing from the lenses of her dark glasses. Always smiling, showing off the gap in his teeth, his thick fair hair standing up on his head. A winter's day in the garden. Snow cushioning the lawn, and Owen with Marianne and the others. Chris and Róisín and that friend of theirs, Ed. Wasn't that his name? A quiet, shy boy with a slight stammer. And Owen pointing to the tracks in the snow, a regular line of small pawprints, his face suffused with joy, as he points for the camera.

'Look Daddy. Look what was here last night. I saw her from the window. And I was right, you didn't believe me, did you? You thought I was making it up, didn't you? But she was here. The fox was here in our garden. And this proves it.'

Proves it, proves for ever that Owen did exist. For those eight years he was my son, my child, my beloved. And what about after those eight years? Nick pulled another wallet from the bag and spread its contents out on the bed. So many pictures of so many other children. Boys who might have been Owen's age. Boys who could have been Owen. Same hair colour, same eye colour. Same build. Same look. Photographs taken thousands of miles away from the last place that Owen was seen. Months, years afterwards. As Nick travelled, first to London, then to New York, then to Toronto, then to Boston, Washington, Chicago, then to Los Angeles. Then to small towns scattered like handfuls of pebbles across America. Here and there, backwards and forwards. Anywhere the fancy took him. Finally to New Orleans. Midsummer, too hot to be in the city, should have left after Mardi Gras. Should have been anywhere other than here. But it was here he saw the girl in the fox mask. And here, for the first time for years, that he had any connection with everything he had left behind.

Except for his collection of photographs. His pictures of Owen, and the boys who Owen might have become. He pulled a last file from his collection. The most recent batches of photographs he had taken. There was a student who had come to his class. His skin was a light brown, and when he bent forward Nick could see the way that his vertebrae protruded through and above the top of his T-shirt. His hair was cut short and clung to the shape of his head, growing into a point at the nape of his neck like the head of an arrow. Nick knew what he would look like if he took off his clothes. There would be a dusting of fairness over his arms and legs, and at the base of his spine. Nick had watched him. He had wanted to get close to him. The boy's ears were small and shapely, and there was a gap between his two front teeth. As he sat and drew, he jiggled one foot constantly. And from time to time he would put down his pencil and fiddle with the crown of his hair where a few strands stood up.

'Don't do that, Owen. You'll make it worse. Leave it alone and it will flatten down by itself. And stop fidgeting with your foot all the time, you're distracting me. Stay still, for God's sake, will you?'

The boy's name was Ryan. He was eighteen. He lived across the river in Algiers. His mother had a coffee and curio shop. His father was a dentist. His parents had divorced when he was ten. His mother had remarried, then separated again. There were two younger children, girls. Nick had bent over his easel to look at his drawing. He could smell the boy's aftershave. It was aromatic, spicy. As if he needed to shave at all, Nick had thought, noticing the smoothness of the kid's cheeks. He looked at the drawing. The boy was good. His movements were sure and deft. He had a finished study of the model way before the others in the class had even begun. And he had decorated the margin of the paper with birds, animals, fish, in an intricate, interlaced spiral.

'I like it,' Nick said. 'It's like something you'd see in one of those old Celtic manuscripts.'

'Like the Book of Kells,' the boy said.

That's right. Do you know it?'

The boy had nodded, sharpening his pencil with a small knife and blowing the shavings off the page.

'My Mom sells all those things in her shop. Postcards, dishcloths, posters, all decorated with stuff from the book. Her family comes from Ireland. We went there when I was a kid and we went to that college to see it. It was neat. I wanted to go back every day to see the next page. You know.' He turned to look at Nick. 'I told her you were from Dublin and she said any time you're passing you should call in and say hi.'

The boy's hands fiddled with the pencil and a soft yellow rubber, all the time drawing and erasing, sweeping away the crumbs of rubber and graphite. His fingertips were stained and blackened.

'So do you remember much about Dublin? Did you like it?'

But the class had ended and Ryan had stood, packed up his pad and his pencils, moved away, gone off with the other kids who were waiting by the door for him. Suddenly embarrassed by this uncalled-for conversation with the teacher. That weird Irish guy, Nick had heard them call him. He had followed Ryan as he ambled down the corridor, his baggy jeans flopping over his trainers, his baseball cap jammed backwards on his head. He had watched him as he and his friends disappeared through the trees, towards the car park. He had wanted to follow, to see where they went and what they did, wanted to listen in to their chatter, try and learn their language, the language that Owen would have been speaking too. But he had seen the way they moved away from him when he got too close. They had sensed his need. He knew.

He lay back on the bed, the photographs spread out beside him, and clasped his hands behind his head. There had been a period of time when he had been a suspect. It was his own fault, he knew it. He hadn't wanted to tell the police where he had been that afternoon. He had prevaricated, hedged and dodged, then lied. Said he'd been in the city all afternoon. Said he'd been having discussions with a publisher about a new project. Said anything he could to avoid telling the truth. Saw the steady way the guard in charge of the investigation, a superintendent called Matt O'Dwyer, had looked at him. Heard him say that they wanted him to come to the station with them for a formal interrogation. That they were going to arrest him. Could still feel after all this time the clutch of fear in his stomach, and the squirming bile of self-disgust.

'All right, OK. I'll tell you where I was. I have an alibi for the afternoon. You can check it if you want.'

   'The way we checked the others, you mean, Mr Cassidy?'

   'No, no, this time she'll bear it out.'

   'She?'

   'Yes, you bastards. She. Now are you satisfied?'

*

He had got to know them well, these policeman who had taken over the running of their lives. One of them, a young woman, new to the force so she had told Susan, had moved into the house. Her name was Min Sweeney. She was twenty-two. It was she who monitored the phone, fending off the constant stream of calls from the inquisitive, the callous, the vindictive. The people who phoned late at night, spewing obscenities at them. Making suggestions as to where Owen might be and what he might be doing.

'You're on a learning curve, you two,' she said to them.

And she was right. They learned so much during those long months while they waited for something to happen. How kind and thoughtful people could be and the extent of the cruelty that could be visited upon the hapless.

They came to question everything they had once taken for granted. The guards had drawn up a list of suspects. All their neighbours were on it. And everyone with whom Owen had come into contact. His teachers, his classmates, his friends and their parents. Their friends. Their extended family. All were visited, all were questioned. All alibis were tested and challenged. They saw the piles of questionnaires that were filled in by everyone who lived within a mile radius of the house. So much information. Times, places, journeys, visits, visitors. Everyone logged in and out of the area. Surely, they asked each other, it must be possible to find Owen, with so much knowledge.

All the houses in the square were searched. And their gardens. Attics, basements, garden sheds, probes driven down into newly dug herbaceous borders and vegetable patches. Heat-seeking equipment brought in to scan anything suspicious below ground.

'Which do you want,' Susan had said to him one night,

a few weeks later, when they had finished their second bottle of wine and he had begun to pour out the whiskey, 'which do you want, Nicky? A dead child or no child at all?'

'Which do you want?' He stood in front of her the bottle in his hand.

'Well.' She held out her glass to him. 'Well, dead children hold no fear or mystery for me. I see them every day of the week. I've sat with them while they breathed their last breath. I've washed their wasted bodies. I've wrapped them up. I've cut them open to find out why they died. I've handed them over to their mothers. I've watched them be buried. I've mourned them. I've seen the equal amounts of relief and despair with which their deaths have been greeted.'

'So that's your answer?' He sat down beside her and took her hand.

'No, you bastard. It isn't. My answer is that I want my son back. I want him back alive and whole and beautiful and perfect the way he was that morning I left and went to work and left him in your care. Remember, Nicky, remember. Remember that you promised you would look after him. That I would go on working because you would be here at home and you would take responsibility for him. Not Marianne or anyone else. But you. And what did you do? You forced Marianne to look after him, didn't you? She told me she wanted the afternoon off. I said it was all right. But that wasn't good enough for you. You didn't want the responsibility of Owen that day. You wanted something else. So you told Marianne she had to look after him. That was what you were paying her for. But she had her own plans. Just like you. She followed your example. She knew what you were getting up to. So go on, now tell me. Tell me all the details. Was it fun what you were getting up to with that woman that afternoon? As my son's life was being put to an end, did you have an orgasm? Did you have one or more than one? Tell me, tell me. Go on, tell me.'

He gathered together his pictures and carefully placed them back inside their plastic covers. Dawn light was beginning to filter through the blinds. He watched it play across the ceiling. Already it was warm. Soon the heat would be unbearable. He got off the bed and picked up a towel. He opened the door and walked down the passageway to the bathroom. Around him the house was silent. He stepped into the shower and turned on the cold water. He gritted his teeth and let it sluice over his head and down the length of his body. Had the girl, Róisín, made the mask herself? he wondered. They had all made masks that Halloween. Marianne and Chris, Róisín and Eddie. Animals and birds, perfectly constructed out of feathers and papier mâché, painted and decorated with beads and embroidery. They had asked him for help and he had drawn the shapes for them, shown them how to make the papier mâché, given them paints and crayons. Marianne was a cat; Chris a magpie; Róisín was a squirrel; Eddie a badger. And Owen? He was the fox. They'd even made him a tail, a big bushy red brush, to be stitched to the back of his coat. They had tin whistles to play and Owen had a bodhrán to beat.

'And when it gets dark,' Marianne had told him, 'we are going to process from the house to the bonfire. Listen to the tune we've made up. Do you like it?'

He had lain in Gina Harkin's bed all afternoon. There

was a familiar smell of oil paints and the dusty sweetness of pastels and chalks. From time to time he was sure he heard the sound of the music, the thud of the drum. And every now and then a sudden bang as one of the kids tried out their fireworks. He had nuzzled his face into the softness of her breast and breathed slowly and deeply until he slept. Warm and satisfied, peaceful.

Now he stepped out of the shower and towelled himself dry. There was grey among the thick hairs on his chest and when he looked at himself in the mirror the blueprint for an old man looked back at him. Creases across his forehead and between his eyebrows, cross-hatched lines around his eyes and deep grooves on either side of his nose and mouth. He had been thirty-five when he lost Owen. Now he was into his forty-fifth year. The youngest of five children. His father dead for many years, his mother gone too. Three years ago. Suddenly. He had got a letter from her a couple of months before she died. As always she had asked him, first and last, when he was coming home.

I miss you, Nicky, she had written, her handwriting still perfectly legible. *We all miss you. We always talk about you, and wonder how you are. You should come back, you know you should. Your place is here with your family.*

He knew what she really wanted to say.

You should never have left. You ran away. You should have stayed and made your life anew here, where it matters.

She had said it to him the day he went to see her, to tell her he was leaving. It was a cold afternoon and he had knelt at her feet to light the fire. He had broken up pieces of kindling, coaxing sparks from small pieces of coal, feeding the small, thin flame until it needed no further help. Watched the way the updraught sucked the flame towards the dark space of the chimney, the sudden flare of gas, blue, green, yellow against the dark orange of embers, until the heat was so intense that he had sat back against her chair, his head resting against her knee.

'You're making a mistake,' she said to him. 'There's no point leaving, you can't get away from your feelings. They'll follow you. You know that, don't you?'

He didn't answer.

'And what about Susan? What is she to do now?'

'She won't leave, she won't leave the house. She says she has to stay there just in case. Just in case what? I said to her. But she won't listen to me.'

'Just in case what?' he had screamed at her. 'Who are you kidding? He's not going to come back. He's gone for ever. You know that. I know that. The police know that. Everyone fucking knows that.'

'Do they?' She had sat still, looking up at him. 'I don't. I'm waiting for my child. I will wait for ever if I have to. And if you loved him the way you say you do, you'd wait too, with me.'

He had seen the posters all over the French Quarter. The Foxy Lady they called her. She must be all of twenty-eight now. And Owen would be eighteen. The eleven hundred block of Royal Street, that's where she lived. He stood across the road and looked up at the shuttered windows and wrought-iron balcony. What path had she taken, he wondered, that had brought her here, all those thousands of miles from that quiet, comfortable street in Dublin? He would be waiting for her when she left for the club this evening. And this time she would talk to him. And together they would go back all those years to that afternoon. Halloween, 1991. The bonfire, the masks, the costumes, the anticipation. And all those questions, asked but still unanswered. He took a deep breath and braced himself against the pain of the memory, still so overwhelming that it knocked the wind from his body.

'Owen,' he whispered. 'Owen I'm coming to find you. Wait for me, wherever you are. Because soon I'll be with you. Remember that, my child. Remember that I love you still and I want you to be with me. Remember that, Owen, because I'm on my way.'

Six

It was Susan who had chosen the house. Number 26 Victoria Square. She had gone to see it one Saturday just before Owen turned two. It had been on the market for months. She could see why. It was dirty, neglected. A rabbit warren of bedsits carved out of the once grand, high-ceilinged rooms. But she could also see through the plaster-board partitions to its original graceful proportions. And when she raised her eyes she could see that the beautiful egg and dart plasterwork of the cornices was still intact.

She had phoned Nick immediately.

'I want it,' she said. 'We need to get out of that flat. We can't go on living in the city with a child. I know you don't want to live in the suburbs, but we're going to have to move sooner or later. So I'm going to make an offer on it. It needs work, but we can do it together slowly. We can take our time. Make it perfect. Make a real home out of it. After all, we're only going to do it once. Aren't we?'

And he had grunted something noncommittal. And thought. She means me, when she says we. She never has any time. And sighed and said, 'All right, if that's what you want, go ahead.'

But he had to admit that he was pleased once the deal was done. Victoria Square was one of the squares, terraces and gardens that had been laid out in a hopscotch fashion between the Dublin mountains and the Irish sea. The houses had all been built in the last quarter of the nineteenth century. They were three storeys high, with long, narrow back gardens leading out onto a network of lanes and mews where once horses had been stabled and grooms had lived.

The Cassidys moved in when Owen was two and a half. It was April. Springtime. Warm and sunny during the day, but cold and damp at night. They camped in the front room. They cooked on a primus stove and washed in a tin bath in front of the roaring fire that Nick built and tended every evening as darkness closed in around them. Susan always remembered those first few months. She had been very happy. Owen was so easy. He played and smiled and chatted nonstop. He scrambled up and down the long staircases, and never fell. He loved the back garden. He rolled around in the long straggling grass. And he watched while Nick stripped wallpaper and paint. And demolished the partitions. And badgered plumbers and electricians, carpenters and painters. Every day when she came home from the hospital he would show her what had been done while she had been away from them. And Owen would take her on the guided tour. 'Look Mama, look what Dada did,' he would crow. And she would stand with her arms around both of them, and kiss them and tell them how much she loved them. How happy she was in this, their new home. And how they would always live here together. The three of them. For ever and ever. Amen.

Now, when she opened the door after her long day's work, she paused on the threshold. And listened. And waited. For Nick's welcoming shout.

Hi, how are you? You're home. Wait till I tell you.

And the sound of Owen's feet, running across the bare

sanded boards. *Mummy, Mummy, guess what I did today. Guess what happened to me.*

It was stupid. She knew that. She had tried not to. She had tried to do what she knew everyone else did when they walked into an empty house. Switch on the lights. Switch off the alarm. Reach down and pick up the post. Walk quickly to the kitchen. Put on the kettle. Sit down. And wait.

For what? What on earth was she waiting for?

Perhaps it was for this. The letter which lay on the doormat along with the rest of the post. A long envelope, the address hand-written. The stamp and postmark American. No name of the sender on the top left-hand corner, or when she turned it over, scrawled across the flap. Coward, she thought as she threw it down on the table. As if I don't know who it's from. As if I can't guess, that the only person who would be writing to me from wherever in America is likely to be him. As if I can't remember all the other letters. The birthday cards, the Christmas cards, the anniversary cards that he sent. Once. Years ago. After he left here. After he ran away from me and Owen and his responsibility to us both.

She sat and looked at the letter. She poured herself a glass of wine and went upstairs to the bathroom. She turned on the taps and closed the shutters. It was dark outside. It was the beginning of October, the month she dreaded. Today there had been nine hours and fifteen minutes of daylight between sunrise and sunset. Tomorrow there would be less. The day after less again. And on the last day of the month, the anniversary of her son's disappearance, there would be the least. The light would go. The darkness would begin to overwhelm her.

She lay back in the bath and closed her eyes. The house was quiet. A relief after the noise of the hospital. No one here to badger her with questions. No one here to demand answers and explanations. No one here to crave her attention, her time, her ability to comfort. No one here at all. Paul would not come tonight. He was working late. He would come tomorrow night and they would talk again.

'Why can't I move in with you?' he would say. 'I love you. I know you love me. Let me share your life. If you won't move out of this house, then let me move in. Please, Susan, it would work. I know it would.'

She pulled herself up and out of the bath and wrapped herself in a towel. Downstairs the letter was waiting. She stood at her bedroom window and looked out at the night sky. The moon was up. It was new and slender. Its light was feeble and fragile. She looked down into the garden. She had spent the last Sunday tidying it, settling it down for its winter hibernation. She had cut back and cut down. She had begun to divide some of the perennials. Cranesbill and chrysanthemum. Campanula and rudbeckia. She had dug down into their fleshy roots and separated mother from offspring. Time to spread them around the beds. Give them room to grow.

Now she dressed quickly. Jeans and a heavy sweater. A pair of comfortable boots, the leather soft and well worn. Downstairs she pulled on her sheepskin jacket and wrapped a scarf around her neck. She took a long beeswax candle and a box of matches from the dresser. She opened the back door. Below her was a flight of wooden stairs which led from the kitchen down into the garden. In summer she would sit out on the top step, and enjoy the sunshine. Her neighbours all did it too. The new couple, the Whelans on the left, who had moved in sometime last July. They would exchange pleasantries. Make small talk. They had three children. Two were teenagers, a boy and a girl. And there was a little one, the youngest, a four-year-old. Just about to start going to school. The same school that Owen had attended. His parents were embarrassed, awkward with her. They didn't want to upset her, hurt her feelings. She tried to put them at ease. Show them it was all right. She could talk about children. She didn't need protecting. But it didn't work. She could see how they avoided her. The way Chris Goulding on the other side avoided her too. Had been nervous and edgy when he told her about the woman he had met and fallen for. She's Bosnian, he said. A refugee. With two kids, he said. They're coming to live with me. It'll be good to have kids on the square again. And she had agreed. Said, of course. She hoped they'd be happy. If there were ever any problems, health problems that is, make sure you give me a call. And he had nodded and smiled, his thin, good-looking face lighting up. The way it used to light up all those years ago when he came to call for Marianne. And he had told her that he had a surprise for them. He was putting up a summer house in the garden. It had been his grandmother's. Her old house had been sold and he was moving it here. So the kids could play in it. Make it their special place. And she had been pleased to see him show compassion and care for these children, not his own.

But there was no one outside in the gardens tonight. Her breath hung in front of her face and her tread left silvery prints in the dew on the grass. She pulled back the bolt on the gate in the high granite wall and stepped out into the lane. It was dark here. No lights, and hardly any sign of life in the houses that backed onto it. She walked quickly out into the tree-lined streets, her hands in her pockets, holding onto the matches and the candle. The houses here were large and detached, set among their own extensive lawns and gardens. Dogs barked as she passed, and she saw the flash of a cat's iridescent eyes from a branch high up in a beech tree. Today was the first day of October. A time of memory, of dread, of fear. A time to think of another death. Another child. A girl this time. Barely fifteen. A girl called Lizzie Anderson, who had died here eighteen years ago in a dilapidated garden shed, strangled, abused, violated.

She walked quickly for fifteen minutes. Then she stopped and looked around. Ahead was a gate. It was padlocked, a thick chain looped around and through the bolt. Behind it in the darkness she could see the outline of the building. She looked down at the ground. Flowers had been left there. Some were withered. Some were fresh. She squatted and struck a match. It flared up and flickered in the night air. She cupped her hand around it and held it to the candle wick. It flickered again, then took hold, burning with a soft, buttery glow. Then she rocked back on her heels and closed her eyes.

'For you, Lizzie. To keep away the darkness at this dreadful time of year. For you, Lizzie, to keep away the fear at this dreadful time of year. For you, Lizzie, to let you know that you are remembered. Now and for always. For ever and ever. And so be it.'

A place to go. A place to mourn when she had no place to mourn her own son. A small scrap of comfort. A sense of belonging. Of being one with others in their grief.

She rocked on her heels, her eyes closed, then stood and

leaned against the granite wall. She would return tomorrow and every day for the rest of the month. It was her duty, her responsibility, her habit. But now it was cold and she was hungry. And the letter was waiting for her. She turned away, turned her back, walked to the end of the road, where the street light cast its orange sheen along a line of parked cars. She shoved her hand into her pocket and pulled out the envelope. She ripped it open. Nick's elegant writing flowed across two sheets of flimsy airmail writing paper. She began to read.

Dearest Susan,

It's been a long time since I've written to you and for that I apologize. I had meant to stay in close contact, but I'm sure you can imagine the reasons why this hasn't been easy. But please believe me when I say that I think of you constantly. In fact, if anything, I've thought more and more of you and about you as the years have passed. And sometimes, Susan, I have felt as if you have been very close, but just beyond arm's reach. It's a strange and disconcerting feeling, but very real all the same.

She lifted her head and looked around her. Then dropped her eyes again to the letter.

I often try to imagine your life in Dublin now. I presume you're still working in the hospital and I know you're still living in our house. I hope that some of the pain has abated, that some of the memories are not as savage as they once were. However, if the experience of your life is anything like mine, then I would guess that the pain is still as present and terrible as ever. And I suppose that's why I'm writing this letter. I want to come home. I want to be at home to mark the tenth year of Owen's passing. I want to be close to where he spent the last days of his life. I want to breathe the same air, feel the same rain and cold, see the same houses, the same faces, the same streets, the same stretch of coast and grey-green sea. To live in the same world as he did in the days before he went.

Can you understand this, Susan? I hope you can. I also hope you can grant me a favour. I want to stay in the house for a while. A few weeks, a couple of months, just enough time for something, I'm not sure what it is, to happen. It won't be peace of mind or contentment, and I have no hope or expectation of solving the mystery, or of finding out finally what took place all those years ago. But perhaps there are questions that need to be asked again, perhaps, with the distance of time and place. And for some reason that I can't quite understand now is the time for me to come back and ask them.

Why this anniversary? you are probably asking yourself. What makes the tenth different from the fourth, the sixth, the eighth or the ninth? Typical, you're probably saying, of the melodramatic bastard to make a big deal about the number ten. And you are probably right. But maybe it's just that ten years is a long time to be away from the place that I still call home. Or maybe it's because I saw someone recently from that world and for some reason it made Victoria Square suddenly very real and alive to me again. You remember Róisín Goulding, of course? Well, I came upon her one night. She's a dancer in a bar here. I didn't recognize her immediately. She's not that mousy little girl who used to hang around the house. Seeing her made me realize just how much time has passed, that I am ten years older now and I don't have for ever to come to terms with the way our lives were devastated by Owen's disappearance. Does this make sense to you? I'm

*not even sure that it makes sense to me. But whatever the
reason, since seeing her all I have been able to think of was
coming home.*

Susan, do this for me. Please.

With love,
Nick

She shivered, a sudden tremor running down her spine. It
had begun to rain, a gentle drenching drizzle, and the
pages between her fingers were damp and spattered with
water. She folded them carefully, returned them to the
envelope and put them in her pocket. She walked back
towards the shadowy outline of the flowers. She stood and
looked down again. The candle by her feet spluttered and
its fragile flame wavered, then died. She squatted again,
lifted it up and lit it. She shielded its golden glow with her
hand until it began to burn brightly. She would wait until
the rain had passed and then she would leave it beside the
flowers. An image to hold in her mind's eye, through the
darkness still to come.

Seven

It was raining too just as the taxi driver dropped Nick and his bags at the end of the square. He shivered in the sudden cold breeze that blew the raindrops against his face. He had forgotten what Irish weather was like. He wasn't dressed for it in his jeans and open-necked shirt and leather jacket.

'Will I take you all the way? It's no bother.' The taxi driver leaned out of the window and looked at him, frowning with concern. But Nick said no, here was fine. He wanted to get a bit of fresh air. He was feeling pretty dodgy after the flight.

'A bit too much of the free airline booze, eh?' the taxi driver said, grinning sympathetically as he fumbled for change. And Nick agreed, as he handed him back the handful of coins, wishing it was that simple.

But it wasn't. He stood on the footpath and waited until the taxi had driven off, its wheels sending up a dirty spray of water as it splashed through a puddle. He looked around him. On the way in from the airport the driver had delivered what Nick was sure was his standard 'introduction to Dublin' spiel. Amazing economic growth, house prices going through the roof, car and mobile-phone ownership the highest per head of the population in the EU. All that familiar poverty and depression supplanted by a 'greed is good' mentality, which dragged in its slipstream an increase in crimes of violence and rampant drug abuse.

'Right,' Nick said a couple of times, followed by 'You don't say' and 'Is that so?' The last thing he wanted was any questions. The kind that begin with, 'Where are you from?' move on to 'Where have you been?' then arrive finally at 'So what brings you back now?' Anything to save him from having to answer the queries which, as he stood shivering, the rain now running down his wrist and dripping off the handle of his bag, he knew he had already asked and failed to answer himself.

His keys were in his pocket. He pulled them out and held them in his hand as he walked slowly past the terrace of houses. He and Owen used to play a game once upon a time. They called it nosy neighbours. Or who's in and who's out. He tried to play it now as he hefted his bag onto his shoulder. Number 2, used to be the Butler family upstairs, and Mickey and Jo Deenihan, the bachelor brothers from Kerry in the basement flat. Butlers out, no car, Mickey and Joe, in, curtains still drawn even though it was nearly five in the afternoon. Number 3, the O'Gradys. In or out? He couldn't tell. There was no longer the sound of a radio coming from their big basement kitchen, or a row of bicycles chained to the front railings. Number 4, divided into five small flats, a floating population of students, always a dustbin overflowing with takeaway containers and beer cans. But not now. Nick stopped to take a look. The scruffy front garden, all dandelions and dock weed, had been transformed into a perfect replica of an eighteenth-century knot garden. Privet hedges, clipped to within millimetres of symmetry, were intertwined and surrounded by a border of lavender, the vestiges of last summer's flowers still clinging on in the grey seed heads which nodded in the wind.

So this was what the taxi driver meant. He could see it now everywhere, in the shiny new cars jostling for parking space by the kerb, in the clean, freshly painted facades of the houses, in the designer interiors he could glimpse through uncurtained bay windows. Where were the sagging nets and dingy blinds, the cracked and crumbling granite front steps, the old ladies – the basement ladies, Owen called them – who lived in dampness and gloom? They used to come out to greet them as they passed by, offering a chocolate biscuit or a piece of home-made Madeira cake. Even the ginger tomcat who howled and spat, resisting all Owen's attempts at friendship, had vanished along with the square's population of sparrows, who once had hopped on stiff legs ahead of them until coaxed into flight by a shout and a wave of Owen's arms.

He paused outside the house where Gina Harkin had lived. There had been no contact between them since those November days. He knew that she and her husband had somehow or other made their peace. They had moved away as soon as the police had cleared them of any suspicion. He didn't know where they'd gone, but he did know that they weren't the only ones to move in the months after Owen's disappearance. Soon there was virtually no one left on the square who had known the child and his parents. It was something of a relief. At least with strangers there need be no pretence, no pathetic attempts at living a normal life. Strangers stared openly and muttered behind their hands as they passed the house. Strangers slowed their steps and even stopped to peer in through the basement's uncurtained windows. Strangers brought their friends around to gawp too and nudged them in the ribs when they bumped into him in the corner shop. Sometimes he just stared right back and took pleasure in their disquiet and embarrassment. Mostly he ignored them.

Now at last he reached their house. He stopped and gazed up at it. It looked unchanged. The door was painted the same canary yellow, the colour he had chosen. The windows were clean, the paintwork around them fresh. The cast-iron railings were rust free and the area in front of the basement was still neatly paved with the cobbles he had found in a skip and carried home, load by load, in a rucksack on his back. But where was the hawthorn tree he had planted on Owen's first birthday? Hawthorns are lucky, he had told Susan. They bring the good fairies. Now its place had been taken by a miniature Japanese maple in a terracotta pot. Its scarlet leaves had begun to drop. They lay in a soft, bright heap on the grey stones.

He put his bag down on the pavement and hitched his computer case higher on his shoulder. He straightened his back. He looked up again, and this time he let his gaze drift to the right to his neighbours. The Gouldings. And saw a face peering over the windowsill from the upstairs window above the door. He stepped back a couple of feet to get a better look. The face belonged to a child, a boy, he could see, with a cockscomb of fair hair. Nick looked up at him and the child stared back. His expression was cold and unresponsive. He held Nick's gaze, his eyes unblinking. Nick stared too and felt tears prick at the back of his eye sockets and the muscles begin to spasm with the effort. And then the child moved away from the window slowly, step by step, showing a slight body wearing a blue sweat-shirt and jeans. He stopped for a moment, still gazing down, then turned quickly and disappeared. And from somewhere inside the house Nick heard the sound of a door slam, as if a gust of wind had suddenly blown in from the garden.

He had seen faces at that window many times before. In the summer the sash would be pushed right up and he remembered that first year, when he and Susan and Owen had just moved in, the Goulding kids hanging over the sill. Often they would spend all day there. And they'd be joined by others from the square. They'd bring out their cassette player and blast the latest teeny-bopper pop at high volume, swigging from litre bottles of Coke and 7 Up and eating popcorn and crisps. Chris would swing his legs from the window, whistling and shouting. A cheeky adolescent, trying out his growing stock of swear words. And Róisín giggling at his side, small, pale, her hair cut in a straight fringe just above her eyebrows. No remnant of that girl in the woman with the fox mask and the whip, the exquisite body and the marks of savagery etched in her skin.

'Won't it be fun,' he had said to Susan as they watched Owen run as fast as he could from one end of the garden to the other, 'when he gets to that age. There are so many kids around here. He will always have friends.' And the thought unspoken between them. Even if you won't have another child. Even if you insist that one is all you'll have. That your work, your life, your duty is to care for others and not your own. That you're doing this only for your husband.

He picked up his bag again and put his left foot on the first of the flight of granite steps which rose up in front of him towards their own front door. He counted them off. One, two, three, four, and he stopped, turned his back to the house and stared out across the square in front of him. Light was beginning to drain away from the sky and a cold wind tugged at the few remaining leaves left on the cherry trees planted at regular intervals inside the railings. In the middle of the muddy grass, wood was piled into a haphazard heap. That time of year again. Coming up to the anniversary of Owen's disappearance. When bonfires were lit across the country, banishing darkness, keeping the winter at arm's length for one night at least.

He looked up again towards the Gouldings' house and saw that the child was back at the window. He lifted his arm and waved. But there was no response. Only the cold, hard stare, the impassive set of the face.

Christ almighty. He turned his face to the leaden sky and felt the rain begin to trickle down his collar. Why had he come back to this god-forsaken place? Why had he opened himself up to all this again? He walked up the five remaining steps. The knocker, the letterbox, the lock, were all polished and shining. As he leaned forward he saw his own face reflected back at him in the oval of metal surrounding the bell. Distorted, swollen, eyes bulging. He cupped his keys in the palm of his hand. He selected one from the bunch and put it to the lock. He pushed, but it would not enter. And as he lifted his hand to press the bell, the door opened and Susan was there. And behind her the house, and within it the remembrances that he had tried to put behind him. Tried and miserably failed.

'Why did you come back?' she said. And inside his head he heard his own voice, tinny and echoing. Saying, I don't know. I don't know anything.

*

It was dark when he woke. He had no idea what time it might be, but he knew it had been long after midnight when he got around to making up the sofa bed in the basement, with the sheets and quilt which Susan had left for him.

'You've a month, that's all, Nick. I'll give you a month here. You can stay downstairs, you can do what you want. All your stuff's still there and all Owen's things are there too. Yours I was just about to throw out. But don't do anything with Owen's. Do you hear me?'

They sat in the kitchen. She had not asked him into the sitting room. She had poured him a glass of wine and pushed the bottle in his direction. She had produced brown bread and some Cheddar cheese, made him a sandwich, but hadn't offered anything else. Her tone was abrupt, her manner cold and circumspect. She made it plain how she felt.

'Look, you made a choice, I made a choice. I chose to stay here. This is my home. You left. I don't know what you've been doing and I don't care. I have my own life now and to be blunt, Nick, you're not part of it and I don't want you to be.'

At least the kitchen hadn't changed. The pine dresser and the units he had built to match still looked good. They were sitting at the table he had bought for a fiver at an auction and sanded and stained. The cutlery was part of a set his mother had given them. Stainless steel from a designer in the north of England. And on the wall there was an etching of Owen as a toddler, which he had framed as a Christmas present for Susan when their son was three. But there were other pictures on the wall too. Holiday photographs pinned to a cork board. Susan, very tanned, wearing shorts and a bikini top, and beside her a small, dark man, sunglasses masking his eyes, bisecting his face. His arm was around her shoulder and she was leaning against him. They were smiling, not at the photographer but at each other. They looked happy, carefree, and very much in love.

'Who's he?' Nick jerked his head in the direction of the photos.

'His name is Paul O'Hara.'

'Do you mind?' Nick picked up the bottle and gestured towards his empty glass.

'Go ahead, help yourself.' The silence was broken by the tinkle of the wine as it splashed into the glass.

'Has it been going on for long?'

'Is it your business?'

'Probably not, but I see no need for you to be so defensive. It's not a trick question.'

'OK, if you want to know. I've known him for the last year and a half. We work together. He's a pathologist at the hospital.'

'So he deals with all your failures, is that right?'

'It's not the way I would choose to describe it, but if you want to put it like that, feel free.' She stood and picked up his plate from the table. She moved towards the sink, then opened the dishwasher and stacked it carefully inside. She closed it, knocking it into place with her knee. She gestured towards the glass-panelled door that led from the kitchen, and took a bunch of keys from the dresser.

'Here. Keys to the back door and to the basement. You can turn on the radiators and warm the place up if you want. I've left you bedlinen and a towel. As I said, Nick, you've a month. After that you'll have to find somewhere else to stay. I don't want you around here for any longer. Now, it's late, I'm up early. Take the bottle down with you, if you like.' She moved away towards the door to the hall and the stairs. 'Oh just one thing. Don't interfere in my life. Stay out of it. Don't get in the way. Don't try anything on. I'm doing you a favour, for old time's sake or some such thing. Don't take advantage. Do you hear me?'

He lay very still, feeling the cold air around his head and neck, listening to the small sounds which filtered through the darkness. Outside the wind blew, sending small draughts of air quivering through the sash windows. Somewhere a door squeaked as it opened and above his head he heard floorboards creak and water pipes shudder as a tap was turned on and then seconds later off again. Music drifted down to him, followed by a burst of what he recognized as radio chatter. And from further away, towards the harbour, the regular toll of the bell for the first Mass of the day.

Now he could hear a voice, Susan's, and another joining in. He heard a laugh, her laugh. He remembered as he listened the way she would gulp for breath as her laugh died away to a giggle, how she would cover her mouth with her hands and close her eyes, her shoulders and breasts shaking. He pulled the quilt up around him, trying to keep out the cold as the sounds from upstairs became louder and more intrusive. Feet traced a measured path from stove to table, to sink, to dresser. Susan would be cooking. She loved breakfast, he remembered. Her favourite meal. Often the only decent meal she'd get all day. In the early days, before they had Owen, he would get up with her, even though mornings were his least favourite time. He would sit hunched up in his dressing gown while she grilled rashers, fried eggs, buttered thick slices of toast, poured mugs of coffee. They had a cat in those days, a sweet-natured tabby, a female who would sit on his shoulder, rubbing her whiskers against his morning stubble and purring loudly. Then, after Susan had gone, after the sound of her footsteps had died away, he would go back to bed, the cat running ahead of him, leaping onto the quilt, curling up in the space Susan had left behind, kneading the bedclothes with outstretched claws, then snuggling into his back, as the two of them drifted off into sleep.

It had been early one morning that Susan had told him she was pregnant. She had thrown up her breakfast, her face a sickly shade of grey, her forehead slick with sweat, as he sat beside her on the edge of the bath and massaged her shoulders.

'I didn't want to tell you until I was sure.' She rested against him. 'But look at this, I got it yesterday.' The black and white image was like something an astronomer might have captured from a deep-space telescope. He stroked the glossy paper with his fingertips.

'Can you see it?' Susan whispered. 'It's our baby.'

The tread of footsteps upstairs was heavier now. The timbre of the voice above him was low. It vibrated with a different frequency from Susan's light tone. Nick stared up at the ceiling. He must have come during the night while Nick was sleeping. To share her bed. And now he was sharing her breakfast. Nick listened again. Taps turned on and off. Then the light and the heavy tread of feet, together along the hall above his head, and the hollow thud of the front door closing. He pushed back his bedcovers and crept to the window. He peered out into the early morning gloom. They were standing outside the gate. Dressed for work. He had a briefcase and a mobile phone in his hand. She was brushing her hair, pulling it back from her face, flipping it into a rubber band. She was laughing. He put one arm around her shoulders and pulled her close. Kissed her on each cheek and then on the mouth. Turned and walked to the car parked in front of the neighbour's gate, while she picked up her bag and fumbled with the lock on her own car. And turned, and just for a moment looked towards the basement windows. And met Nick's gaze. And smiled. And looked away, walked to the car, opened the door, slid inside, slammed it shut.

He stepped back then. He was cold through and through, shivering uncontrollably, his mouth dry and foul. Susan had never looked at him like that before with that curl of her lip, that glance of triumph. She had always been shy and tentative, unsure of her physical presence. But he had seen the way she moved her body towards the man, whose name he knew but could not bring himself to say. She had lifted back her hair and tilted her breasts towards him. She had swung her hips like an adolescent schoolgirl. And he had laughed and kissed her and stroked her. And Nick felt sick at the sight of it.

Róisín had told him. He had waited for her again outside the club and followed her back to the house on Royal Street. And this time he had been quicker, better prepared. Instead of calling out her name he slammed his hand hard against the gate and pushed through behind her.

She showed no surprise.

THE GUILTY HEART

'Come in, why, why don't you?' she said, her voice breathy and with that slight stammer of her childhood. And she turned and walked away from him along the cool, dark passage towards the wooden staircase.

Her apartment upstairs was large and spacious. High ceilings, polished floors, elegant modern furniture. He sat down uninvited on a sofa covered with cream linen. She came out of the kitchen with two bottles of beer, opened. She handed him one. He tilted back his head and took a deep swallow. She sat on a hard-backed chair and stared at him.

'So? To, to what do I owe the honour?'

He wiped his mouth with the back of his hand. The room was cool, the hum from the air conditioner loud. He felt chilled, the sweat on his back suddenly cold. He shrugged his shoulders.

'I saw you in the bar. That's quite an act.'

She smiled. 'Don't tell me you're shocked.' She sipped her beer.

'Shocked? Yes, I am. Not by what you do, but by the fact that it's you doing it.' He paused and looked around him. The room's white walls were bare. 'I would never have expected it. Of you of all people.'

'No? What would you expect?'

He shrugged again.

'You don't know, do you? You don't, don't know anything about me. You never did. I never counted for much in your world, back then, did I?'

He looked down at the floor. He tried to remember.

'I was just the girl you'd ask to babysit when you were stuck and you'd no one else. But you didn't know me, did you? Or anything at all about me.'

'Look, I'm sorry.' He put his bottle down on the floor. 'I shouldn't have barged in like this. It's just, when I saw you in the bar, when I realized who it was in that mask, well, all I could think about was Owen. And the way it used to be. Before.'

'Before?'

'You know, Róisín, you know what I'm talking about.'

'Yeah, I know. Before, before your wife discovered what kind of person you really were.' She smiled at him and her small face lit up. 'Poor Susan. She was such a good person. So kind to us. And you were knocking off that slag from up the square. Gina, wasn't that her name? She was an artist, wasn't she? Like you. We all knew about you two. We used to watch you with her. From the lane at the back of the houses. It was such a laugh. Even Marianne, who was your greatest fan, who wouldn't believe it of you, even she was dis-disgusted.' She crossed her legs and leaned forward. 'But now, Nick, you'll be pleased to know that Susan is happy. I have it on good authority. So you can rest easy in your bed. Because she does.'

He stared at her.

'Your wife,' she said, her lip curling away from her small white teeth, 'has a boyfriend. Did you know that? She has him living in the house. Your house.' She paused and looked up at him. 'You look surprised. Did you not think she'd get lonely and want someone else in her life? Well' – she lifted her glass and saluted him – 'she has now.'

He stood up. He moved towards the door.

'Oh dear.' She leaned back in her chair. 'Going already? That's a shame. I thought you wanted to wander, to wander down memory lane a bit longer. Reminisce about your lost boy. Question me again about that day, that afternoon. But you don't, no? Shame, what a shame. Not that there's anything I can tell you that you don't already know.'

He stopped and looked back at her.

She lifted her beer bottle and waved it in his direction.

'You did the right thing. Leaving, that is. No point in hanging around. I followed your example. I left too. This is the place to be, don't you think? The land of opportunity, the streets paved with gold.' She stood up and moved towards him. She reached out and placed her hand on his chest, just over his heart. 'But you don't have to go, to go now, I'm on my own tonight. Why don't you stay here with me?' She began to undo the buttons on his shirt. He could feel the coolness of her skin against his. But when he looked down at her, a child's face looked back up at him. A child with dull green eyes and mouse-coloured hair. He pulled away quickly. He did not speak. He began to move towards the door. She followed him.

'Oh dear.' Róisín hung her head with an expression of mock sorrow. 'Oh dear, not your type. Oh well.' She raised her bottle and saluted him. 'Just remember, pieces of eight, pieces of eight.' She laughed loudly, a raucous incongruous sound. He stopped and turned back.

'Don't you remember, Nicky, pieces of eight? Don't you remember that old book of yours? *Treasure Island* or something, wasn't it? Long John Silver and the parrot on his shoulder. We all used to be the parrot.' She put her head to one side and flapped her arms like wings, then hopped from one foot to the other and shrieked. 'Pieces of eight, pieces of eight.'

Nick turned away. He could find nothing more to say. No words would come. He opened the door and walked out onto the landing. Water trickled gently from a small fountain in the patio below. The sound was like a child's toy xylophone. He took the stairs two at a time and hurried out into the wet warmth of the street. And when he looked up at the windows he saw her small, slight silhouette.

Still hot there in that town by the river. Hot and humid, sticky, right through September and into October. Even though the ladies of the town took their fur coats out of storage. But as he walked those streets all he felt was the cold of an Irish autumn. Felt the rain on his face, and heard the rustle of fallen leaves beneath his feet. And the sun's light slanted at a low angle to the earth as the evenings crept further back into the day.

He was cold now, here in this familiar room, in this house he knew so well. Chilled to the bone and over-whelmed with sleep. His eyelids were beginning to close, his body to droop. He turned to the bed and pulled the quilt up over his shoulders. He buried his face in the pillow. The breath flowed from his mouth and darkness closed over his head. He slept.

Eight

It was one of those cases that wouldn't go away. No matter how many years passed, still people remembered. The eight-year-old boy, his parents, such a nice couple, weren't they? And what happened, what really happened that afternoon, that Halloween?

There's an exhibits room, a storeroom really, in the basement of the headquarters for the Dublin metropolitan region in Harcourt Square. It's there that everything that was collected during the Owen Cassidy investigation is kept. There's a massive amount of stuff. Five filing cabinets filled with statements and questionnaires. Sheafs of photographs taken: of houses, cars, streets, lanes, open spaces, derelict sites, public buildings, churches. And a hundred-page report written by Superintendent Matt O'Dwyer, detailing everything that had taken place since the time that Susan Cassidy phoned the Garda station at six-thirty that evening until the eventual scaling down of the investigation six months later. The report included a description of the four teams into which the guards were divided. The questionnaire team, the search team, the enquiry team and the office team. It told in clear narrative form what had happened and when. A number of appendices supplied supplementary information: the list of areas, schools and checkpoints where questionnaire forms were completed; all the alleged sightings with dates and locations; all the places searched; the possible involvement of sects, religious or otherwise. And then there were the diviners, the clairvoyants, the soothsayers, the dowsers and the dreamers, who also volunteered their opinions. Statements were taken from them, and each was treated on its merits. In all, there was a total of four hundred and twenty statements. However, the report concluded that despite the hundreds of man-hours and the massive amount of media attention which the case had received, there was still no real clue as to what had happened to the child.

Then there was the list of suspects. It was simultaneously huge and tiny. Everyone and no one was on it, from the child's father and mother to the retired postman who manned the school's pedestrian crossing. If only there had been a crime scene, it would have made everything so much more straightforward. At times it seemed as if the whole coastal strip from Dublin to Bray, fifteen miles to the south, was the crime scene. But even limiting it to that huge area could be considered a mistake. Who knows where the child might be and, if a crime had been committed, and it was hard to believe that one hadn't, where that might have taken place.

The list of suspects? Men were at the top of it. They had targeted all the men and boys in a mile radius of the house. There was a map somewhere rolled up in the exhibits room. It was huge, eight feet by four. It was the street map of Dun Laoghaire enlarged. They had taped it to the wall of the incident room. The occupants of each house were listed, with sex and age. They went after the men. One by one. Soon every one of them was as familiar to the team as their own families. They knew all their good points and all their bad ones too. They'd found out a lot in those weeks of questions. Who was having it off with whom. Who was gay and hadn't come out to their wives. Whose businesses were going badly. Who was creaming it off the top and putting it in a separate bank account. A lot of confessing was done by a lot of people who seemed on face value as if they had nothing secret at all in their ordered suburban lives. One of the team, an enthusiastic rookie, the same Min Sweeney who'd stayed in the Cassidys' house, had taken it upon herself to make up a grid. She had drawn up a calendar of events for that day and the subsequent week and slotted every single person on the map into it. It was very impressive. It looked really good.

But none of it shed any light on what had happened to Owen Cassidy.

Two of the team, older men this time, had the unenviable task of discussing with the husband of Gina Harkin the nature and frequency of Nick Cassidy's visits to her house. For one brief, happy moment they had thought that perhaps the child's disappearance might be linked to the affair. It might be a revenge kind of thing, a tit for tat. But it didn't seem likely. Her husband was an actor. TV commercials, and a part in a popular soap. A heavy drinker by the look of him. And a casual attitude to his wife's infidelities. Not surprising as he'd had a few of his own, he told them.

They also found out that Gina was not the first of Cassidy's extra-maritals. How was it all the local women described him? Min was sent to talk to them.

He was lovely, he was sweet, he had such a good sense

of humour, he was so sensitive. He was a great father to Owen.

'He was,' one woman said, 'just like one of the mothers. Just like one of us.'

And it was fun the way he joined in with everything. He did the school run, he helped out at the school fête, the sports days. He'd always be available to look after a child if a mother was ill or something suddenly came up. He was so nice, that was what they all said. And a number of them, three to be exact, when pressed, stated that, yes, their relationship with Nick had been more than just platonic.

'Of course,' they had all said, 'things have changed a bit since Marianne came to live with the Cassidys.'

'Changed? In what way? Was there something going on between Cassidy and the girl? Is that what you mean?' Min Sweeney had asked each of them.

Oh no, they didn't mean that. No, he was very paternal towards her. No, there was nothing like that about it. It was just, well, he wasn't around in the way he had been. The girl brought Owen to school in the morning and picked him up in the afternoon. It was the girl they liaised with about visits and sleepovers and trips to the seaside. Not Nick any longer. And they missed that.

'So who was she, this childminder? Where did they get her? From an ad in the paper, from an agency?'

Oh no, it was nothing like that. They thought that the impetus for it had come from Marianne's mother. Apparently the girl, who was eighteen or so, had wanted to come to Dublin and there were concerns about her ability to cope on her own.

'Because, you know,' they said, 'she'd been so ill when

she was younger. Leukaemia or something like, it was, and she'd been a patient of Susan Cassidy's for years really, in and out of hospital, and they'd all got very close. The parents used to come and stay with Susan and Nick when she was in hospital. It was that kind of relationship. The father was a painter, or a sculptor. Something arty, anyway.'

'And tell me,' Min had wanted to know, 'did the child's mother not spend time at home with him? Was she always so dedicated to her job?'

'Oh, absolutely,' was the answer that she got from everyone. 'Ever since we can remember Susan always put work first.'

'And Nick told me,' someone else said, 'that they had an arrangement. You see, Nick was really mad keen to have children. But Susan wasn't so sure. You know, she looks really soft and motherly, but she's actually very tough. Well, you'd want to be if you were going to do that job. And she felt, apparently, at least that's what Nick said, that she had made her commitment to the children in hospital and she wasn't so sure that she wanted or needed children of her own.'

'Oh?' Was there something here that might lead them somewhere?

'Oh, don't get me wrong.' A hint of anxiety in the voice, a nervousness in the sudden frown. 'She was, is, I mean, a devoted mother. You can see it in her when she and Owen are together, but . . .' a shrug of the shoulders as the words trailed off.

'So, how come Owen?'

'Well, the way I understand it,' there was a pause while more coffee was poured, 'Nick said that he would be prepared to take the lion's share of day-to-day responsibility for looking after the baby. That he could manage it himself and she wouldn't have to worry. And he did.'

Until Marianne came to stay.

And what of the girl herself? More statements taken. Min Sweeney pressed into service again. She flicked through her pad fluently, reading back her shorthand.

'She's devastated. She loved the child. He loved her. They got on really well. Usually she was quite happy to spend all her time with him, but that day she had made arrangements to spend the afternoon with the kids from next door. Chris and Róisín Goulding and some other friend. But Cassidy had insisted that she mind Owen. He told her he had a meeting with a publisher or something, but she knew he was lying. And she was furious. So she got rid of the kid, her words not mine, gave him some money, told him to get lost with his friend. Then she went off with the others.'

'Went off? Far?'

'No, not far at all. Next door. Basement. Apparently the Goulding kids use it as their own playpen, my words not hers. They listen to music, there's a kitchenette down there where they can cook, they've a few old mattresses and a sofa. Generally they hang out with their friends. Their parents were away for the weekend. So—' She paused and looked at O'Dwyer over the top of her pad.

'Don't tell me, let me guess. Sex, drugs and rock and roll?'

The drugs were cannabis resin. And there was acid too. Apparently Chris always had a ready supply. The sex was true love, Marianne told her, and Chris her first real boyfriend.

'So, do they have alibis or do they not?'

Each one was questioned. Each one confirmed what the others had said. Chris Goulding was initially defensive about the LSD. He admitted to the cannabis, but they could tell he wasn't giving them the full story. A few threats and he caved in, even offered the name of his regular dealer. Róisín Goulding tried to deny the drugs and sex part, then broke down, said her parents would kill her if they found out, and confirmed what had been said by Marianne and Chris. As did Eddie Fallen, a quiet boy with long dark hair and bad acne. Their names and movements were added to the grid.

'Do you dream about Owen Cassidy?' Min Sweeney asked her boss sometime into the third month of the investigation. 'Because I certainly do.'

'Dream about him? I don't think so, but I think about him a lot. And if you mean do I think about him when I'm sleeping, well, I suppose you could call that dreaming.'

They all thought about him when they were sleeping and when they were awake. When they were at work and when they weren't. And even six months later, when the investigation was operating with a fraction of the staff, and even a year, two years, three years and more later, when all that was left was the exhibits room in Harcourt Square and the archives of newspaper cuttings, video and audio tapes, and the memories of the child's family and friends, those who had been involved from the beginning still wondered and waited for the moment when something would change. Something would happen.

Most of them carried on meeting for a long time afterwards. A pint and a sandwich at lunchtime, or more than a few pints on dark winter evenings. They'd got something of a reputation for difference, oddness, notoriety, call it what you will.

'They all fucking fancy themselves,' some would say.

'Not that's there's much to fancy,' others would add. 'After all they didn't get a result, did they?'

So was it a stain or a halo they carried with them from station to station, from shift to shift, from case to case? Maybe both, Min Sweeney always thought. She never mentioned it, never talked about it. She didn't relish the curiosity of others. But it followed her anyway. And every time there was an anniversary some bright spark would be bound to say loudly, 'Hey, you want to talk to Min. She knows all about it.'

But what did she know? At the end of the day all she knew was that the child had gone missing and had never been found. No more or less than the boy's father, whose face, suddenly familiar to her, she saw again for the first time in years, looking through the plate-glass door that led from the public waiting room in her Garda station back to where her office was.

'What does he want?' she asked Hennigan, the duty sergeant, who had come to get her.

He shrugged. 'What do you think he wants? What do we all want?'

'But I can't help him, not now.' She held back, hoping that he hadn't seen her.

'You may think that. I may think that, but the chief says you're to talk to him. He'll remember you. You can get rid of him more quickly and painlessly than any of us, can't you?' And he held open the door for her and stood back to let her pass through.

A stain or a halo? She knew as she looked at Nick

Cassidy's face which it was he would pick. She swallowed hard, walked briskly towards him, held out her hand and said,

'Good afternoon, Mr Cassidy. I understand you want to see me.'

Nine

Loss becomes no one, Min thought as she sat across the desk from Nick Cassidy. She remembered him the way he was the first time they met. He was stunning. Even the lads were impressed. Some of them were obviously jealous. It wasn't just that he was physically handsome, although of course he was. Tall, lean, muscular, with long legs and narrow hips. Bright blue eyes in his thin dark face. Long hair, wavy, parted in the middle and flopping on his shoulders. And a smile that would render you helpless, able to do nothing except smile weakly back at him.

But it was his manner that was special too. He was a really nice man. Charming, of course, although his charm had been stripped away by the grief and a kind of mad frenzy which overtook him in those first few days and weeks of his son's disappearance. But once the charm had gone there was something else which was even better left behind. Depth, warmth, sincerity. Hard to square it with the boyo who had worked his way through all those women without, it seemed, a qualm or a thought for his wife and their husbands.

But he wasn't that man now. He looked bruised and damaged. It wasn't just the lines beneath his eyes and around his mouth, and the streaks of grey in his hair. He was different now, that was plain to see. As I am different, she thought as she looked down at her hands, which fiddled with the piles of paper on her desk. Loss doesn't become me either.

She looked up again and saw that he was staring intently at her.

'You're not listening to me, are you?' His voice was suddenly loud in her small office. 'You know, this may not mean much to you, and to you it may all be neatly filed away under case closed or whatever you call it. But it's extremely important to me and I expect at the very least a bit of courtesy in your response.'

'Hey, hold on a minute.' Stung by the accusation she half rose in her chair. 'Just hold it there, right there. For your information your son's case is not closed. Like all other cases where there has never been a successful prosecution resulting in a conviction, the case is still officially open. The problem is that we have exhausted all possible lines of enquiry, as you yourself know, and until we have any fresh information there's very little we can do about it.' She paused, her hands bracing herself on the desk. Then she sat down again and cleared her throat.

'Look, I remember what you and your wife went through. If you remember, I too was very affected by what happened. If you remember, I was the one who spent most time with the two of you during that period. I know what it was like and, believe me, I and the others who worked on the investigation have never forgotten about it and all of us most fervently desire an end to it all. We're not proud of the fact that we never, at the very least, found your son's body and confirmed his death. We're not proud of that fact at all. And if there was anything we could do to change that we would.'

'So why won't you open the investigation again?'

'As I've just explained to you, the investigation is not closed, it is just inactive and it cannot be activated until there is fresh information or some new piece of evidence upon which we can act.'

'Bullshit.' He stood up. 'I just don't believe that. I just don't believe that you couldn't go back over all the stuff that was collected then. All the statements you took, all the questionnaires you collected. I remember everything you had. I remember the knowledge that you put together about that day and the days afterwards. I refuse to believe that somewhere within it there isn't the key to Owen's disappearance. For Christ's sake, I remember what it was like being questioned by that smarmy bollocks of a sergeant, what was his name? Carroll, O'Carroll, Callaghan, was that it? If he could reduce me to a confessing wreck in the space of half an hour, why couldn't he do it to anyone else?'

'He did and he couldn't.' Her voice rose in exasperation. 'Andy Carolan tried everything, all the tricks he had up his sleeve, but the problem was the only information that you and the others like you coughed up was about what could be described as petty crimes and minor misdemeanours of a moral and ethical kind. We didn't get any substantial confessions and admissions. We didn't even get anything that we thought might lead to any. We got, as you remember, Mr Cassidy, absolutely zero.'

'So.' He sat down again and crossed his legs, taking out a cigarette packet. 'What are you going to do about it?'

'There's no smoking in this building.' She pointed to the sign on the back of the door.

'Oh, for Christ's sake.' He stood up again, shoving the

packet back into his pocket. 'Look, I'm telling you once and for all. Something has to give here, and if you won't make it happen, then I will.'

The door slammed behind him and there was a sudden silence. That smarmy bollocks of a sergeant, that was a typical description of Andy. The suspects he questioned never had a good word to say for him. The first time they met him, if they had been asked, they would have said he was a nice guy, reasonable, understanding, easy to get along with. But there was always a point in the interview when things got out of hand. Andy had described it to her many times. There was that moment when he'd up the ante, change gear, put on the pressure. Stop being Mr Nice Guy and start being a real gobshite.

'You enjoy it. Go on, admit it,' she'd said to him.

And he'd smirked at her, the corners of his mouth turning up and his cheeks suddenly very red and round, like a kid.

'Yep, Min, my sweetheart, I love every minute. It's the best. It's almost as good as, well, you know what.'

He was good, very good, reckoned to be among the handful of the best interrogators in the whole of the force. They missed him after he died. But not half as much as she missed him. She'd worn out all the clichés. The broken heart, the heart scalded, the wooden heart. Truth to tell she had no heart for anything much after Andy died. Or she wouldn't have if she hadn't had the kids to look after. Andy's lucky double was how he described them when the twins were born and he held them, cradled each one in the crook of an elbow looking down at their identical crinkled faces.

'Lucky we had two,' he said. 'Can you imagine the row

over whose father would be the namesake? At least this way we can cover all the bases.'

And they had. The babies were named James Patrick after Andy's father and Joseph Malachy after hers.

'Jim and Joe, that's what we'll call them, short and sweet,' Andy said as he raised his can of Guinness to her the night they brought them home.

They were six now. In senior infants at school. Two years to go before they'd match Owen Cassidy's age. Sometimes she wondered if she'd have had more insight into the Cassidy case if she had been a mother herself at the time. Back then, ten years ago, she'd barely got her badge. She didn't know her arse from her elbow when it came to police work. Every day was a new adventure. Every situation mint. She'd had no experience, no prior knowledge against which to assess the situation. But that's why you had superior officers, Min, she chided herself. You were only a tiny cog in that whole investigation. You were a foot soldier, a form-filler, a slogger. The only reason that you got as close to the action as you did was because you were a woman. And they needed, or thought they needed, a woman, a female as they would put it, to handle the whole thing.

'You go, Min,' they'd say. 'You go and talk to the mother again. She'll find it easier to talk to you.'

Or 'You go, Min. You go and stay the night with them because they're being driven mad by nutcases on the phone. You go and sleep in the house with them. It'll be easier if they have a female about the place, someone who can make tea and answer the door and be polite and kind.' And the other comments unspoken. You're young, you're very pretty with your short, shiny black hair and your big brown eyes and your athlete's figure that looks good in even the crappiest navy blue uniform. God knows what he might say to you if he's feeling bad and he's feeling guilty and he needs a shoulder to cry on.

It was always like that, right from the beginning.

'You go to the domestic violence unit, you get trained to handle the rape cases. You look after all those messy family situations like incest, wife beating, emotional stuff that the lads don't like.'

'But hang on a minute,' she wanted to say. 'I don't want those kinds of job. What about burglary, larceny, assault, murder, for fuck's sake? What about Special Branch? What about the Emergency Response Unit? Why can't I be like everyone else? Why can't I be a real guard?'

And then she had the twins, and even then she managed. She and Andy worked opposite shifts. He did his bit. He loved it. He could talk nappies and bottles and wind and colic and sleepless nights and teething with the best of them. He could cook a meal with a baby on either hip. He could bathe and burp and kiss just as well as she could.

And then he died. No warning. No illness. No nothing. Just the sound of the kids trying to wake up their Daddy as she arrived home after the night shift. When she opened the door to the sitting room, the television and all the lights were still on. And he was lying sideways on the sofa. A bottle of beer open on the table in front of him and a ham sandwich, half eaten, still in his hand. And Jim was looked up at her and saying, 'Dadda's fast asleep, fast asleep.'

But he wasn't fast asleep. He was dead. A brain haemorrhage, the pathologist said. A sudden catastrophic bleed. Nothing to be done. And she knew they were all saying to each other, although not to her, 'Just as well he went when he did. He'd have been no use to man or beast if he'd survived.'

But, she thought, at least I could have said goodbye to him. I could have kissed him and held him close and told him how much I loved him. And his body would have been warm and responsive. Not cold and stiff to my touch as it was when I found him. And maybe I could have nursed him back to life. My love for him could have woken him from his sleep. And when I kissed him he would have opened his eyes and been mine again.

She looked at her watch. It was coming up to lunchtime. She was lucky with her job these days. Managing Matt O'Dwyer's life, taking care of his appointments, his diary, keeping ahead of the posse of demands that landed on a chief superintendent's desk, might not be the most exciting way to spend her days, but at least it gave her time and space with the kids. Although she'd heard rumours, canteen gossip, that there was a view further up the line that it was about time she made a decision. Did she want to go on as a member? Or did she want to make a move into civilian life? She'd get a good job as a PA or office manager. She was bright, computer literate. She understood the nature of large organizations. She could work in the civil service or even private industry. The money might be better. She'd thought about it herself. But there was something about being a guard that she loved. It had been Andy's life. If she left now, she'd be leaving him behind. And she wasn't ready for that. Not yet. And if they told her they were moving her back to shift work, back to the beat, back into uniform, what would she do? She looked at her watch again. If she hurried, she could get home in time to grab a sandwich and a cup of tea with the kids and the au pair.

Or maybe not enough time for the sandwich. But time enough to see how they'd got on at school, to make sure that Jim's cough hadn't got any worse and that Joe had got over his nightmare of the night before. Just enough time to tell them she loved them. To make sure that they were safe. Just enough time to do that.

Ten

Dark nights were the best time to see the fox. Nights with no moon and a fine film of cloud which made the stars seem even more distant and remote than usual. If Susan switched off the lights inside the house and stood at the door from the kitchen and waited, soon the animal would appear. Long nose to the ground, snuffling, hoovering up earthworms, beetles, slugs, grubs, anything it could find in the grass and the overgrown flowerbeds. Then, when it had satisfied itself that nothing had escaped its attention, it would turn tail and head towards the back wall, where the rubbish bins were stored. This was the moment to move, to open the door and close it quietly behind her and, taking one step at a time, ease herself forward.

Of course, this fox, the vixen, that had moved into the garden in the last few years was almost tame. Susan fed it regularly. Kitchen scraps. Bowls of bread and milk to supplement its diet. Somehow she felt she owed it to Owen to look after it. She remembered how he had got so mad with her when she had told him that foxes were just scavenging vermin. That in the countryside, where she had grown up, the farmers welcomed the local hunt.

'You have to keep the population down, Owen,' she said. 'Otherwise the hens and chicks would be annihilated by the fox. They're an awful nuisance. And they're completely savage when they get into a henhouse. You've no idea the mess they make. Feathers and blood all over the place. They kill far more than they can possibly eat. They go crazy.'

But he wasn't convinced by her argument. The fox could do no harm as far as he was concerned. Nick had drawn him a beautiful fox to hang on his wall.

'She's a vixen,' he said to Susan as she was sitting on his bed one night. 'She's the best. Because she can have babies, cubs, that will grow up to be beautiful too. Just like her.'

'And does she have a name?' Susan asked, as she picked a book from his shelf.

'Of course she does. Everything and every person has a name.'

'So what's hers? Tell me.'

He paused, his head on one side, one finger to his mouth in deliberate imitation of his father.

'I think I'll call her Susan after you. Because sometimes Mummy, sweetie pie, when the sun shines on your hair it looks almost red and it's very pretty too.'

And she had leaned down and kissed the top of his head, then tucked him in and lay back on the pillow beside him as she began to read.

'Do you like this one? It's *The Star Child*. It's the one with Daddy's drawings. Do you remember it?' she asked. And he nodded, exaggerating the movement, his small round chin jutting out and up and down.

'Of course I do. It's the story where the baby comes from the sky and the woodcutters rescue him and take him to the nice family who look after him.'

'And do you like the pictures? Do you think your Daddy's clever to draw pictures like that?'

Again the exaggerated nod. And the finger pointing to the drawing of the boy.

'That's me. My Daddy took my face and he put it into a book. Isn't that right?'

'That's right,' she said, then snuggled him to her and began to read. 'Once upon a time two poor Woodcutters were making their way home through a great pine-forest.'

Tonight there was no moon. The sliver of silver that she had seen the night before was covered by dense cloud, so when she made her way down the steps to the garden she held carefully onto the wooden railing and watched where she put her feet. She was expecting Paul in an hour or so. He had said he would come and spend the night again. She knew the reason. He didn't like it that she had let Nick stay in the basement. When she had told him what was in the letter he just grunted in a noncommittal way, muttered something about it not being his business to object, but . . . And when she pressed him, he shrugged and said that he couldn't understand why her husband was coming back now, and anyway why did he want to stay here, in the house? Wouldn't he be better off with one of his sisters?

'That's hardly likely,' she replied. 'They were so furious and upset that he didn't come home when his mother died. I told you about it, didn't I? How they put off burying her for a week while they tried to track him down. How they got in touch with the Irish ambassador in Washington, and all the consulates around the country. You know, I honestly think right up until the moment when they filled in the grave they thought he'd show up.'

'And did you too?' Paul's gaze was direct. She looked away. She didn't answer. Of course she had. Expected any minute that she would see his long, lean figure and his head of dark wavy hair, pushing through the mourners to be at her side.

And now he was here again. She turned towards the house. All the lights were on in the basement. She could see right through from one end to the other. Nick was standing at the cooker. He was stirring something in a large red pot. The table was laid. There was a bottle of wine open and a bunch of flowers in a jar. Supermarket flowers, she thought. Rusty orange chrysanthemums that would last in water for an unnaturally long time. As she watched him, he moved away from the cooker and walked to the far end of the open-plan room. Another set of walls he had demolished back then. By himself with a sledge-hammer. Now he switched on a lamp and perched on the edge of a high stool. His long body hunched over his drawing board. She moved closer to get a better look. He was working. It was the usual mess. Large sheets of paper discarded on the floor, and beside him on a small table an array of pens, pencils, paints, brushes, inks. She moved still closer. The light shone on the white of the paper and on the jar of water in which he swirled his brushes. The smell of paint came rushing back. He always smelt like that, pigment ingrained around his fingernails, no matter how thoroughly he scrubbed his hands. Now he straightened up and squinted at what he had done. Then he stood and stretched, reaching back over his head to pull off his sweater and the white T-shirt underneath. He undressed as he moved towards the small bathroom across from the kitchen, dropping his clothes as he walked. His skin was very brown, apart from a strip of white across his groin and buttocks. She felt the shock of seeing him naked after so long. Involuntarily she put her hands to her eyes and covered them. Then dropped them to her side and stood and looked. Then turned away. Time was passing. She had to go. Lizzie was waiting for her.

It was late when Nick heard the sound from the garden. He couldn't identify it immediately. Perhaps it was the rustle of branches in the wind. Or maybe the scrabble of claws on the granite wall. He got up from his drawing board and walked to the glass doors. He opened them and stepped out. There was a sudden flurry of movement in the back corner where the bins were kept. The scurry of an animal fleeing. A cat maybe, or maybe the fox. He remembered that they were similar in size, the fox much smaller than he had expected. And similar in other ways too. Much more like a cat than a dog. Well able to jump, climb, scramble, slither, crawl, squeeze. Sneak into all kinds of holes, nooks, crannies. He walked quickly across the grass, but whatever had been there was there no longer. Only a scattering of tin cans and a torn plastic bag with the scraps from last night's dinner. He bent down and picked them up, putting them back in the bin and wedging the lid on tightly.

He turned back towards the house. Lights were on in the kitchen upstairs and the small study next to it. Susan was seated at a computer. She was wearing glasses. That was new. She'd never needed them before. They gave her an old-fashioned, scholarly appearance. She looked like a bluestocking, her hair pulled back into a knot at the nape of her neck and an intense frowning expression on her face. He supposed she was working. All those children with all those needs.

'Playing God, that's what you're doing,' he'd said to her on more than one occasion. 'Why don't you just let them die? With dignity and grace. You know they'll die sooner or later. What are they getting out of you and your needles and your drugs and your magic potions?'

'A chance to grow up,' she snapped back at him. 'A few more years with their families. An opportunity to be the ones to benefit from all the new treatments as they come on-stream.'

'Yeah, right,' he had jeered. 'Guinea pigs for your drug company friends. That's what you mean, isn't it?'

And had been sorry immediately that he'd said it. Knew that she was right. Knew that if it was Owen who was ill he would have done anything to pull another day of life out of her magician's hat of treatments.

She looked tired, her shoulders hunched. He would go in to her. Offer to make her tea, or perhaps a drink. They would sit and talk. He would tell her about his life in America. The people he'd met on his travels. He'd try and explain to her again why it was that he had gone. He'd tell her of his grief when eventually he heard that his mother had died. She'd understand. She always understood him. They'd sit together in that small, quiet room, surrounded by her books, lined up neatly on the shelves he had built himself. He'd reach out and take her hand. He'd kiss her, first on the cheek, then on the mouth. She'd put her face close to his. It would be like it once was. He would feel that same rush of emotion. He'd pull her to her feet and lead her out to the stairs, kissing her again, kissing her as they walked slowly up to the bedroom. It would be good. For both of them.

But as he watched he saw the door open. He saw the man she'd called Paul come in. He saw her smile of welcome and the way she reached out to him. He saw him stand behind her, put both hands on her shoulders, then slide them down to cup her breasts. He saw the way she leaned back against him. Smiling. Saw her stand and turn towards him. Saw him undo the buttons of her shirt. Watched him bend his head, pulling away her bra, kissing her skin, pushing up her breasts and taking them in his mouth. Saw that she closed her eyes, let her head fall back so her hair hung free of its band. Saw her reach out over the man's bent head, reach for the heavy curtains, pulling them closed. But not before he had seen the man, Paul, tug at the zip on her skirt, and the way the material began to slide down over her thighs.

He stepped back quickly into the cover of the trees. He turned away and moved to the gate. He opened it and stepped through into the darkness of the lane. He closed the gate behind him and leaned back against it. He felt sick. He shouldn't have looked. No good would come of it. He turned and moved away. The gate to the Gouldings' house stood open. He was surprised. In the old days, the days before, he remembered that Brian Goulding had been obsessed with security. There was barbed wire along the top of the wall and an automatic light that came on when anything, man or beast, broke its beam. The light was still there, but its bulb was shattered and the wire was rusted and broken, trailing carelessly down to the tangle of weeds that crowded up against the base of the wall. He reached out to pull the gate closed. And saw as he did that there was something different now about the garden. There was a building on the place where before Hilary Goulding's vegetable patch had been. He walked towards it. It was wooden with a pitched roof. Square, with windows on three sides and, on the fourth, double doors which stood open.

He stepped up to it and peered inside. A smell of decay filled his nostrils. Dead leaves, and something else perhaps. Perhaps the musty smell of fox. He put his foot on the step and as his weight transferred to the floor it rocked gently. Of course, he knew what it was. He'd had an old aunt who lived in a large house in Blackrock. A spinster aunt. A maiden aunt his mother called her. There was a summer house in her large, beautiful garden. It was made of wood, creosoted black. It was mounted on a pivot. There was a wheel beneath. It could be turned to follow the sun's progress on a hot summer's day. He remembered going for afternoon tea there with his mother. They had sat on canvas deckchairs and every now and then he would be told to put his shoulder to the door and push. And the house would move.

'Enough, enough,' his aunt would call out. 'Leave it there, Nicholas. That's grand.'

Until the sun had moved again. And again he would push. He pushed this one now. But it did not move, just rocked from side to side. Old, he thought, broken, seen better days.

He moved away. Suddenly lights went on. First in the small bedroom at the top of the house. Then on the stairs and landing. The child he had seen before at the window was standing looking out at the garden, the same distant expression on his face. Beside him stood a tall thin woman with short black hair. There was another, younger child in her arms. A girl perhaps. She was crying. The woman began to walk down the stairs. She switched on the light in the kitchen, opened the fridge and took out a carton of milk. She moved to the cupboard, the girl now clinging monkey-style to her hip. She put a mug on the table and began to pour. The boy moved towards it and reached out and grabbed the mug. Milk flowed across the floor. The woman turned on him. Her face held fury within its pinched features. She reached down and grabbed the mug from his hand. He tried to grab it back, but she pushed him hard and he fell. She began to pour the milk again, this time holding the mug high out of the boy's reach. She sat down on a chair and held it to the girl's small mouth, but the boy was having none of it. This time he climbed up onto the table and began to tear at the woman's face with his fingers. And this time she pushed him harder and he fell again, backwards head first. Nick cringed, feeling the pain in his own skull, imagining the crack as the child hit the tiles. He should do something. He should intervene. It wasn't right, that kind of behaviour. But just as he began to move towards the house he saw that now there was another figure in the room. A young man whom he recognized. Hardly changed from all those years ago. When Marianne had been in love with him. When he had been in and out of the house with her. Mugs with the dregs of coffee and ashtrays filled with cigarette butts left on the kitchen table and the sitting-room floor. And the radio tuned into whatever was the favoured rock station of the time. And Marianne's conversation always beginning with 'Chris says', 'Chris thinks', 'Chris wants'.

'She could do with a bit more independence from Chris Goulding,' he remembered he had said to Susan once, and Susan had shrugged and replied along the lines that it wasn't surprising that Marianne would be needy, would look for reassurance.

'After all, she's been through more pain and suffering, more uncertainty, in her young life than many go through in their three-score years and ten. And don't forget, Nick, she's been mollycoddled by her parents, wrapped in cotton wool for years, ever since she left hospital. It'll take her a while to stand on her own two feet. Give her time.'

A small lithe figure. Brown hair which fell over his forehead and dark-rimmed glasses. A mouth which widened into a smile, as he bent down to pick the boy from the floor. Soothing him, comforting him, lifting him up and swinging him around, then sitting him down on his knees, ruffling his cockscomb of hair. Reaching over to take the hand of the woman, then handing her a cigarette and lighting it. Pouring her something from a bottle, vodka maybe, raising a glass, saluting her. Then standing, the child draped over his shoulder and ushering the woman with the girl out ahead of them. Lights off in the kitchen, and on the stairs as all four walked slowly upwards. Lights off in the bedroom at the top of the house. Lights out everywhere. As Nick stood by himself in the dark and felt the cold seep into his body.

Later he sat in front of the stove with a glass of whiskey in his hand. The bottle was at his feet. He listened. There was no sound from the house above. No sound from the street outside. Just the constant low mumble of traffic from the city.

'Owen,' he whispered, the breath of the word warm on his lips. 'Owen,' he said again, this time just a little bit louder, 'Owen, my child where are you? Tell me, tell me now.'

He listened. But there was no reply. Only the familiar, crushing, leaden silence.

Eleven

It would never be dramatic. It would always be painstaking and slow. Only the events being investigated were dramatic, frightening, different. And even they became run of the mill and routine as the years passed. This was how Min had come to think of her work.

In the beginning she had been excited, full of antici-pation. But she had come to see it all so differently.

Andy had spelt it out for her.

'It's about attention to detail,' he had said many times. 'It's about being able to read a statement and read between the lines. It's about being able to break down a statement into jobs. And then breaking down all those subsequent jobs into more jobs. So the net of interest spreads out and out and out, until eventually it catches not just the min-nows and sprats, the crabs and whelks, the seaweed and slime, but the real, live, big fish. The fish that has made it happen. The fish that can be examined, filleted, skinned and fried.'

The call had come to the chief superintendent's office. The canteen gossips had been right. They wanted to move her from her cosy desk job. They wanted her to go to headquarters, to get her hands dirty again. They thought she'd be ideal for the work.

'We need you,' they said. 'We need women members

like you in the front line. You've no idea how the world has changed in the last few years. It's the World-Wide Fucking Web. It's out of control. Or it will be if we can't get a handle on it.'

She said nothing. She didn't want to go.

'We need you,' they said again. 'It's about time you moved on.'

'But why there? Why can't I just go back to the beat? I'd work the streets. I wouldn't mind. Why this?'

'Oh, come on, Min,' they said. 'Where's your ambition, your guts? You were a detective once, before Andy died. You should be using your skills and your ability.'

There was no further argument. She was told to turn up for training.

'To update your computer skills,' they said. 'You'll need it.'

'Oh, for God's sake,' she said, 'I can use a computer. I know my way around the Internet. What do you think I've been doing in the super's office? Polishing my nails?'

Her teacher was young and good-looking. He introduced himself. Conor Hickey, Detective Garda. He had dark hair cut close to his scalp, heavy-lidded grey eyes and a neat gold stud in one ear. She noticed his skin was smooth and sallow, his cheekbones were high and angular and he had a deep indentation in his chin. He waved her to a chair beside him. His long legs sprawled out beneath the desk. He seemed to take up every bit of available space. She sat down gingerly and looked around.

'Where's everyone else?' she asked

He shrugged. 'Busy, out, doing their job.'

She nodded towards his screen. 'So, tell me. What's all this?'

He shoved his chair back on its castors and swivelled from side to side.

'Oh, just a little something I'm working on. The boss told me to bring you up to speed. He said you wouldn't have much of a clue. But he said you'd catch on quick.'

'Right, well.' She sat up straight. 'I'm here. I'm all ears. In fact, I'm all yours. What are we waiting for?'

She tried not to show it, but quickly she was lost. He spoke a language that made little sense. She understood the principles all right. Painstaking, slow, attention to detail. Find the crime, then find the criminal. That was straightforward enough. It was the medium in which the crime was committed. That was the problem.

'Do you have to?' she asked, as he lit up his fifth cigarette in a row.

'Yeah, I do. So what?' He squinted sideways at her through a fog of smoke.

'Here.' She rummaged in her bag and threw a packet of chewing gum on the keyboard. 'Give them a go before I feel the urge to take out a case against you for damages due to passive smoking.'

Not a good start.

'Slow down, slow down,' she found herself shouting at him, her patience exhausted by the way his fingers skipped across the keyboard. Newsgroups. Bulletin boards. Internet relay chat. Direct client to client. Fserves. Listserves. File transmission protocols. 'Explain, explain all this to me.'

He just laughed and clapped her on the back, unwrapped a stick of chewing gum and simultaneously lit another cigarette.

When she got home her clothes and hair stank. She

poured herself a large gin and tonic as she cooked dinner. Fucking little gobshite, who did he think he was?

They ate at the table in the kitchen. The boys were always trying to get her to let them eat in front of the TV, but she insisted they sit down together. What would Andy have done? she always asked herself. Would he have cared? Would he have insisted on some kind of order and structure in their lives? But if Andy had been there the question would never have arisen. Because he was their order and structure.

The au pair was at her evening class. She was a nice girl, Russian. Her name was Vika Petrovna. She was small and very thin with bleached blonde hair and skin the colour of skimmed milk. She was from St Petersburg. Or so she said. Min wondered. But she didn't ask too many questions. She couldn't manage the kids on her own. And childcare was expensive and hard to come by.

The kids ate well. Tonight they had lamb chops, mashed potato, spinach and carrots. And sliced bananas and ice cream for afters. They fought as always. They fought about everything. It wasn't just competition. It was war.

'Stop it.' Her voice was sharp as Jim sneaked the last spoonful from Joe's plate and Joe hit him, a stinging punch to the nose, which brought an outburst of tears.

'Get upstairs and get undressed. It's bathtime.'

You've got to stop wondering, she scolded herself. You've got to stop the 'what if'. 'It's not doing anyone any good, least of all them,' she said out loud as she poured herself another large drink and followed them up to the bathroom. At least they still enjoy this, she thought as she sat on the closed lid of the loo and watched them. Soon they would be too big to fit in together. Already it was a tight squeeze. She turned on the taps and topped up the hot water. They still had their favourite toys. The frog that swam when you pulled the string from its mouth. The tugboat that hooted. Even the old rubber duck that once had a clutch of baby ducks inside its tummy.

'Don't forget what the soap is for, will you?' She stood up. 'Don't forget to wash.' Two wet faces turned towards her, both smiling, mouths open, baby teeth shining white.

And she saw just for a moment what she had seen that afternoon on Conor's computer screen. A boy, the same size as her boys. In a bath, in a bathroom that could have been her bathroom. His mouth was open. But he wasn't smiling. His face was turned towards a man's naked body. The man was kneeling up in the bath beside him. The man's hand was holding the boy's chin. He was guiding his mouth towards him. The boy's eyes gazed frantically towards the camera. His expression was one of panic and absolute fear. But there was no escaping what was to happen. Conor moved the mouse and clicked on the down arrow. The image unfolded. She saw what happened next, and next, and next, and next. She saw it all.

They left headquarters for lunch. Conor wanted to go to the canteen. He patted his stomach thoughtfully as he stubbed out his cigarette.

'You're right,' he said, as he picked up his denim jacket. 'I'm thinking about chips.'

But she insisted they go somewhere else.

'Not a fucking sandwich bar. Christ, spare me,' he groaned as she led the way towards Stephen's Green.

She ignored him and turned off into one of the lanes

that connected Harcourt Street with Camden Street. There was a cafe she remembered run by a couple of gay guys from Cork. Italian food with a few concessions to the local cuisine. She ordered minestrone soup with a mozzarella salad and thick crusty bread. He had lasagne and a side order of chips. She was tempted to go for the half carafe of house red, but the thought of the long afternoon ahead put a stop to that.

'So, go on,' she said through a mouthful of cheese and tomato. 'Tell me all about it. In English this time. Irish even, if you prefer. But in some class of a language I can understand.'

He didn't respond immediately. He continued to shovel food into his mouth with the concentration of a starving orphan. She sipped her soup delicately from the side of her spoon. He speared a thick chip and offered it to her. She shook her head and offered him in return a piece of mozzarella. He shuddered.

'Hate that stuff. Like cheesy chewing gum that you have to swallow instead of spitting out.' He put down his fork and looked at her.

'You were married to Andy Carolan, weren't you?'

She nodded. 'Did you know him?'

'No, not really. I knew who he was. We all knew who he was. We were all very sorry about it. His death, I mean.' He smiled and she found herself smiling back. 'It was a real sickener what happened.'

She nodded with that familiar sense of tears welling up, of her throat closing over.

'There are so many stories about him, aren't there? He must have been involved in practically every big murder case in the last twenty years.'

'Thirty years actually.'

'Yeah, right. He was a class act. Everyone says that.' He finished the chips and wiped his fingers on the large white handkerchief he pulled from his trouser pocket. 'I knew he was married to a member. I'd heard about you. But I somehow thought you'd be, well, different.'

'You mean older, don't you?'

'Yeah, well.' He reached for the cigarette packet, but her stare stopped him. 'Well, he must have been, at least, I dunno, at least . . .' He paused. His voice trailed away.

Stop digging, Conor, she thought, looking at him. Don't make it any worse.

'At least twenty years older than me? Is that it?'

He shrugged, his fingers pleating the check tablecloth

'Actually it was nineteen years and six months. I was thirty-three when he died and he was just two months off fifty-three. If you want to be strictly accurate about it.'

'OK.' He nodded. 'Well, I'm glad we've cleared up that little misunderstanding.' He leaned back in his chair and looked at her. 'They were right about one thing.'

'Right?' She cut across him. She didn't want to hear what was coming next. 'About what?'

'They warned me when they heard you were coming to the unit. They said you were very direct and you didn't take any shit. They said I shouldn't be fooled by your big brown eyes and your smile. They said you were a hard woman.'

'Is that right now?' She pushed away her bowl. 'That's a terrible slur on a woman's good character. It's not an expression I'd use about myself. Difficult, irritable, cranky, bad-tempered. They're more my style. Impatient is another word I'd use. So come on, order us some coffee and tell me what's really going on with all this computer shit. What makes it any different from any other form of criminal activity.'

'Tell me about your sons.' Conor stared hard at her. 'Their age, their interests, their school, their daily life. Tell me about their teachers, the lollipop man who stands outside the gate, their friends, their friends' fathers, their friends' older brothers, the friends of their older brothers. Tell me about your children's uncles, cousins, grandparents. Tell me about the man in the corner shop, the man who delivers the milk, the man who collects the rubbish, the old man who lives in the house next door. Tell me everything, and I will tell you what it all means.'

Min sat and listened.

'Do you have photographs in your house? Pictures of the kids at the beach or playing football. Pictures of them on the swings in the park. Pictures of them in the bath. Pictures of them at a mate's birthday party or on an outing to the zoo. Do you have all these?'

She nodded.

'Well, out there – ', he waved towards the busy street beyond the steamed-up plate-glass windows – 'there are people, men usually, who collect pictures like yours. They have literally hundreds of thousands of such images. They keep them. They store them. They swap them with others. To you they are innocent. They are memories to be cherished. But for them they are something else. They are erotica. They are objects of extreme sexual gratification. They are aids to masturbation. They are stimulation. They are the stuff of life itself.'

He put his hand into his inside pocket and pulled out a plastic wallet.

'We raided a house in Galway the other day. The guy had been passing some of these around. On the Internet, that is. They'd been spotted by a cop in Oklahoma. A mate of mine. He was doing some routine monitoring of a selection of newsgroups that were known to feature paedophilia. He didn't know where they'd originated, but eventually he worked out the game the subjects were playing and he sent the material on to me. One thing led to the other and we found an email address for Mr Connemara. Here, have a look at what we took from his attic.'

She picked the wallet up from the table. It contained photographs of boys playing hurling. And the same boys in the changing room. Boys of twelve, thirteen, she wasn't sure. They were in various stages of undress. Underpants, shorts, vests, socks, T-shirts. They were not naked, although there were a couple of shots of boys wrapped in towels. They were ordinary boys. Irish boys with white bodies. With freckles and spots. With mousy brown hair. They weren't beautiful. They were just boys.

'So?' she shrugged. 'So what? Where's the crime? My house is full of pictures like this. Everyone I know has stuff like this.'

'Really? Boxes and boxes, all with the same subject-matter? All boys between the ages of ten and fourteen. And boxes and boxes of magazines, the kind that were produced in Sweden and Denmark in the sixties. Before there was a crackdown on child porn and it was no longer safe or profitable to publish it. Do you have them too?'

She said nothing.

'He also had stacks of computer disks. When we get back to the office I'll show you what we found on them. We don't print from them. We don't make copies for ourselves or for other police forces. Because we feel that to do that is to exploit the image again. And we won't be party to that.'

She stared at the pictures on the table.

'I don't understand,' she said. 'I don't understand what's going on here. Are you saying that these, whatever they are, these family snaps, are sold? Is that what this is? And if so who's the distributor? Who's the supplier? Who's making money out of it? Where's the profit margin?'

He smiled at her. 'It's funny you should say that. Because until recently I would have said that money didn't count. That none of this was about making money. That most paedophiles are into it for something else. Love they'd call it. But all that's changed recently. Which is good for us. Because now we have another way of tracking people. You know, all the guys who do this, they all have security, they use proxy servers, they're all heavily password protected. It's as much luck as skill that can get you through their defences. So using credit cards is great. It's much harder to disguise a transaction that involves a bank. But it also means that, with the amount of money being generated now, we'll be coming up against not only big business but serious criminals, the finger-in-every-pie sort and that's bad news. Child pornography was never the income generator that adult porn was, but all that is going to change.'

She sat very still, staring down at the tablecloth. She began to sweep the crumbs from her bread into the palm of her hand, then emptied them onto her plate. Then she spoke. 'Love, you say? What do you mean by love?'

He shrugged. 'Well, you might call it obsession. You might call it sick. You might call it evil. But they call it love. And I'm afraid, Min, sometimes it helps your work as a guard to see it in their terms. Only then can you begin to see what you're up against.'

Her boys had a strict bathtime routine. Joe got out first because he was the younger. By six minutes. He sat on Min's knee and she dried him and hugged him and whispered endearments into his ear. Then sent him off to their bedroom to get his pyjamas. Jim lay back, the bath to himself and luxuriated in his older son status. He swished his legs from side to side and stretched his toes down towards the taps. He talked of serious matters. He liked to know about what she had done all day. He wanted to know if she had caught anyone bad.

'Did you, Min?' he asked. 'Did you earn your crust today?'

Andy's phrase.

'I don't know. I don't think so. Not really. You know I've moved now. I'm working in a different unit. It's a special place.'

'Oh.' Jim lay back in the lukewarm water until he was almost submerged. A sticking plaster on his big toe, the adhesive loosened by the soaking, floated just under the surface like a scrap of pink seaweed. 'Is it good? Is it scary?'

'No, of course it isn't.' She leaned over the bath and looked down into his round blue eyes. 'Of course it isn't scary. It's all very safe. Safe as houses. Now.' She reached in and took hold of his hands, standing and pulling him slowly upright. 'Now, mister big boy, time for you to get out.'

They walked back to the office. She listened while Conor talked. She thought she'd never get him to shut up. He told her all about his undercover work.

'Online, that's where I go. None of your hanging round street corners in the rain. This is chat rooms and news-groups. That's my world.'

'But hold on a minute, Conor,' she said. 'None of this is new. There's always been child pornography. When I worked here before years ago I remember we seized all kinds of stuff.'

That was so, he agreed.

'And, if I remember rightly, a lot of it was old even then. The anti-child-porn laws passed in Denmark and Holland in the late seventies put an end to it.'

He agreed. They had. But it was what had happened to the material that was in those books and magazines that was really interesting.

'Oh yeah?'

'Here, pull up your chair. I'll show you.'

She looked at her watch. It was getting late. She'd need to think about facing the rush-hour traffic if she was to get home at any reasonable hour tonight.

They had, he said to her, something like eighty thousand images stored. They were putting together a database.

'What do you mean? What are you talking about?'

'Here.' His hands moved across the keyboard. The screen began to fill up. Thumbnail images. Boys and girls, every age. Babies, infants, toddlers, children of school age, pre-

pubescent kids, and young teenagers, their bodies beginning to show their sexual maturity. She stared, her mouth
dry, her hands wet.

'These children,' she said, 'they're not all different. Look
at this row. They're all the same child.'

'It's a series, that's what they call them. They like to
collect them. Like football cards, or stamps. Do you see this
boy?' The cursor settled on the face of a child whom Min
thought was probably about four or five. His fair hair was
cut very short and he was smiling. He was seated cross-
legged on a shaggy hearthrug in front of an open fire.

'Now,' Conor's hand moved quickly. 'Look at these.'

The screen filled with more and more photographs of the
same child. In spite of herself Min groaned. She pushed
herself back from the desk. She covered her eyes.

'We have five hundred of him. But it's possible there are
many more. Now,' he paused, 'let's look a little more closely.'

Again his hand moved and this time the picture grew so
it filled the monitor's oversized screen. In magnification the
boy's blue eyes were misted over, his features smudged.

'Now, look at this.' Conor moved the cursor again, this
time to the background of the photograph. 'What do you
see?'

Min shifted her gaze from the child to the wall behind
him. It was patterned with paper, with an embossed surface.

'I don't know,' she said, 'it's wallpaper, it's fairly ordinary. I don't know.'

'And what else do you see?'

She shrugged. 'I don't know. What else is there to see?'

He half turned towards her. 'You surprise me. I thought
you were supposed to be good at this kind of thing.'

She was silent.

'Come on, we haven't got all day. Use your eyes, for Christ's sake. What do you see?'

She shrugged again. 'Wallpaper, plug sockets, carpet, there's a picture on the wall too. A country scene. Mountains, sea.'

'That's right, good girl, mountains, sea, bog. And the plug sockets. What are they like? Come on, come on.' He clicked his fingers.

'Three-pin plugs with a switch.'

'Congratulations, girl. You've hit the jackpot. At last a bit of observation. A little bit of police work.'

'So?'

'So that's everything. We have to go on everything that's in the picture. Three-pin plug. So it's British or Irish. Picture on the wall, looks to me like a Connemara scene. Wallpaper, carpet. Vintage seventies. And look at the toy the kid is playing with. I bet neither of your kids plays with an Action Man like that, do they? But maybe your brother or your cousin did, way back then, when this series, the Billy series we call them, when this series of photographs was taken.'

'Billy, why do you call them Billy?'

'I'll show you. Hang on a minute.'

The image changed. It was a birthday party. A cake with six candles. And a name written in pink icing. Happy Birthday Billy it said in a flowing script. This time the child was naked. This time he was not alone on the shaggy rug in front of the fire. And this time the tears were running down his face.

Min stared at the screen. She tried to find her voice. She swallowed hard.

'So,' she said to Conor, 'every picture is a crime scene

and should be analysed thus. For example, three-pin plugs mean Britain or Ireland. Connemara scene on the wall probably narrows it down further. Only a few hundred thousand toys like that one sold. Gets you a long way, doesn't it? I'd say it'd be bound to get you an identification, and get you a result? Isn't that right. Another little notch on your mouse, eh?'

He looked at her, the light from the screen reflecting back from his deep grey eyes.

'Depends what you mean by "result". In fact we did identify the kid. We did a routine search on children at risk between the ages of four and ten, and children who had died from non-natural causes, both here and in Britain. And bingo. Billy O'Reilly popped up. Turned out that his family were Irish, originally from Mayo, emigrated to Manchester in the sixties. Parents split up. Mother was an alcoholic. Father got the kids. Billy, his big sister and his little brother.'

'So, did you get the bollocks?' She gestured towards the picture on the screen. 'Who was he? Father, uncle, parish priest?'

'To answer your first question, we didn't get him. Because we didn't get Billy. Billy is dead. He has been since 1975. He died when he was six, not long after his birthday party. He was killed by a drunk driver as he was crossing the street to the chipper. With no Billy we'd no witness, no accuser. Not enough to go on from the pictures alone. So, what do we have? We don't have a living victim, we have no perpetrator. We just have the pictures. And the pictures will remain. For ever and ever, as long as there are computers, those pictures of Billy will stay out there. And bad bastards like the bad bastard who did those things to that little boy will carry on getting pleasure out of looking at them.'

He began to close down the file, his hands moving rapidly with keyboard and mouse.

'They're famous those pictures. They're the Mona Lisas and the Sistine Chapel of the child-pornography world. They are the penny blacks and holy grail. They are the most sought after, the most coveted. To get copies of those pictures you would have to donate thousands and thousands of other images to the club. And do you know why?'

She shook her head, unable to speak.

'Because Billy is dead and gone. He will never grow up. He will never change from being a special little boy into a great ugly, hulking, hairy, spotty, smelly adolescent. And for the paedophile, the person fixated on the body as it exists before puberty, that makes him the most desirable. And they will do anything to get their hands on him.'

She sat in the darkness and watched the twins as they slept. They still had a night light.

'It's so if I wake up I'll be able to see Daddy sitting on the end of the bed watching over me,' Jim explained to her when she suggested turning it off. 'He might not be able to find us if our light wasn't on. He might not remember which room we sleep in.'

'You're right,' she agreed. 'That's very sensible. You keep the light on for as long as you want.'

She lay down on the bed beside Joe and took his hand in hers. Outside, beyond the curtains and the trees at the end of the garden, she could hear the mutter of passing traffic. A gust of wind rattled the sash windows. Today the streets had been filled with the golden swirl of falling leaves. Soon that brightness would be gone and it would be winter. She lifted her head and looked towards the night light. The shade turned slowly, casting pretty silhouettes across the ceiling. Children playing with bats and balls. A cat jumping, a dog running, its tail streaming out behind its body. Beside her Joe stirred and whimpered, his hands clenching into fists. She stroked his hair and kissed his forehead.

'Shh,' she murmured, her lips against his silky skin. She mouthed the words of the song her mother had always sung to her. On nights when the wind roared in from the sea and the house shook and seemed as if at any moment it might lift up from its foundations and sail off towards the stars.

'V'la l'bon vent,
V'la l'joli vent,
V'la l'bon vent,
Ma mie m'appelle.'

Her voice died away to a whisper as Joe's breathing slowed and he turned on his side, one small hand slipped beneath his cheek. She inched her way carefully to standing and moved towards the door. She closed it behind her, pulling the handle until the latch clicked into place. Next door was her own room and bed. She was tired. She should sleep. But she could not bear the thought of the empty space beside her. She leaned against the wall and closed her eyes. 'Please come back, Andy,' she whispered. 'Please come and look after us. We need you now, more than ever.'

Twelve

It was a small white face which was looking at him through the glass doors from the garden. A boy's face. The face of the boy whom Nick had seen next door, in the Gouldings' house. He stared at Nick, then opened his mouth and breathed hard, so a white mist fogged the glass and he all but disappeared from view.

Nick got up from his drawing board and walked towards him. He squatted down so he was at the same level as the child. Then he too opened his mouth and breathed out. He pulled back from the misted area and put up his finger. He drew quickly, a smiling face. Two eyes, a blob of a nose and a curving arc for the mouth. He waited. The boy's hand moved. And then his index finger. And he too drew. Two eyes, a blob of a nose, and a mouth. But this time the arc curved in the opposite direction. A sad face, not a smiling one, looked in at Nick.

Nick stood up and opened the door. Outside it was bright but cold. The child was dressed in faded red pyjamas. The remains of an embossed Mickey Mouse pattern showed faintly on his chest. His small white feet were bare. It had rained heavily during the night and the grass was still wet. The child's pyjamas were soaked up to his knees and he looked chilled to the bone, his slight body shaken by the shivering tremors which ran through his frame.

'Here.' Nick stood back from the open door and gestured towards the room behind him. 'Come on in. It's much warmer than it is out there.'

He waited for the child to make a move towards the door. But he just stood there staring up at him, clasping and unclasping his hands in an oddly grown-up manner.

'Come on.' Nick swung open the door and bowed from the waist. 'Join me, do.'

Still the child made no movement.

'OK, suit yourself.' Nick walked back into the kitchen, opened the fridge and took out a carton of milk. He poured some into a pan and set it on the cooker. He switched on the kettle and took a packet of ground coffee from the cupboard. He measured it out into a glass jug. He opened the cupboard again and this time found a packet of biscuits. He pulled the wrapper apart and fanned them onto a plate. Their chocolate-covered surfaces gleamed. He hummed loudly as he put out two mugs, poured boiling water onto the coffee, sniffing exaggeratedly, holding his face into the steam.

'Wow, that smells good,' he said as he pushed down the metal plunger and turned to lift the pan of milk from the heat.

'Now, how do you like it? Lots of milk or just a touch?' He paused. 'Or maybe you're too young for coffee. How about drinking chocolate, would that be better?' Again he went to the cupboard. He had bought some yesterday. For old times' sake, really. He poured milk into the mugs and two heaped spoonfuls of chocolate into one. He spoke again, this time not looking in the direction of the child.

'I remember when my little boy was about your age he loved coffee. But his mother said it wasn't good for kids, so

I used to give him this and we'd call it special coffee, Owen's coffee. I'd put extra sugar in it too. Of course,' he paused again, 'his mother said sugar wasn't good for him. Or chocolate. But we never paid any attention to her. She was a bit of a nuisance really. She was always trying to stop our fun.'

He sniffed again. 'Delicious, that's what I say. What do you say?'

He picked up the two mugs, balanced the plate of biscuits on top of them and walked carefully back to his drawing board. He sat down on his high stool and put a mug and the plate down on the floor. He broke a biscuit into pieces and dunked them into the coffee. He sucked on them, then chewed and swallowed. He licked his fingers, drank some more. Then put the mug down and turned back to his drawing. It was a doodle really, nothing more. An idea for a book. Preliminary sketches, charcoal on sheets of scrap paper pulled from a pile on the desk. Swift strokes, not too much detail. A fox cub and a kitten, brought up together, their den a nest of dried grass and leaves beneath an old wooden summer house. And the small boy who finds them and loves them. Outlines, nothing more at this stage. But it interested him. It had been a long time since he had wanted to tell a story.

He reached out his hand for his coffee and leaned down to pick up another biscuit. The chocolate had begun to soften. He could feel it sticking to his fingertips. He lifted them to his mouth and sucked them clean. The chocolate left a strangely salty taste on his tongue. He looked down at his drawing again. He smoothed out the heavy charcoal lines, using a piece of rag to vary their tone. He whistled softly through his teeth. And heard the sound of footsteps, bare feet tiptoeing towards him. He put down the cloth and picked up the charcoal. He began to draw. A boy with short hair that stood up from his head, long thin legs and arms, and hands that were reaching out towards the fox cub. The charcoal squeaked as it slid across the paper, and as he put more pressure on the stick it broke, with a brisk snap, half of it rolling onto the floor. He glanced down and watched it drop beside the child, who now was squatting at the plate, lifting up the mug and drinking deeply from it, then grabbing the biscuits and shoving them into his mouth.

Nick drew some more, another picture. A boy sitting cross-legged, holding the cub gently, his hands stroking the creature's head, his mouth open as he whispered in its pointed ear. Beside him the child grunted softly as he ate. Crumbs spattered across his pyjamas and chocolate dribbled down his chin. Nick's hand moved swiftly over the paper, filling it up with pictures of the boy and the animals. As he finished each sheet he let it fall to the floor and started immediately on a new one. Beside him the child sat back on his heels. He wiped his mouth with his sleeve, chocolate smearing his cheeks. His gaze shifted from the empty plate to the pieces of paper. His small hands spread them out in a circle around him. Nick watched him, how his fingers touched the charcoal marks and traced their outline, his expression rapt.

'Here,' Nick said. He pulled some paper from the pile on the shelf and picked a couple of long charcoal sticks from the box. He laid them down on the floor. He turned away and went back to his own work. The boy drew quickly. Stick figures marched across the paper. Men and women, children, animals. There were cars and bicycles, and houses with steep gables, pointed roofs and chimneys. Smoke spiralled from them, up into the sky where birds flew, their necks elongated. Nick watched him, his own hand stilled. The child knelt, squatted, half stood, lay on the floor, changing position as he moved around the paper. Soon the charcoal was reduced to small pieces. The boy wiped his hands across his chest and stood up.

'That's brilliant, that's really good.' Nick got up from his stool and bent down to look. He reached out to pick the papers up, but the child quickly scooped them up, gathering them into a bundle, crushing them to him, his face distorted, his eyes wild.

'All right, it's OK.' Nick stepped back. 'I'm not going to take them. Here, put them down again. It's fine, I promise.'

But the child had already turned and was heading towards the garden, running, his bare feet slapping on the wooden floor. Struggling with the handle, unable to open it, both his hands full, so he kicked out at the glass, then shoved his shoulder into the jamb.

'All right, OK, if that's what you want. Hang on, hang on, I'll do it for you. There's no need to hurt yourself like that.'

Nick moved towards him and pressed down on the handle as the child pushed past, running across the grass towards the thick shrubs against the wall. Nick followed, curious to see where he was going. He could see the bushes shaking as the child struggled through them, and then, as he looked over the wall he saw him on the other side, still holding onto his pieces of paper, torn and muddy now, as he headed for the steps up to the kitchen. His feet slipped on the wood, and for a moment Nick thought he would fall backwards and tumble down onto the ground below. But just as he reached the top the door opened, and the thin dark woman he had seen through the window the night before was standing there. She screamed at the child, words that did not make sense, and reached out and grabbed him by his shoulder, shaking him, tearing the paper from his grasp, then pushing him into the house. She turned back towards the garden and saw Nick. She nodded in his direction, then followed the boy inside. The door slammed hard behind them and there was silence.

Nick stepped away from the wall and walked towards the thicket of shrubs. He bent down and crawled beneath. He had planted this buddleia himself, all eighteen inches of it. Bought in a plastic pot from the local supermarket not long after they had moved in. Now, he reckoned, it must be fifteen feet high, and spreading outwards the same distance. An ugly shrub he thought, except in midsummer when its purple sprays exuded honey and attracted butter-flies which clung, wings slowly fanning open and shut as they thrust their long tongues deep into the flowers. He got down on his hands and knees and struggled beneath the shrub's low-growing branches. It was dark in here. A secret place. A hiding place. Easy enough for a child's small body to wriggle through. And there, at the point where the back wall met the boundary wall, there was a gap. Or there had been one before. Hidden by the buddleia on one side and a large red-flowering fuchsia on the other. Big enough for a cat or a small dog or a fox or a boy to scramble through. The Goulding kids had used it when they were young. Owen had used it too. As had his best friend Luke and the other children who had come to play in the garden. Nick inched his way forward and felt with his hands. The hole was still there. And now this kid had discovered it, was using it, making his way from one garden to the next. Just like all the others.

Slowly Nick backed out from beneath the branches. He stood up. He was wet and muddy. And cold too. He walked back inside and closed the door. Pieces of charcoal were scattered across the floor. He got the brush and began to sweep them up, emptying the fragments into the bin. Owen had liked charcoal. He loved opening a new box and lifting back the tissue paper, seeing the fresh, untouched sticks lying side by side, like little bundles of twigs. He had liked the black and white. Nick had offered him colours, sticks of pastel, crayon, soft pencils in every shade of the rainbow. But Owen refused. That's colouring in, he would say. Girls do that. I want to do real drawing, like you do, Daddy. That's different stuff.

Nick turned now to the cardboard boxes that were stacked up against the wall. They were sealed with wide tape and tied up with heavy string. Susan's speciality, the packing of boxes. He remembered when they had come to this house from the flat in which they had spent the first years of their marriage, she had taken charge of the packing and the moving.

'Go on, get out of here,' she had said, as he surveyed the pile of empty boxes in the middle of their tiny sitting room. 'Go on. Go off and play football or meet the boys for a pint or whatever it is you get up to when I'm not around. It's easier to do this on my own.'

And as he reached out for her, taking her by the waist and pulling her close, she laughed at him and batted his hands away, and pointed to the door and said, 'Get thee gone, old Nick.'

And when he came home, singing as he swayed in through the door, he found her asleep on the sofa, the packing taken care of, their new life ordered and categorized. And he had felt, he remembered suddenly, irritated not grateful. Annoyed not pleased. And he had gone through to the kitchen, and ripped open the box that said 'alcohol' and found a bottle of whiskey and tipped some into a mug with a broken handle, the only one that had had been left out, to be thrown away he assumed. And sat down and watched her as she slept. And wondered. Could he spend the rest of his life with a woman who made a fetish out of order? As he dropped cigarette ash down his shirt. And watched her stir and sigh, her eyelids flutter as she dreamed. And then felt sorry, felt love and gratitude for her difference from him, for how she would look after him and mind him and keep their feet on the ground when all he wanted was to have his head in the clouds. Or so she always said. And when he had finished his cigarette and his drink, he gently woke her and half carried her into the bedroom and laid her down and wrapped her in his arms, and slept too, her smell of soap and cleanliness the last thing he knew.

Now he could see that she had been just as thorough with all Owen's belongings. His clothes, his books, his toys. When Nick had left this house his son's room had been untouched. Everything had been just as it always was. Dusted every week. The windows washed, the carpet Hoovered, even the sheets on the bed changed. Now it was all parcelled up in each of these labelled boxes. He stepped close to them and read the inscriptions in Susan's neat capitals. And found the one he wanted. 'Paintings, drawings, art materials,' it said. He pulled the box from the pile and dragged it into the middle of the floor. And stepped over to his drawing board and picked a small curved knife from among the pencils and brushes, and slashed through the tape, ripping back the cardboard flaps. And stepped away then, to the kitchen, taking the bottle of whiskey from the cupboard and slopping a large measure into his coffee. And, sitting down on the floor, he delved into the box as if into a lucky dip. Grasping hold of piles of loose papers, and drawing books, spreading them around him. Kneeling up to see what else there was to find. And realized there was everything, from the first scribble that the toddler Owen had done, the pencil clumsily held between his chubby fingers, unable to control the angle of its sharpened point. Each scrap of paper was dated on the back. Susan's work he knew. Susan's obsession with collection, with the record.

'Let's set the record straight,' she would always say. And there would follow a list of his misdemeanours and his failings. She would push her hair back from her face and strike the index finger of her right hand against the fingers of her left hand as she counted them out. And he would shrug and laugh and try to change the subject.

But he had been a good father. He would not allow anyone to gainsay that. The evidence was here in the boy's own work. He had forgotten how gifted Owen was. Some of these pictures showed a real and mature talent. The child could see and he could draw. Even at the age of five his pictures were original, his vision unique. He liked close-ups. Big faces covered the pages. Their features made them easy to identify. He saw himself, with his wavy black hair needing to be brushed, his cheeks and chin needing to be shaved, and a cigarette in his mouth. He saw Susan, two parallel lines of a frown between her eyebrows, and the phone in her hand. He saw Luke Reynolds, 'my very best friend' as Owen called him, his face round and fat, a sweet bulging in one cheek. And here was Marianne. Instantly recognizable, her eyes large and brown, a wide smile across her face and, he laughed out loud, a small crown resting on her dark head. And here were all the others who had featured in Owen's short life. His favourite schoolteacher, Miss Murphy, big pink freckles across her snub nose. And some of the other children in his class whose names Nick had now forgotten. And here was Chris Goulding. Glasses with thick black rims and a triangular wedge of brown hair across his face. A camera slung around his neck. Beside him stood Róisín, or at least Nick supposed it was her. The figure in black had the same face as her brother, but the body of a woman, with very obvious breasts and a narrow waist. How strange, he thought as he sat back on his heels, and looked again at the pictures. He had never really noticed Róisín, certainly never seen her in that way until that night in the club in New Orleans. But somehow Owen had and he had drawn her thus.

Nick stood up and poured more whiskey into his mug. And felt his foot crunch on something on the floor. Another piece of charcoal, one that he had missed. He bent down to pick up the small pieces, the tips of his fingers blackened, the whorls and ridges of his fingerprints showing clearly as the fine black powder clung to them. He moved to the drawing board again and laid each one down in turn on a clean sheet of white paper. He pressed them carefully, from side to side, watching as the distinctive pattern of his skin was transferred onto the smooth surface. The police had taken his fingerprints during their initial investigation. A routine procedure they assured him. They had fingerprinted Susan too. She had not protested. She had been rendered dumb and passive by the ritual. They had asked for something that Owen had touched. So they could harvest his prints too. Nick had given them his GameBoy. Its plastic surface was perfect for the collection of oils from the hands. They had asked for his dental and medical records. Number of baby teeth still remaining. Number of new teeth. Any X-rays that had been taken of his bones or internal organs. They had asked for any identifying scars or marks on his body. Nick had remembered. The child had been in an accident at his nursery school when he was nearly four. A large wooden doll's house had collapsed and fallen on his leg. Although bruised and sore he had seemed fine. But later, Nick remembered, Susan had noticed that he was limping. An X-ray had revealed a partially healed greenstick fracture, a bend rather than a break in a young bone. He had felt so guilty that he had not spotted it earlier. Would it still be there, that mark on his bone? he had asked Susan and she had nodded. There was nothing else. A few scars on his knees where he had fallen from his first bicycle. Other than that his body was perfect, unmarked. But I would know him, Nick thought. Even now, if I saw him, I would know him. Even if his face was unrecognizable, I know I would know him. By the quality of his skin, the shape of his feet, the line of his ribs and his shoulder blades pushing through the skin of his back. I would know him.

'Daddy, tell me the star child story again. Tell me how the little boy was found in the forest, and his mother came to look for him,

but she was a beggar woman and she was wearing rags. And the star child was mean and nasty and he said he didn't know her. That he didn't recognize her, that she couldn't be his mother because she was a beggar woman. And he turned away from her and said he would rather kiss a snake or a frog than kiss her. But tell me then what happened, Daddy, didn't he get turned into a nasty scaly thing like a snake or a frog? And that was good, Daddy, wasn't it, because he was bad and it was only when he started to be good again that he went back to being a boy. Draw the pictures for me, Daddy. Put my face onto the star child's body. Please, Daddy, please.'

They were all there in the other boxes. The sketches, the roughs, the preparation for the final finished pictures for the book. But he couldn't bring himself to look at them now. He would instead take comfort in some of the books he had loved as a child. The copy of *Treasure Island* that had once been his own father's, the William books that his Uncle John had passed on to him, *The Thirty-Nine Steps*, which was another old favourite, and a selection of stories about horses that his mother had loved and read to him at bedtime. *My Friend Flicka*, *Thunderhead* and *Green Grass of Wyoming*, all illustrated, all full of comfort. They must be here too, packed away, but he could find none of them.

He sat down on the floor again and leaned against the wall. And heard the sound of footsteps above his head. The floorboards creaked and doors opened and closed. He looked towards the garden and saw Susan appear. She had a wicker basket in her hands and she moved slowly towards the washing line. He watched her pull sheets from it, folding them neatly in half, and half again, and half once more.

Laying them carefully in the basket, her hair falling forward over her face. He got to his feet. He walked to the doors and opened them. He stepped outside. She didn't turn her head. She continued with her task. Methodical and ordered. He moved towards her. She was wearing an old Aran sweater that had stretched out of shape and hung loosely now around her hips. He recognized it. It had been one of his. His mother had knitted it for a Christmas present one year. Susan had taken it over when she was pregnant and it had changed shape as she had changed shape. Now, as she bent down then reached up to the line, he could still see the swell and curve of her stomach in the off-white wool of the sweater.

The sun had come out and the garden was filled with light. A cluster of blue tits darted towards the bird feeder filled with peanuts, which swung from the end of a branch of the old apple tree in the middle of the lawn. Nick stopped and watched them, how they hovered like planes in a holding pattern at a crowded airport. How as each bird finished feeding the next was ready to take its place. Polite, considerate, organized in their approach. He had watched sparrows one day with Owen. It must have been spring. There were fledglings perched on the nearby branches and, as they watched, the parent birds presented their beaks and allowed their babies to feed from them. But spring was a long way away, he thought, as a large grey cloud blotted out the brightness and the garden was cast into gloom again.

'Susan,' he said. There was no immediate response. She carried on with her task.

'Susan,' he said again. Still no sign that she had heard him.

'Susan, please, I'd like to talk to you.'

'Oh, really? What about exactly?' She did not turn her head.

'Look, this isn't easy, you know, coming back like this after so long away. It's not easy at all. I feel very strange and out of place.'

'Yeah, is that so? Well, if that's the way you feel, why don't you go back to wherever it was you came from? No one asked you to come home. No one wanted you.' She turned towards him. Then picked up the basket and began to move towards the house. She looked exhausted. There were deep circles beneath her eyes and her shoulders were slumped.

'Here.' He moved towards her. 'Let me help you.' He made as if to take the basket, but she stepped out of his way.

'Look.' Her voice was loud. 'Am I not making myself plain? I don't want any cosy chats with you. Any meanderings down memory lane. I just want to be left alone to get on with my life. The way you got on with yours.' She put the basket down on the ground between them and straightened up. Her gaze was cold and direct. 'You know, you really amaze me. You write me a letter. You tell me you want to come back. And why? Some nonsense about the anniversary. Some rubbish about meeting Róisín Goulding in a bar. Some innuendo about what she is doing there. As if I care, Nick. As if I give a damn about what you were doing then, or now. You're down there in that basement as if you had never left. And for what reason? Tell me that? Wallowing in self-pity, no doubt. Beating yourself up over what happened. Satisfying your grotesquely inflated view of your own importance. That's it, isn't it?'

Nick didn't reply. The blue tits were shrieking loudly. A cat was creeping across the grass towards the apple tree. His body was flattened, close to the ground, his tail thrashing from side to side. Susan's voice had a quality that raised the hairs on the back of his neck. He was suddenly very conscious of the windows which looked down into the garden. He glanced up. He could see someone standing in the bedroom above.

'Oh,' he said, 'that's it, is it? Lover boy is getting upset.' He jerked his head. 'Jealous, is he?'

She took a sharp intake of breath.

'You bastard,' she said, her face very white. 'How dare you? You don't know the meaning of the word jealous. You really have absolutely no idea what you did to me, do you? You know something, Nick, I don't know why I said you could come back here. I must have been crazy. But there's one good thing that's come out of it. I know now that I want a divorce. For some reason I didn't before. When you were away and I hadn't seen you for so long it was easier. I suppose I thought you'd ceased to exist. A bit like Owen. You'd vanished into thin air. But unfortunately you haven't vanished, have you? You're alive and well and as much of a shit as you always were. And now that I see you clearly for what you are, I want to end this for good. You know, Nick, I wish I'd never met you. I wish I'd never married you. And I wish most of all that I'd never had a child with you. Because if I hadn't I wouldn't have all this pain.'

He felt cold, sick, the whiskey sour in his mouth. He moved towards her again. 'You don't mean that. I know you don't. You don't mean that you wouldn't have wanted to have Owen with me. You don't mean that, do you?'

'I mean just that. If I hadn't married you, I'd have

married someone half decent. Who wouldn't have betrayed me the way you did. And I'd have had a child with someone who would have put that child first, not last the way you did. And none of this would have happened to me.'

The kitchen door opened. Nick looked up. Paul was standing at the top of the steps.

'I mean it, Nick. Stay away from me. I don't want anything to do with you. I thought I could handle seeing you again. I thought there was enough scar tissue to protect me from the pain. But there isn't. The wound is still open. The flesh is still raw. It still hurts far too much. And I can't bear it.'

He opened his mouth to speak, but there were no words. She turned away, picked up the basket. Her feet were loud on the wooden steps. The door slammed shut behind her. The cat lunged forward, its claws biting into the ridged bark of the tree's trunk. The birds flew up. They squeaked and clicked their displeasure, circling around before clustering on the highest branches. He looked up at the sky. Clouds were layered, one huge pile behind the other. Light turned their edges to silver. Small patches of dark blue showed between them, then they too were lost as the greyness became complete. He looked up at the windows. They were dark, almost opaque. He shifted his gaze to the house next door. And saw the boy's face again. Nick smiled up at him, then pulled a face, crossing his eyes and sticking out his tongue. The child looked back, then leaned towards the glass and blew out. And drew. Two eyes, a blob for a nose and the curving arc of a smiling mouth. Nick lifted his hand in salute. And turned away and walked inside.

Thirteen

The book was where it had always been. In the wide shelf. The shelf where all Nick's children's books had once been kept. She had got rid of them after he left. Only *The Star Child* had been allowed to stay. And now it was surrounded by medical journals and textbooks. When Owen had still been there they had been put away, out of the sight of curious eyes, out of reach of curious fingers. It was because of the illustrations and photographs. She found them fascinating, enthralling, even beautiful. But Nick had insisted.

'They frighten the living daylights out of me. God knows what a child would make of them.'

She had argued, insisted that they were no more upsetting than his collection of Hans Christian Andersen and the Brothers Grimm. Or his vividly coloured edition of *Struwelpeter*, blood spurting from the stumps of the wild haired child's fingers, amputated by the huge scissors which lay on the floor, its blades red and glistening. But his view had prevailed, as it so often did where Owen was concerned.

Now she stood in the sitting-room window, the book in her hands. She turned the pages slowly. Owen's baby face looked up at her. Wrapped in a cloak of golden tissue wrought with stars. A shaft of sunlight glanced through the low clouds and fell across her hands, warming them. She looked up. Two boys were dragging a wheelbarrow across the square. It was filled with wood, offcuts from the builders' suppliers two streets away. She watched as they began to fling it onto the heap. They were laughing and shouting, clowning around as they worked. Below her she heard the sound of the basement door closing. She peered out and down and saw the top of Nick's dark head as he walked along the path towards the road. He stopped for a moment, fiddling with keys, checking the pockets of his leather jacket. She drew back into the shadow of the room. He did not look up. She closed the book and moved away towards the shelves. When she looked out again he had gone.

It had taken longer than Nick had anticipated to find Luke Reynolds. The family no longer lived in the last house on the square. In fact there was no longer a family in the sense that there had been ten years ago. Luke's mother and father had separated, recently divorced. Luke's mother, Bridget, had remarried and moved to London with her new husband and son and her daughter by her first marriage, Luke's sister. Luke was in his second year at university, and had elected to stay behind in Dublin with his father and his father's girlfriend, in an apartment in Temple Bar.

Nick had remembered that both the Reynolds were solicitors. They had worked together: he specialized in conveyancing and personal injury cases; she covered family law, separation agreements in the days before divorce was legalized along with custody claims and barring orders, all the messy, painful baggage that went with the territory. Nick had gone through the phone book looking for their names, but it was only after he rang the Law Society that he discovered that their joint practice had ceased and that Pat Reynolds was now working for one of the biggest firms of solicitors in the city. In fact he was a partner. 'Raking it in,' he told Nick, when Nick eventually reached him on the phone. Never had it so good. Should have made the move years ago.

Nick wasn't sure which of the moves in his life Pat meant. Until he stepped out of the lift into the lobby of his penthouse apartment. Maple floors stretched to the wall of windows, which gave an uninterrupted view down the river towards the docks and the sea beyond. Sprawled on a white leather sofa, glass in hand was a woman, a girl rather, all tousled blonde hair and bare midriff, who barely raised her eyes from the wide-screen television in the corner. Nick remembered Bridget from before. He had never seen her belly bare. And she never watched MTV.

'Jan, meet Nick, an old friend from way back. Nick, this is Jan, the new lady in my life.' Pat beamed with self-satisfaction as he offered Nick a seat and a drink. Jan rolled over on her stomach, and changed channels. Of Luke there was no sign.

'Oh, he's here all right.' Pat gestured towards the spiral stairs which snaked up towards a mezzanine floor. 'Well, he's up there if truth be told. Stuck in front of the computer. If it's not games it's the fucking Internet. Don't understand a word he says these days. Another language altogether. Jan, now, she can make more sense of him than I can.'

Nick resisted any comment.

'And his mother,' he asked, 'how's she?'

A mood of gloom cast its dead hand across the room.

'Jesus, don't mention the bitch. Took me for every penny. Gave up work. Insisted on being supported. Got the house, the car, the bank account. Got the kids too. Then gets the divorce, and wham bam, suddenly she's with this new bloke, she's married, she pisses off to London and leaves me lumbered with Luke. After years of making sure we've hardly any contact.'

He paused and glanced guiltily towards Nick, as he took a long swallow from his glass. 'Look, don't get me wrong. I love him, I really do. The problem is I don't know him. All those Saturday afternoons eating pizzas and going to whatever crap kids' film was on at the Savoy doesn't exactly prepare you for a one-to-one relationship. I try.' He raised his hands in a theatrical gesture towards the ceiling. 'I do my best, don't I, love?'

There was no verbal response from Jan, who rolled over onto her side and changed channels again.

'But you know the way it is. Teenagers, Christ, they don't make it easy for you, do they? I mean when his mother pissed off to London I thought maybe he could stay on in the square, maybe with one of his friends out there. But he wouldn't. He actually insisted that he come to live with me, with us. And now, well.'

The awkward silence which followed Pat's words was only broken when he lumbered to his feet and shouted loudly up the stairs. Nick's gaze moved to the view. Streams of light crossed the river, north and south, and flowed in a continuous line along the quays. And above the city the illuminated outlines of cranes hung like early Christmas decorations.

'Luke.' Pat's voice sounded more and more desperate. 'Get your arse down here, now. There's someone to see you.'

'Look.' Nick half rose. 'I don't want to cause any hassle. Maybe I should come back another time.'

'Not at all, stay where you are. I'll go and root him out. It's always the same. From the minute he gets in from college he's straight up the stairs and into his room. I don't know what's the matter with the kid.'

Nick listened to the sound of Pat's fist on a closed door, then the mutter of voices. Jan rolled over onto her back and folded her arms behind her head.

'He's homesick, that's what wrong. He misses his mother. Who can blame him?'

Nick looked at her, surprised by the gentleness of her tone.

'Pat tries, but he hasn't a clue. And the kid hates me. Again, who can blame him? There's no denying, the whole situation is a mess.'

'What's a mess, eh? What are you complaining about, my pet?' Pat's feet thumped loudly on the stairs, but his tone was jovial, 'You wanna see the mess in Luke's room. I dunno, kiddo, it's like something from the dirty protest up there.' He turned back and gestured to the boy who followed him slowly. 'Hey, look who's here to see you, Luke. Remember Mr Cassidy, Nick from Victoria Square? Remember?'

The boy said nothing. He stood and stared at the floor, his face sullen, his hands shoved in the pockets of his baggy trousers. Pat reached down and took the girl's hands, pulling her to her feet.

'Hey, come on, chicken, let's get out of here and leave these two old friends to talk about the past. I fancy a pint.' He began to usher her to the lift door, the palm of his hand flat against the small of her back. 'Help yourself to anything from the fridge, Nicky me lad, and don't put up with any crap from my son. He's all yours.'

The door slid to behind them. The sound from the television was suddenly very loud. Nick got to his feet and picked up the remote control. He pressed the mute button.

'There, that's better,' he said, as he took the place on the sofa where Jan had been lolling. He looked up at Luke, who was still standing, his eyes fixed on a large knot in the smooth, shiny maple. 'How are you, Luke? Nice to see you after so many years. Nice to see that you've grown up into such a fine-looking young man. Why don't you come and sit down beside me? There's a couple of things I'd like to ask you. Nothing difficult, nothing complicated. I just want to talk to you about Owen, about that day. You don't mind do you? I'm sure you don't.'

What did he remember about the child as he was then? He remembered that he was a year and half older than Owen, nearly ten. That he was plump and round. That his hair was strawberry blond, cut in a pudding-bowl style. That he liked to gather his saliva in his mouth and dribble it out so it lay on the floor in frothy pools that resembled cuckoo spit. That he was rude and gave cheek, stole money from his mother's purse. Tried to get Owen to do the same from Nick's wallet. And that Owen loved him, took great pleasure in Luke's naughtiness and wanted to be just like him.

Now his plumpness had been converted into muscle. His biceps pushed through the sleeves of his T-shirt. His legs were rock solid and although he slouched there was no denying his height. He must be well over six feet, Nick reckoned. Takes after his mother's family. She had been tall too. And very big. Not fat exactly, but strong and well built. The pudding-bowl hairstyle had gone. Now his hair, still on the red side of blond, was tied back in a ponytail, and a reddish stubble gave a sheen to his jaw and neck. So this is how they change, Nick thought, as his eyes moved towards Luke's feet, encased in trainers that it seemed only a giant would wear.

'Your laces are undone,' he said. 'You could trip if you're not careful.' He lifted his gaze to the boy's face, and noticed the look of casual contempt that had replaced indifference.

'Yeah, right, whatever.' Grunts rather than words came from his mouth as he turned his head towards the television. The tendons in his neck stood out as he moved and a rancid and slightly aromatic smell drifted from his body.

Nick sat back. He said nothing. He waited. The boy shifted from foot to foot. Nick looked away and then back up at him.

'He loved you, you know, Luke. He looked up to you. He wanted to be like you. Did you know that?'

There was no reply. The boy picked up the remote control and pressed the volume button. Sound flooded from the speakers, changing from speech to music to gunfire to the screech of racing cars' tyres to the roar of a football crowd, as he flicked from channel to channel. Pictures and noise filling up the space so there was no room for anything else. No room for emotion, for sorrow, for regret, for everything that accompanied the tears that Nick now saw begin to seep from Luke's eyes, roll down his cheeks and drop slowly onto the floor at his feet.

It was Halloween. For weeks now they had all been waiting for the moment when the bonfire in the square would be lit. That would be later. After they'd gone trick or treating earlier in the evening. Everyone on the square knew that

Owen was the fox and Luke was the horse. They all liked Owen, Luke said, he was everyone's favourite. So when they saw the fox and the horse coming there'd be loads of sweets and even money for them.

But that was later, much later too. None of that ever happened. That was just the way it was to be.

'So what did happen? What happened that day? Tell me. You were the last person to see him. The last we know, anyway. You must tell me what happened.'

'Look, I've told you already. I told the guards all about it at the time. I told my parents. I told everyone who asked me. I don't want to talk about it any more.'

When the tears had been shed and wiped away they left the apartment and walked. Across the river and down O'Connell Street. Into McDonald's. Nick watched Luke as he ate. A Big Mac with cheese. Two portions of fries. A strawberry milkshake and an apple pie. Nick had coffee, thin and bitter and far too hot. He could feel, as he swallowed, the skin stripping from the roof of his mouth. He watched the way Luke wolfed down the food, exhausted after the tears, occasionally gulping breath into his lungs, his broad shoulders shaking like those of a child.

They walked again, further down O'Connell Street. It was crowded, busy. Pedestrians jostled them. Romanian women with babies swaddled in shawls on their backs, begged at street corners, and men with dark faces clustered in shop doorways, their words fragments of languages Nick had never heard before. On the plinth where Nelson's Pillar once had stood there was the familiar figure. The woman who sang hymns to the Blessed Virgin, her face transfigured with joy. They stopped to watch and she opened her arms and included them in her petitions for mercy and grace.

'My dad thinks she should be locked up,' Luke said as they stepped out into the traffic. 'He says she's a relic of a bygone age.'

'And what do you think?'

Luke shrugged. 'I think if Fellini was making Irish movies, she'd be one of his stars.'

Nick smiled and gave him a small shove in his back as a bus swerved to avoid them. 'Hey, Luke, I take it you're old enough to drink now?'

The boy grinned.

'OK.' Nick grabbed his arm and they turned right into Parnell Street. 'I haven't been here since my student days. It used to be me and Owen's mum's favourite place. It was cheap and it was mercifully free of other students.'

He held open the door to the Blue Lion pub. 'As long as you're sure I won't be accused of leading you astray.'

It was obvious from the way Luke polished off half his pint in one swallow that Nick need not have worried. He waited until he had reordered and the barman had set them up in front of them. Then he began again.

'So, tell me. What happened?'

'Do I have to? Haven't I already told you and everyone else everything that I can remember. It was ten years ago, I was only a kid.'

Nick looked at him. 'A very bright kid, I seem to remember. A kid who was up to all kinds of schemes and mischief. A kid who was hell-bent on rewriting the rules of kid behaviour, isn't that so?'

'You didn't like me though, did you?' Luke's broad fingers drummed on the table. 'I remember you always got a real disapproving look whenever I came around. You weren't the only one, everyone was like that to me. They all loved Owen, though. He was the favourite. It used to really make me sick.'

'Oh?'

'Yeah.' Luke drank again. 'He was teacher's pet at school. He was always asked to do special jobs, things that got him out of class. Carry messages to the head teacher, go to the storeroom to get things, art equipment and stuff. Silly little things.'

'Sounds like he was a real pain in the arse?'

'He wasn't. It was everyone else and what they thought of him that was a pain. My mother was always moaning and nagging and going on at me.' His voice rose and his features took on a pinched look as he mimicked. 'Why aren't you more like Owen Cassidy? Why isn't your home-work neat and tidy like Owen Cassidy's? Why don't you say please and thank you like Owen Cassidy? And I used to wish that someone would snap their fingers and fucking Owen Cassidy would disappear in a puff of smoke.'

His face flushed, a sudden colour washing across it. 'Sorry, sorry, I didn't mean that. Really, I don't know why I said it.'

'It's OK, Luke.' Nick smiled at him.

'It isn't OK. None of it was Owen's fault. I could have been a better friend to him. I wasn't that day.'

It was quiet in the bar. The television was tuned to a news programme, with the sound turned down. A panel of dark-suited men were sitting in an arc at an angle to a woman with straight blonde hair and very blue eyes. Nick looked at the faces as the camera shots changed from wide to close-up. He watched for the give-away signs of tension. The tightening of the jaw, the narrowing of the mouth, the defensive hand to the back of the neck.

'Tell me,' he said.

He pulled a pencil from his pocket and began to doodle on the beer mat. He listened.

It had begun to rain while they were in the pub. The streets were empty now and a chill dampness had settled over the city. He walked Luke back to Temple Bar and waited until he saw him close the heavy street door behind him. He turned away then, pulled the collar of his leather jacket up around his face and shoved his hands deep into his pockets. He looked around him. So much had changed in the years he'd been away. Everywhere there were new bars and restaurants, and people spilling out onto the street with a wild gaiety, fuelled by the contents of the glasses they clutched. He felt alone and lost. And out of place. But beneath the surface gloss, the shiny new prosperity, he knew that this was the city he had always loved, as familiar to him as the lines on his own face.

They had both felt the same about it, he and Susan, when they were students. They had walked the streets, holding hands, deep in conversation. Their courtship had been a public affair, taking place in pubs and alleyways, in the neglected city squares and depressed docklands. They had shared cramped bedsits and rundown flats in Georgian houses with rudimentary plumbing and no heating. And they had lain at night, wrapped in each other's arms, listening to the wail of ambulances and police cars, the shouts, curses and wild laughter of drunks, secure in their love for each other.

It was, he realized now, only a short walk to the hospital where Susan had worked and still worked. He would go and see her, the way he always used to. He would call in and drink tea with the nurses on the night shift, wait until she was ready to come home. Carry her briefcase and let her rest her tired body against his. The way she always did before. All those years ago. When life was full of hope and wonder.

He moved quickly through the narrow lanes and back alleys, his feet slipping and sliding on the worn cobbles. Stephen's Green was quiet, the trees around the perimeter of the square dark, spindly shapes, the wide pavements empty. He ducked through the traffic and began to jog up towards the lighted sign above the stone portico and carved marble angel, which spread its wings over the street below. He stopped, catching his breath and looked up at the rows of lighted windows above him. The building hadn't changed, unlike so much of the city. Still the crumbling, converted Georgian houses that had been donated by a benefactor at the end of the last century. He pushed open the swing doors. The porter behind his polished mahogany desk looked up from his evening paper.

'Will you look who it is?' His smile was instant and warm. 'How are ye, long time no see.' He reached over, his hand out, his palm warm and welcoming. 'Are you looking for herself? She's up in the Purefoy Ward. D'ye remember the way? Sure of course you do, sure nothing's changed around here, nothing at all, not even meself.'

He was right about that. Nick took the stairs two at a time. The walls were still painted mushroom and the lino on the floor was cracked and stained. And the smell, of course, nothing could change that. Disinfectant and chemicals, with just a hint of fear that snatched at the back of his nose.

On the first landing there was a large statue of the Virgin Mary. A red lamp glowed at her feet, and a halo of stars shone around her head. Beside her, on a hard wooden bench, a young couple sat huddled together. Their faces were pinched and worn. The girl clutched a large teddy bear, holding it against her stomach and crooning as she rocked backwards and forwards. The boy pulled her head onto his shoulder and kissed her cheek, one hand stroking her hair, while the other fiddled with a packet of cigarettes. Nick stopped and looked down at them. Then turned and moved away, his shoes squeaking on the shiny floor as he walked down the long corridor towards the glass doors at the end.

It was very quiet here now. During the day this was a busy, noisy place. Children everywhere, in and out of their beds and cots. Toddlers in playpens, older kids walking up and down, pulling their intravenous drips behind them on wheeled stands. Even the sickest children seemed to have the energy to talk or play. They always amazed him, how they coped with their pain and their fear.

'They're very honest with themselves,' Susan had told him, 'and we're very honest with them and their parents too. They can stand knowing much better than not knowing. We could all learn a lot of lessons from these kids.'

But now each of the wards was in semi-darkness. A dimmed light cast a bluish glow across the sleeping children and their mothers and fathers, who lay beside them on fold-up beds. At the end of the corridor heavy doors barred his way. He tried the handles, but they were locked. He stepped up close and pressed the sides of his hands against the cold glass of the large square windows set into each one. He shielded his eyes and looked inside. Susan was standing beside a high metal bed. She was wearing a green gown, her hair pulled up into a cap, a mask across her face. She was leaning down to check the flow from a bag suspended on a metal hook. The thick, red liquid slipped, drop by drop, through a transparent tube. It was bone marrow. He knew that. A child lay curled on its side. Hard to tell whether it was a boy or a girl, with its bald and shiny head, its skin whiter than the sheet which covered its slight body. Susan pulled up a chair and sat down. She pulled down the child's green gown, exposing the tube which ran into its chest. The child's eyes opened and it reached out towards her. Susan picked up the plastic figure which had fallen onto the floor. Barbie doll's hair was stiff, blonde and full. The child held her up, then kissed her and laid her on the pillow beside her own bald head. Susan sat still. She laid her hand across the girl's forehead. Nick could see the movement of her lips against her mask, but he could hear no sound through the heavy glass doors. The room was sparsely furnished, with little of the paraphernalia of the other wards. It was sterile in there. It had to be. He knew what the little girl had already been through. Her body had been blasted with radiation, killing off her own bone marrow, leaving her defenceless, her immune system anni-hilated. The thick viscous liquid in the bag was its replace-ment. The child, her family, the doctors and nurses would wait, hold their breath for the next seven days. She would remain in isolation. Until, with everything that modern medicine could do for her, and with luck, her body would begin to replicate the new, uncontaminated bone marrow in her system.

'Sometimes it takes, sometimes it doesn't,' Susan had tried to explain, 'often we don't know why. And often we can do nothing except watch them slip away.'

He drew back from the door. His reflection hung in front of him and behind it Susan stood, picked up a clipboard and began to make notes on a chart. Her body, its outline unclear swathed in her hospital clothes, slipped in and out of view. She began to move towards him and he stepped back into another doorway, suddenly not wanting her to see him. A kitchenette was to his left and on the wall a peg board covered with photographs. 'August Bank Holiday, 2000, the Millennium Year' the printed caption said. A picnic, an outing of some description. Children in summer clothes sitting on rugs, eating burgers and sausages. A barbecue, a row of adults behind it, smoke obscuring their faces. Groups of nurses in uniform, and another group, doctors perhaps because Susan was there, laughing, her arm around a girl whose face was suddenly familiar. Brown eyes, with thick black lashes. A wide mouth with a deeply indented upper lip. Dark hair cut so close to her head that her scalp shone whitely through. But she, of all of them, was not smiling. Her face was sad, reflective. Her eyes shadowed. He remembered when he had first met her. She had been a patient here. She had gone through what the little girl in the isolation unit was experiencing. And she had been lucky. She had survived.

Her brother's bone marrow had saved her life. Given her a second chance. And when she was eighteen she had come to them.

'We'd be doing her parents a big favour,' Susan had said. 'They don't want her to come to Dublin and be by herself. They want her to have some friends, a safe place to live. And just think, Nicky, it'll be great for you. You can take time off just for yourself. She'll be there for Owen every afternoon. You can get up to all kinds of mischief, can't you?'

And although he had protested that he didn't want someone else in the house, that he didn't need help, that he liked everything the way it was, Susan had worn him down. So he found himself painting the boxroom at the top of the stairs, putting up bookshelves, shifting in a bed and a wardrobe. Even finding her a portable television and a CD player and radio. Making her welcome. Noticing how she slipped into their lives as if she had always been there. So, six months later he lay in bed in the mornings and heard, through a fog of sleep, her footsteps on the stairs, her voice hurrying Owen into his coat, finding his schoolbag, his football boots. Got up to a kitchen that was clean and tidy, a freshly baked loaf of brown bread cooling on the table, knew that when he came upstairs from the studio in the early evening dinner would be in the oven, Owen would have done his homework, the fire in the sitting room would be lit, and a bottle of wine would be open, with his glass beside it.

'See, wasn't I right about her?' Susan had said to him that summer as they sat in the garden and watched Marianne and Owen lying on a rug, their heads close together, as she read aloud to him.

Nick reached forward and pulled the photograph from the board. He had blamed her for what happened. And she had blamed him. There had been a dreadful row. In front of Susan. Each riven with their own special guilt. Each desperate to shed it somehow. And he remembered what Susan had said.

'I thought it was you, Marianne. That he was in love with you. I thought it was you he was having sex with. I didn't want to believe it. I didn't think you could be so cruel. But I'm sorry to say I did think it was you. And I'm so glad, the only good thing that has come out of this is that it wasn't you.'

It wasn't Nick who was in love with Marianne. It was Owen. That was what Luke had told him in the pub.

'It was love. It wasn't infatuation or a crush or whatever you call it. He was cracked about her. He wanted to be with her all the time. And she sent him out to play with me because she had a date with that guy, Chris from next door. And he didn't want to be with me. And I was mad with him. So I said to him, I told him.'

He had stopped and drunk some more. Nick waited.

'What did you tell him?'

Luke's eyes filled with tears again. Nick waited.

'We'd gone to the shopping centre. Marianne had given us money. I wanted to buy some more fireworks and we knew there was a guy who sold them down in the basement. But we couldn't find him. We were hanging around, then Owen said he wanted to get his photograph taken in the automatic machine thing. So we went and he did it. He made a big fuss about it. He went into the toilet and put water on his hair so it wouldn't stick up. And when he got the pictures he said pick one, pick the best one. He said it was for Marianne. He got me to tear it off. I laughed at him. I said he was stupid. He was a wimp. And then I told him. I told him she had a big cunt. I'd heard the older kids talking about girls and cunts. I didn't really know what it meant. I think I thought it was tits. But the funny thing was Owen knew what it meant. He screamed at me that I wasn't to say that, that I didn't know anything about her. And I said that I did, that she had shown me her cunt. That she'd let me touch it. He went crazy then. He started hitting me and kicking me. And do you know what I did? I ran away from him. I was scared and I ran away. I thought he'd follow me, that he'd forgive me and follow me. But when I looked back he'd gone. There was no sign of him anywhere. We weren't supposed to leave the square without an adult. But we did. All the time. I ran away and when I looked back there was no sign of him anywhere. I stood on our steps and I looked, but he wasn't there any longer. That was the last I saw of him. That was the last thing I said to him. I lied to him, but he believed me.'

Nick looked at the photograph again. Owen had drawn her as a beautiful princess with a golden crown. She was still beautiful now, but her eyes were filled with pain.

Susan's green-gowned figure passed in front of him. She walked quickly towards the young couple on the landing. She squatted down in front of them, her head inclined towards theirs. He could sense the urgency in her voice. She straightened up. She motioned to them to follow her. He drew back again until they had passed. And felt suddenly, inadequate, intrusive, out of place. Quickly, before she should see him, catch him out, he hurried out towards the stairs.

'You didn't tell the police about that, did you, Luke?'

'No, I couldn't, I felt so bad. I just said that Owen had gone to look for more stuff for the bonfire, but I had to go home. Well, that was true too. We were going to look for stuff for the bonfire. I did have to go home. It was all true.'

True but incomplete. Like his own first version of the events of that day.

The porter was gone from his desk as Nick ducked through the hall and out into the dark street beyond. The rain had stopped now, but it was cold and cheerless. He looked at the photo in his hand. He slipped it into the inside pocket of his jacket and felt the other picture that was there. Luke had handed it to him as they said goodbye. Took it from his wallet.

'I kept it. But you can have it now,' he said as he pressed it into his hand. Owen's eight-year-old face looked up. His smile was broad.

Nick pulled it out and stared down at it. He checked his watch. It was after eleven. Just time, if he hurried, to find a pub still open. He needed a drink badly. A mistake to come here. He didn't belong any more. He didn't belong anywhere. He shrugged his collar up around his ears. He turned away and quickened his pace and headed for the lights in the distance.

Fourteen

He woke. It was dark. He was so stiff he could barely move. His cheek was resting on the worn velvet of an old cushion. The smell of damp filled his nose. His body was sprawled out along the floor in front of the stove. His hip bones felt bruised from their contact with the bare boards and his feet were cold. He stirred gingerly and lifted his head. The sound of banging filled his ears. Blood thumped in his temples. He pushed himself slowly up till he was sitting. The noise continued. It was loud and repetitive. He put his head in his hands and pushed his fingers into his ears. But still he could not shut it out. His mouth was dry and foul and whiskey coated his tongue.

He tried to stand, but his legs were weak and collapsed beneath him. He rocked backwards and forwards. And still the banging continued. And now there was a voice too. Calling his name. And the sound of the flap of the letterbox rattling as it was lifted then dropped. The voice again and his name repeated.

'Mr Cassidy. Are you there? It's me. It's Min Sweeney. From the guards, Mr Cassidy.'

He tried to stand again, and this time pushed himself up and leaned against the wall for support. His stomach turned over and he bent his head and retched.

Again the banging on the door, again the voice, then

the sound of footsteps, getting more faint, on the concrete path outside.

'Hold on, hold a minute. I'm coming for Christ's sake. Hold on.' He tried to remember. What time was it that he had got home? What day was it? What time was it now? He lurched uncertainly to the door and opened it. A gust of wind snatched it from his hands, slammed it shut again, catching his two fingers in the lock.

'Shit.' The pain shot up his arm, down his shoulder and felt as if it had lodged somewhere in his heart. He pulled his fingers free, unable to speak and bent double, clutching one hand with the other.

'Dear, dear, that looks sore.'

He looked up. Min Sweeney was standing on the door-step.

'Here, let me.' She put down the large plastic bag she was carrying and moved him back into the light. 'Nasty, very painful. I've done it myself and it's agony. Your fingers need to be washed under very cold water. I doubt if they're broken, but you never can tell. Maybe a trip to casualty is in order.'

She made no comment on how he looked or the state of the room. She turned on the tap in the kitchen sink and despite his protests held his hand firmly under the cold sluice of water, until his fingers had turned translucent and the bruises showed up blackly against the pallor of his skin. Then she put on the kettle and dropped tea bags into two mugs. She took a carton of milk from the fridge and sniffed it speculatively before pouring. She handed him a mug. He winced as he took it.

They drank in silence. She noticed the pallor of his face, the redness of his eyes, that he needed to shave and the smell of alcohol that seeped from his pores. He was very thin. He looked, she thought, the way he had looked before, all those years ago. As if he was beaten.

He finished his tea and dumped the mug in the sink, then walked towards the other end of the room. There was a cigarette packet lying on the floor beside the velvet cushion. He squatted down and picked it up, shaking it, then throwing it with an expression of disgust into a small wicker bin. She followed him as he sat down on the sofa. He leaned back and stared up at her, cradling one hand in the other.

'I don't suppose you smoke, do you?'

She shook her head. The floor was covered with sheets of paper. She bent down to look more closely. Some of them were drawings of a small boy and a fox cub. They were beautiful. So real the figures seemed as if they could walk off the page and into the room. The other pictures were obviously done by a child. But they too were lovely.

'These are terrific,' she said, looking back at him over her shoulder. 'You did them, I suppose.'

He didn't reply.

'You know I have some of your books at home. My kids love them.'

He shrugged.

'They were very impressed when I told them I knew you.'

'Is that right?'

'I told them about you and your little boy.'

'Did you now?'

'They said I should do anything I could to help you. They told me I should move heaven and earth to find him.'

'Move heaven and earth, that's a great phrase.'

'Isn't it? It's one of my father's favourites. My boys are great mimics. Copycats really. Like all children of their age. They soak up everything around them. Words, expressions, mannerisms, tics. I'm always seeing people I know and they know coming out in them. But you know what I'm talking about, don't you, Mr Cassidy. You remember, of course, the way your own child was.'

'Nick, please. Call me Nick. I'm sure you did before.'

She smiled and shrugged. 'Wouldn't want to presume anything, wouldn't want to step on any toes.'

'Really? That's not the way I remember you lot. I seem to recall that you did a fair amount of stepping on toes. No hesitation at all. You sure as hell stepped on mine a few times. What was it your boss called me? A womanizing adulterer. A disgrace as a husband. A suspect in the murder of my own son. My toes, I can tell you, were properly crushed.'

She pushed herself back onto her heels and stood. She said nothing. She walked to the front door. He heard it open. There was silence. He leaned back and closed his eyes. Pain throbbed through his fingers and hand. He felt sick. He heard the door close, and then her footsteps as she walked back into the room again. He opened his eyes and looked at her. She was carrying the large plastic bag. It banged awkwardly against her legs as she moved. She reminded him of a child with a heavy schoolbag. She dumped it on the floor and it fell over on its side with a soft thump.

'Look,' she said, 'whatever you may think about what happened we did our job as best we could. It might surprise you to know that all over the country there are men and women who have never stopped thinking about your son and wondering what happened to him. And they've never stopped berating themselves for what they might or might not have done differently at the time. And, yes,' she nodded her head vigorously, reminding him again of a child, a good child trying to do her best, 'yes, you were a suspect. So were your wife, your neighbours, your childminder, your friends, your acquaintances, your lover and her husband. You were all suspects, as I would be in a similar situation. And it wasn't very nice, it wasn't very comfortable, but it was very necessary.'

There was silence again.

'OK.' Nick held up his hands in a gesture of conciliation. 'I accept what you say. I'm sorry, forgive me for my rudeness. I'm not feeling the best.'

'Yeah,' she smiled, 'understatement of the year, I'd reckon. What's been going on here? The place stinks like a pub last thing on a Saturday night.'

'Ach' he shrugged, 'I think it's called old habits die hard. Or maybe it's just called facing the past and not liking what you find.'

'Oh yeah? Do you want to tell me about it?'

He shook his head and smiled warily. He didn't want to tell her. He didn't want to remember. Could he even remember? He had left the hospital. He had headed for the nearest bar. He had got into conversation with a couple of guys. Car salesmen, they said they were. They'd taken him to a club. He'd lost them then, somewhere in the maw of noise and alcohol and deep, dark shadows. He'd found a woman. He'd bought her drink. She'd listened to him, let him rest his head against her shoulder, held him up as they staggered out into the dawn. Got a taxi and taken him back to her flat. He closed his eyes. He didn't want to remember the rest of it. It had been bright and sunny when he left her, but there was a cold breeze that made his nose and eyes run. He'd stopped to buy a bottle of whiskey on the way home. And he'd drunk most of it before he passed out on the cushion on the floor.

'Here,' she said and pushed the bag across to him. It was filled with beige folders. She sat down beside him on the sofa and pulled a few of them out, dumping them on his lap.

'I'm working in Garda headquarters at the moment,' she said, 'and I have occasion to take myself down into the archives, and when I was there today I came across these and it occurred to me that you might have time on your hands and you might be usefully occupied having a look at them.'

He sat forward. 'They let you take all this stuff with you?'

'Well,' she shrugged, 'I wouldn't say that "let" was the most accurate of terms to use. But what they don't know won't hurt them. Anyway – ' she wagged her finger and looked at him with mock sternness – 'I know I can trust you not to damage any of this material in any way, or to divulge any of it to a third party. Isn't that so?'

He nodded. 'Of course. Of course I won't.'

He put one hand down flat on the smooth buff cover. 'Statements, is that what they are?'

'Photocopies of statements, reports of searches, alleged sightings of Owen, reports of information given by psychics, all the crazies who came forward. The questionnaires that your neighbours filled in. Pretty much everything that I could carry. There's still a ton of stuff left there, but I picked anything that I thought would be useful to you. Not, I have to say, that I honestly think you're going to find anything that we didn't. But who knows?' She smiled at him. 'Fresh eyes and all that.'

'This is great, this is really fantastic.' He smiled back at her, and she saw it again, as if for the first time. The charm, the warmth, the blue eyes that looked directly into hers.

'You know what?' He pushed the files onto the seat beside her. 'This calls for a celebration. A bit of showing of gratitude and mending of fences. I don't have any chocolates or flowers, but what about a drink? Something nice, festive, a hot whiskey or an Irish coffee maybe?'

'Oh yeah.' She pulled a face. 'Hair of the dog is what you want, isn't that right?'

'That's it, be cynical. Look a gift horse in the mouth.' He stood up. 'Suit yourself, but I'm going to make it anyway.'

'OK, OK, keep your hair on. I'd love a hot whiskey, but only if you have cloves and brown sugar. Only if you're going to do it right.'

'Well, if you're so fussy, come here. You can take care of it yourself.' He reached down and took hold of both her hands. He pulled her to her feet and led her to the kitchen. He opened the cupboard above the sink. 'Now, let's see what we have. Sugar, cloves. And look.' He picked a lemon from a bowl with a very black banana and a shrivelled apple. 'Now you can do that cute thing where you stick the cloves into the slice. Very posh lounge bar. Very seventies.'

She laughed.

'Shut up,' she said. 'Here, fill the kettle. And where's the alcohol, the special ingredient? Don't tell me, you drank it all yourself?'

They sat at the kitchen table, steaming glasses in front of them.

'This is nice,' she sipped, careful not to burn herself. 'This time of the day it's usually peeling spuds over a cup of tea and trying to stop the kids from killing each other until after we've all had dinner.'

'How old are they?'

'They're both six. They're twins. Boys.'

'So you've got married since.' He peered at her left hand. 'Ah, there is a ring, I hadn't noticed.'

'Since, that's right. Seven years ago.' She fished a clove from her glass with her teaspoon. It lay on the metal surface like a tiny black bone.

'And what does he do?'

'Did. He's dead. He died three years ago.'

'Oh God, I'm sorry. I didn't realize.'

She shook her head, stirring the grains of sugar around in her glass.

'Why should you? You weren't to know.'

There was silence for a moment. He sipped his drink carefully.

'Was he ill? Was it sudden? An accident?'

'Sudden, but not an accident. A brain haemorrhage. Completely unexpected. He was very fit, very healthy. Never a day's sickness in his life. And then, bang. Just like that. He's gone.'

They drank in silence. She looked tired, he thought. Suddenly younger, vulnerable. Her scars visible.

'Must be hard to manage your job in the circumstances.'

She shrugged. 'You get on with it. You do whatever has to be done. But you don't have much time for yourself. My mother's up visiting for the week. She's mad about the boys. She practically throws me out of the house when she's here. Can't wait to get her grandmotherly paws all over them.' She smiled. 'God knows what they make of her. She's a devil for the cleanliness and the godliness.'

'A traditional Irish mammy is she? One of the old school?'

'No, not at all. In fact she's anything but. She's French for a start. That's where I get the name. Min, it's short for Mignonne.'

'Oh, I'd assumed Minnie as in . . .'

'Yeah, don't remind me. Minnie bloody Mouse. The bane of my childhood.' She laughed. 'But it isn't.'

'No,' he said. 'It's lovely.'

He got up from the table and went to the fridge. He squatted down, opened the door and peered inside. His face in the cold clean light looked exhausted. Dark bruises beneath his eyes and his skin flecked with stubble. He turned back towards her.

'Are you hungry? I am. Let's see what I can find in here.' He reached inside and rummaged, then stood up. 'Now. What's this? I've some Brie, some goat's cheese and a few other bits and pieces. And these are nice, these black olives.'

He laid crackers on a plate and she cut chunks from the cheese and offered them to him.

'My mother wouldn't approve,' she said as she bit into a biscuit, crumbs scattering across the table.

'No?' His mouth was full as he spoke.

'No, in our house you don't keep cheese in the fridge and you don't eat it with these.' She waved her hands in the air. 'Zees ridiculous bits of zomesing or other. You eat cheese only with bread baked at home, according to the recipe that was handed down from your grandmother to your mother to yourself.'

'Right, I get it. No sliced pan for you?'

'Wash your mouth out at the very idea of it.'

'So she's not the traditional Irish mammy, she's the traditional froggy one, all pink cheeks and gingham apron, baguettes in the bicycle basket and fifty varieties of foie gras?'

She laughed and her cheeks flushed. 'Wrong again, but you can't be faulted for trying.'

'All right then, give me another go. She's the quintessential Parisian. Petite, elegant, languid, perfectly groomed *à la* Coco Chanel. Always the touch of white at the throat and the wrist, *n'est-ce-pas?*'

She threw back her head and laughed, loudly this time. 'Coco Chanel, where did you get that from? You don't look like a dedicated follower of fashion.'

'Thanks.' He assumed a look of wounded pride. 'Thanks very much. Have you forgotten, you who know so much about me, that I'm an illustrator? I cut my teeth on drawings for designers years ago when I was a student. I know my Chanel from my Givenchy and my Schiaparelli from my Yves Saint Laurent.'

'Really? You don't say. So those trousers, are they from the Milan or the Paris or perhaps the New York collections this year?' She gestured with her knife at his paint-spattered jeans.

'OK, OK, you've made your point. Actually, to be honest it was my mother who always said that about Chanel. And, do you know something, I think she was right. It must be the way the light is reflected back onto the skin from the white. Must be something like that.'

He paused. His mouth drooped.

'Your mother,' Min said. 'She died, I heard. A few years back, wasn't it?'

He nodded.

'I remember her. She was a quite a beauty. And I remember the house. It was lovely. And the garden. Stunning.'

He nodded again.

'What happened to it all?'

'My older sisters took care of it. They organized the sale. They got rid of the furniture and everything else. I let them at it.'

'You didn't come back for it? You didn't want any of it?'

He shrugged and stared at the floor.

'I don't know. I couldn't face it. So I did what I always did when it came to the family. I behaved like the indulged little brother, the spoilt brat. They sent me a large cheque. They exonerated me from all responsibility.' He fiddled with the spoon again, then looked at her.

'Another?' He stood up and held out his hand. The drink was going down well. She could feel her cheeks flushing and a sudden gaiety in her voice. She nodded.

He set the steaming glass down in front of her and she raised it in salute.

'Anyway,' she said, 'you still haven't worked out my mother, have you?'

'Oh, all right, I give in. Put me out of my misery.' He sat back and crossed his legs.

'Well, the way it was, she was the cook on a fishing boat that came into a little place called Slievemore, down in west Cork. They'd engine trouble and the weather was bad and they were stuck there for a few weeks, *et voilà*, she met my father, fell madly in love and when the weather cleared and the engine was fixed she decided she'd stay on and marry him. He's a fisherman too and his family owned a pub, had done for years. So she started working in the bar, completely transformed their attitude to food, opened up a restaurant specializing in fish, unheard of at the time, drove everyone mad with her perfectionism, and made a huge success out of the whole thing. She's quite something, my mother. Quite something indeed.'

'And you get on well with her?'

Min shrugged. 'Yeah mostly, I mean she's bossy as hell. Completely dogmatic. Despises the Irish, so she says, although she's lived here for the best part of forty years. Doesn't think anyone's good enough. But underneath it she's a dote. And I'm the only girl in the family. And I'm the only one who doesn't live near them. And I'm the one doing this crazy job, so she says, and I'm the only one who's given her grandchildren.'

'So you're the pet, the favourite.'

She smiled, drained her glass, glanced at her watch. 'Won't be for much longer if I don't get home soon. She'll think I've been up to mischief.'

'Is that something you often do? Get up to mischief, I mean?'

She giggled. 'Well, I haven't recently. Too bloody busy. But once upon a time when I was in my youth and prime . . .'

'Come on, don't give me that. Once when you were in your prime, pull the other one. If you're not in your prime now, I can't imagine what you will be like when you are.'

She laughed out loud. 'Flattery, it'll get you everywhere. Every time.' She looked at her watch again. 'I suppose I could stay a bit longer.'

He drained his glass. 'Well, I don't know. I don't want you to get into trouble on my account. Perhaps another time might be better.' He stood up and held out his hand. 'Look, I'm sorry about earlier. I didn't mean to take my feelings out on you. I appreciate this. It means a lot to me. I hope you didn't stick your neck out too far to get hold of them.'

She felt the smile stiffen on her face. She stood up, suddenly light-headed. She picked up her coat and bag.

'Well, I did, but who knows?' She turned away and began to walk towards the front door. 'Maybe something good will come out of all this in the long run. I'll give you a call in a couple of days.'

She stopped and turned back. 'Have you been doing much since you've come home?' she asked.

'Much?'

'Yeah, asking questions, going back over what happened. The kind of things you thought we should be doing.'

'Well, actually – ' He bent down and picked up one of Owen's pictures from the floor. 'In fact I went to see him yesterday. Do you recognize the face?'

She took the piece of paper from his hand, and stared at it. 'It's that boy who was his best friend, isn't it? The one who was with him that day.'

'That's right. We had a very interesting conversation about Owen. He told me something I didn't know.'

'Oh?'

'He told me Owen was in love with Marianne O'Neill. I'm not sure whether I believe him or not. I'm not sure that it's possible for an eight-year-old to be in love.'

She handed the picture back to him. 'My boys fall in love. They have deep and intense crushes on people. They can become quite obsessive.'

'Yes, but love, that's different surely?'

'Is it? Or maybe it's just that we don't recognize that what they experience is love. We call it a "crush" because we don't accept that children can feel with such intensity. Because if they do, then so many of our attitudes towards them and our behaviour towards them would be not just unacceptable but cruel and wrong.'

She opened the front door and stepped outside into the darkness.

'It's interesting, anyway, that he should, after so many years, still describe Owen's feelings as love. It must have been very powerful then for him to remember it that way.'

'Yes.' Nick followed her outside. 'But does it mean anything? Is it significant?'

'Well, probably not. But it was something that we didn't know, it's something new. Remember it when you're going through all that stuff I brought you. OK?' She opened the car door. The interior light gave it a warm, inviting appearance. She got in. She slammed the door and it was dark again. He walked out onto the footpath. He watched her drive away, the rear lights red and cheerful and the winking orange of the indicator as she turned onto the main road. He looked up at the windows of the house. The sitting room was bright. He could see the glow of a fire in the grate and hear music. He recognized the tune. It was

'My Funny Valentine'. He stepped closer and inclined his head to listen. Miles Davis on trumpet, Bill Evans on piano and Paul Chambers on bass. His CD, perhaps even his old LP. He turned away and walked back inside. He closed the door behind him.

It began to rain as she drove from Victoria Square towards the centre of the town. The wipers hustled the water efficiently from the windscreen, their noise a familiar comfort. She had, she thought, an infinite amount of pity for Nick Cassidy. She hoped she wouldn't regret giving him the files. It was strictly forbidden, she knew, and it wasn't like her to be so reckless. What would Andy think? she wondered. They had talked about Nick and his wife from time to time over the years. She had asked Andy the big question.

'Did you ever seriously think he might have had something to do with it?'

'No, not really. His problem was his other secret. It was that which was eating him up. He kept on trying to find a way not to reveal it. For good reasons. He didn't want to hurt his wife. He didn't want to add insult to injury. But eventually it had to come out.'

'So what about Susan? What did you make of her?'

'Now, there was a puzzle. If she hadn't had such a strong alibi for the whole period of time I might have wondered a bit more about her.'

'Really, why was that?'

'I don't know. There was something cold and detached about her. He cried a lot more than she did. And she was so cool when she found out about the affair. I remember when I told her. And I didn't do it very gently. I smacked her in the face with it. I read Cassidy's statement to her. All the details we'd extracted from him. Times, dates, meetings. And feelings. I'd gone into all that with him. And he'd told me. Once he got started he couldn't stop. How his relationship with his wife had cooled over the years. How she was so involved in her work. How he'd really enjoyed the friendships he'd built up with all the other women in the square. And how inevitably one thing had led to another.'

'He didn't really say that, did he? He didn't really use that bloody cop-out line.'

'Yeah, sorry. I know you like him. But he did.'

'And this last one, Gina. Was she casual? Was she like all the rest?'

'Well, I suspect she was, but he kind of made out that she wasn't. I don't think he wanted to admit to me just what class of a shit he really was. But when I told Susan Cassidy about it, when I read the statement to her, she just looked back at me and raised an eyebrow and said something like, not that again.'

'But you didn't really think she was involved in Owen's disappearance did you?'

'No, it would have been quite out of the ordinary. Not unheard of, of course. Women are just as capable of killing their children as men.'

'Just as capable, maybe. But not as likely, surely.'

'Well, statistically I suppose you're right, but you wouldn't want to rule it out. Not completely.'

'OK, not completely. We won't rule it out completely.

But we'll put it on the back burner until we need it. So, apart from that, give us a theory, give us the benefit of all your years ferreting around among other people's secrets.'

What could he say? The child was dead, that much was clear. Or almost clear. The child had probably been killed by someone who knew him. Otherwise there would have been a struggle, a scene, a fuss that would have been noticed. And there wasn't. No one saw anything that afternoon that was a cause for comment. It was, to all intents and purposes, a perfectly ordinary autumn day in a perfectly ordinary suburb.

'I still can't believe,' she said more than once, 'that no one saw anything. That still perplexes me. Even after all this time I still can't get my head around the fact that not a single one of all the hundreds of people we questioned, that no one saw the child, saw where he went after he and his friend split up. It doesn't make sense.'

So what would Andy think about her trip to the archives and the bundle of files she had left on Nick Cassidy's kitchen table?

'Come on, Andy, tell me.' Her voice was loud in the car.

There was silence. Was it disapproving? She listened. And heard the crack of fireworks and saw a sudden sunburst of colour hanging in the night sky. It was that time of year again. She must remember. A pumpkin, a few bags of nuts, packets of sweets, and what was it Joe wanted? A witch's mask made of hard plastic.

She slowed down and turned left into the cul-de-sac that was home. She stopped outside her house and turned off the ignition. The curtains were pulled over the large downstairs windows. A sudden gust rang the bells of the Japanese wind chime that she had hung outside the front door. Inside it was bedtime. The boys would be warm and snug beneath their matching duvets. They would be waiting for her goodnight kiss before they would allow themselves to go to sleep. She walked to the door and put her key in the lock. She turned back just for a moment and looked up at the night sky. The red lights of a plane turning to make its descent to Dublin airport flashed, then flickered and disappeared as a cloud passed in front of them. She turned away, let herself in and closed the door on the outside world.

Nick looked up from his laptop screen. He had begun to read through the stack of files, making notes as he went. It was quiet now. No more music from upstairs. The rain had stopped and the wind had died away. He stood and stretched. He needed some exercise. One thing he liked about America. The way that everywhere you went there were running tracks. He'd got used to his daily jog. It cancelled out the other bad habits.

He picked up the glasses and plates and carried them to the sink. He washed and rinsed them carefully. He was drinking far too much. He'd want to watch it. He remembered before. That year between Owen's disappearance and his decision to leave. He remembered that he remembered virtually nothing of it.

He put on his jacket and walked to the front door. Outside it was cold and very damp. The footpath gleamed with a bright wet slick. He crossed the road to the square and pushed open the wrought-iron gate. He began to run, criss-crossing the grass, his breath loud in his ears, dodging around the wood piled high for the Halloween bonfire.

Backwards and forwards he ran, feeling the sweat begin to gather in the small of his back and across his chest. Someone had left a child's football abandoned beside one of the wooden benches. He kicked it, then followed it, kicking it again, then catching it on his instep and bouncing it up, dodging backwards and forwards, keeping it in the air. And saw that he was no longer alone. Someone else was running towards him. He kicked the ball hard, and watched how it was flicked away, pursued, then blocked and then kicked back towards him again. He lunged after it, caught it with his toe, stopped it, then booted it high and wide, and saw the other figure running, getting beneath it, his body arching, his neck elongated, as he caught the ball on the crown of his head and flicked it back. As he turned the street lights shone on his face and Nick recognized the angular features, the dark hair flopping over his forehead, the dark-rimmed glasses, the irregular grin which made his face look lopsided. And a salute and a voice calling out across the square.

'You're back. I heard you were coming. I see you haven't lost your touch. Bet you, bet you can't beat me to a goal. Bet you, bet you can't.'

And remembered Owen, running full tilt towards him.

'Bet you, bet you can't. Bet you. Bet you.'

As he lunged again, the side of his shoe flicking the ball up, then the sound of his toe connecting with the wet leather as it flew through the air, and landed, wedged against the railing.

'Cassidys one, Gouldings nil.' He shouted and heard Chris's laugh as he ran towards him, his arms outstretched.

Fifteen

Susan stood at the window and watched them. She heard them laugh. She heard the dull thump of the ball. She watched their agility, their grace, their fluid movements as they lunged and jumped and chased and kicked. From this distance it was hard to tell that Nick was so much older than Chris. Or it would have been hard if she had been a casual observer. But she could see the slight stiffness in his knees, the way he caught his breath as he ran. She knew that the sweat would be running down his back and gathering beneath his hair where it flopped over his jacket collar. She knew all this. And she knew more.

She watched them, saw them walk away from the muddy grass of the square, still kicking the ball ahead of them as they crossed the road and disappeared beneath her view into the basement. She moved then into the hall and stood by the door which had once connected the upstairs of the house with the downstairs. It had been locked and sealed for years, but when she pressed her head against it she could clearly hear their voices. Hear laughter, hear music.

She walked into the kitchen. Poured herself wine from the half-empty bottle on the table and began to clear away the remains of dinner. Paul had cooked it. Fillet steak with potatoes and a salad. He had finished his. She had barely touched hers. She would keep the scraps and take them out to the fox. Later. When the moon was up.

She stacked the plates and cutlery in the dishwasher. Then sat down, looking through the glass door towards the garden. The house around her was silent. When Paul left he had slammed the front door so hard that the windows had rattled. She could still hear the echo. He had shouted at her that he would not be back. She felt sick, a hollow in the pit of her stomach. She should call him. Apologize. Tell him she knew he was right. But somehow she couldn't bring herself to stand up, to move towards the phone.

He was right. Of course he was right. Her head told her so. But her heart refused to acknowledge it. She raised her glass. The woman reflected in the glass door raised hers too. They saluted each other.

'You're all I've got,' she said out loud. 'Just you. You're all I can depend upon.'

She drank some more. She was tired. She felt as if she could lay her head on the table and sleep. She had been tired when she came in from the hospital. The child in isolation was not doing well. It was touch and go whether she would survive. She had delayed leaving the ward, so it was late when she got home. She had rushed to get the candle and the lighter. She had been just about to leave the kitchen when she had heard Paul's voice in the hall.

'Sue, are you there? Where are you? I've got something for you.' Bursting through the door, a large bunch of lilies in his arms, a bottle of wine wrapped in tissue paper and a supermarket bag. 'Lovely to see you. Sit down now, I'll get you a drink and then I'll cook. How about that?'

But the smile on his face faded as he saw her, standing like a guilty child at the back door, her hands full.

'No,' he said, 'no, not this again. You can't keep on doing this. It's crazy. What on earth is the point? You're just tormenting yourself. You've got to stop.'

She said nothing, backed away from him, her fingers already reaching for the handle.

'Susan, listen to me. Your child has gone. But mourning this girl, who you didn't even know, it's senseless. All it's doing is dragging up those feelings which by now you should have put behind you. What is the point to this ridiculous ritual you go through every October? Susan, please. Listen to me. I know what I'm talking about. I know what I'm saying is right.'

But she had turned and opened and closed the door, running down the steps, across the grass and out into the lane. Not stopping to look behind. Not letting herself think about his words. Running through the darkened streets until she came to the place. Kneeling to light the candle. Waiting until the flame had struck. Saw the flowers and cards that someone else had left. Recognized the writing. Knew who it was. Stood and closed her eyes. Remembered that evening five years ago when she had gone to the meeting in the local church hall. The Church of Ireland clergyman had suggested it to her. He had come to call. She had been rude and offhand. He had been patient. He told her he had known her father. He remembered a sermon he had preached one Easter. It was on forgiveness.

'He was a lovely man, a good man, a man of God. He believed in reconciliation,' he said, his plump cheeks colouring.

'I don't believe,' she replied bluntly. 'I don't have any faith. I stopped believing when I was twelve. There is only darkness after death. That is all.'

'Fine,' the young man said. 'If that's what you want. But what about the living? You need help. You need to share your grief. You're not alone in this. Come along some evening. Meet others who are suffering like you. It may help.'

So she had gone. Sat on a hard folding chair. Looked around her at the faces whose agony was laid bare beneath the harsh strip lighting. And it was there she met Catherine Matthews.

'I'm here because my friend is dead,' the young woman said. 'She was my best friend. She was wonderful. She was pretty and funny and talented. I trusted her with my life. But I didn't know her. She betrayed my trust. She fell in love with my father. He betrayed my trust and the trust of my mother and the rest of the family. All the time when Lizzie was with me she wanted to be with him. When she came on holidays with us, he wanted to be with her. And then it happened. One night. They were together, meeting, in the shed next to the house where she lived. And she died. Someone killed her. Someone put their hands around her neck and squeezed tightly until she could breathe no more. The police thought it was my father. They arrested him, charged him with her murder. He was tried, but he was found not guilty. Because they had discovered that she was also with someone else that night. Another man. There was another sample of semen on her sweater. It didn't match my father's. So he was found not guilty. But not guilty of what? Not guilty of putting his hands around her throat and stopping the air from flowing into her lungs. Not guilty of that. But guilty of betrayal, of seduction of an innocent, of corruption of a girl who was young enough to be his daughter, of destroying my mother and us, his children too. Guilty of those sins and more.'

That night, after they had all left, Susan had followed Catherine Matthews down the road. She had put out her hand and touched her arm. They had gazed at each other. No words were needed. Catherine had taken her to the place where Lizzie had died. That was five years ago. And every October since Susan had gone each evening to light her candle and to remember.

Paul had been in the kitchen when she returned. His face was flushed. He had been drinking. The atmosphere was heavy with disapproval. He had laid the table and cooked the potatoes. The salad was prepared. The frying pan was smoking. He slapped the steaks down on it.

'Paul, please, I know that in many ways what you say is right, but . . .'

'Yeah, but,' he interrupted. 'It's always "but" with you, isn't it? You never listen to me. You never respect what I say to you. It's always "yes, but" this and "yes, but" that. I told you what I felt about him.' He stamped his foot on the floor. 'And what did you say? "Yes, of course I agree with you, but he does still own half this house. He was my husband. He was Owen's father. He needs this."' He turned towards her. 'He needs it? What about me? What about us? What about our relationship, Susan? Our future? Tell me that.'

She tried to eat, but the food stuck to her palate. She tried to speak, but no words would come. She reached out to take his hand, but he stood, dropping his knife and fork on the plate in front of him with a loud, discordant clatter.

'I've had it with you. I can't take it any longer. It's your choice now. Your decision.' He turned away, wiping his hands on a cloth and dropping it on the floor. She lowered her eyes from the fury of his gaze. She heard his footsteps retreat along the hallway. She heard the door slam, the reverberation of the sound through the house. Then the silence.

When the moon had risen above the house, she took the plate with the scraps of meat and walked down the steps into the garden. She would leave them beneath the buddleia. The fox would find them there and take them away. She bent down and laid her offering on the ground, then straightened up and turned again towards the house. Lights were on in the basement. Nick and Chris were sitting at the table. They were talking, laughing, their faces animated and expressive. She stood and watched them. She saw them get up and leave. She moved back towards the steps and walked up them slowly. She sat down on the doorstep and leaned back against the cold glass. She waited. Until she saw the shiver of the bush's lower branches, heard the snuffle of the long snout. Saw the quick flick of the tail. Then she stood and went inside. She was cold now. And deathly tired. She climbed the stairs to the bedroom. She dropped her clothes on the floor and slid beneath the covers. She wrapped her arms around her body. The moonlight lay in cold, bright blocks across the floor. She sighed and closed her eyes and waited for sleep.

Sixteen

'So, do you ever see her these days?'

'Who?'

'Marianne, of course.'

They sat at the table where Nick had sat earlier with Min. He offered Chris whiskey. Chris shook his head.

'Not my drug,' he said, 'not any longer.'

'Ah.' Nick poured himself a shot. 'I remember. That's right. You were into other stimulants weren't you? Nearly got you into big trouble. A certain reluctance to come clean with the police when Owen went missing. You had us all going there for a while.'

Chris looked down at the table for a moment.

'Yeah, secrets, we all had our little secrets.' He took a packet of cigarette papers and tobacco from his jacket pocket, and a small rectangle of silver foil.

'You don't mind, do you? I'd rather this than the drink, if it's all the same to you.' He unfolded the foil and began to break fragments of hash from the sticky black block. He bent down and sniffed it appreciatively. He joined two cigarette papers together and filled them with tobacco, then sprinkled the dope into it.

'Nick leaned forward to get a better look. 'I haven't

seen stuff like that for years,' he said. 'It's all grass in the States.'

Chris picked up the joint, carefully rolled the papers together, then ran his tongue along the adhesive edges, twisted the end and lit it. He inhaled deeply and passed the joint over. Nick felt the sudden hit of the drug as he drew the smoke into his lungs. A rush of sensation swept through his body. His head felt so light that it seemed as if it was floating towards the ceiling and his fingers tingled.

'Wow, that's strong. Where did you get it?'

Chris shrugged. He took the joint from Nick, sucked hard, then screwed up his eyes against the smoke.

'Oh, you know. Here and there. Would you like me to get you some?'

Nick nodded. Minutes seemed to pass. Then he spoke again.

'What are you doing these days? I seem to remember, maybe it was Susan told me years ago, that you were teaching. Doesn't seem to fit, the blackboard and the cannabis resin. At least, teachers weren't like that in my day.'

'No they weren't, were they? They were all secret drinkers and paedophiles. Dirty great Christian Brothers getting their jollies at the expense of poor little boys, and nuns with a liking for a slap across the knuckles with the rosary beads. It's not like that now.' Chris exhaled slowly. 'Now I teach in this fantastic school for girls. Lovely girls. All of them. Laurel Park. Do you remember it? Beautiful big old house up the hill. Formal gardens, tennis courts, swimming pool. Everything money could buy.' He stood up and walked over to the drawing board. He sat down and pulled

Nick's laptop towards him. His fingers rested on the keyboard.

'Nice one. Nearly as nice as mine. I love them, don't you?'

Nick shrugged. 'Love isn't the word I'd use. They're useful, that's what I'd say. Handy for emailing work around the place. Quick and simple if you want to do something in a hurry. But they don't give me the pleasure that I get from pencils and paper and charcoal and ink and paint. No way.' He held out his hand towards Chris. 'Hey, what you doing with that joint? Keeping it all for yourself? Very uncool. Very, very unhip.'

Chris stood and moved towards him. Nick reached out and took the joint from Chris's drooping fingers. He drew hard on it. The air was filled with the smell of burning. He held his breath for as long as he could then let the smoke dribble from his mouth.

'Yeah,' he said, when he could control his speech again, 'yeah, the school. I remember it. And I remember that your grandmother lived next door.'

'That's right. When she died the school bought the house. It's dormitories now and classrooms. I even have my own little study there, down in the basement. Very cosy.'

Silence fell over the room. Nick sat back in his chair and closed his eyes. The sound of Chris inhaling and exhaling was loud in his ears. His body felt heavy and sated. He could have put his head down on the table and slept. He was so tired. His limbs felt as if they no longer belonged to him. He moved his feet slowly, crossing and uncrossing his ankles. They seemed as if they were a very long way away. A sudden hunger made his stomach rumble.

'Hey.' He opened his eyes. 'This is crazy. I've got the munchies like you wouldn't believe. I haven't felt like this for years. Come on, let's go and get some fries and maybe a cheeseburger.'

It was quiet on the main street. It wasn't closing time yet. In half an hour the footpaths would be jammed with drinkers meandering home, and the air would be thick with loud conversation and shouted insults. They stopped at the chipper. Chris pushed open the glass door and bent low in an elaborate bow. They stood at the high counter. The smell was overwhelming. Saliva filled Nick's mouth. They ordered.

'Owen loved this place,' he said. 'Do you remember? Marianne used to bring him here as a special treat. Susan was never keen on him eating what she considered junk, but Marianne loved chips. I seem to recall that she specially loved that curry sauce you could get with them.'

'And I loved the spice burgers. And Owen loved the sausages fried in batter. We used to come down here all the time with him. Those nights when neither of you were at home we'd bring him here for his tea. He'd sit up at one of the tables and as a concession to healthiness he'd have a big glass of milk. He always reckoned the milk tasted different here.'

Nick watched how the large dark woman standing at the bubbling fryer stirred the chips with a perforated spoon. Round and round they swirled like scraps of twigs in a whirlpool. He was so hungry he wanted to put his hands into the boiling oil and scoop them out and stuff them into his face. He felt if he had to wait much longer his legs would no longer hold him up.

'Marianne,' he said, casting around for something to distract him. 'Marianne. Where is she now? Do you know? Do you ever see her?'

Chris did not reply. He turned away and walked to the jukebox, which was hanging on the wall. He took some coins from his pocket and fitted them into the slot, then punched a combination of buttons.

'Owen loved this too. Do you remember?'

John Lennon's voice filled the air. Nick sang along with the simple, persuasive melody. Boats, rivers, marmalade skies, diamonds, a kaleidoscope of images.

And saw the child, the girl, the teenage boy as they sat at the Formica-topped table. Saw the child reach out and pick up the tumbler of milk and drink from it, the white froth coating his upper lip, the tomato ketchup red on the plate, on the golden chips, on the child's small fingers. Saw the way he held up his fork and waved it in the air, conducting an imaginary orchestra of singers and musicians.

'Marianne? You want to know about Marianne?'

Chips swirled in the boiling oil. They tumbled from the ladle in a gleaming pile. Nick saw his face reflected back at him from the greasy mirror above the till. He looked old and tired. Spit was gathering in the corners of his mouth. He swallowed.

The woman scooped the chips up into a brown paper bag.

'Salt and vinegar?' Her voice was suddenly loud. He

nodded, unable to speak. He watched the shower of fine white crystals cover the golden fried potatoes. The smell of the vinegar burnt his nostrils. He took the bag, felt its heat through the thick brown paper. He counted out the change. He stepped outside into the damp night. His hands fumbled. He felt the grease cling to his fingers. He ate. He tasted. He stuffed his mouth with food. He swallowed.

'Marianne,' he said, 'yes, tell me about her. I'd really like to see her again.'

It had been bad after Nick left for America. It had been bad before then too, but somehow Marianne had held it all together while there was some semblance of the way they once had been. And then, when Nick left, the world as she had known it ended. She had gone home to Galway.

'But we were on the phone to each other the whole time. And I'd go and see her every second weekend. She wouldn't come to Dublin. She wouldn't come here to see me at home or anything. She wanted me to move down there, to transfer to college near her. But I didn't want to leave. This is my home.'

They walked down to the sea. Out in the middle of the bay container ships were at anchor. Their lights moved slowly up and down as the boats rode the swell. Nick could feel the motion of the water through his own body. He closed his eyes and surrendered himself to the waves.

'So what happened?'

'There are lots of fancy names for it. Paranoid schizophrenia is probably the one most commonly used. But I prefer to think that she went mad. I like that expression much better. What happened to Marianne O'Neill? She went somewhere. Where did she go? She went mad. Where's mad? Mad is the kingdom of the unknown, of the unknowing. Mad is also a place of safety and refuge.'

'You mean she had a breakdown, is that it?'

'No.' Chris turned to him, his face wild with fury. 'No she didn't have a breakdown. She didn't break. She didn't crumble. She didn't collapse. She didn't do anything pathetic or weak or negative. She did something positive. She went fucking mad. She changed into another person. A crazy woman. She spoke, she wrote, she painted, she sang, she made up songs and verses. She lived without sleep or food. She became beautiful, rather than just pretty. But they wouldn't leave her alone. They wouldn't leave her like that. They took her, her parents, and they put her in an institution. They sedated her. They drugged her. They gave her all kinds of junk so she became a thing instead of a woman. They made her fat and ugly and stupid. And like nothing I'd ever seen before. They took her away from me.'

The ships rose and fell. Nick watched their lights. He could no longer tell where the sea ended and the sky began. The pinpricks of brightness formed into patterns. He lifted his head and looked at the shapes of the constellations far, far away.

'Strange isn't it,' he said, 'that we can at one and the same time be inside the Milky Way and yet we're able to observe it as if from outside. I've never quite been able to grasp how that can be.'

They leaned against the harbour wall. Neither spoke. The clock on the town hall chimed the hour. It was one. Nick turned and began to walk away. Then he stopped and looked back at Chris.

'So where is she now? Do you see her?'

'What's it to you? Why do you want to know? The last person Marianne needs is you. After what you did to her?'

'That's not fair, Chris. It wasn't intentional what happened. Whatever happened. I didn't mean to hurt anyone.'

'No, you're like everyone else. Never mean to hurt. But hurt they do.' He scuffed his feet over the footpath. 'I'm not the person to ask about Marianne. I never see her now. But she comes to visit your wife sometimes. They keep in touch. If that's what you can call it. You can't touch Marianne. You can't make contact with her. It's as if the sensitive part of her, her quick, has been coated with a thick insulating layer. Nothing gets through it. Nothing. Not voices or words. Not letters or music or songs. None of the stimuli that once would have had her nerve endings firing. Nothing. Now she goes in and out of hospital. And when she's out sometimes she's OK and other times she sleeps rough. Or lives in a hostel in town. Ask your wife, she'll know where she is.'

'So the drugs don't work?'

'No, the drugs don't work the way everyone wants them to work. They don't bring the old Marianne back and they don't allow a new Marianne to be brought forth. They hold her in a kind of a limbo where nothing is real and nothing is unreal. Where there is only nothing.'

They walked in step together through the darkness towards the square. Drifts of leaves lay against granite garden walls and fallen conkers shone like stones polished by sea water in the glow from the street lights.

'I had forgotten,' Nick said, 'how much I love this place.'

They stopped outside Chris's house.

'Come in,' he said. 'Meet Amra. You've met Emir already, I do believe.'

'Is that his name, the little boy? Is he yours?'

Chris shook his head. 'Hardly, he's nine. He's Amra's son. And the little girl, Sanela, is her daughter. She's nearly five.' He walked ahead up the steps, took keys from his pocket and opened the front door. 'Come in, it's cold out there.'

There was a row of slippers lined up in the hall. Chris slipped his shoes off and gestured to Nick to do the same.

'She's very fussy is Amra. She doesn't like the way we Irish bring our dirt inside. She thinks it should be left out-side, where it belongs.'

They walked in their socks into the room on the left. It was dark. A woman sat beside a dying fire, her head bent, her hands caught tight between her knees. She did not look up.

'Amra, I've brought someone to see you.' Chris squatted beside her and kissed her gently on the cheek. She did not respond. He stood up and tousled her short black hair, then ran his fingers through it, clenching his fist so her head was pulled back towards him. Still there was no response.

'Oh dear.' He let go and she slumped again. He looked towards Nick, who hung back uncertainly in the doorway. 'She's having one of her little moods. Come on, we'll leave her to it.'

The kitchen was cold. The sink was piled high with dishes. The remains of a meal lay on the table. Baked beans congealed on plates and scraps of toast. A bucket filled with dirty clothes gave the room a sour smell.

'Your parents,' Nick asked, 'what happened to them?'

'You didn't hear? The gossip mill didn't reach as far as wherever it was you took yourself off to?'

Nick shook his head. He was tired. All he wanted now was sleep.

'Sit down. I'll make some tea if I can find anything to make it in.'

'No, don't bother, not for me. I've got to go.'

'Oh, I see.' Chris's face was set. His voice was irritated. 'Fussy are we now about a bit of domestic disorder? Not what we're used to, is that it?'

Nick shrugged. 'It's not that, it's just I've a lot to do tomorrow.'

'Oh yeah, doing what? Playing amateur sleuth, is that why you came back here? A bit of Miss Marple, or maybe Hercule Poirot.' His accent slipped into a parody. 'Exercising ze leetle grey cells. Searching for ze cluez and ze beets of evidence zat will bring back ze leetle boy.'

Nick shoved his hands in his jacket pockets and turned towards the door.

'Sorry, sorry.' Chris clenched his left fist and banged it hard against his forehead. 'I didn't mean it. I'm being an idiot. It's the fucking dope, you know. I shouldn't smoke so much of it. But sometimes I just can't stand it. I can't bear to think about Owen and all that. Please.' He stood up and held out his hand. 'Please stay, I really do apologize. Stay and I'll make some tea.'

They sat together in an uneasy silence. The tea was strong and black. There was no milk.

'She forgot to get it. And I forgot too. I'll have to go out first thing in the morning, before the kids wake up.'

'Who is she and what is she doing here? Are you together? I mean, are you a couple?'

'Yeah we are, unlikely as it may seem. She's Bosnian. She came here in 1995. The boy had been badly injured during one of those terrible mortar attacks in Sarajevo. The Irish government did the decent thing and offered to take a number of families. Amra was lucky to get out when she did.'

'And you, how did you meet her?'

'I was brought in to teach English to them. I became very friendly with her. And with the kids too, although Emir is a real problem. He doesn't speak, you know.'

'Ah, I see. I thought it was just me.'

'No, not just you. Everyone. He's mute. It's not a physical thing. There's nothing wrong with his vocal cords or anything like that. And he's very bright. Very high IQ. A total nut with the computer. But for some reason he's made a decision not to communicate verbally. It makes it very hard for his mother.'

'I bet.' Nick sipped the tea warily. 'He's been coming in to me, you know. I've been giving him paper and pencils. He's been drawing pictures. I didn't really understand what he was doing, but it makes more sense now.'

'And what does he draw?'

'Lots of ruined buildings, houses, office blocks. Lots of men with guns. Lots of fires. His pictures are very expressive.'

Chris took out his packet of tobacco again.

'Not for me.' Nick held up his hand. 'I've had enough.'

Chris began to roll himself a joint. 'You must tell me if he begins to draw any pictures that involve his mother.'

'Why's that?'

Chris concentrated on his task. 'She was raped, you know. Emir was little more than a baby. They were living in a small town outside Sarajevo. Serb soldiers came. They took away her husband. They hurt her. They did it all in front of Emir. She ran away and got to the city. Then she discovered she was pregnant. She doesn't know who the father of her daughter is. She could have had an abortion, but she wasn't sure. So she went ahead with the pregnancy. And now every day she's looking at her and wondering.'

'But the boy doesn't know that, does he? Surely he doesn't remember what happened?'

Chris shrugged. 'Who knows? He didn't have enough language at the time to express his feelings. But the social worker and the psychologists who have seen him say that the emotions are all there. It's just there's no way for them to come out. But I'd appreciate it if you'd tell me if his pictures seem to have any sexual content. It would be useful to know.'

He took his glasses off and laid them on the table. He rubbed his eyes and massaged the bridge of his nose. Without them he looked like the teenage boy Nick remembered. His gaze was unfocused as he held a match to the twisted end of the joint. He inhaled deeply.

'Do you love her?' Nick asked. 'You must if you're prepared to put up with all the grief that goes with other people's children.'

Chris exhaled, a long grey stream of smoke. 'She needed help. She was very alone. She was destroyed by what had happened to her. I wanted to do something to make up for—' He paused and picked a flake of tobacco from his lower lip. 'To make up for Owen.'

There was a sound from the hall behind them. Nick turned and looked over his shoulder. The woman was standing staring at them.

'I go to bed,' she said, her voice flat.

'You do that, darling. I'll be up soon.' Chris waved the joint at her.

'I'll go.' Nick stood. Chris leaned back in his chair. He smiled up at him.

'It's nice, isn't it, that sensation of being the man of the house. I never thought I'd enjoy it. But I do.' His mouth widened into a grin.

Nick said nothing. He began to walk towards the front door. Then stopped and walked back to the kitchen door.

'Your parents,' he said, 'you never told me. Where are they?'

'They're both dead. They were on holiday in Spain. They were in a hire car, going from Malaga to Seville. They were in a head-on collision with an articulated lorry on the motorway. They were both killed instantly. My mother was driving. The police said she probably forgot which side of the road she should be on.'

'God. I didn't realize. I'm sorry.'

Chris's face set. He put his glasses back on.

'Don't be,' he said. 'Please, no hypocrisy. I remember you didn't like them. Wasn't there some row over loud music at night time or something? Empties left in the front garden? Something like that?'

A confrontation at the front door. Nick in his dressing gown, a hangover, the house littered with empty bottles and dirty glasses. Owen screaming in his cot upstairs. Brian Goulding's face puce with rage.

Chris continued. 'I didn't like them either. They died and they left me this house. I've got Amra and the kids now. They're all I need. All I want. I have my own home and I have my own family.'

'And your sister? What about her? Is she still part of it all?'

Chris drew heavily on the joint again, then looked up at Nick.

'Oh yes, my sister. You met her. She told me. She told me you didn't approve.'

Nick shrugged. 'I thought it a pity that she was doing what she was doing. That's all. I was surprised. I wouldn't have thought it of her.'

'Oh yeah.' Chris sniggered. 'But you watched her, didn't you? You and all the rest of them. You couldn't take your eyes of her. She told me. She had you spotted right off. She said you couldn't get enough. You kept on getting closer and closer and closer to the stage. Drooling, you were, she said, fucking dying for it.'

He giggled loudly, his shoulders shaking. 'Bloody drooling. She told me. She phoned me and she laughed and laughed. And I laughed too. And I said, that fucker, still up to the same tricks. Never changes.' He stood, the legs of his chair grating on the floor. He pushed past Nick towards the front door. He turned back to look at him. 'You know, when I think of all you had. A wife, a child, a house, a mistress, is that what you'd call her? A career, a reputation, a future. And what do you have now, Nick? Tell me. What do you have? And then I look at myself and I think that I had nothing. And now I have all this. Not bad, eh? Not bad at all.'

He opened the front door and leaned back against the wall.

'Now let's say bye-bye, Nicky baby. Oh.' He turned towards him and put one hand on his shoulder. 'There is just one thing. Don't forget your shoes. It's a dirty wet night out there and I'd hate for you to catch cold.'

Owen's pictures were still strewn where Nick had left them across the floor. He bent down and began to gather them together. The child had done his subjects justice. Who had taught him to see like that? Nick had boasted to Susan that Owen had inherited the Cassidy talents.

'Runs in the family,' he had said. 'All the Cassidys can draw and paint.'

And she had laughed at him and said, 'Yeah right, all the Cassidys are good at making things up, aren't they? Dreamers, fantasists, creatures of whim, that's what you are.'

And he had replied, with not a little rancour, 'Don't you mean that we're creative? Dynamic, mercurial, intuitive, expressive, not bound by the fetters of empiricism like you.'

He picked up the picture that Owen had painted of Marianne. He sat down and felt in his inside pocket for the photograph which he had taken from the noticeboard in the hospital. He compared the two. Owen had seen her as a princess with a little crown on her head. She was smiling, her mouth open in a wedge-shaped grin. Her eyes were round and brown, and her hair, which was parted in the middle, fell down on either shoulder in two thick plaits. Owen had painted big red ribbons on the end of each of them. He had given her a dress of silver and her feet peeped delicately out from beneath its long skirt. A different creature looked back at him from the shiny photographic paper. Her hair was cropped, shaved almost, so closely did it shadow the bones of her skull. And there was no smile on her small face. Once it would have been described as heart-shaped. A term which was overused, he always thought. This face was more like an equilateral triangle, the cheekbones sharply defined, the chin pointed, the forehead revealed by the paucity of hair. He put the pictures down and walked over to the files that Min had brought him. He flicked through them until he found the one with the name Marianne O'Neill printed on it. He walked back to the sofa and sat. He opened it. He began to read.

Statement taken by Detective Sergeant James Fitzgibbon, 2 November 1991

My name is Marianne Gemma O'Neill. My address is 26 Victoria Square, Dun Laoghaire, Co. Dublin. I am aged 19. I am a childminder employed by Nick and Susan Cassidy. On Wednesday, 31 October, I was in the house with Owen Cassidy until 12.30 p.m. Both Nick and Susan were out. Susan was at work in the South Dublin Children's Hospital. Nick had told me he had an appointment in Ranelagh with his publisher, to discuss a new book he was planning. Susan had left for work at 7 a.m. as she always did. I did not see her before she went, but I heard her in the bathroom, which is next to my room. I got up at nine o'clock. I usually got up earlier than that, but because it was mid-term break Owen did not have to be at school so I stayed late in bed. He came into my room at about eight-thirty. He got into bed with me and asked me to read to him. I said no, because I know he is well able to read for himself, but eventually I gave in and read a couple of chapters of his book. I could hear Nick downstairs in the kitchen. When Owen and I went down Nick had made breakfast for us all. We ate scrambled eggs and toast. I drank coffee and Owen had orange juice. After breakfast I did the washing up and put a load of washing into the machine. Owen had gone upstairs to get dressed. I went and had a bath, then I got dressed and went downstairs again. Owen and Nick were having an argument. Nick had told him he had to go out, and Owen was upset because he wanted his father to go with him and look for firewood for the bonfire. He also wanted him to help him finish off his costume. It was a fox and he wasn't very happy with the colour. He thought it should be a brighter orange and he had asked Nick if he could use some of his paints on it. Nick had got cross and said those paints were very expensive and there was no way that he would waste them on a silly old Halloween costume. Then he said he had to go, and that I would help Owen with whatever he wanted. But I said to Nick that he had told me I could have the day off. I wanted to spend some time with my boyfriend Chris Goulding, who lived next door. But Nick said no way, that it was my job to look after Owen when he and Susan weren't able to, that they had made that plain to me when they had me to stay with them. That they were really doing me a favour and it was the least I could do. I protested that I had already made my arrangement, but he just got furious and began to shout. Then he picked up his bag and said he didn't know what time he would be home, and would I make sure that Owen had a proper lunch, that I wasn't to take him to the chipper, that I was to cook him something. Then he left. It was about eleven o'clock although I can't be sure. Anyway I was pretty mad with him. So I did some housework, some ironing, and then at about twelve I gave Owen a tin of spaghetti hoops which he really likes and then I rang his friend's mother. Her name is Mrs Reynolds. They live on the other side of the square and Luke is Owen's best friend. I said would Luke like to come over to play. He arrived about fifteen minutes later. Then I told them that they could go out and look for firewood and not only that, they could go into the town and buy themselves some fireworks. That there were lots of people selling them in the shopping centre. I know I shouldn't have, because I know they're illegal and they're also dangerous. But I just wanted to get him to go off by himself and leave me alone. So I went to the jar in Nick's studio, where he keeps all his small change. He usually has about fifty pounds' worth of it there. And I tipped out the jar and found about a tenner's worth and I gave it to Owen and said he could spend it. But he was cross with me. He said he wanted to spend the day with me, that I had promised that I would help him with his costume. He got really upset and began to shout and scream. And I got really cross too. I hit him. I know I shouldn't have but he was annoying me. He was being really clinging and babyish. He kept on wanting to hug me and sit on my knee and I told him to grow up. And he said why couldn't he come with me to the Gouldings, that I usually let him, that he liked being with all of us. But I was determined that he wasn't going to come with me this time. So anyway, at about one o'clock I went next door to the Gouldings. Owen and Luke Reynolds left the house at the same time. I said I'd be back at about five and if they got tired or hungry or anything they should go to the Reynolds' house. So I went into the Gouldings and I spent the rest of the day there. There was Róisín, Chris's sister and her boyfriend Eddie Fallon. Chris had got some acid, and we all took some.

It was my first time and it was amazing. I felt the way I used to feel before I got sick, when I was a little girl. It was as if I had gone back to being that person again. I wanted to stay like that all the time. I didn't want to come out of it. But I fell asleep and when I woke I wasn't sure what time it was. But I knew I had to go back to the Cassidys' house. Susan Cassidy was there. She'd come home a bit earlier than usual because it was Halloween, and when she asked me where Owen was I couldn't answer her properly. I was still pretty out of it. I said that I thought he was at the Reynolds', although I actually didn't know. But when she phoned Mrs Reynolds, she said she hadn't seen Owen and she said Luke had come home at about three and he hadn't seen Owen since. So we waited for a bit and then Nick came in. It was dark by now and they were getting worried. So I went out and walked all around the square and then went into the back lanes where the kids often went to play and I kept on asking people everywhere if they had seen Owen, because everyone around the place knew him. He was very popular. But no one knew where he was, so I went back to the house and then at about seven o'clock, I think it was, when Nick and Susan were getting really worried, they decided to phone the guards.

The signature was clumsily formed. He remembered that Marianne had missed a lot of school when she was ill. She had found it hard to fit in when she went to secondary school. She was always lagging behind the other girls. Her parents had worried so much that she might not be able to manage, that she would never be able to function as an adult. But Susan had tried to reassure them. He remembered hearing her on the phone. Always patient, always kind. She'll be all right. She's a bright girl. She just needs a bit of confidence.

He remembered the row that morning. The way she had stood up to him. He had been furious with her. It was all planned. He did have a meeting with the publisher, but it would last at most for half an hour. Then he would go and buy a few treats. A good bottle of wine. Some nice bread and cheese. To take with him to Gina.

He walked over to the drawing board. He laid down a fresh sheet of paper. He rummaged among his boxes of brushes. The finest of sable was what he wanted. He unscrewed a bottle of dense black ink. Marianne's story appeared before him. In black and white. A frieze of images. That day as she had described it. Sheet after sheet of paper dropped to the floor beside him. When he had finished he bent down and picked them up, then taped them in sequence to the wall above the fireplace. He stood back to look. Then he lay down on the sofa and pulled a blanket over his body. He closed his eyes. He slept.

Seventeen

Did he recognize her, the girl who stopped in front of him on the pier and said his name out loud? She was wearing a knitted hat, rainbow stripes, pulled down low over her forehead so it almost covered her eyebrows. And although it was yet another warm, bright day, a long grey overcoat, which fell to the toes of her heavy, laced black boots.

He had woken with the sun falling across his face. He had showered and eaten. It was late. It was past noon. When he walked outside the sky was pale blue, washed clean by last night's rain. The boy was sitting on the front steps next door. Nick stopped. He held out his hand. The child took it.

'We'll ask your mother, will we? We'll ask her if you can come with me down to the sea.'

He looked up. Amra was standing in the doorway.

'Would that be all right with you? I'll take good care of him. He just needs a coat.'

She nodded. She disappeared inside and came back a couple of minutes later. She handed Nick a faded red anorak.

'He be good,' she said. 'He be nice boy with you.'

*

They had walked to the pier. Emir had dropped Nick's hand and skipped ahead of him. There were groups of men fishing from the granite walls. Emir squatted down, inspecting their bags of bait. Nick sat on a bollard and turned his face to the sun.

And then he heard her voice and saw her face.

'Nick, Nick, Nick, Nicky, Nicky, Nicky.' The girl repeated his name over and over again, as if savouring the sound of it in her mouth. At her feet a small black dog slumped, then looked up at him with the same intense brown stare as the girl.

'Nick, I heard you were back. Susan told me. I wanted to see you. I've come to find you. I went to the house, but there was no one there. No one person, no single person. Not a person in all the world. And then I thought. I wondered. If I was Nick and it was a sunny day and the world looked beautiful and I wanted to see it and enjoy it the way I used to see it and enjoy it, where would I go? And if I wanted to find my boy and be with my boy the way I used to be, where would I go? And of course, then it was so simple. Once I was inside your head I knew where to come and it was here.'

She held out her arms and spun around and the pier and the blue of the sea and the huge white ferry and the seagulls in the sky and the lifeboat rocking at anchor and the women walking their babies in their buggies spun with her. A kaleidoscope of colour and desire and warmth and brightness and happiness, all moving and changing shape as she moved. And the dog leapt up and down beside her, barking and barking, his long pink tongue flopping from the side of his wet black mouth. And Emir ran towards Nick and clung onto his legs, his mouth opening and closing, making no sound, his eyes squeezed tightly shut, his small thin fingers digging through the cloth of Nick's jeans as he held onto him.

And Marianne looked down at the boy's blond cockscomb, then back up at Nick's face, and dropped to her knees and reached out to touch the child, muttering so Nick could hardly hear the words.

'Is it you, my treasure? Is it you, my little boy? Is it you, my lordling? Is it you, my Owen, the light of my life, the stuff of my dreams, the apple of my eye, the song of my heart?'

But the child reached out towards her face, his fingers twisted into claws and drew red marks down her cheeks, so she fell back with a cry, losing her balance and sprawling on the pier's warm granite stones.

'Shh, stop it, Emir, calm down. It's all right, no one will hurt you.' Nick bent and picked up the child, holding him awkwardly, trying to gather in his legs and arms, so he wouldn't kick or reach out to scratch or bite.

'It's all right. She's friend, Emir, a nice person, a good person. She won't hurt you.' Waited till the child's heart had stopped fluttering and skipping like a panicked bird, then placed him carefully down again, and reached out to what looked like a pile of old clothes flung down and found Marianne's small hand and took it, then squatted beside her, murmuring words of comfort for her too.

'It's all right, Marianne, he just got frightened. He doesn't speak any English. He doesn't speak at all. He's from Bosnia. He's been through a bad time. He saw some terrible things when he was little. He needs lots of love and affection. He needs help.'

She lifted her face. The scratches were deep. Tiny beads of blood oozed in a dotted line across her cheek.

'Come on, now. Would you like to come home with me? You need to have those bathed. I wouldn't think that Emir's fingernails are the cleanest. You know what little boys are like.' He reached up and stroked the top of her head, let his hand drop down, felt the bones of her shoulder, the thinness of her upper arm. Waited as she gathered herself together and stood, slowly, wrapping the heavy coat around her body, straightening up, tears still washing from her eyes.

'Where's Timmy?' she asked, pulling a piece of rope from her pocket. 'He should be on a lead. They don't like dogs running around by themselves here. They get in people's way, they get very cross here when dogs go off by themselves. And they take them away and you have to pay lots of money to get them back. And I don't have any money, not enough to pay. Can you see him anywhere?'

He hadn't gone far. He had made friends with a black Labrador and was cavorting beneath the bandstand. Nick ran after him and caught him by his collar and tied one end of the rope to it. Emir watched, his thumb in his mouth.

'Come on.' Nick held out his hand. 'Let's all go home.'

He lit the fire in the stove and waited until it had caught and there was a dull red glow from behind the glass door. Then he began to cook. His favourite pasta sauce. Marianne and Emir sat at the kitchen table and watched him. The two pairs of eyes, dark brown, light green, followed his movements. The dog lay curled in a corner, from time to time cocking one ear stiffly.

He chopped up rashers of bacon and fried them in olive oil. He added garlic, then tinned tomatoes and small slices of bright red chilli. He added more oil and let it all bubble away together. He cut bread from a long French stick. He boiled the kettle and filled the saucepan with the water, then threw in handfuls of pasta, penne, quills with sharp diagonal ends. The kitchen windows whitened with steam. The smell of the food drew down saliva and tummies rumbled in anticipation.

He sang as he worked.

> 'You are my sunshine, my only sunshine,
> You make me happy when skies are grey.'

Marianne's voice took up the song.

> 'You'll never know dear how much I love you,
> Please don't take my sunshine away.'

Nick looked over at her as he stirred the pot. She had taken off her hat. Her skull was very white through the dark stubble of her shaved head.

'Your coat, Marianne, you can take it off now. It's warm in here.'

She shook her head and pulled it even more closely around her thin shoulders. But she was smiling for the first time as she sang, the words flowing from her large soft mouth, one booted foot keeping time beneath the table.

Beside her Emir too beat out the rhythm with a wooden spoon. He watched her closely, his mouth opening and closing in a mirror image of hers.

Nick spun around and waltzed over to Marianne. He held out his hand and pulled her up to dance, singing loudly,

> 'The other night dear as I lay sleeping
> I dreamed I held you in my arms,
> But when I awoke dear I was mistaken
> And I hung my head and I cried.'

She laughed out loud as they whirled around the room, dodging the sofa, the drawing board, the table and chairs. They sang together

> 'I'll always love you and make you happy
> If you will only say the same
> But if you leave me and love another
> You'll regret it all some day.'

He felt her fingers gripping the flesh of his upper arms and he pulled her faster and faster, repeating the words of the song while the room spun around them, boy, dog, bubbling pots on the cooker, scarlet glow from the fire in the stove. Everything warm and bright and their voices loud and tuneful. Then, as they came to the end of the chorus again, he dropped her hands and stepped back with a bow, then led her to her place at the table, pulling out the chair and seating her carefully. He turned back to the cooker and speared one of the quills with a fork and held it up, his teeth sinking into the softness of the cooked wheat, feeling the heat on his tongue and on the delicate pink flesh of the inside of his mouth. The dog sat up, all attention focused on the food. Nick held out the piece of pasta, then flipped it towards him. The dog jumped up, his jaws snapping together as he caught it, and gulped it down with one swallow.

'Yes, nice one,' Nick cried out and Marianne clapped her small hands. And for a moment Nick felt a surge of all that old familiar happiness and contentment. Then heard above his feet in the kitchen upstairs the sound of footsteps. He looked up and Marianne looked up too, the smile fading from her face as she heard the boards creak. And her eyes brimmed with tears and she dropped her head down towards the dog, who was once again slumped by her feet. Nick turned back to the cooker. He lifted the pot and began to strain the pasta into a sieve. Behind him Emir got up from the table. Nick looked over his shoulder and watched as the child began to draw with one finger on the steam-covered window. Two circles for the eyes, a blob for the nose and the mouth, a convex curve turned down at the corners. Then he turned back and put his hand on Marianne's shoulder and held his face up close to hers. He opened his mouth and put out his tongue and began to lick away her tears.

They ate and it was good. Nick opened a bottle of red wine. He offered a glass to the girl. She nodded eagerly. He poured. They drank. He poured again. They shovelled the bright orange of the sauce and the pasta into their mouths. The evening sun angled through the glass doors. The steam slowly vanished and with it the face. Marianne giggled and smiled. Nick told her stories. Of his travels in America. The places he had lived. The people he had met. He told her about the classes he taught. The pictures he had painted.

'But you've come back,' she said. 'I always knew you would. I knew you wouldn't leave Owen for ever.'

He didn't answer. He pushed away his plate and refilled his glass. He stood up.

'Come here, Marianne.' He held out his hand. Her face was filled with apprehension.

'It's all right, I just want to show you something.'

They walked together to the wall above the fireplace.

'Look, what do you see?'

'There's me,' she said, pointing. 'And there's my boy. And there's him from next door and her from next door and her boyfriend, the Fallon person. And there's the angel Susan and you and that bad woman you were with.'

'And who's that, Marianne?' Nick tapped his finger on the paper. His nail rested just above the head of Luke Reynolds. 'Do you recognize him?'

'He is another bad one. He told lies. He was naughty. He was bad for Owen. He taught Owen bad things. He made Owen do bad things. Owen was always good until he met Luke Reynolds, then things started to go wrong. Luke was not good.' She began to whimper, wrapping her coat around her body and swaying from side to side. 'Not good, not good, he was a bad boy. He was a bad boy. Not good, not good.'

Her voice began to get louder and louder. Emir got up from the table and approached slowly, on tiptoes. The dog had risen too. Now it was Emir's leg he was pressed against, his tail pulled in underneath his skinny haunches.

'Why doesn't he speak?' She turned towards the child.

'Speak to me, boy, tell me your story. Tell me your past, your seed, breed and generation. Tell me who you are.'

She knelt down in front of him and placed both her hands on his shoulders. She put her face close and pressed her nose to his.

'Breathe me into you, little boy, and I will protect you from evil. Here I will give something that will save you from harm.' She fumbled beneath her coat and pulled out a circular disc made of a green stone. She held it up and showed it to him.

'Do you see this?'

He didn't respond.

'This has come from the farthest ends of the earth. It is warmed by my body and when I put it around your neck it will carry with it my warmth and make you warm too. It will carry with it my spirit and my soul and my life's blood and it will save you the same way that I was saved by another's life blood. Here.'

She slipped it over his head, then pulled back the round neck of his sweater and fed the cord beneath the faded wool. She pressed her palm flat against his chest.

'Do you feel it? Does it feel nice and good?'

He stared at her, his eyes as green as the stone. Then backed away and sat down on the floor. He leaned against the wall and pulled the disc from beneath his clothes. He pressed it to his lips then rubbed it over his small face.

'Here, Emir, for you.' Nick picked up a pad of heavy cartridge paper, turned it to a blank sheet and sent it spinning across the room. 'And this too.' A thick pencil followed, turning somersaults over the floorboards. 'Draw something for me. Something you like.'

He sat down on the sofa and motioned to Marianne to join him. She shook her head and stood in front of the frieze on the wall.

'I see the day,' she said, 'I see it all.'

'What do you see?'

'I see the morning, I see the moment when I said goodbye to the boy. I see me standing at the door and knocking. I see Chris asking me to come in.' She stopped. She lifted up her hands and placed them, palms flat against the drawings. 'Where is what happened next?'

He filled his glass from the bottle.

'You'll have to tell me, Marianne. You know. I don't.' He held out his glass to her and she raised it to her lips and drank deeply. The wine ran down her chin and dripped onto the floor. She put the glass on the mantelpiece and took off her coat. Beneath it she wore a padded silk jacket. It had once been a vivid turquoise with a dragon embroidered in red across the back. He knew it. He had bought it for Susan from a stall which specialized in antique clothes in Portobello Market in London, a long time ago. Before they had married. It was faded and tattered now. Covered with patches and other embellishments. Crystal beads had been sewn on the sleeves, and stars and circles embroidered around the high collar. With it she wore a pair of jeans which clung to her legs. They, too, had been patched, worked on, lozenges of bright colours that gave her the look of a harlequin. She picked up the glass again and held it out to him. He filled it. She drank. She began to speak.

'This is the way it was that day. When the leaves were dropping in golden cascades from the trees, I sent my boy away with the bad boy Luke. I gave them money for fireworks. My boy cried and I hit him. He cried some more.

He said he hated me. I laughed at him. I said I hated him too. I went to the next door. I knocked. Chris answered. I went in and down the stairs to the basement. It was dark but it was warm because Chris had made a big fire. The room was filled with heat. The fire was very red. I took my clothes off. He took his clothes off too. Róisín was there and the other boy, Eddie. They took their clothes off. We drank some vodka. Chris had rolled lots of joints. We smoked and drank. We were so happy. We were laughing, all of us. There was music. We were dancing. We were so funny without our clothes. We were so beautiful too. Chris especially. His skin was smooth and very white. I wanted to kiss him, I wanted him to kiss me. Then he said he had something special to give us. He opened his fist. There were pills. He said not to be frightened. That this was the best thing there was. I took the pill and so did everyone else.'

She paused. He waited. He looked across the room to Emir. His head was bent over the pad. One hand was scribbling, the other was twisted through his hair.

She began again. She started to walk in a square shape, from corner to corner. She placed her feet carefully, one in front of the other.

'Awash my body, awash with pleasure. I am so happy. He has taken away the scars of my world. I am not scarred any longer. I am not scared any longer. I am not scared that the cancer will come back and will consume me again. Scared that the magic marrow will stop working and I will be feeble and weak and helpless. Scared that there is nothing in front of my eyes except blackness and night, coldness and pain. We lie down together in front of the fire. He is part of my body. We are growing into one creature with two heads, four arms, four legs. We will be like Siamese twins, inseparable. Together. There will never be anything outside this room ever again. Then something happens. I'm not sure what it is. I open my eyes. I am lying on the mattress. I am cold. There is dust and dirt. The sun cannot shine through the windows because they are so filthy. I sit up. And I see Chris. He is standing above me. He has a camera. He is taking photographs of my body. He pushes me this way, that way.'

She lay down on the floor her legs spread-eagled. She turned over and lay flat, then rose onto all fours. She crouched down and curled into a ball. She twisted one arm back behind her head, the palm facing outwards.

'No, Chris, don't. I don't like it. Not now. Not like this. I know you can see right through me with your cold glass lens. You can see into my blood. You can see what is happening there. I don't want to know. I don't want you to tell me. Don't do this to me any more. Not like this.'

She stood up again and put her hands over her eyes.

'Chris, stop. Don't do this. I am cold, Chris. Warm me with your warmth. Put your arms around me.'

She reached out.

'Lie down with me now, Chris. Hold me.'

She lay down again on her side.

'Be with me. Be thou my beloved. Chris of my heart. I am so frightened. There is blood on the walls. Blood on the floors. Someone is screaming. I heard screaming. It is so loud in my ears. Someone is calling out for help. Someone is frightened. And then it is as if there is a mirror hanging down from the ceiling and I see, suddenly I see it's me. I hear it's me. It's my voice. It's my cry, my shout, my fear. It's me.'

She sat up and began to shriek.

'Help me, help me. Please, someone help me. I'm dying. I don't want to die. I'm scared. I'm helpless. Please, someone make it stop, rescue me. Make it better.'

Her eyes were open, but they looked through him, beyond him. In spite of himself he turned and looked over his shoulder, in the direction of his gaze. Then looked back at her. Tears were streaming down her face.

'So what happened to Owen, Marianne? You were with Chris and Róisín and Eddie. I was with Gina. Susan was at work. Luke was at home with his mother. So where was Owen and what happened to him?'

But she bowed her head and began to shake it slowly from side to side. And Emir was beside her. He knelt down and put his arms around her shoulders. He held her as tightly as he could. He rocked from side to side. And the dog crouched too, one paw resting on her thigh. Nick watched. He waited. Slowly her cries began to lessen. Her eyes closed. She began to breathe deeply.

'Here.' Nick got up and knelt beside them. He lifted her from the child's grasp and laid her down on the floor. He turned her on her side and folded her arms around her body. He soothed her gently with his voice and his hand. Then he pulled a rug from the sofa and covered her carefully from head to toe. She shuddered, her mouth opening, then closing again. A dribble of saliva rolled down her chin.

'Shh,' he said and the boy held a finger to his lips.

'Shh, quiet,' Nick whispered and the boy nodded. Nick stood up and moved away. He walked over to the stack of files. He picked one out and flicked through it. Then he sat down on the sofa and opened it. He began to read.

Statement taken by Detective Garda James Fitzgibbon, 4 November 1991

My name is Christopher Andrew Goulding. My address is 27 Victoria Square, Dun Laoghaire. I am aged 21. I am a student at University College, Dublin, studying English and Philosophy. On 31 October 1991 I had taken the day off because it was Halloween that night. I left the house at about 10.30 that morning and went to meet a friend called Dermot O'Dwyer, at his house in Belgrave Square in Monkstown. Dermot had got me some LSD and some cannabis resin. I walked back home along the seafront, then went to the Quinsworth supermarket in the shopping centre and bought a litre bottle of vodka, some orange juice and some cans of Heineken. I also bought tobacco and cigarette papers. I got home at about 12.30 p.m. My parents were away on holiday in Spain so it was just me and my sister Róisín in the house. I went down into the basement and lit a fire. My sister came and we were joined about half an hour later by her boyfriend Eddie and my girlfriend Marianne O'Neill. Marianne was upset because earlier she had a row with Owen Cassidy, the little boy she looked after. She was very angry because she had asked for the day off and then at the last minute Nick Cassidy, her employer, had said he had to go out and that she would have to stay with the kid. She knew that he was having a relationship with a woman who lives just a couple of houses away. She felt her loyalty was being abused. She felt she was betraying his wife, Susan. She said she was going to tell Susan what was going on. Anyway we all went into the basement and we smoked a few joints and drank some vodka. Then we took the acid. I had taken it lots of times before. But it was Marianne's first time.

I was a bit worried how she would be, because I knew she was very vulnerable after having been so sick when she was a kid. I thought she might be freaked out by it but she said she was fine. So we stayed there in the basement all afternoon. We all had sex, and at one point Marianne did get a bit upset and I had to make sure she was calmed down. I was worried about her. I'd heard about people having bad trips and I thought I might have to take her to the hospital, but I sat with her and comforted her and after a while she was fine again. Anyway at about five o'clock she said she'd better go home. I said I'd go with her, but she said she was OK. That she'd better go and get Owen. She thought he was with his friend Luke Reynolds across the square. So we said goodbye and then about an hour later she phoned me and said they were all frantic because they didn't know where Owen was and would I come and give them a hand to look for him? So I did. I searched all around the square and all the back lanes. There are quite a lot of old mews and garages there. Some of them are nearly derelict. I used to play in them all when I was a kid and I knew that Owen was in and out of them all the time. I thought he might have fallen and hurt himself. So I searched them carefully, but there was no sign anywhere. And when I got back to the Cassidys' house they had called the guards. At first when I was questioned I wasn't completely honest about what had happened because I didn't want to admit the dope and the acid. But that's what happened. That's what we did all day.

Nick lifted his head from the page. The child was crawling across the floor towards Marianne's sleeping body. He lifted the blanket and wriggled beneath it, snuggling into the curve of her stomach and breast. He looked up at Nick, put his finger to his lips, then closed his eyes.

Nick got up and filled his glass again. He walked to the drawing board and pinned down a clean sheet of paper. He sorted through his pencils, then opened a wooden box and took out a brush. He stroked the fine black sable hairs, and rummaged through the row of inks on the shelf. He dipped his brush into the bottle, and drew a fine line on the paper. He stood back and looked at it. Then leaned forward and began.

Time passed. Light drained from the sky outside. Inside, the lamp above his desk glowed. The sleeping bodies on the floor stirred, muttered, turned. The dog shifted and twitched. Soft growls came from his mouth and the flesh of his lips lifted back to show his sharp white teeth. Page after page covered with figures dropped to the floor by Nick's feet. When they were dry he pinned them to the wall and stood back to look.

'What happened next?' he said out loud. Then heard the doorbell ring. Amra was outside. She had the little girl by the hand. Nick beckoned to her to come in and gestured towards the sleeping forms.

'You can leave him here for a bit longer if you like,' he said. 'My old friend Marianne O'Neill has come to visit me. She is not very well. She was tired so she lay down for a rest and Emir was tired too. Don't you think they look very comfortable together?'

She shook her head.

'It is late. Chris is home. He wants his dinner. It is time for Emir to come back. He spends too much time with you in your house.'

She walked to the child and shook him briskly by the

shoulder. He raised himself up, his face crumpled and creased. He looked at her and began to cry. She pulled him to standing. She picked up his coat and roughly began to bundle him into it. He started to protest, but she spoke to him, her voice harsh. His shoulders slumped and he allowed himself to be dressed, rubber boots crammed onto his feet.

'We go now. We say thank you and goodbye to nice Mr Nick. We say we see you soon.'

'I say thank you and goodbye to master Emir. I say maybe we go to the pier again. Maybe next time we go fishing.' Nick squatted down in front of him and did up his zipper. 'Maybe we catch a whale. What do you think, Emir?' He stood up and rumpled his hair.

He sat in the darkness. Through the trees he could see the moon rising. He waited for the light to flood into the garden. Above his head the floorboards creaked and cracked. Music floated down. He recognized the melody. It was Mozart. One of the symphonies, forty or forty-one. He could never remember which. And all the while the girl still slept. Cars passed slowly along the square, their head-lights arcing across the walls, revealing his work, the shapes of the figures he had drawn with black ink on the white paper. What would he draw next? he wondered. What would he find?

Outside in the garden a shadow moved among the shrubs. He stood up and walked quietly to the door. The little dog was at his feet. He sniffed the air and whined, then reached out with a paw and scratched at the jamb.

'No,' Nick spoke sharply. 'Not for you.'

The dog gave an insistent yap. Nick pushed him away with his foot. The dog sat back on his haunches and pressed his nose against the glass. Outside the fox moved confidently forward onto the lawn. She raised her head and looked around, then trotted quickly to the wall and with a quick flick of her haunches was up and over. And gone. Nick opened the door and the dog rushed ahead and disappeared into the dappled darkness. Above them the moon rode high.

'Follow me, moon,' Nick said as he walked away from the house. He looked back and up and saw the moon move with him. And Susan standing in the bedroom window looking down. He lifted his hand and waved. He waited for the response. She stepped back and pulled the shutters closed. He turned away. He whistled and waited. He whistled again and began to walk towards the house. The dog rushed ahead, its long tail wagging, its nose pressed to the grass. Nick clicked his tongue against the roof of his mouth. Then he closed the doors behind them.

What was it that woke him? A sudden cold sensation as the covers were slid away. The feeling of soft skin next to his, of lips on his neck, of a palm slipping down the flat of his stomach. He sighed and turned towards the warmth, feeling the swell of a breast beneath his hand, the smoothness of a thigh beneath his own leg. And heard the girl's voice in his ear, whispering his name, her breath against his mouth. And woke. And sat up, pushing her away, quickly. Violently, so she cried out as she hit the floor.

'No,' he shouted. 'No, not this. Not with you, Marianne. Never with you.'

'But please, please, Nick, my Nick.' She crawled towards him, her hands reaching out. She pulled herself up his body. Her fingers scrabbled at his chest, but as he tried to peel them from him she dug her nails into his skin, ripping downwards, tearing at him. Screaming. 'Please, Nick, you told me you were lonely. You were lost. Please, Nick, I always wanted you. Didn't you know? Didn't you see? Didn't you understand? And you wanted me too, didn't you?'

But now he was on his feet, moving away from her. Repeating again and again. Louder and louder.

'No, Marianne, not you. You were like my daughter. You were a child to me then and you're a child to me now. And it was Owen who loved you, not me. This is wrong. This is not for you. Don't do this.'

She stood, her arms crossed over her nakedness, her close cropped head bowed like a penitent. She bent and gathered her clothes together, hastily scrambling into them. Then picked up her coat, her hat, her bag, called the dog to her with a whistle and a shout. Tears spurting from her eyes. The front door slammed behind her. And she was gone. And all that was left was her face staring down at him from the picture pinned to the wall. A questioning glance, a half smile, and a gaze that passed through him and beyond.

Eighteen

'So, what happened? What do you want from me?'

Nick stood awkwardly at the top of the steps that led into Susan's kitchen. She was standing by the cooker, a kimono tied tightly around her waist, her feet bare, her hair loose and untidy on her shoulders.

'Can I come in? Just for a couple of minutes?'

She shrugged and picked up a cup of coffee.

'If you must,' she said.

'You're not at work today? That's not like you. A day off midweek?'

'I'm not well. I've had a bad throat for the past few days and I can't risk going into the hospital like that.'

'Yes, I remember. The demands of your job. Physical as well as intellectual perfection, isn't that right?'

But it wasn't that. They both knew. She stared at him for a moment and didn't speak. The sun glanced through the windows and shone on her face. He looked at her closely. He could see how she had aged in the ten years that he had been away. The skin of her neck was looser and creased. Her cheekbones weren't as clearly defined as they once had been. Her eyelids were heavier and there were deep lines between her eyebrows. She was very pale today. She looked exhausted, he thought. Vulnerable and delicate. He could imagine the phone call she had made that morning to the hospital. She would have phoned her secretary. And her secretary would have passed on the message to the ward sister and the registrar.

'It's that time of the year again. It's October. We won't see much of her until after Halloween.'

And the response.

'Poor thing. Thank God for email. We'll just send her everything at home.'

'I'm sorry,' Nick said, 'I don't want to keep you out of bed. But there's something I need to ask you.'

'Oh?'

'Yes. It's about Marianne. I'm wondering if you know how to find her.'

He had woken early with a sensation of deep loss. For a moment he lay on his stomach and tried to think what had caused it. A sparkle of brightness caught his eye and he reached out a hand. A small glass bead was lying on the floor. And he remembered. It had been sewn onto Marianne's padded jacket. A decoration, a trim at her wrist. And then he remembered.

He got out of bed. He was naked. He looked down at himself and felt the shame of what had almost happened. He had wanted it. He had wanted her. For a full half-minute or so he had wanted her more than anything else. Years ago he would have had her. He wouldn't have thought twice about it. Indeed, he remembered that it had crossed his mind more than once when she was living with them. It would have been easy to cultivate adoration in her. He had indulged himself in a joking flirtation for a while. If he hadn't already been involved with Gina, he might have taken it further. Even though it would have been risky as hell, dangerous, foolish.

He walked into the kitchen. It was still dark, the garden in shadow, a scattering of stars visible in the sky. He would have to find her and apologize. He would have to make sure she was all right. He couldn't leave it like that. Owen would never have forgiven him if he hurt her. He stepped into the shower and turned on the hot tap. Water poured over his head and down the length of his body and he felt again the smoothness of her skin and winced. And winced too as the scabs on the small scratches which ran down his stomach softened and began to bleed again. He turned the tap to cold and gasped out loud, his skin wrinkling and contracting in the sudden iciness.

What was it Chris Goulding had said about her? That sometimes she slept rough, sometimes in hostels? He would ask him later when he came back from work. What else was it he said about her? That it was Susan she kept in touch with. Susan would know where to find her.

'Do you know where I can find her? I need to see her.'

They sat together at the kitchen table. Susan's head rested on her hand. She listened while he told her what had happened. There was silence.

'You surprise me,' she said eventually. 'Able to resist a warm body. What's come over you?'

'Oh, for Christ's sake.' He stood up. 'Give us a break, would you?' He turned towards the door.

'OK, OK.' She held out her hand and took hold of his arm, 'Look, I'm sorry. I shouldn't have said that. Here, sit down again and have some coffee. There's a full pot on the stove.'

He filled their mugs and picked up the carton of milk. She nodded and watched as he added a generous amount.

'That's right, isn't it? You always liked milky coffee.'

She smiled. 'I still do, and I suppose you still drink it black?'

'Some things never change.'

'And some things do, isn't that right, Nicky?' Her hand rested close to his. 'I'll give you a list of places to try. She's well known out on the street.'

'Is she? Poor kid. What a way to end up.'

'No, you don't understand. She's not as helpless as she seems. Or as mad as she often appears. She has a network of supports, some institutional, many personal.'

'You mean she has friends?'

'Friends, patrons, households all around the city where she's a fairly regular and welcome visitor.' Her wrist was so close to his he could almost feel her warmth. 'I used to worry about her all the time. I used to feel very responsible for the way she was.'

'Well, it was you who cured her. You who gave her a second chance.'

'Playing God. That's what you used to say, didn't you?'

He shrugged and sipped his coffee.

'Bit hard of me really, wasn't it?'

'I don't know. More I think about it, the more I agree with you. Anyway, I did feel responsible for her. And then, after Owen went and she fell apart, I felt even worse. But as time passed I began to see that Marianne, no more than the rest of us, has made choices. And she has chosen to live like this.'

'That's a bit extreme, isn't it? Surely someone like her has a diminished sense of free will?'

'Well, it's not the same as yours or mine, but she has had that explained to her many times. She knows that her thought processes are different, that the way she handles information does not conform to the way the rest of us do. And she knows that if she wants to approximate to the way we think she must take her medication and live with the consequences and the side effects. So there is choice in it.'

Nick sipped his coffee again.

'Not a very comforting set of explanations for her parents, though, I would have thought. I remember what they went through when she was a child and so ill. Her survival must have given them high hopes for her future. They wouldn't have wanted their daughter to end up a wandering vagrant on the streets with a mangy mutt at her side.'

Susan looked at him.

'No, you're right. They wouldn't. But isn't that the first rule of parenthood? To accept difference and to let go?'

He stared past her out of the window for a moment, then looked back at her face.

'We didn't get that far, did we? We never had the opportunity to put the theory into practice.'

She sighed. She moved her hand. He felt her skin brush against his.

'I don't know about that. I think we did. Like Marianne, Owen knew much more than we gave him credit for. I really believe that. I don't see him as a victim any longer. I see him as someone who made some kind of decision that day. I don't know what that decision was. Maybe it was to get into a car with someone he didn't know. Maybe it was not to shout for help. Maybe it was to keep on walking when he could have come home, when it was getting dark. But, whatever it was, I don't believe that Owen was helpless and pathetic. Not any longer.'

A blue tit flew up to the window. It hovered, swift darting pecks seeking out insects trapped in a spider's web.

'You don't mean that. You can't really mean that?'

'No?' Susan sipped her coffee. 'Can't I? Why not?'

'Because you can't be suggesting that an eight-year-old child could have any control over what is done to him by an adult, can you? You couldn't be saying that Owen wanted any of this to happen to him or to us? Could you?'

There was silence in the kitchen. Then the fridge motor began to hum. Loudly, vibrating.

'Do you remember, Nicky, when Owen went through that phase when he was always threatening to run away? Do you remember it? If he was challenged or checked or punished, he'd storm upstairs and appear with a plastic bag with his pyjamas and his teddy. And do you remember you went out and bought him a little suitcase, a cute little cardboard thing? And you said to him, the next time it happened, you said, go on then, off you go. Have fun. And he was so mad. He packed the case and slammed the door and stomped off down the front steps. And we waited. How long was he gone for?'

'It was a good hour at least. You wanted me to go and look for him. You said it was stupid and dangerous. But I said no, that he had to learn. And he did. And he came home. He was wet through and he was hungry, but there was something different about him. He never threatened to run away again. He never behaved like that. So.' Nick got up and leaned against the fridge, shifting its weight. It shuddered violently and the vibrations stopped. 'So what does that prove?'

'It doesn't prove anything, but it says to me that even a small child is capable of making decisions, of choosing. I don't know what he did or didn't do that day. But I know that for me it is extremely important that I do not see him purely and simply as a victim. I just can't do it any longer.'

'So where is he then? Why didn't he come home to us?'

Her fingers moved gently, slowly, touching him. He held his breath. She shifted on the hard kitchen chair and the folds of her kimono slipped.

'I think we both know where he is, Nicky. He's at peace. He's safe and warm and loved by us all. He's loved by God and his Son and his angels.'

She crossed her legs, one long shin wrapping around the other, one bare foot arched on the tiles.

He leaned closer to her, spreading out the fingers of his hand on the table so they almost touched her arm.

'You don't really believe that? You never believed in God. You were vehement in your disbelief. Active in your disbelief. You wouldn't get married in church, you wouldn't let Owen be christened. You wouldn't allow for my agnosticism. You were adamant. There was no proof, you always said. Don't you remember the rows with my mother over it?'

'Oh, I remember all right, vividly, and the way you took her side. But don't be so disingenuous. Think for a moment what I used to say. I wouldn't be married in a Catholic church just for the form, for the ceremony, for the event, for the big hats and the day out and the presents and the white dress and the bridesmaids and all that crap.'

'Who said anything about being married in a Catholic

church? Your father wanted to marry us. Don't you remember? He was so hurt when you rejected his offer. I wouldn't have minded. I liked him a lot. He was a nice man, a decent man, a good man. He would have given his eye teeth to have been able to marry us. But you wouldn't have that either would you? You and your bloody principles.'

'Oh yeah, since when have you been so bothered about all this? It was the vows that were important. The promises. We made those vows and those promises. We made them to each other. And it was you that broke them, if you remember. Not me. I wasn't the one who was interested in the form. I was interested in the content. The meaning. And I was proved right, wasn't I?'

'OK, here we go again.' He straightened up and stared at her. 'That's you all over isn't it, Susan? Having to demonstrate that you were right. Having to nail it down. Having to prove once and for all that you were the good one, I was the bad one. Go tell it on the mountain. Shout it from the rooftops. Never for an instant let me forget that I made a mistake.' His voice rose into a shout and he slammed his hand down on the table so the mugs of coffee jumped. A sudden cold silence fell over the kitchen. Susan lifted both hands and pushed her hair back from her face. She twisted it into a knot at the back of head, held it tightly for a moment, then let it go so it spiralled loosely onto her shoulders again. And as she did so he saw through the wide sleeves of her gown, the white inner edge of her arm, her armpit and the soft heaviness of her breast. His mouth went dry. He swallowed, his throat tight and constricted.

She coughed and crossed her arms over her breast.

'You should be in bed.' Nick said, 'It's too cold here for

you if you're not well. Why don't you go up and I'll bring you more coffee or something. Would you like that? Would you like something to eat?'

She smiled at him and reached out again, resting the back of her hand against his.

'You were always a good nurse, weren't you, Nicky? One of the lovely things about you. You were always so kind when we were sick. It brought out the best in you. All your practical skills and qualities. Do you remember when I was pregnant and I was ill all the time? There was always a slight smell of vomit everywhere. But it never seemed to put you off.'

He smiled at her. 'How could it? You were beautiful when you were having Owen. I loved you big and heavy. You reminded me of Stanley Spencer's angels.'

'So what was it that put you off? Was it when I went back to work? When I wasn't your milkmaid any longer. When I wasn't lying around in bed with my breasts dribbling. Was that it?'

'Don't, Susan, please don't. I can't explain it to you. I can't tell you why I did what I did.'

'Can't, Nicky, or won't?'

Her hand rested against his. She shifted again, and again her kimono opened.

'You were beautiful when you were young.' she said. 'Not just handsome. But truly beautiful. Your hair was so wavy and thick and so black. And your skin was always so smooth. Your mother had skin like that. All your family, men and women have it. Owen didn't have it. He had my skin. Inclined to redness, to flush in the winter, to burn in the summer. He wasn't going to be handsome like you. He was going to be much more like me. Fair and plump once he'd got over his childhood skinniness. He would never have had your long legs and your narrow waist and hips. Rock-star hips, weren't they? Tight jeans and shirts undone to the navel. And leather belts and boots with pointed toes to go with them. You know, I remember when we started seeing each other, when we were students, my friends were all amazed. How did you get him? they used to say. And I knew what they were up to behind my back. They tried to seduce you, didn't they?' She smiled. 'It was an uphill battle keeping all those women at bay and at some stage I gave up. I decided you were on your own. I had my work and my son. And that was enough for me. I made peace with the idea that you were unfaithful.'

He gazed down at her feet. They were broad, the toes strong and well developed. There were still, even now in October, the marks where she had worn sandals during the summer and the exposed skin across her instep was tanned.

'Nothing to say? No clever justification at the ready?'

He shook his head.

'I'm shamed by you, Susan. I have been for a long time. I've had plenty of opportunity to think about myself and what I did. And none of my thoughts are good. But unlike you, I can't accept that Owen isn't a victim. And I can't accept that he is at peace. He won't be at peace until he can tell us what happened. Whether he is alive or dead I need to see him. To hold him. To know.'

Her hand moved against his again. He could feel her bones as they rocked backwards and forwards. And the hard unyielding circle of gold that she still wore on her finger. The clock in the hall chimed the hour.

'Where's your watch?' She turned his wrist over. 'The one I gave you for your birthday. Did you lose it?'

'No, I took it off a couple of days ago. The strap is very worn. I didn't want to lose it. I'd hate to think of it dropping off, falling and breaking or just lying abandoned somewhere.' He touched her hand with his finger. 'After all we've been through together I'd hate that. So I've put it away somewhere safe until I get round to going to a jeweller's for a new strap.'

She smiled at him.

'Come with me,' she said and stood up. 'I'll make that list for you.'

He followed her along the corridor to the small room just off the sitting room. She sat down at her desk. She picked up a pen and began to write. Through the cotton of her robe he could see her spine as she bent forward. Her hair fell down on either side of her neck. He remembered that there was a black mole just above her first vertebra. That there was a small scar just below her left shoulder blade where she had cut herself when she had fallen from a tree when she was a child. He knew she had broken her right arm when she was a teenager. And that she had a neat appendix scar from an operation when she was twelve. He knew how the skin on her stomach had puckered after Owen's birth and that she had silvery stretch marks on her breasts.

'You know all my secrets, don't you,' she had said to him once. 'The telltale story of my life that is written on my body. That no one else knows about.'

He moved closer. She pushed back her hair with one hand. Her fingernails were cut short. Her cuticles were shiny half moons. She never wore polish on them. He could hear the sound of her breath moving in and out of her nose. He wanted to breathe it in as it left her and breathe it back into her lungs again. He wanted to smell her hair, taste her skin, feel the soles of her feet against his leg. He wanted the push of her hip bones against his. He closed his eyes and felt sweat prickle in his armpits and moisten the skin of his forehead.

Her chair moved harshly on the floor.

'Here.' She stood and held out the list to him. 'This will get you started.'

He glanced down it. There were names, addresses, some phone numbers.

'Thanks.' He folded it in half and stuck it into his shirt pocket. 'Will I let you know how I get on?'

She shrugged. 'If you wish. She'll probably show up at the hospital some time soon. We let her bring the dog in to visit the bigger kids.'

'So you'll tell me if you see her?'

'Well, I'll ask her if that's what she wants. She is an adult after all.'

'But,' he started, then broke off as the phone on the desk began to ring. She reached down and picked it up. He turned away and walked towards the door. He could hear her voice. She sounded surprised, pleased. She followed him out into the corridor and towards the kitchen, holding the receiver close to her face.

'Thanks,' she said, 'thanks for phoning. I appreciate it. Especially after, well, you know.' She paused and listened. 'I'm fine really. I would love to see you. Why don't you come by later? That would be nice. You'll cook? How lovely. Hold on. Just a moment. I'll have a look and see what's here.'

She rested the phone on her shoulder. Nick opened the back door and stepped outside. He lifted his hand to her.

She waved, then turned away, and stretched down to open the fridge. He could still hear her voice as he reached the garden. He stopped, his hand on the carved newel post at the end of the wooden banister. A blackbird perched on the pyracantha which covered the back wall of the house. It gazed down at him from its eye ringed with yellow. He didn't move. He waited and watched as the bird bent its head and began to pull at the scarlet berries which decorated the dark green foliage. It reminded him of an illustration from a medieval Book of Hours that his mother had given him when he was a student. The colours were all so clear and vivid, undimmed by the passing of the years. Colours like feelings, he thought. Untouched by time.

A clean sheet of paper was waiting for him. He picked up a pencil and began to draw. Stick figures. A car on a street with trees whose leaves had fallen into soft drifts. A man leans out. A boy leans in.

A car with a man and a boy drives along a motorway. A car stops. A boy tries to get out. A man raises his hand in a fist.

A boy walks along a terrace of houses. It is getting dark. The street lights glow. There is a crescent moon in the sky. There is smoke coming out of chimneys.

A boy goes into a shop. He stands at the counter. He holds out his hand. There are coins on his palm. He takes packets of sweets.

A boy stands in the street. There is a man with fireworks in a bag. Rockets peep from the top. The boy is looking at them. He holds out money, notes this time. The man takes them, gives him the rockets.

A man stands with a shovel. He is digging. Behind him there are mountains. The sky is dark. There is a huge pile of earth and more earth is flying off his spade. Beside him on the ground lies a boy. The fireworks lie beside him. There is a hole in the ground, and the boy lies in the hole. His arms are crossed over his chest. His eyes are closed. The fireworks are at his feet.

There is a hole in the ground, but the boy cannot be seen. He is covered over by earth. Above it hovers an angel. He is singing. He is smiling.

The clouds have opened and the boy is flying up through a gathering of more and more angels. He is smiling too. His mouth is open and he is laughing. Nick can hear his laughter. He can see that he is happy and he is at peace.

He sat back and looked at his work. He picked up the sheets of paper and pinned them to the wall. Then he sat down again and again began to draw. His pencil moved more slowly across the paper.

There is a man's face. It is his face. He is crying. Beside him is a woman. It is Susan. His hand is outstretched, but she has turned away. She is looking at the woman who squats in the corner. Her hair is very black and thick. It hangs down her back in a long untidy plait. Her dress falls open and reveals heavy breasts. One hand is touching her nipple. She holds it out to him as a mother would to a nursing child. But it is not milk which jets from it. It is dark and viscous. It is blood.

He sobbed as he drew. Choking cries that stuck in his throat and made him feel as if he was about to vomit. His chest heaved and he gasped for breath. He flung down his pencil and staggered to the door and out into the garden. And saw the child, Emir, scrambling through the shrubs, a football in his hand. Man and boy faced each other. Then Emir dropped the ball and ran towards him, grasping him around the knees and clinging onto him so tightly that Nick began to sway and lose his balance.

'Hey, kiddo, it's OK. Everything's fine. Come on, let's go inside and see if we can find you something nice to eat. Would you like that?'

He pushed back the child's head and looked down into his eyes. Emir reached up, stretching onto his toes. Nick dropped to his level, squatting. The child pulled down the sleeve of his sweater and carefully wiped the tears from Nick's cheeks with the frayed rib. He leaned his face in close to Nick's and pushed his nose up against his. He scrabbled at the cord which hung around his neck and pulled out the disc of green stone that Marianne had given him. He began to drag it over his head, but Nick stopped his hand.

'No, not that,' he said. 'She gave that to you, only to you. She gave it to you as a present and she wanted you to have it. She gave it to you so that you would look after it. And keep it safe. Here.' He pushed it back feeling the child's skin warm to his fingers as he settled it beneath his vest. 'Now, come on, would you like some lunch? I'm hungry.'

He went into the kitchen and began to make sandwiches. The child wandered around the room. He sat down on the sofa. He lifted the lid of the laptop. He pressed the power button. Nick heard the hum as the computer began to boot up.

'Hey, Emir, not that.' He walked over to the boy. 'I hear you know all about these, but not today.' He switched off the computer and closed the lid. The child looked up at him, his bottom lip thrust out.

'Here.' Nick squatted beside him and touched his cheek.

'There's plenty of paper and loads of pencils. Help yourself to them. OK?'

He moved back towards the kitchen. The child got down on his hands and knees and crawled over to the drawing board. He reached up and pulled down a pad and a box of pencils. He lay with them on the floor. Nick watched him. Emir frowned with concentration. Now and again he would get up and pace around the room, sometimes stopping and gesturing, making sudden swift movements as if in preparation for flight. Sometimes he would lie down and curl into a small tight ball, pulling his head down towards his knees, reminding Nick for all the world of the hedgehogs which once lived in his mother's garden. He wondered as he watched him what had made him like this. And he thought of the images he had seen of the war in Yugoslavia. The straggling refugees. The women and children whose husbands and fathers had been taken away from them and slaughtered. Nick watched the way he gripped the pencil tightly between his thin fingers, how he slashed at the paper so the sharpened point made spiky holes. How he scribbled backwards and forwards across the images, creating a thick black mass of lines. How he flung the paper away from himself, then got up and stamped on it, grinding it into the floor with the heel of his rubber boot. He doesn't need words, Nick thought. His body was his mouthpiece. More articulate than most of the sounds that could come from a child's mouth.

'Are you right, kiddo? Lunch is ready.' He was just about to put plates and glasses on the table when the doorbell rang. Suddenly, loudly, catching Nick unawares so that he jumped and smiled at his own surprise.

'That'll be your mother, master Emir. She'll be wanting

you to go home.' He walked to the door and opened it. Two men were standing outside on the front path.

'Yes?' Nick leaned towards them. 'Can I help you?'

The older of the pair looked up from the notebook in his hand. 'Are you Mr Nicholas Cassidy?'

Nick nodded.

'We're from the guards, Mr Cassidy. Can we come in? There's something we'd like to ask you about.'

Nick said nothing. He stepped back to let them pass. They introduced themselves. Detective Garda Sean O'Rourke and Detective Garda Vincent Regan. O'Rourke, the older of the two, put his hand in his jacket pocket and pulled out an envelope. He opened it and took out a transparent plastic bag. He held it up. 'Can you tell me, these credit cards and this chequebook, are they yours?'

Nick reached out and took the bag from him. He smoothed it down and turned it over. He nodded. 'Yeah, they look like mine. Where did you get them?'

'You haven't noticed that any of these are missing?'

Nick shook his head, 'I've been in all day. I haven't had any reason to use them. Hold on a minute, I'll just have a look and check.' He reached into the back pocket of his jeans and took out his wallet. He opened it and flicked through its contents. 'Yeah, the cards, they're all gone. And I had, I don't know how much, about fifty quid or so and I also had some dollars.'

'And the chequebook?'

'I keep it somewhere, usually in my jacket. Just a minute.' He pulled the coat from the back of a chair and felt through the pockets 'Yeah, it's also missing. That's strange. Where did you get it?'

This time it was the younger man who spoke.

'The body of a young woman was found early this morning on the railway line just past Dalkey village. She appears to have been killed by one of the trains. Your credit cards and chequebook were found in her bag. We were wondering if you might be able to help us with her identification.'

Nick felt the blood drain from his face.

'What do you mean "found"? What do you mean "killed"?'

'Well—'. The younger of the two men paused and looked at the floor. 'To be honest we're not that sure ourselves about any of the details yet. There will have to be a post-mortem and we're waiting for the availability of the chief state pathologist. He's a bit backed up at the moment. So we can't really say what happened. But – ' he looked at Nick – 'what we are trying to do is to establish, first of all, her identity, then her movements before and leading up to her death. So we're visiting everyone who we think had some contact with her. Now.' He stopped, looked down at the plastic bag again. 'It may very well be that your cards were stolen from you. But we did think that perhaps you might have given them to her, that there might have been some contact between you and the girl. So that's why we're here.'

Nick felt suddenly as if he was watching the scene unfold from a vantage point high up. His stomach heaved and his mouth was filled with saliva. Emir grasped his hand, digging his fingernails into his palm. Nick looked down at him.

'If you don't mind,' he said, 'I'd just like to take him home. He lives next door. Make yourselves comfortable. I'll be back in a minute.'

'Fine. We'll wait.' O'Rourke sat down on the sofa and motioned to Regan to join him.

It was bright outside, the sun shining from a clear sky that was the palest of blues, like a watercolour wash on textured paper. Nick hurried the child up the stairs. He lifted the knocker and let it drop. He waited and saw through the glass panes on either side of the door that Chris was hurrying to answer.

'See you soon, kiddo.' Nick gave Emir a gentle push in the small of his back.

'Not staying?' Chris's tone was sarcastic.

Nick didn't answer. He turned away and saw that one of the guards had followed him outside and was waiting below in the front garden.

He took the steps two at a time and pushed past him. He slammed the door shut behind them both.

'OK,' he said. 'Why don't you cut out all the bullshit and tell me what this is really about?'

Nineteen

They walked the line from Dalkey station, their feet slipping and sliding on the heavy loose stones on which the track was laid. On either side the embankment rose to the road above. And above again were the windows of the houses which looked down onto the railway. Ahead was the mouth of the tunnel and dimly visible in the gloom the shadowy figures of the technical team, their white overalls giving a ghostlike quality to their presence. A plastic tent had been erected over the body. Beside it lay a small black dog. Curled up tightly, its head pressed against its flank, only a cocked ear showing that, unlike its mistress, it was still alive.

They approached slowly. The flap on the tent was pulled back. They bent down to get a better look.

'Oh my God.' Min's voice sounded unnaturally loud. It bounced back from the tunnel's curved stone ceiling. 'The poor kid. How on earth did that happen to her?'

She'd got the call on her mobile just as she was leaving home. It was Conor Hickey. He explained quickly. There was a request in from the Bureau of Criminal Investigation. Would they go to Dalkey? There'd been a death. Circumstances were far from clear.

'And besides that, Min, they think you'll be interested

in this. They think it's that girl. You know, the one who was the childminder in the Cassidy case? They've asked specifically for you. OK? I'll meet you there. Fifteen minutes. Oh.' There was a pause. She could hear the sound of traffic spilling from his mobile. 'Hope you've had your breakfast. You won't feel like eating after you've seen this.'

It was the first commuter train of the morning, from Greystones to the city centre, that hit her. The driver had noticed what looked like a bundle of old clothes dumped across the line in the tunnel. And there was a dog. Small, black, its ears pricked up, its eyes gleaming an unnatural red, flattening its body against the curved wall.

He had done what he could. Slammed on the brakes, pressed the alarm button in the cab, resisted the temptation to cover his eyes with his hands. But he was travelling too fast. A slight bump was all he felt before the train slowed to a standstill. He shut everything off then and stayed where he was, stuck to his seat, trying to control the shake in his hands, listening to the rapid bang of his heart in his chest, his bladder suddenly so full that he felt as if he might behave like a three-year-old and let his own hot urine trickle down his leg. Until eventually he could wait no longer and climbed down from the cab and hurried along the track, away from the thing that lay now beneath the train's wheels, fumbling with his fly in the darkness, letting out a sigh of pleasure as eventually he was able to relieve himself. Relieve himself, he'd never understood before what those words really meant. But now this morning he did.

He was back in the cab by the time the police and the

ambulance men and the officials from the railway company
had all arrived.

'Stay there,' they shouted at him as he made to jump
out. So he did. Until they gave him instructions to move
the train, slowly, carefully back and away from the body
which lay beneath. Then they questioned him, quickly,
abruptly, dragging from him the few words he could find
to describe what had happened.

'It's very important,' they kept on saying, 'that you tell
us everything you can remember. Everything.'

But he knew that. This wasn't the first time he'd hit
someone. At least he hadn't seen this one's face. Not like
the old lady who jumped out in front of him a year or
so ago. It had all happened so quickly, and at the same
time so slowly. Her face had hung in front of the windscreen. For ever, so it seemed. She had looked right into
his eyes and opened her mouth. But he hadn't heard her
scream. All he had heard was the thump as the train hit
her body. And then his own voice. Screaming, calling out
for help.

But there really wasn't much he could tell them about
this one. He sat in the cab and put up with the questions.
And then they let him go. The dog followed him down the
track towards the tunnel exit. He turned and tried to shoo
it away. And called out to the guards to take it. A woman
had joined them. She was young and very pretty, with short
black hair cut like a boy's and long legs and a nice smile.
The dog kept on jumping up and trying to lick his hands.
The woman caught hold of it by its collar and pulled it
away.

'Last thing you need, I'm sure, is this to look after,' she
said, with a sympathetic grin. She put her hand on his arm.

'Look, this is awful for you, isn't it? It wasn't your fault. She shouldn't have been there. Don't blame yourself.'

He began to cry then, her unexpected warmth melting the cold sense of unreality which had overtaken him.

'Here.' She handed him a bunch of tissues and a card. 'Listen, my name's Min Sweeney. This is my mobile number.' She tapped it with her fingernail. 'Give us a call if you need anything. Really, anything at all.' She smiled and picked up the dog, tucked it under her arm. 'Whew.' She nodded in its direction. 'Something needs a bath.'

He reached out and stroked its narrow forehead. 'I suppose I could take him. My kids would probably love him.' He held out his hands. 'Here, give him to me. I probably owe him one anyway.'

She watched him walk away towards the light, a lanky silhouette. It was rough, she thought. Burdened by that dreadful sense of responsibility. He'd feel better when they told him. And they would when they had it confirmed by the post-mortem. But it was pretty obvious to everyone already. Marianne O'Neill was dead when that train hit her. Otherwise her blood would have pumped out all over the tracks. She turned and looked back towards the place where the girl's broken body lay.

'Poor kid,' she said softly. 'May she rest in peace.'

It was her old boss, Matt O'Dwyer, the Chief Superintendent from Dun Laoghaire, who had asked for her.

'Don't know whether it's significant or not, Min, but you might as well be in on this. The Bureau need all the help they can get. Your unit will release you for as long as you're needed, and they've offered Conor Hickey too. So

I've told Jay O'Reilly, the inspector I'm putting in charge, that if you want in you'd be very welcome. How about it?'

'Great, thanks. I appreciate the offer.' She raised her mug of coffee in his direction. She remembered O'Reilly. He'd been promoted recently. He'd kind of fancied her once. Asked her out a couple of times after Andy had died. She'd refused him.

The super smiled at her. 'How's the babysitting these days? Working out OK?' he asked.

She laughed out loud. 'You wouldn't want to let some of the more feminist members hear you saying that, boss. They'd look upon it as an infringement of their privacy.'

'Is that right now.' He gazed at her with an expression of mock ruefulness. 'Isn't that funny? And there's me just trying to be friendly.'

It had been a while since she'd attended a post-mortem. Years probably. But in that time nothing had changed. It was all intensely familiar. The smells, the sights, the sounds. The screech of the saw as it bit through the skull. The clang of stainless steel on stainless steel as scalpels and knives were dropped into dishes. The click of heels on the tiles and the stickiness of rubber gloves being peeled on and off again.

She had wondered as she and Conor had driven into the morgue what she would feel. He was uncharacteristically silent, his face pale as they stood in a semi-circle around the table. She noticed beads of sweat breaking out on his forehead, although the room was chilly. And when the green scrubs were removed from what was left of Marianne O'Neill's body he gagged and excused himself quickly.

'OK, fine, one down. Any other takers?' Johnny Harris, the pathologist, raised his grey eyebrows above his mask and looked around. He smiled at Min, deep lines radiating like the spokes of a wheel from the corners of his eyes. 'How are you today, Min. Long time no see. *Et ta maman, ça va?*'

'*Bien, toujours bien,*' she replied, conscious suddenly of the prickle of interest from the others around her. They weren't to know that she and Johnny were old friends. Had been since she was a child. He'd come to Slievemore as a young man, stayed in the nearby youth hostel. Spent every evening in their pub. Gone fishing and sailing with her father. Swapped recipes with her mother in his schoolboy French. Talked to her about his job, about his passion for forensic pathology. Discussed the great athletes of the past who were her heroes. He was the first person she confided in when she decided to go into the guards. Supported her when her mother railed against her choice and said she was wasting her abilities. That she should go to university. Become a teacher or a lawyer. But she listened when Johnny said he thought it was a great choice. It was a noble calling to serve your community. 'And anyway, Noelle, you know Min hates to be indoors. She loves to be active, to be doing something. Let her at it. She'll be good at it. You'll see.'

He had comforted her after Andy died. Explained to her how he had died, how there was nothing that she or anyone else could have done. How there was no explanation for the bleed in his brain. That it wasn't because of his age. Or the forty cigarettes he smoked a day. Or the pints of Guinness he drank every evening. That he wouldn't have suffered, would have known nothing of what was to come.

Now he looked down again at the body in front of him. He cleared his throat.

'Interesting, very interesting. The train severed the legs just around the knee joint. So as you can see we have a complete torso, upper body and head. From my preliminary examination I think I could say with confidence that the young lady was dead by the time the train hit her. Cause of death was a skull fracture with consequent internal haemorrhaging, causing initially loss of consciousness followed some time, thirty minutes or so later, by death. If you look here,' and he pointed with the tip of his scalpel to the brain which had been exposed, 'you will see the cause.' A small black clot lay like a slug across the grey brain tissue. 'And here,' he lifted her head and turned it 'you will see the extensive bruising, laceration and damage to the skull, caused I would imagine by her head being smashed repeatedly against something hard. Would I be right in that?'

Min swallowed. There was blood on the tunnel wall, a dark smearing that shone redly when their torches were turned upon it.

'Apart from that, she has other injuries. She has weals around her wrists showing that she was held tightly, against her will, probably as she struggled to free herself. She has bruises around her neck, probably showing how she was held while her skull was fractured. She also has extensive bruising to the abdomen and stomach, probably caused by a fist. And there is reason to think she had non-consensual sexual intercourse within the immediate period before she died.'

There was silence. Min looked down at Marianne. She tried to remember when she had last spoken to her. It wasn't that long ago. Sometime during the summer. She had been living rough in one of the car parks down by the sea. She'd made a kind of shelter from a large sheet of plastic, draped over a couple of bushes and held in place with bricks and large stones. The weather had been good. Soon she was joined by a group of others. Travellers of the traditional and the New Age variety. A couple of the local drunks dropped by from time to time. It had got out of hand one hot, bright night. There were complaints from the expensive flat complex nearby. Reports of drunkenness, of drug taking and of couples having sex in full view of their middle-class neighbours. A car had been sent down to break up the party. The response had been hostile and in the ensuing melee Marianne and her friends had been arrested. Brought into the station. Kept there overnight until they sobered up. Min had brought her a cup of tea and some toast the next morning. They had talked. About old times. Min had told her to go home for a bit. Start taking her medication again. Try to get hold of her life.

'I'm telling you, Marianne, you'll get into serious trouble if you keep this up. Or else you'll get hurt.'

Marianne had been contrite. Tearful. She had phoned Susan, who had come to take her home. But her contrition hadn't lasted long. She was back on the streets the next week. And Min had heard that she'd been seen soliciting. Working the canal and the areas around the city centre.

A grim silence had fallen over the room. Johnny Harris broke it.

'So.' His tone was brisk. 'Any questions?'

She cleared her throat.

'Yes, Min. What can I do for you?'

'I was just wondering? Is there any DNA? Anything that could pinpoint a suspect?'

Harris held up a plastic sample bag. 'Well, we've found a few hairs that didn't originate on her body. And we have scrapings from beneath her fingernails. We've taken swabs for body fluids. It'll take a bit of time before we know what we have.' He rubbed his forehead with the back of his gloved hand. He looked down at the girl then back up at Min's face. 'Just one thing to say. She was murdered. There's no doubt about that. Whether she was deliberately placed on the railway line to try to disguise that fact I have no idea. Or perhaps she was killed there because it was quiet and out of the sight of prying eyes. Whichever it was, I don't particularly care. But I do care about the terrible punishment that this girl received. I haven't seen anything like it for quite a while.' He sighed deeply, his mask blowing out then collapsing back against his wide, soft mouth. He rested his hand for a moment on the girl's arm. Then he turned away.

Conor was waiting for her outside. His colour had improved. He was leaning against the car, a cigarette in one hand, a copy of the *Sun* in the other.

'Wow, look at her.' He waved the page in front of her nose. 'Something else, isn't she?'

'Something else all right.' Min took the paper from him, 'Ninety per cent silicone and ten per cent wishful thinking, I'd say. Not a pleasant combination. And a sight more nausea-inducing than a poor dead girl who's been run over by a train.' She folded the newspaper in half and half again. 'But therein lies the difference between you and me, Conor. Ain't that so?' And she smiled at him as she shoved it into his chest.

They drove out along the sea road towards the Garda station in Dun Laoghaire, where the incident room had been set up. Conor told her the latest. One of the residents of the houses that overlooked the railway line had seen Marianne. It was about three in the morning. Apparently she was singing loudly. Sounded as if she was drunk. And then ten minutes or so later a man was seen in the same place. Dark, medium height, medium build. Probably wearing jeans and a jacket. No distinguishing features.

'Great,' Min said. 'That really narrows it down, doesn't it?'

'Yeah, well this does.'

'What?'

'They found some credit cards and a chequebook in her bag. They belonged to Nick Cassidy, your old friend. Apparently she spent most of yesterday with him, including most of yesterday evening and night. He says that she left in the early hours. He says they had a row. That she wanted to have sex with him and he wouldn't. He says she stormed off in a rage, that he's been trying to find her ever since. That he doesn't know anything about what happened after she left. So what do you make of that, eh?'

She didn't reply. She turned towards the sea and let her eyes rest on the deep blues and greens that stretched across the bay towards Howth. It was busy out there today, a line of container ships waiting to enter the port through the narrow river mouth and in among them the distinctive red quadrilateral sail of a Galway hooker. She wondered who was at the helm. She'd met most of the hooker crews down through the years at the pub in Slievemore. Her father was something of an expert on traditional sailing boats. He shared that interest with Johnny Harris. But Harris was a purist. Everything on his thirty-two-foot herring drifter was as it once had been. He'd only recently allowed himself to be convinced that he needed a diesel engine.

'There'll be DNA, won't there, from her? That'll show, surely, what happened. I find it hard to believe that if she came on to him as he says she did that he wouldn't have been interested. What do you think?' Conor's fingers drummed on the steering wheel.

She'd sailed with Harris many times out into Roaring Water Bay, then further, past Cape Clear as far as the Fastnet rock. He must be fifty at least, she thought but he was still very fit. Thin, wiry, supple, strong. He could do everything on that boat. Rushing from bow to stern, his long legs in cut-off denim shorts keeping him balanced as the boat bucked and lunged beneath him. Hauling on the sheets as she pushed the tiller away and sang out, 'Lee ho,' the bow swinging round, followed by the great rust-coloured mainsail, which blotted out the sun's rays and cast a dense cold shadow across the deck. While he cleated off the sheets, checking and rechecking the angle of the sails to the wind as the long wooden bowsprit rose and fell, scything through the Atlantic rollers.

'Harris is a lovely man,' she said. 'I'm very fond of him.'

'You've known him for long?'

'Long enough.'

'So you know a lot about him?'

'Enough.'

'So you know everyone reckons he's gay?'

'They do, do they?' She glanced across at him. He reached for a cigarette from the packet on the dashboard. He flipped it into his mouth and pushed in the lighter.

'They do,' he said.

She shrugged her shoulders. 'Well, I reckon that's his business. Not yours, not mine. Not anyone else's.'

The lighter popped out. He held it up. The element

glowed a dull orange. He held it to the tip of his cigarette and sucked hard.

'You think so, do you?' A plume of smoke funnelled from the side of his mouth.

'Why, don't you?' She held down the button on the door's inside panel and the window slid open. Cold wet air poured into the car. 'You don't? You think that you, and whoever else, has a right not only to know the intimacies of Johnny Harris's life but also the right to comment and to judge.'

He didn't reply.

'Harris is a great forensic pathologist. He's been responsible, virtually single-handed, for getting us the evidence that we've needed, not just to get a charge to stick, but also to get a conviction. He could write the textbook on fibres, hairs, bodily fluids. And he's the best person I've ever come across for analysing head wounds. His sexual preferences have nothing to do with that. Nothing at all.' She stared out across the bay again. The hooker was making steady progress now, the brisk westerly carrying her out towards the horizon. An awkward silence fell. The car slowed to a crawl. A traffic jam stretched ahead.

'So.' She turned towards him again. 'Why the problem with gay men?'

He didn't reply. He reached across her. 'You don't mind do you? We've had enough fresh air for the time being.' The window slid shut. He stubbed his butt into the ashtray.

'Who said I have a problem?'

'Well, you obviously do. The very fact that you're bringing it up with me means that.'

'Really? Can it not be raised, talked about in the same

way as a personality characteristic, or a physical difference can be discussed? You're bloody typical, aren't you?'

'Typical of what?' Her voice rose.

'Typical of all the politically correct. The man is a homosexual. That makes him different. His interests are different. The way he lives his life is different. His desires are different. Why can't I say that?'

'OK, say it if you want to. Say it as loud and long as you like. But don't think that it gives you the right to judge him because, if you really want to know, Conor, Johnny Harris has a relationship that would be the envy of practically every heterosexual couple I've ever come across.'

'Yeah?' Conor sniggered. 'Slippers and cocoa eh? And cosy chats and back rubs before the heavy stuff. His and his leather gear, is that it?'

She didn't reply.

'I've shocked you, haven't I?' He leaned back, one arm trailing along the top of her seat.

She sighed. 'No, not shocked. Disappointed that's all. And I think you're wrong. I think you spend too much time at your computer. And what you see doesn't make you happy.'

'Oh, that's what you think, is it? You think I need to get out more. Well, let me tell you, Min, whatever's between your friend Dr Harris and his soulmate, there's an irrefutable truth about gay relationships. They are fundamentally predatory. They are based on power and exploitation. There is an element of physical force about them, which is undeniable. And if you don't believe me, then go into any of the gay bars or clubs in town any night of the week and take a look for yourself. Because the Johnny Harrises of that world are few and far between.'

His voice was cold and very hostile. But when he turned to look at her she saw that his eyes were shining with an unnatural gleam and his face was flushed.

The traffic lights ahead turned green and the car began to move slowly forward. Conor reached for the cigarette packet.

'Do you mind?' he asked.

She shrugged. 'Suit yourself. It's your lung cancer not mine.'

'Well, if you put it like that. Got any more of that gum?'

She fumbled in her bag. Her phone rang. She pulled it out and looked at the display.

'O'Reilly,' she said and pressed the button. She listened. 'OK, no problem. See you there.' She put the phone down on her lap. She took a packet of Polo mints from her coat pocket. She stripped back the foil wrapper and held them out to him.

'Thanks.' He fumbled awkwardly with them, so they scattered on his lap.

'Shit,' he muttered, his eyes on the road. 'Would you mind?'

She gathered them up and selected one for him. He crunched it noisily, then spoke. 'So, tell us, what's up.'

'O'Reilly wants us to meet him at Cassidy's house.'

'He's not bringing him in?'

'No. He says he thinks he'll get more if he keeps it informal for the time being. He says he wants me to be there because I know him better than anyone else.'

'And why me?'

She smiled. 'Because, and I'm quoting here, "Bring that guy, Hickey with you. I've heard so many excellent reports about him I want to see if they're true."'

'Wow.' Conor bobbed his head with mock humility. 'I am honoured. A commendation from a gobshite like O'Reilly. What is the world coming to?'

'Go 'way.' She laughed at him. 'He's not that bad. But you know he's of the old school. I hope you've got your notebook with you. Your real honest-to-goodness Garda issue. None of that personal organizer stuff. He wouldn't approve. Do you need a pen?' She rummaged again in her bag. 'I've a few here. Blue or black? Take your pick.' She held them out to him.

'Black of course. Black, black, black is the colour of my true love's hair.' He sang loudly. 'Black like yours.' He looked over at her and smiled and the car picked up speed as the traffic began to move again.

Twenty

Nick walked the way that Marianne had walked. Early that morning. When it was quiet, still and cold. Her warm breath turning to droplets of mist in front of her face. The moon still hanging above her. He followed the path he imagined she must have travelled. Along the top of the embankment, trying to see where it was that she climbed and slithered through the brambles and the bracken down onto the line. And found the place. A muddy track strewn with empty beer cans and plastic cider bottles and, in the middle of it, the blackened remains of a fire.

He walked on, past Dalkey station towards the tunnel where her body had been found. And just before the spot saw that it was easy to get onto the line. Ten concrete steps down the slope and a small metal gate, padlocked but no bother to climb over. An electricity substation beside it, and a few yards away the curve of the tunnel's stone roof visible. Still the crime scene tape fluttering and a uniformed guard leaning against the wall.

It would have been all right to begin with, he thought. Marianne wouldn't have minded the darkness or being on her own as she walked along the line. She had the dog at her side. She was singing, so they said. She would have been buoyed up by her own madness. So who was it who had come up behind her? Did she turn around and see him? Did she know him? Did she greet him with pleasure or with fear? What did he say as he came close to her? The guards told him that she had been attacked. That she had been beaten and probably raped. That her head had been smashed against the tunnel wall. That she had not died immediately, but had probably lived for an hour or so afterwards. Nick closed his eyes and tried to conjure her up as she had been when she was a teenager. As she was when Owen was still with them. As she was that evening when he danced her round the room, fed her with pasta and tomato sauce, gave her glasses of wine to drink, tucked her up with a blanket. And turned her out onto the street.

He moved closer. The guard looked at him and made as if to come forward. Nick stopped.

'No entry here.' The guard's voice was loud. 'Restricted area.'

Nick stepped back. He smiled.

'Sure thing,' he said. 'No problem.'

He moved back up the incline towards the road. From above, the entrance to the tunnel looked even darker and more threatening. He turned away, then stopped. He bowed his head.

'Forgive me, Marianne.' His voice was low, barely audible. 'Please forgive me for what I did and for what I didn't do.'

Then he turned and walked away.

'What was the point in going there? I don't understand why you'd want to do that.' Susan's manner was cold and unfriendly. There was no comfort in her words. He hovered on the doorstep. Over her shoulder he could see Paul O'Hara watching him.

'You blame me, don't you,' he said.

'Are you surprised?' she replied. 'If you hadn't turfed her out at three in the morning, she'd probably still be alive. How could you do that? How could you let someone as vulnerable as Marianne leave you like that?'

'Hold on a minute.' He moved towards her. 'You were the one who only yesterday was lecturing me on free will and her ability to make her own decisions, live her own life. That's a bit much coming from you now, don't you think?'

'No, I don't actually. What I think is that you did what you always do. You suited yourself. You obviously made her feel that you loved her and cared for her, and then you let her down. No wonder the poor kid did a runner like that.'

He stared for a moment at the floor. The smell of coffee brewing came from the kitchen. It turned his stomach.

'Susan, listen to me. Don't you think it's significant that she is dead now? Don't you think that it proves something?'

'Like what?' Her voice was harsh. 'Like some crazy Agatha Christie detective story, some theory about plots and counter-plots? Something like that?'

'Like I don't know, but it can't be a random killing. It just can't.'

'Maybe not. Maybe it has something to do with the life that she has been leading for the past few years. But I don't really see that it has anything to do with Owen. That's what you're getting at, isn't it? That's what you mean.'

'Sue.' O'Hara put his hand on her shoulder. 'The coffee's ready. Come on now.'

She moved back into the kitchen. Her eyes filled with tears. She reached out to pull the door shut. Nick stepped out of her way. His throat was tight. There was a large, hard lump in it which threatened to choke him. He turned and walked slowly down the steps to the garden. He'd had a call from the guards, from Jay O'Reilly, the inspector. They wanted to talk to him some more, he said. They'd a few more questions to ask him. They'd come to the house.

'Are you sure?' he asked. 'Are you sure you don't want me to come to the station? Are you sure you're not arresting me?'

And there had been jovial laughter in reply. Not at all. Just a friendly chat. Nothing formal. Nothing to be worried about.

But he wasn't so sure. He remembered being questioned before. He remembered how important it was to be certain in his recollection of what had happened. To be consistent in his answers and his descriptions. Now was not the time to be casual or careless, hesitant or halting. He sat down at the kitchen table. Might be a good idea to spend five minutes with a pen and a piece of paper, to write down a chronology of events. To make a note of times and incidents, to forestall anything that might lead them to suspect that he had an involvement in Marianne's death.

He was surprised when the three of them showed up together. O'Reilly, the inspector, and with him Min Sweeney and another young man. Tall, burly, handsome. Casually dressed in jeans and anorak. Introduced as Conor Hickey. Nick invited them in, offered tea and handed around a plate of biscuits. Then took his place on the sofa and waited for the pleasantries to be dispensed with. That didn't take long. All three sat and looked at him. Min smiled, but he thought he detected a wariness in her eyes that hadn't been there before. She shifted awkwardly on her chair, crossing and recrossing her legs, the leather of her long boots squeaking as she moved. He wanted to say to her that this whole thing was ridiculous, that he had absolutely nothing to do with Marianne's death, that he was distraught about it. And could they not just step outside and sort the whole thing out between themselves? But he could see that they had gone beyond that stage.

O'Reilly cleared his throat. 'We wanted to see you, Mr Cassidy, because there are a couple of areas that we are unclear about. If you know what I mean.'

'Not really.' Nick stared hard at him. 'If you wouldn't mind explaining. I thought I told everything I knew to the two guards who came here earlier to tell me that Marianne was dead.'

'What did you explain to them, Nick?' Min leaned forward, her notebook resting on her knee, her pen poised.

'I explained to them that, yes, Marianne was here last night. She had been going to stay, but then we had a difference of opinion and she became very angry and she left. I tried to stop her. I tried to reason with her. But you know, at least I'm sure you do, that Marianne has, had, I mean, serious emotional and psychological problems. She was not open to reason. And the more I tried to restrain her, control her, the more angry and violent she became and eventually I had no option but to let her go.'

'Angry, violent. What exactly do you mean by that?' Conor Hickey chipped in.

Nick looked at him. When he spoke his words were carefully chosen.

'Anger, a profound emotion expressed forcefully. A sense of outrage, of hostility. Violent, the translation of that emotion into physical activity. The use of fists on flesh, the use of hands, slapping, the use of feet kicking. That's what I mean.'

'So you are admitting that you were violent towards Marianne O'Neill?' Conor's tone was direct.

'No, I'm not, not at all. She was violent towards me. She hit me, she scratched me, she even kicked me with her bloody great boots. That's what happened.'

'So, Mr Cassidy.' It was O'Reilly's turn now. 'So what was it that precipitated this violent behaviour?'

'Look.' Nick put his head in his hands. 'I told the two guys who were here earlier. I told them exactly what happened. We had spent the day together. I had cooked a meal. It had all been very pleasant, very nice, very friendly, very warm. Then she got upset about my son. The memories were very painful for her. She fell asleep here in front of the stove. I made up a bed for her. Then I went to bed here also, on the sofa. But sometime in the night I woke up and found that she was beside me. It appeared that she wanted to have sex. I told her it wasn't on. I told her that I hadn't had that kind of relationship with her in the past and I didn't want it with her now or in the future. I suppose because she woke me suddenly out of a deep sleep I didn't behave as thoughtfully or as sensitively as I might have under other circumstances.'

Min looked down at her notebook, then up at him again.

'What you said earlier was that you threw her out of the

bed. Is that what happened, Nick?' Her voice seemed to have lost some of its warmth.

He paused again and looked down at his notes.

'It was a metaphorical use of the word. I didn't actually pick her up and throw her out. I woke up. She was beside me. It was immediately obvious what she wanted, I pulled away. I tried to get up, but she was between me and the floor. So I pushed her. She fell out. She landed heavily. She was shocked, hurt. I was shocked too. I was half asleep. I didn't really know what was going on. She came on to me again. I pushed her away again. It was at that point she became angry. She lashed out. I tried to restrain her. I took hold of her wrists and tried to stop her from hitting me.' He sighed. 'Look, this doesn't make me sound good, I know that. But if you can just try and understand it from where I'm standing. I didn't mean the girl any harm. That was the last thing I meant.'

'So why did she leave like that? Your wife heard her, you know. She heard the sound of raised voices. She heard the front door slam. She heard her shouting out abuse. She must have been making quite a commotion for your wife, who was on the top floor of the house, to hear her.'

'She was. In fact, I'm surprised the whole square didn't hear her.'

'And your wife heard something else a few minutes later. She heard the sound of another set of feet. She said it sounded like a man's.'

Nick shrugged. 'What can I say? She may have heard something, but it wasn't me. I didn't follow her.'

'And then Marianne was seen half an hour later on the railway line just past Glenageary station. A young mother up nursing her baby saw her clearly, she said, from the window. And fifteen minutes later saw a man on the line. A man who answers your description. What do you say to that?'

Nick rubbed his face with his hands and rested his fingertips on his eyelids. He could feel his pulse through the fine skin. He put his hands down on his knees.

'What can I say? What can I say to you that will convince you? It wasn't me. I didn't follow her. After she left I went back to bed and tried to go back to sleep. That was all I did.'

There was silence for a moment, then Min leaned forward.

'Nick, I know that if we look at what happened from your point of view it all makes perfect sense.' Min's voice was soft and neutral. 'And it explains very neatly some of the injuries on Marianne's body. The marks around her wrists, for example, possibly some of the bruises on her back. And it would really help us if you would give us some hair samples, some tissue samples, a swab from which we could get your DNA. Then we'd be able to match up whatever we find on her body and eliminate you from our enquiries.'

'But,' O'Reilly interrupted, 'your version of what happened doesn't explain this.'

He reached into his pocket and pulled out a plastic evidence bag.

'Do you recognize this, Mr Cassidy?' He passed it to him. Nick held it up.

'This?' he said, a tone of surprise in his voice, 'Where on earth did you get this?'

'So, you do recognize it?'

'Of course. It's my watch. But where did you get it from?'

'Nick, your watch was found just a couple of yards from Marianne's body. It was lying beside the track.' Min's voice was gentle, soft. Understanding.

'But this is ridiculous, extraordinary. The last time I saw it I had taken it off because the strap was very worn and I needed to get a new one. I've had that watch for a long time. It was a birthday present from my wife.' He turned the plastic bag over and smoothed it down. He looked at the inscription on the back. *N.P.C. from S.M.C. 30th January 1985*, it read. He looked up again at the three faces, which were all staring hard at him. 'So I took it off a few days ago. And I put it here.' He got up and walked to his drawing board. 'Here, in this box. I keep all kinds of bits and pieces in it. Here.' He held up a wooden pencil case. An old-fashioned kind with a swivel lid. He opened it. He rummaged through the contents with the tip of his index finger. Min got up and came to his side.

'I just don't understand this.' He handed the box to her. 'I swear I put it there, oh, I don't know exactly when, a few days ago at least.' He turned back towards O'Reilly. 'Look, there's really been some mistake here. I took the watch off because the strap was worn. I was going to get a new one. I put it in the box for safe keeping. Look.' He held the bag up in front of them. 'This strap is broken, but it wasn't broken when I took it off. And look here.' He paused. 'The glass of the face is broken. It wasn't broken when I last saw it.'

'That's right.' O'Reilly's voice was loud. 'Not only is the glass broken, but we found pieces of it in the treads of

Marianne's left boot. You see, Nick, you've given us your explanation and very plausible it is too. But if you don't mind I'd like to suggest another scenario to you. Why don't you sit down again and listen to me? We won't take up too much more of your time.'

After they'd gone Nick could do nothing but sit and stare at the floor. He had agreed that the next morning at ten o'clock he would present himself – their words, not his – at the Garda station. He would volunteer a number of samples. Hair, tissue, blood, saliva. They had told him he could refuse. But he knew there was no point. Not after O'Reilly had spelt out for him what they thought had happened last night.

'You see, this is the way we think it went, Nick. We think, we suspect, that it was you who attempted to have sex with Marianne. It was she who rejected you. That was why she left the house at three in the morning and rushed out, screaming, into the night. Took off by herself. We think that perhaps you were worried what she was going to do. Worried who she might tell. Might she tell your wife? Might she go to the police? Might she accuse you of all kinds of things, behaviour that was completely out of keeping with your usual practice? Perhaps she might even start making allegations about the past. Did she know something that so far she hadn't revealed? We don't know because Marianne is dead. But we have an eyewitness who saw a man on the railway line minutes after she had seen Marianne. The description fits you. And we found your watch a couple of yards from her body. It could be suggested that the reason the strap broke was because you were engaged in some kind of violent struggle with the girl. The strap broke. The watch fell to the ground and as she fell over she stamped on it, breaking the glass.'

Nick had shaken his head in disbelief as he listened. He had tried to catch Min's eye, but she stared resolutely at O'Reilly as he spoke. He continued to shake his head as he listened to O'Reilly's words.

'You were angry with her. You grabbed hold of her by the wrists. You pushed her into the tunnel. You forced her to have sex with you, then you smashed her head against the stone wall. You left her there on the track. You came back here, you cleaned yourself up. You waited until the morning. Then you went and spoke to your wife, told her your version of what had happened and asked her for help in finding Marianne. And that was that.'

He had wanted to laugh. It was all so ridiculous. All so crazy. But as he listened to O'Reilly he had to agree. It was also all very plausible.

'If you like we can arrange legal representation for you, Mr Cassidy.' O'Reilly stood.

Nick shrugged. 'I don't know. I'll think about it.'

He opened the front door. They filed out past him. Min put out her hand to touch his arm, but he pulled away from her.

'We'll see you in the morning,' O'Reilly called back over his shoulder. 'Ten o'clock. Don't forget.'

He stood on the doorstep and watched as they walked towards their cars. Then he heard the sound of Chris Goulding's voice. He walked up the path towards the gate. Chris was running down his front steps, calling out to the guards, waving to them. Nick stopped and watched. He couldn't quite hear what Chris was saying, but the three of them, O'Reilly, Min Sweeney and Hickey, all turned and walked with him back up to the house. The heavy door slammed behind them, its brass knocker lifting and falling with a sound that was almost musical.

Nick walked across the road and leaned against the railings. He looked around the square. Everywhere he could see windows which were bright and welcoming. A cold wind tugged at his hair. The bonfire in the middle of the muddy grass was growing steadily. Now it towered above him. He turned around and stood and faced the houses. He could see Chris standing in his front room talking to the guards. He was gesturing, pulling Anna forward, including her in his conversation. The boy was there too. He leaned back against Chris's legs. Chris's hands played with his hair, then rested on the child's thin shoulders. As Nick watched, he saw O'Reilly leave the room, leave the house, pass by Nick with barely a glance, get into his car and drive away. And Min go out of the front room, the woman following slowly behind her. While Chris and Hickey sat down together, the child standing between them, his gaze shifting from one face to the other. Then moving to the window and standing looking out at Nick, until Chris stood with an abrupt movement and took hold of the curtains and pulled them quickly together. So there was no more for either to see.

Nick turned towards his own house. Susan and Paul were clearly visible in the sitting room. He was standing at the mantelpiece, a glass of wine in his hand. She was sitting on the sofa.

'Look at me,' he said out loud. 'Turn your head and look at me. See me for what I am. A man who was weak and flawed. But a man who loves you still. Look at me, Susan. Please.'

But she did not move. She did not respond. He shivered. The wind blew, gusting through the trees. There was rain coming. He could feel it. He pushed himself away from the railings and crossed back to the house. He walked inside and closed the door. He sat down on the sofa and stared at the floor. He felt cold and sick. And suddenly very frightened.

Twenty-one

Min had never liked the Gouldings' house. She had been in and out of it many times back then, before. It was always very clean, but cold. It was always quiet. There was no television in the large sitting room, which looked out over the square. Hilary Goulding had a small transistor radio in the kitchen, shoved onto a shelf next to pots of homemade marmalade and jam. The volume was always turned down low. The two teenagers seemed to spend all their time in the basement. There was no sign of them upstairs. Even their bedrooms at the top of the house looked as if no one ever disturbed the smooth surface of their patterned bedspreads or took items of clothing from the neat piles folded in their matching chests of drawers

She didn't like the Gouldings either. Brian was small and slight. He had a jutting goatee beard, which gave his face an aggressive air. Hilary was even smaller. She seemed old to Min then. But she wasn't, Min thought, as she sat and looked at her son. She must only have been in her mid-forties. Yet her hair was greying, cut short in an unflattering, masculine style. And her clothes looked as if they had come from a charity shop. Clean, but faded, as if washed many times.

What had she thought of Chris and his sister? she asked herself. Of the sister not much. She seemed like her mother, a pale and colourless character. Retiring, shy and nervous. She cried a lot and chewed her fingers, stripping the skin from her cuticles and around her nails until they bled. She let Chris do all the talking. He was good at that. He, unlike the rest of his family, had personality. He was attractive if not handsome. Charming, entertaining, his large blue eyes shining behind his dark-rimmed glasses. He had managed to talk his way out of a 'possession with intent to supply' charge and had been convicted of the much lesser crime of 'possession for personal use'. His case had been heard at the district court. He had been warned and fined. Told off, had his knuckles rapped and sent home to do penance.

Of which Min was sure there was plenty in the Goulding household. But now the parents were dead, the sister away and Chris ruled the roost. And ruled it well by all accounts. The sitting room into which they were invited was warm. Children's toys were scattered across the carpet, which was worn but clean. There was the smell of cooking from the kitchen down the hall. Chris had a drink in his hand. Vodka or maybe gin. Something colourless. He called down the hall.

'Amra. Come here. There are people who want to speak to you.'

The woman stood uncertainly in the doorway. She had a dishcloth in one hand and a lighted cigarette in the other. A small boy hung back behind her. Chris drew her forward, including her with a wave of his arm.

'This is Amra,' he said, 'and this is her son, Emir.'

He reached down and took hold of the child's hand and pulled him forward. The child leaned back against his legs and Chris tousled his hair.

'Amra's daughter, Sanela, is upstairs asleep,' he volunteered.

The woman offered coffee.

'Why don't I give you a hand?' Min asked.

The woman shook her head, but Min followed her down the hall into the kitchen. While, behind her, Chris motioned to Conor to sit.

'So, what did you make of him?' Min sat into the car and shivered. It was colder now. The wind had turned to the east, bringing rain and, possibly, she thought, snow.

Conor drove slowly towards the main road.

'Well, he'll make a good witness. He had it all. Times, identifications, the lot. What about her?'

Min folded her arms tightly around her chest and shivered again.

'She was asleep. She heard nothing. Saw nothing. She went to bed at eleven-thirty. She takes sleeping pills, she said. She has nightmares. She woke at seven-thirty when the alarm went off. That was that.'

But it wasn't really that. Even now, sitting in the car with Conor's bulk beside her, Min felt anxious, nervous, ill at ease. Amra had begun to cry as soon as the two of them got to the kitchen. The tears had tumbled from her eyes, her slight frame shaking. She filled the kettle and plugged it in, opened cupboard doors, spooned coffee into a jug. Did it all with her back turned to Min.

Min waited until the coffee was made and the room filled with its pungent smell. Then she put out her hand and took Amra's.

'I'm sorry,' she said, 'this is obviously very painful for you. I didn't realize that you knew Marianne O'Neill.'

The woman lifted her head and looked at her. Her eyes were red and streaming. She pulled a ball of tissues from her sleeve and wiped her nose.

'I didn't,' she said, her accent strong, 'I didn't know this girl. But I know many girls who have died, very bad deaths, very painful deaths, very lonely, sad deaths. Deaths where they have not had the comfort of their mother, their husband, their brother, their sister. No comfort, no hand to hold, nothing but fear and darkness.'

She poured coffee into small cups. It was strong, aromatic. Min sipped hers warily.

'Do you like?' Amra asked. 'Most Irish don't like. They want it from the jar. Instant. Disgusting.'

Min smiled. 'Yeah, that's it all right. My mother is French and she complains all the time about the standard of coffee-making here.'

Amra's face brightened for an instant. 'She is French? That is good. I would have liked to go to France. I learned French at school. But then the war came and we could go nowhere and then when Emir got hurt the Irish government offer to take some families from Sarajevo. So we come here.'

'He was hurt? How did that happen?'

'We were at the market one day. You know we have to go, although it is so dangerous. There is no one I can leave him with. He won't stay without me. He screams and cries every time. So we are in the queue. I hear there are potatoes to buy. And there is an attack. I was all right. I was just thrown to the ground, very shocked. But Emir was bad. He was hit in the stomach. Blood everywhere. I try to stop the blood, but the wound was very big. So he go to hospital, but hospital in Sarajevo is like no other hospital in the world. There is no electricity, no water, no drugs. No painkillers. They do everything they can for him, but they tell me it is most likely he will die. And you know I am pregnant. I have so little to eat while I am carrying my daughter. I think there cannot be a baby in my womb because there is no food for my baby. And then, like miracle, I am sitting by Emir's bed. He is crying and crying and a doctor comes in and says you can go now to the airport. There is an ambulance waiting. You can go away to Germany. And after that to some other country. So we go.'

'And you came here. And you met Chris? Yes?'

The woman nodded.

'We have classes to learn English. Chris is the teacher. He likes me and he likes my children. He asks me to come and visit him here in his house. Then he asks me to come and live with him here. He says we will be family. Like family before in Bosnia.'

'And is it, like before?' Min looked at her. Amra bowed her head.

'What do you think?' she asked.

Min didn't answer. She drained her cup.

'You could go back,' she said. 'The war is over.'

But Amra shook her head.

'There is no going back. There are too many memories. Too much betrayal. No trust any longer.'

'I'll take you home,' Conor said. 'You could make me dinner.'

'Now there's a thought.' Min turned to look at him.

'Dinner, I like the sound of that. Problem is we have tea in our house. Tonight it's fish fingers and oven chips followed by ice cream. And, if I'm lucky, between the cooking and the eating there'll be time to sit down and watch the evening news with maybe a glass of wine. That's if Vika doesn't have a date.'

'Vika?'

'My Russian au pair. She's a big hit with the local lads. I'd say she'll be announcing her engagement any day now. And then there'll be the baby. Or maybe there'll be the baby first and then the engagement. Either way she's guaranteed a visa and I'm guaranteed more hassle trying to replace her.'

'So I take it that's a polite refusal.'

'Well, it's a refusal, not so sure that polite is the term to qualify it. I've kind of run out of politeness these days.'

'Rain check then?'

'Rain check.' She looked at him. 'Conor, you've been watching too much American telly. It's not a rain check, it's a definite no. Anyway, you're young, single and free, why aren't you heading off into some hot spot in town filled with twenty-somethings, all Wonderbras and Bacardi? Make the most of it, for God's sake. One day some nice girl will have memorized your PIN number and convinced you that a joint account is the modern way.'

He sighed. 'I should be so lucky.'

'Oh, come on, don't be giving me the poor mouth. Take me home and drop me, and then go off and have some fun. But listen, before you go, answer my question. What did Chris Goulding tell you? Is he certain it was Nick Cassidy he saw?'

Chris was certain all right. He had been reading in bed.

It was late. Amra was asleep. He was just about to turn off the light when he heard loud voices. Heard Marianne shouting. Heard Nick shouting back at her. Heard the door slam, heard footsteps.

'I couldn't resist it,' he said, 'I did the nosy neighbour thing. I got out of bed and peeped around the curtains. I saw her leave. I was going to go after her and see if she wanted to come and stay with us, but I thought better of it. Amra has enough on her plate coping with Emir. She doesn't need another disturbed person to handle. So I went back to bed. But I still wasn't sleepy. So I read some more. And then about five minutes or so later I heard the door again. I got up and looked. I saw Nick Cassidy go down the path. He was hurrying. He took off in the same direction as Marianne. I assumed he'd gone to try and bring her back.'

'But would he have known where she was going? She could have taken any route out of the square. She could have gone anywhere when she got onto the main road. He wasn't to know that she'd end up on the railway line, was he?'

'Ah, now there you see. That's where you're wrong. He would know. He did know. Because — ' Chris's expression was triumphant — 'you see, all the kids around here go through a phase of hanging out on the railway line. It's the ultimate in bad behaviour. We all did it at some time or another. Drinking down by the track, then going into the tunnels. It's dangerous, but it's fun. And, you see, Nick knew all about it because there was an incident with Marianne. She took Owen onto the line with her once. And someone, one of the neighbours, saw them and told the Cassidys and they went ape about it. And I reckon, if Nick really thought about where she'd go, he'd be thinking of the railway line and he'd be pretty sure that he'd find her there. Pretty sure.'

'That's a new one.' Min tapped her forehead with her index finger. 'I never heard anything about railways lines and the like before. I think he's pulling a fast one.'

'Well, I don't know. It all sounded pretty good to me.' Conor changed gear and slowed for the traffic lights. 'And added to what we already have, I'd say it's all pointing one way, wouldn't you?'

She didn't reply.

'Funny, isn't it?' He turned to look at her, his fingers drumming on the steering wheel.

'What?' She turned to look at Conor again.

'This area. Lovely place to live. Lovely place to bring up kids. Middle class, affluent, safe and secure. And yet.' He paused as the car moved off quickly again. 'And yet. Your old friend and preoccupation Owen Cassidy disappears off the face of the planet in the middle of the day. No reason, no clues. Nothing. And ten years later the girl who used to look after him is attacked, beaten, has her head smashed against a wall and dies. Yards away from all those nice, comfortable homes with nice, comfortable families fast asleep inside them. Kind of thing that's supposed to happen in the inner city, where the wild people live.'

'Wild people, that's a nice way of putting it.' Min smiled in the dark. 'Reminds me of that lovely children's book, *Where the Wild Things Are*. Do you know it?'

He shook his head. 'They weren't big on kids' books where I was reared.'

'Oh?'

'Oh, forget it. Some other time maybe.' The car slowed

and turned into her cul de sac. 'This is you, isn't it? What number?'

'Just here, number six. Thanks, Conor.' She bent down and picked up her bag. 'You know,' she said, 'funny what you were saying about the area, its niceness and all that. That woman Amra said something similar.' She began to button up her coat and wrap her scarf around her neck.

'"I don't like it here, you know." That's what she said to me. She said, "In the daytime it all seems so pretty and so safe. But it's like Sarajevo became. There you never knew from day to day. Which building would have the sniper. They moved around, you know. So one day you can walk this street and it's safe, but the next day you walk the same street and a bullet smashes into your skull. Or maybe you're even more unlucky and there is a sniper who has a special skill. He only shoots at women. And he only shoots at their private parts. He shoots women in the lower abdomen so they cannot have babies. Or he shoots women in their breast. He does it to hurt and maim, not to kill."

'"So," I said to her, "but it's not like that here. It's safe here."

'"No," she says, "it isn't. You know there is a place not far from this square where every day there is fresh flowers laid and candles lighting. I walk there often with the children. It is the place where a young girl was murdered. We stop and look. We bring flowers too. The girl was called Lizzie. They never found who killed her. No one saw a thing. But someone must know what happened to her. Someone must have hidden that person. Just the way someone lets the sniper into the building. Someone pretends that he is plumber or electrician. So there is someone, maybe not far from here who knows who killed that girl."'

'Oh, of course.' Conor took out his packet of cigarettes, and pushed in the lighter. 'That was a famous case. Years ago, before you and I were in the force. Do you remember it?'

Min looked out the window at her house. She could see shadows moving behind the curtains.

'Yeah, I do indeed. Lizzie Anderson. It was the early eighties I think. Eighty-three, eighty-four, around that time. It's another one that's still talked about. The jury's out on whether or not your man, Matthews, should have been convicted. Some people are convinced that he killed her and he was just lucky that there wasn't enough evidence to get a result. But others are sure that it was the second man she was with that night, that he was the one.'

'It was eighty-three, actually. I know that for sure. And do you know how I know?' He held the lighter to the tip of his cigarette and inhaled. 'There's a website dedicated to her. All kinds of pictures of the girl. Baby photos, school photos, the works. And there's a newsgroup, one of many such, that's all Lizzie Anderson fantasies. It's the pits. The police have tried to shut it down, but it just keeps on popping up again. It's like most of them. It's unstoppable.'

'Unstoppable? That's a very defeatist attitude to take.'

Conor shrugged. 'Yeah? You think so? Well, I know so. Unstoppable is what it is.'

Min opened the car door. She got out. She bent down.

'Well, you're the expert I suppose.'

She straightened up, looked away, then turned back to him again.

'Thanks,' she said.

'What for?'

'Well, by my count there's at least fifteen cigarettes that

you didn't smoke today when I was with you. So, just to let you know that I noticed and I appreciate it.'

Conor exhaled. 'Yeah, well, I'm going to make up for it now. You'd better go quick before the oxygen content in the car goes below danger levels.'

She laughed and walked away, then turned back and waved. He watched her open her front door, saw the two small figures who appeared, their arms up, saw their faces, the love in their expressions. Saw her crouch down and envelop them in her hug. Saw the door close behind her. Closing them in. Closing him out. He put the car in gear and slowly drove away.

Twenty-two

The procedure was simple and straightforward. It was also painful. Nick sat on a stool while the laboratory technician pulled a sample of hairs from his head and placed them in a plastic evidence bag. At least ten to twenty were needed, he had been told, for the sample to be representative. Next he was instructed to undo his belt and unzip his flies, pull down his underpants, and allow the technician's gloved hands to pull the same number of hairs from his pubis. He winced and let his eyes drift over her blonde head towards the printed notices on the wall. He focused and read. It was a list of specimens to be taken in case of rape. His eyes scanned the notice. Penile, perianal, rectal, anal canal, fingernails, urine, mouth, skin, head hair, pubic hair, vulval, vaginal low and high. Each of the most secret and private parts of the human body probed and penetrated. A further invasion, it seemed to him.

'Now.' The technician turned to him again. 'Open your mouth, just for a moment.'

He put his head back and did as he was told. She rubbed the inside of his cheek with a cotton bud and placed it carefully in another bag.

'That's grand,' she said, 'that's the fun bit over. Now if you wouldn't mind, would you just roll up your sleeve? This won't take a minute.'

He didn't look. He felt the rubber strap tighten around his upper arm and her first two fingers slapping the vein in his inner elbow.

'Deep breath,' she said, and he did as he was told. He could feel the tip of the needle sinking through his skin and even deeper. He breathed out slowly, then in again, counting silently.

'Now,' she said, 'all done. You can relax. You can open your eyes.'

He looked up at her. What does she think of me, he wondered? Does she think I'm a murderer, a rapist, a brutalizer? Does she feel nervous of me? Is she judging me already, making up her mind, slotting me into the bad-guy section of her memory? He couldn't tell. Her grey eyes were calm and trouble-free and her smile was warm but neutral.

'All done,' she said, turning away from him to her work bench. 'You're free to go.' And she smiled again.

He had woken early. It seemed as if he had barely slept. He had lain for a while in the dark, the bedclothes wrapped tightly around him, listening. He heard the sound of the radio in the kitchen upstairs and Susan's quick footsteps moving backwards and forwards. She must be going to work today. He hoped she was feeling better. But he doubted that was the case. He lifted his left arm from the covers, to look at his watch. Then remembered. There was a wide white band around his wrist which marked where the strap had been. He looked at it. He tried to remember. When had he last seen his watch and where? For an awful moment he wondered. Were they right? Had he done what they accused him of doing? Had he followed Marianne down to the railway line, crept up on her, attacked her, smashed her head against the tunnel wall, left her to die. Had she reached out and grabbed hold of his wrist, struggling with him, clawing at his hand so the weakened strap of his watch broke and it fell to the ground? And as they toppled backwards and forwards, locked together, had her boot smashed the face, small rough splinters of glass wedging in its deep treads? Perhaps this was where he had to accept responsibility, punishment, make recompense for all his past sins and crimes. Perhaps the time was now.

He pushed away the covers and got out of bed. He made tea and cleaned out the stove, taking comfort from the familiar ritual of fire-making. He reached into the boxes of papers stored against the wall and pulled out handfuls of his old drawings. He tore them into strips, twisted them and knotted them, piling them into a heap in the grate. Then he lit a match and watched them as they flared up, the brightness of the flame brighter than any of the colours he had employed in their construction.

He sat back on the floor, his mug in his hand and watched the fire light. There were other pictures scattered around him. Sketches for the star child book.

'Why are you picking that one of Wilde's stories?' Susan had asked him. 'Why not the happy prince or the selfish giant? They're the best loved of them all.'

'Yeah.' He had justified his choice to her. 'But they're all too goody-goody. The star child rejects his mother because she comes to him in the guise of a beggar. Because of this his beauty is taken from him and he is despised by all. In order to redeem himself he must take on a series of apparently impossible tasks, all of which do good. And then at the end of the story his beauty is restored and he is reunited with his father and mother.'

'Yeah and they just happen to be the king and the queen. Nice one, Oscar.'

'Yeah, OK, but it is a fairy story. It lives in the realm of the fabulous. But it does have an important message. Goodness counts for more than beauty.'

She looked at him with incredulity on her face.

'Extraordinary coming from a man for whom surface is everything.'

'Well, just goes to show you can't judge a book by its cover.'

'Yeah, but I don't like the ending. What does it say? The star child doesn't reign long as king because he has suffered so much. And the one who came after him ruled evilly. What on earth does that mean?'

'It means, I think, that every action has its consequence. There's nothing neat and tidy in this world or even the world of the fairy tale or the children's story. That's why I like it. It's an opportunity to show that you don't get away clean as a whistle.'

He had been happy down here in his studio, with his son at his feet as he worked on his pictures. Or he thought he had, but now he wondered. Was his memory failing him? Did he really remember all that happened that day? Now he got up and went to the pile of photocopied statements in the plastic bag on the floor. He flicked through them and found his own. He sat down again. He began to read.

JULIE PARSONS

My name is Nicholas Patrick Cassidy. I live at 26
Victoria Square, Dun Laoghaire. I am a freelance illustrator and graphic artist. On 31 October 1991 I left
home at around 12.30 p.m. I went first of all to Gog-
gins pub in Monkstown, where I was due to meet my
publisher, Alison McHenry. We had a drink and discussed a new project I was about to start working
on. I left the pub at 1.30 p.m. I then went to the
Quinsworth supermarket in Dun Laoghaire and bought
two bottles of wine. I walked back to Victoria Square,
but my intention was not to go home. I remember that
as I turned into Victoria Square from the main road at
about 2 p.m. I saw my son, Owen Cassidy, walking
across the square with his friend Luke Reynolds. They
did not see me and I did not draw attention to myself.
I assumed that our childminder Marianne O'Neill was
probably somewhere close by and I did not want to
alert Owen to my presence because I was going to the
flat of Gina Harkin at number 23 Victoria Square. I
had been having a relationship with her for the last
two months, seeing her regularly at least three times a
week. My relationship with her was not just platonic.
We had been sexually involved for most of the time
I had known her. I arrived at Gina's flat at about
2.10 p.m. I left her flat at about 5.20 p.m. I had
meant to leave earlier but I had had quite a lot to
drink and I had fallen asleep at about 4.15 p.m. When
I got home my wife Susan was there. She was very
anxious because she did not know where our son was.
I had thought that Marianne O'Neill, who was our
childminder, was looking after him. But when Marianne came back to the house she told Susan that she

had sent him out to play with his friend Luke. Marianne's understanding was that Owen and Luke would play around in the square together and then go to Luke's house. However when Susan phoned Mrs Reynolds she told her that Luke had been home since approximately two-thirty that day and neither of them had any idea where Owen was. My wife was very upset and anxious so I immediately went out to see if I could find him. I searched the square and the neighbouring streets and asked in all the local shops. When I came back I called on Chris Goulding, who lived next door, and asked him to help me. A number of the other neighbours joined in and between us we searched all the obvious places where we thought Owen might have gone. My wife decided while I was out that she should phone the guards, but because it was Halloween it took an hour for them to arrive. During this time I went out again and again looked wherever I could think that he might be. But by now it was very dark and by the time I got home again the guards had come and decided to mount a full-scale search. I spent the rest of the night by the phone waiting to see if there would be any news of him. But there wasn't. I have absolutely no idea what happened to Owen that day and in the days since then.

Shame flooded through him as he read. He had wanted to forget the betrayal of that day. How he had slunk back against the wall and stood and watched Owen and Luke as they were wandering aimlessly across the grass. How they stopped to look at the bonfire and Luke picked up a few small pieces of wood that had fallen from it and were lying scattered around. He had flung them as hard as he could across the square and Owen had run to them and picked them up. Cradling them in his arms like a newborn and rushing back and replacing them carefully. Making sure that they wouldn't fall down again before turning and following Luke as he ambled towards the road. And he had waited until they were no longer in sight before continuing on down the square towards Gina's flat. Squashed the nagging doubts about the two boys. Sure that Marianne was somewhere close by and anyway Bridget Reynolds obviously knew where the boys were. Sure, hadn't they looked after Luke many, many times? Had him to tea and to sleep over. Put up with his bad manners and his rudeness. Perhaps it was her turn to shoulder some of the burden.

But knowing all along somewhere inside himself that he was wrong about that. That he had denied his son. Turned away. Ignored him. Suited himself. And he would pay for it eventually.

He walked from the Garda station feeling the ache in his arm. Outside in the car park he heard his name called. He turned and saw Jay O'Reilly coming towards him, a bundle of files in one hand, a mobile phone pressed to his ear.

'Mr Cassidy, a minute of your time, if you wouldn't mind.' A wave of the arm that turned into a beckoning finger. Nick stopped and waited. O'Reilly ended his call and put the phone in his pocket.

'Mr Cassidy, I'm glad I've caught you. I was just going to give you a call. There's been a new development in the case.'

'Yes?' Nick's heart jumped. 'And what might that be?'

'We have a witness who says you were seen leaving your house just a few minutes after Marianne left it. This witness says you were seen walking in the same direction as the girl. I'm afraid we're going to have to ask you to come into the station for further questioning. You don't mind, do you? We need to clear this up one way or the other.'

Nick said nothing. He was tired. His vein throbbed.

'When?' he asked. 'I've just been in to give the samples you wanted. I've co-operated with you so far. I've done everything you asked me to do. So far.'

'So you have, so you have. You have indeed. And we appreciate your co-operation. It has to be said, however, Mr Cassidy, that we already have a lot of evidence against you. There are some jurisdictions in the world, Britain, for example, where by now you'd probably have been arrested, pending a charge. But we're a bit more relaxed about things here. So let me see, perhaps, I'm not sure when, but we'll be in touch. You're not thinking of going anywhere are you? I'll give you a call and we'll arrange a time. OK?'

He didn't want to go back to the house. He wanted to be anywhere other than the basement. He wandered along the seafront. An easterly blew across the bay.

Where does the wind come from, Daddy?

It comes all the way from Russia, Owen. From even further than Russia. From a place called Siberia, where in the winter the snow lies on the ground in drifts ten feet deep and the ground freezes so hard that no one can dig a hole in it for months and months.

And does it ever melt, Daddy?

Of course it does. In spring it turns to water and it flows down the hillsides into the streams and the streams flow into the rivers and eventually after travelling thousands and thousands of miles the rivers flow into the seas and then do you know what happens, Owen?

What happens, Daddy?

The water becomes salty in the sea and every single one of the seas and the oceans mix their waters together, so do you know what that means, Owen, me lad?

It means, Daddy, that the rain that fell in Siberia ends up in the sea that I can paddle in, isn't that right, Daddy? Isn't that what you always tell me, Daddy?

He turned and began to walk back up the hill, through the quiet streets he knew so well. And saw as he walked along the square that Susan was standing in front of the house. A man and a woman were with her. They looked familiar. He recognized them. They were Marianne's parents, Jack and Maria O'Neill. Their faces were white, shocked. Their eyes were red-rimmed. He knew where they had been.

He slowed his pace. They turned.

'I'm so sorry,' he said. 'I don't know what to say.'

His words dropped like lead weights.

'What can you say?' Maria O'Neill turned to him. Her daughter's eyes looked up into his. 'Can you say you're sorry this happened? Can you say you didn't mean it to happen? Can you say you wish it hadn't happened? Can you say any or all of that?'

'Maria.' Her husband put his arm around her. He tried

to turn her away. Susan made as if to walk up the steps to the house.

'Do you know what we've just done?' Maria O'Neill pushed her husband's arm away. 'We've just been into the morgue. We've just identified our daughter's body. The remains as they call it. And in this case it's unusually appropriate.'

'Maria.' Nick took a step towards her.

'Don't you "Maria" me. How dare you?' She stepped backwards, tears beginning to flow from her eyes.

'Maria,' he began again. And saw over her shoulder that Chris and Emir were coming towards them, the boy skipping ahead, Chris with a bag of groceries in each hand.

'I'm so sorry,' he continued. 'Believe me, I had nothing to do with Marianne's death. Please, you have to believe me. It wasn't me who hurt her. Perhaps I was insensitive to her needs, but please, I beg you to believe me, I didn't hurt her. You must know, after all we went through, that I would never want to visit that on another person, another parent, another mother or father. You must know that, don't you?'

She turned towards him. Her mouth was set. Her face was rigid with fury.

'I know nothing like that. All I know is that my daughter is dead.' Her voice rose. 'That's all I know. All I'll ever know. Now and for ever.'

The child ran past her and stopped in front of Nick. He reached out and took hold of his hand. Maria O'Neill looked back and saw Chris. She held out her arms to him and they embraced. She rested her head on his shoulder and began to sob. Chris stroked her hair. He murmured to her and her sobs began to quieten.

'Now,' he said, 'it'll be all right. You'll see.'

He pushed her gently towards her husband, guiding her, shepherding her as if to safety. Jack O'Neill took her by the arm and gently pulled her away. Together they walked slowly up the steps. Susan held the door open for them. They walked inside. The door shut behind them. And all was quiet.

Chris picked up his shopping bags.

'Come on, Emir, time to go.' He reached out and took hold of the boy's wrist, jerking him away from Nick. Emir pulled back, whimpering.

'Leave him alone, Chris,' Nick said. 'And, while you're at it, leave me alone too.'

Chris looked at him and smiled tightly. 'I don't know what you mean,' he said.

'Don't you? I think you do. I think you know exactly what I mean. It was you wasn't it?'

'Me, me what?'

'You who told the police that you saw me leaving the house after Marianne. I saw you, the way you went after them when they left my house. I saw them go back with you. I know it was you. But answer me this. Tell me why, that's what I want to know. Why did you lie like that? What is your reason, eh?' He extended his fingers and poked Chris in the chest. He felt the bone of his sternum, hard and unyielding and he pushed him again, with still more force, so Chris stumbled and swayed.

'Hey, don't do that. Leave me alone.' Chris raised his voice. His arms flailed and he caught Nick on the shoulder.

'Oh, it's like that, is it?' Nick pushed him again, sudden

anger flushing through him. 'Why did you do it? You've no idea the damage you've done. I don't understand you, Chris. What's in it for you?' He pushed him a third time and Chris fell back. Nick bent over him. He grabbed the lapels of his jacket, jerking his shoulders so his head snapped up and down, barely missing the stone steps. Heard Susan's voice, screaming.

'What on earth do you think you're doing? How dare you behave like that? Here of all places. Now of all times. Get off him, you bastard, leave him alone.'

And he looked up and saw her standing in the doorway and in the window he saw Marianne's mother and father. And heard the child whimpering beside him, tears streaming down his pinched white face as rain began to fall.

He waited for the phone call from O'Reilly. He waited all afternoon. He sat in front of the stove and fed his pictures into it. The room was filled with the smell of burning paper and scorched paint. Rain drifted across the windows and light began to fade from the sky. He walked into the kitchen and made tea. He stood and stared out at the garden. And saw the branches of the buddleia by the back wall begin to shake, then a small figure run, bent low across the grass, towards him. Saw the face pressed to the glass. Opened the door and let him in. Felt him wrap his arms around his legs and press his dirty face to his knees. Dropped down onto his heels, and took him in his arms and hugged him and kissed him. Then carried him to the sofa and put him down in the warmth. Gave him hot chocolate and a biscuit, covered him with a blanket and listened to his breath flowing evenly in and out of his mouth. And fell asleep too, his head drooping down onto the child's shoulder.

Woke suddenly. The room was dark except for the brightness of the computer screen. The child was sitting at it. One hand was on the keyboard, the other on the mouse. Nick pulled himself upright and yawned.

'Hey, Emir, what's up? What are you doing?'

The child didn't respond. His back was tense and upright. One hand slipped from the keyboard and tugged at the waistband of his trousers. Nick got up and walked towards him.

'Do you want something, Emir? Are you hungry? Do you want to go to the loo?'

He leaned over him and looked at the monitor. And felt the breath catch in his throat. There was a boy on the screen, about the same age as the child whose hand was manipulating his image. The boy was naked. And he was not alone. A large male hand grasped him and as Nick watched, the hand began to probe the child's body, poking, fondling, pushing, squeezing, grasping, manipulating, finally slapping and hitting.

'Emir, what are you doing?' Nick moved closer and grabbed hold of his shoulders, turning him around. But the child pulled himself from his grasp. He was smiling, a look of triumph on his face. His small hand moved with confident sureness, pushing the mouse this way and that, pulling up more and more and different images. A parade of boys across the screen. A display of cruelty, greed and lust.

'No, Emir, don't.' Nick shouted out at him and tried to drag him from his chair. 'Don't do that. Stop it.'

He pushed the child to the floor and sat down in his

place in front of the screen. He moved the cursor to the back button and clicked and watched as the sequence of events reversed. As the boy moved from a sobbing heap, lying on a bare floor, to a child playing with a toy truck sitting on a sofa. And felt Emir's hand on his thigh, his small fingers squeezing as they inched towards his crotch. He looked down at him. The child was kneeling at his feet. He was smiling up at him. A wide, grin that showed all his teeth. His tongue slipped delicately across his bottom lip. He leaned forward and laid his cheek against Nick's knee as his hand moved.

'No,' Nick shouted and pushed him away. 'No, Emir, no. Not that, never that. No.'

He stood up and crashed his fist down on the table so the pictures on the screen jumped and fractured. And the look on the child's face was transformed. To fear. To panic. To pain. To a bewildered expression of incomprehension. As he scuttled, like a frightened creature, backwards, scurrying across the floor to the doors to the garden. Reached up to grasp the handle, twisted it open and was gone. While Nick's eyes followed his progress, then turned slowly to look down at the screen, at the boy, who gazed back up at him with mute terror stamped on his small pale features.

Twenty-three

Silence upstairs and downstairs. Footsteps on the floor above, occasionally voices. Music for a short while. Then the sound of the front door opening and closing. Voices outside, the car starting up and driving slowly away. And silence again. He lay on the sofa and stared into the stove's burning heart. He knew now he needed help. He stood up and walked around the room. Then pulled the phone book from the shelf, flicked through the pages, searching. Picked up a pencil from his drawing board, scribbled an address on a scrap of paper. Then took his coat from the back of the door, and shoved the police files into his computer bag. Locked the door behind him as he left the basement.

He walked along the seafront, past the railway station, towards the old Coal Harbour, past the lighted windows of the yacht club at the end of the pier, then into the shadows, where the path ran with the railway line on one side and the sea on the other. He kept his head down as he walked, the sound of his feet on the loose gravel and the crash of the breaking waves against the sea wall loud in his ears, so loud that he was no longer able to hear the cries of the child as he ran from the room out into the darkness. The tide was high and spray, carried on the wind, swept across the path in front of him. He ran his tongue along his lips and tasted salt, bitter, astringent, making him shudder and shrink down into his coat. He kept on walking, up onto the road towards Blackrock, when the path by the sea came to an abrupt end, past houses snug against the winter cold, their interiors lit behind curtains, here and there the sound of music or a television set turned up loud. On towards the town, stopping at a corner shop to buy some cigarettes, a sudden craving driving him into the warmth and brightness, finding himself surrounded by a crowd of kids all buying sweets and cans of Coke. Pushing and shoving each other and him as they jockeyed for position at the counter. Until he couldn't bear the noise and the proximity and turned and walked away back into the darkness outside and kept on walking, turning, this way and that, through streets once familiar but now crammed with houses where before there had been fields with cattle and horses grazing and the graceful, arching branches of copper beeches, as old as the century.

He stopped beneath a street lamp and pulled the piece of paper from his pocket. He compared the address he had written on it with the green nameplate on the low pebble-dashed wall. Then he walked past it and took the next turn to the right into a cul de sac, a curved arc around a green space, neat two-storey town houses with shared front gardens and large picture windows. Cars were parked at the kerb and there was a clamour of barking dogs as he walked slowly along the path. He stooped and picked up a child's bicycle left lying on its side, straightening out the handlebars and wheeling it into the nearest driveway. Then he stepped up to the front door, his hand reaching for the bell, pressing his ear against the wooden panels. Then stepped away quickly as he heard the sound of adult voices from within. He moved back onto the pavement and followed the curve of the path until he was directly opposite the house. Then he leaned against the trunk of a half-grown cherry tree and waited.

Lights were on in the bedrooms upstairs. They shone dimly through the curtains. Shadows flitted backwards and forwards, then the lights went off. He could imagine what it was like inside that house tonight. Teeth cleaned, faces washed, bedtime stories read and reread. Small mouths puckered for a goodnight kiss, small arms reaching out for a hug. Entreaties for glasses of water, trips to the toilet, biscuits to be eaten, more kisses and hugs. Then finally the last hushing, the last goodnight and silence.

Still he waited. The front door opened and a girl appeared. She paused on the doorstep, checking her bag, then turning back, calling out, her voice heavily accented. He saw Min standing in the lighted hallway, handing her keys, laughing with her, reaching down to kiss her cheek, watching her walk along the street before stepping back and closing the door.

Now he moved away from the support of the tree. He crossed the road and walked up the short drive. He pressed the bell. He tensed himself. He waited. The door opened. Light fell on his face.

'Oh, it's you. What do you want?'

'I need to talk to you. I need a few answers. To be honest, I need help.'

'Look, Nick, I'm sorry, but I can't. Things are different now. You're under investigation for Marianne O'Neill's murder. It's not appropriate for you to come to my home like this. I'm going to have to ask you to leave.' She drew back further into the house, one hand on the door handle, her weight beginning to push it closed. But he followed her, moved with her, his shoulder forcing the door open so she fell back against the stairs, the expression on her face shocked and scared.

'Get out,' she shouted. 'Get out or I'll call for help.' Her hand reached around for the phone on the small table.

'Don't,' he said loudly. 'Just listen to me. I'm not going to hurt you. I don't want to make any trouble for you. But I need you to listen.'

He picked the phone up and yanked the cord free. He hefted it in his hand like a weapon.

'What are you doing?' she screamed, her voice loud and filled with fear. 'What on earth are you doing? Get out of here. Leave me alone.' And heard, then saw, the wail of a child and a small face appearing through the banisters upstairs. She got to her feet and turned to the boy.

'It's all right, Joe, go back to bed. It's fine.'

But now he had been joined by a second small figure, who stared belligerently at Nick, pointed his finger at him and shouted.

'Go away, leave my mummy alone. Go away, you're a bad man.' Advancing step by step, a battered teddy bear held out in front of him.

'Shh.' Min stood up and held out her arms to him. 'It's all right, Jim. It's all right. Nothing is going to happen.'

Nick pulled back. He put the phone down.

'Look.' His voice was shaking. 'Look, I'm sorry, I didn't mean for this to happen. I didn't want to upset you and your children. I just, I just, I just don't know what's going on any longer.'

She nodded and stared at him, one hand stroking her son's dark head.

'Yeah, OK, I think we should all calm down. You go into the sitting room and I'll put these two back to bed and then we'll talk.'

Inside it was warm and comfortable. A fire burned in the grate. There were clothes drying on an airing frame, and two neat piles of school books, with matching pencil cases, on top of two red satchels. Nick sat back in a large armchair and closed his eyes. The wind blew raindrops in a sudden staccato beat against the windows. He could hear the voices upstairs. Water running, the toilet flushing. A sound of protest cut off by Min's firm tone. The goodnights called out loudly as she walked downstairs again. He got up from the chair.

'No.' She waved him back down again. 'Stay where you are. You're all right.' She sat down opposite him.

'Now,' she said, 'you'd better tell me what all this is about.'

After he had finished she got up and went into the kitchen. He sat with his head in his hands. She came back with an opened bottle of wine and two glasses.

'Here.' She sat down and poured.

'Thanks.' He gulped greedily then spoke. 'So, what do you think?'

'I think you're in big trouble. I think you need good legal advice. Conor Hickey is an expert in the area of Internet pornography. He probably knows more about it than anyone else in the country. If he finds out about this, you won't know what hit you.'

'But I didn't do it. It wasn't me.'

'It's on the hard disk of your computer. That of itself is

an offence. It doesn't matter how it got there. If anyone finds it, you've had it. This whole child pornography thing is absolutely huge. And the detection of it is becoming increasingly sophisticated. You could find yourself implicated in investigations in any number of legal jurisdictions. There are no geographical boundaries to this stuff.' She paused and sipped her wine. 'You know, Nick, I want to believe you, but it's difficult. It's practically impossible to imagine that a child like that little boy is capable of doing what you say all by himself. How old is he? Eight, nine?'

'He's nine, actually, and don't be put off by his apparent confusion. Emir is a bright boy. He's a survivor. I can't begin to imagine what he and his mother went through in Bosnia during the war. After that I think anything's possible.'

He drank again and she held out the bottle and topped up his glass.

'But listen, Min, there's something else. Marianne said something to me the night before she died. I can't stop thinking about it. She said she heard screaming. She didn't say it in her statement. I checked all the statements you gave me. Look.' He reached for his bag and pulled the files from it. He flicked through them, spreading them on the floor in front of her. 'Look, her statement, Chris's statement and the statements of Róisín and the other boy, they are practically word for word the same. None of them mentions screaming anywhere. But Marianne said it to me. She said, I heard screaming. She also said there was blood on the walls, blood on the floor.'

'But for God's sake, Nick, Marianne was out of her skull on acid. She didn't know what she heard, or saw, for that matter. And when she told you this she was crazy, wasn't she? She is a paranoid schizophrenic. She has periods of intense madness. You said yourself to us that her behaviour was strange and erratic. And you told us that her behaviour when you rejected her was totally off the wall. Isn't that what your defence is based upon? Isn't that your explanation for the scratches on your chest, your skin under her fingernails, your hairs on her body? Isn't that what you said? That she was crazy that night. Isn't that it?'

He didn't reply.

'You can't have it both ways, you know that.'

'No, that's not what I know. What I know is that I've been shafted. Someone is doing this to me deliberately. O'Reilly wants to question me again about this witness statement, this person who claims they saw me leave the house just after Marianne. Did you know that? He actually told me that I was lucky that I wasn't already in custody. Can you believe it?'

She drank, then nodded. 'Yes I can believe it. The next time he questions you the gloves will be off. He will arrest you and hold you in the station for six hours, renewable for another six hours. He will be hoping that by the end of it he will have enough to charge you.'

'So it'll be back to the bully-boy tactics, will it? Back to old what's his name? Will they bring him in to have another go at me?'

She looked up at the row of photographs on the mantelpiece.

'I don't think so, somehow.'

His eyes followed her gaze. He looked down at the glass in his hand then at her face, the flicker of the flames reflected in her dark eyes.

'I'm sorry. I didn't realize he was your husband.'

She shrugged. 'Why would you?'

'I shouldn't have said all those things about him, I wouldn't have if I'd known.'

She shrugged impatiently. Her voice was irritated, on edge. 'It doesn't matter. You weren't the only one to complain about Andy. He made a habit of behaving, not exactly badly, but not well. That's just the way he was. He was an old-style copper. It had worked for him for years and he wasn't going to change just because the style of policing had changed. He didn't believe in accountability and transparency. He believed in instinct. In right and wrong. In good and bad.'

'But you loved him, you got on well?'

She looked at him.

'Sorry.' He sat back in his chair. 'Sorry, it's none of my business. Hardly appropriate, to ask you something so personal.'

She smiled.

'You're OK. To be honest, it's kind of nice to be able to talk about him. You know the way it is. It's very quickly an embarrassing subject. Most people shy away from it.'

'Tell me about it, I know what you mean.'

'Yeah.' She sighed. 'You would, wouldn't you?' She looked down at the floor for a moment then back up at him.

'I loved him,' she said slowly. 'I loved him from the first moment I met him. He looked at me and I looked at him and that was that.' She drank some more. The coals in the fire spat and a blue flame flared for an instant, then died down.

'So, your sons, do they take after their father?'

She shrugged again. 'Who knows? Some days they're the spit of him. Others you'd never know they had a father.'

'And do they remember much about him?'

'I'm never sure how much they really remember and how much is just what they've heard and been told. We do the ritual at bedtime. Do you remember when Daddy did this and Daddy did that? Do you remember when Daddy took you out in the boat and you caught a whale? Do you remember what Daddy liked for breakfast, what pro-grammes he liked on the telly? Do you remember what Daddy looked like? But, to be honest, I don't know any longer whether any of it is real.' She looked across at him. 'It must be a bit like that for you with your son, is it?'

He didn't answer. He finished his glass and set it down on the hearth.

'I'd better go,' he said. 'Look I'm really sorry about, you know, earlier. I shouldn't have turned up unannounced like that, but I reckoned if I phoned you wouldn't have agreed to talk to me. And I'm sorry, Min, but I just didn't know where to turn.' He stood and picked up his bag. 'Here are all the files. I thought you'd want them. It's probably not a good idea to have them in my place any longer. And I reckon I've got everything out of them that I need.' He moved away from the fire. She stood too. She nodded.

'But, please, will you think about what I said about Marianne? I told you what that kid Luke had said to me. I don't know, but I just feel that it means something. So, please, for me, for Owen, for whatever. Please.'

She nodded and moved with him towards the door. He stepped out into dark, then turned back.

'And I am truly sorry about your husband. If you loved him, he must have been all right.'

He smiled at her. She smiled back. She didn't answer. She closed the door. She walked back into the sitting room. She picked up the empty glasses from the table and moved towards the kitchen. It was a mess. She filled the sink with hot water and piled everything into it, then stared out at the dark garden. Her own face stared back.

'Whoever would have thought it?' he'd said to her. 'Love at first sight for an ould fella like Andy Carolan.'

'And was it?' she'd asked him. 'Was it truly?'

'Yes,' he said. 'I looked at you that day, the day after the Cassidy kid went missing. You were so beautiful. Your shiny black hair cut like a boy's, your big brown eyes full of life and fun. And your body, well.'

'Go on, what about my body? Go on, flatter me.'

But he just shook his head and held her hand and said again, 'The moment I saw you, I knew you were the one.'

The wine he had drunk with Min had given him the taste for more alcohol. There was no shortage of pubs between her house and his, but with every pint he poured down his throat he felt more desperate, more alone, more defeated. Everywhere there were men who looked like him. Men on their own. Men with slumped shoulders and lined faces. Men with bad consciences, with more of their past that they wanted to forget than to remember. He watched himself in the reflections he saw. In the smeared mirrors behind the bars, the glasses half filled with stout he held up in front of his face, the metal cigarette lighter towards which he bent his head, the dark windows he passed by as he wandered back to Victoria Square. He remembered his own father's face. The way he had looked as he died slowly of cancer. It was as if the flesh had peeled from his bones over those months he had been ill. He had never been a fat man, but as he lay, first of all in his own bed in the room that had been his all his married life, and then in the bed in the hospice, his body began to consume itself, to take him back into its essence, to reduce him to what had been there in the beginning. The embryo. The shape of the spinal column, the eye, the head. So at the end there was only this and nothing more.

The shape of his own head, the eye socket, the cheekbone, the jaw. That was what Nick saw when he looked into all these reflections as he passed them by. And he thought of what he would find if he found Owen. The shape of the head, the eye socket, the jaw, the small teeth, the collarbone and sternum, the ribcage, the ulna and radius, the bones of the wrists and hands. The spinal column and the pelvis, the femur, the tibia and fibula, and the small neat bones of the ankle and foot. He had tested Susan as she learnt their names for one of her exams. More bones in the foot than any other part of the body, she would say. It all starts with the foot, the point where the human being connects with the earth. The place where we realize that we too are flesh and blood, bone and sinew. That we are not just consciousness, awareness, a collection of sensual information, but as much a part of the physical world as every other creature. As easily broken, smashed, hurt and destroyed as the fly or the ant, the maggot or the black beetle.

It was closing time now. He joined the stragglers as they ambled down the main street. Their conversations were loud and aggressive. He stared at the footpath in front of him as he walked, avoiding catching an eye, being drawn into any kind of contact. Too easy for a fight to start. A chance remark, a slighting reference to a football team or a woman. An explosion of fury, a head smashed to the kerb, a boot aimed at the testicles or the kidneys. He had seen it too many times before. There was a certain relief as he turned off towards the square and the interlocking squares behind it. At least he would be safe now in the quiet darkness, where children slept, tucked up in their beds and parents double-locked doors and windows, and turned on alarms for extra protection. Soon he would be home. He would crawl beneath his quilt on the sofa. He would sleep long and wake refreshed. And then he would face into another day.

But as his hand went to the door, the key outstretched towards the lock, he saw that it was already unlocked and, when he pushed it, it swung back. There were men in the room. Jay O'Reilly and Conor Hickey. They were gathered around the table, their heads close together as he stepped into the light.

O'Reilly turned to face him.

'So, you've decided to come back, have you? We were just about to send out a search party to look for you.'

'What on earth do you want? What are you doing here?'

'A complaint has been made against you, Mr Cassidy. A very serious complaint. We have a warrant here and we've just searched your flat.'

'Oh, and what you could possibly find of any kind of interest?'

'These.' O'Reilly stood back. Nick stepped forward. The table was covered with photographs, spread out. His photographs. The pictures he had taken down through the years, of boys, of children, in groups and singly. Boys on the beach, boys playing, boys eating ice cream, girls and boys in playgrounds and parks. Boys with thick fair cockscombs of hair and round blue eyes. Boys smiling and crying. Boys in swimming trunks and shorts, and boys naked, playing in the sea and on the beach.

'And this too.' O'Reilly gestured towards the computer. 'We'll be taking it for forensic examination. Oh.' O'Reilly turned towards him again. 'And of course we'll be taking you. I'm arresting you in accordance with section 5 of the Child Trafficking and Pornography Act of 1998. Perhaps you'd be so good as to step outside and make your way to the car. If you don't mind, Mr Cassidy.'

And as Nick opened his mouth to protest he heard O'Reilly's voice again.

'Now, get outside now, before I find myself in a position to use force against you. Do I make myself clear?'

Min woke. Her heart banged painfully. Her breath caught in her throat. She sat up straight. She reached for the clock. It was four-thirty. She listened for a moment. Then she got out of bed, and reached for her dressing gown.

The landing light was on. She opened the boys' bedroom door and peeped in. They were both sleeping soundly. She closed the door and moved to Vika's room. The girl was snoring softly. Her clothes were tumbled on the floor and there was a smell of alcohol and perfume. Min moved away to the window on the landing. She peered out through the crack in the curtains. It was still raining.

She walked downstairs and checked the locks on the

front door. She put on the safety chain. She checked the windows. They were all locked securely. She moved to the kitchen and tried the handle of the sliding door to the garden. It did not budge. She moved back into the hall and stopped by the alarm panel. She pressed the button. The electronic voice spoke to her. 'System is armed to home,' it chanted. Armed to home, she thought as she climbed the stairs again, a sense of distaste at the term. But there was also a sense of comfort. Armed to protect. Armed to secure. Armed to keep whatever terrors might be out there at bay.

She lay down and pulled the quilt tightly around her. She closed her eyes, but she could not sleep. She muttered the words of the old prayer, over and over and over again.

> 'Now I lay me down to sleep,
> I pray the Lord my soul to keep,
> If I should die before I wake,
> I pray the Lord my soul to take.'

Twenty-four

'What happened?'

'It was bad. They questioned me. Over and over again. Everything I said made my situation look worse. They showed me what they had taken from my computer. The stuff is unbelievable. I'd never imagined in all my life that people were capable of such cruelty. You know, Susan, I thought I was pretty sophisticated, pretty knowing. I thought I'd been around a bit. After all the travelling I've done, particularly in the States, I thought I'd seen everything you could see. But I was wrong. I haven't a clue.'

'And did they have any suggestions as to how it all got onto the hard disk?'

He shook his head.

'All they could say was that I had done it. Even when I demonstrated to them, or tried to, that I didn't have a clue how it worked. I can just about manage email. I only use the goddamn computer for some of my graphic work. And to write letters, that sort of thing.'

'And did they believe you?'

He sighed deeply and buried his head in his hands. 'Well, they haven't charged me with anything. But they left me in no doubt. They will if they can. You can bet your life on it. They will charge me if they can.'

'And the complainant? Did they tell you who it was?'

He shook his head again. 'They didn't. I asked, but they said they couldn't tell me. But I think we both know, don't we? I said had they investigated the child's home situation. Had they spoken to his mother and to Chris. They said they had. They said the child and his sister had been visited by the local childcare worker. They said that because of his psychological problems, his lack of speech etcetera that there was a lot of information available about him. None of it suggested any kind of abuse or exposure to pornography within the home. So that pretty much was that.'

It was mid-afternoon. They sat in the kitchen. Susan poured tea. She had made scrambled egg and toast, but he could barely eat.

'Come on, Nick. You should, you know. Doctor's orders.' And she reached across the table and took his hand and smiled at him.

'Thanks,' he said. 'I didn't know what you'd think. I didn't know who you'd believe.'

She had seen him from the front windows as he walked along the square after he'd been released. She came out onto the front steps and called his name. He looked up at her as if he didn't know who she was. And then he smiled and she came down towards him and held out her hand and drew him after her into the house.

They sat in the kitchen. Rain slammed against the windows. The kettle boiled. Susan made more tea.

'Tell me about the O'Neills,' he said.

She sighed and fiddled with her spoon.

'It was terrible. I don't know how they survived the

identification process. I volunteered to do it for them, but they didn't want that. They were very brave.'

'I'm sorry,' he said, 'about the way I behaved in front of them. It was unforgivable of me.'

'Yes.' She looked at him. 'It was.'

'Can I make it up to them?'

'No, not really. Not for a while. I'm trying to get Marianne's body released so they can bury her. But the pathologist won't let her go until he gets the DNA results back from the lab in Britain. And God knows how long that will take.'

'But surely in a case like this those tests will have priority? Surely it won't take too long?'

'It's not as simple as that, Nicky. There's nowhere here in the Republic that can do them. They have to been sent to Britain. They're extremely expensive and there's probably already a waiting list of cases. So it won't be tomorrow or the next day. But I'm doing what I can. I know the patho- logist of old. He's a great guy. He'll help.'

'And the funeral, you'll go?'

She nodded.

'And should I?'

She looked away, 'I can hardly say to you that it depends, can I?'

He stared at her. 'Do you honestly think there's any doubt about it, Susan? Can you sit there and say to me, you who have known me longer and better than anyone else, can you honestly think that I might have raped Marianne and smashed her head against the side of the tunnel?'

There was silence for a moment. Outside the wind tore through the trees.

'Longer? Better? Is that so?' Susan's voice was low. He leaned forward to hear her.

'Longer, longer than anyone else apart from my older sister,' he replied. 'Better, better than anyone else including my sisters. That was one of the things that I hated most about being away. Every time I met someone I had to begin the story of my life all over again. And even then, Susan, there was no guarantee that any of them would understand. And that once we'd got beyond the superficial, the where, what, why and when, that there would be anything more to say. Do you know what I mean?'

She fiddled with her mug of tea. She nodded.

'And that I would ever stop comparing them to you and to what I had once had with you. I knew eventually I would have to come back. That I couldn't go on without you,' he said.

'So.' She looked up at him, her gaze steady. 'So why did you go in the first place? Why did you tell me you didn't love me and you wanted to get away from me?'

'What?' His face crumpled with disbelief. 'I never said that. Never.'

'Yes, you did. You sat here in this kitchen and you said, I can't stand being here with you. I can't stand it any longer. I can't bear seeing you like this. I can't bear the absence, the lack, the loss. You said I was like a great dark lacuna, an empty space into which Owen had disappeared and you would too. You said you couldn't bear me, you couldn't bear to be near me. Don't rewrite history, Nick, don't pretend it didn't happen. It was me you left.'

'Susan.' Nick gripped the edge of the table. His voice

rose, 'Susan, I didn't say that. Or if I did, I didn't mean it that way. What I meant was that I couldn't bear my shame and my guilt. I couldn't stand that when I looked at you I saw my own weakness and my own selfishness staring back at me. When I looked at you I saw Owen's absence made flesh. But I didn't mean that I didn't love you and want you and want to be with you. I wanted you to come with me. I wanted you to start again somewhere else. We could have, couldn't we?'

She shook her head. 'No, Nicky, we couldn't. The only chance we had was here. In this house. In this street. In this place where our child once lived. The place you said in your letter you wanted to come back to.'

'And does that mean, Susan, that the only chance for us is here, now?' He leaned across the table and took her hand. He lifted it to his cheek. Her skin smelt clean, almost antiseptic. He turned his mouth towards her palm. He kissed it. She picked up his other hand and put it to her own face. He felt her eyelids beneath the pads of his fingers and her chin against his wrist.

'Shh,' she whispered. Her breath was warm and moist. 'Shh, shh.'

It was dusk when they left the house. They walked in silence through the streets. Drifts of leaves lay in their path, sodden now from the afternoon's heavy rain. It was dark by the time they reached Lizzie Anderson's shrine. Susan bent down and removed the stub of yesterday's candle.

'Here,' she said. She handed a new one to him and held out the lighter. 'You do it.'

He cupped the small flame in his hand until it caught.

Then he placed the candle in the glass container. He stood back and looked and bowed his head. He closed his eyes.

'She comforts me,' Susan said quietly. 'She makes me feel I'm not alone. I know nothing of her, of the kind of person she was. I know what she looked like. I know something of what she suffered the night she died. But, for some reason that I can't quite fathom, she comforts me.'

They turned and walked away. Nick looked back. The candle glowed in the darkness. A small point of light.

'Let's walk,' he said. 'Let's not go back just yet. That is—' He paused and looked at her. 'That is if you're not expecting someone. Paul, for instance.'

'No,' she smiled, 'no I'm not, I won't be seeing him this evening.'

They walked on. It was cold now. The sky was clear. The moon was up. The Plough hung in the southern sky.

'Did Gina ever speak of her?' Susan's voice was suddenly loud.

'Gina?'

'Gina Harkin, your Gina.' Her voice was steady.

He tried to keep his tone neutral. 'Did she speak of whom?'

'Lizzie Anderson.'

'No, she didn't. Should she?'

'Well, you did know, didn't you, that Gina gave her lessons?'

'No, I didn't. How did that happen?'

'Well, you know that Gina taught at Laurel Park when Lizzie was there. And apparently Lizzie used to have extra classes twice a week with Gina. Gina knew about her relationship with Brian Matthews and she allowed her to use the classes as a cover story for meeting him.'

He didn't reply.

'And in return Lizzie modelled for her. Don't you remember that painting that Gina had in her flat? Above the fireplace.'

He remembered. A huge canvas. Six foot square. It made the room look small. He had never been able to decide whether he liked it or not. The girl lay with her feet towards the viewer. Her head hung back over the edge of an unmade bed. Her trunk was elongated. Her breasts were flattened against her ribs. Her pubic bone stuck up.

'Her face,' he said. 'I remember that the girl's face was barely painted. Gina had put all her energy into the body. The girl's face was hardly there at all. I didn't like that about it. I felt it was alienating, objectifying the girl's humanity.'

'Did she agree? Did she tell you who the girl was?'

'I don't remember. I'm sure if she had I would have remembered. But I know that she defended the way she had represented the girl. She said it was an abstraction, a study of a body, and that to give her a face would have given her a nature and she didn't want to do that.'

'Do you agree?'

'No, I don't. I've done a lot of work with models over the years. A lot of the time I was in the States, when I was teaching, I used models in life classes. It was always very interesting to see how the students responded to them. Whether they saw them as a complete human being or just a collection of body parts. And the models themselves always knew. They could tell who despised them and who valued them.'

They walked on, climbing the hill away from the sea.

'How do you know that about Gina and the girl?' He looked towards Susan.

'I've become friendly with Catherine Matthews, Brian Matthews's daughter. Lizzie's one-time best friend. She told me. She and her mother went to court every day while her father's trial was on. They heard all the evidence.'

'Did she think—' He paused.

'Did she think he did it?' Susan dug her hands deep in her coat pockets and sank her neck down into her collar. 'She said she didn't know. Her mother staunchly defended her husband. She refused first of all to believe any of it. Then, when he admitted that he had been sleeping with Lizzie, she blamed the girl. Then, when it became apparent that Lizzie wasn't some kind of erstwhile Lolita and that he was the instigator of the whole thing, she still stood by him, put it down to a kind of male menopause, mid-life crisis. Blamed herself for not taking care of her appearance, putting on weight, letting herself go. And Catherine said that when he was acquitted she welcomed him home with open arms. And for a while it looked as if they could put it all behind them and get on with life as a family again. But—'

'But?'

'Well, I think you can imagine. It wasn't that simple. There were always doubts, particularly as the police never did manage to charge anyone else. So eventually he left home, went to England. And that was that.'

'Another man who ran away from a mess of his own making. Isn't that right?'

She didn't reply. It had begun to rain again, a misty drizzle this time. Soft haloes of refracted light hung around the street lamps. She shivered.

'We should go home,' she said. 'We've walked far enough.'

Nick stopped. 'Do you see where we are?' He pointed towards the large house in its own grounds ahead. 'See the sign? It's the school, isn't it?'

'Yes, that's right. Laurel Park. Very exclusive. It's where Chris Goulding teaches now. And do you remember, Nicky?' She turned away from him. 'That house, the one next door that's part of the school now. That used to be Chris's grandmother's. Do you remember? He and Róisín often used to take Owen there. It had the most beautiful garden with a stream and a little woodland area. And it had that lovely summer house, the one that's in Chris's garden now. Have you seen it? He got it moved to his garden after his grandmother died and the house was sold. He did it for Amra's kids.'

'Oh, so that's where it came from. I was wondering. They're not that common these days, the old-fashioned ones on the swivel.'

They began to walk again, quickly now as the rain began to fall heavily.

'I'd forgotten what Irish rain was like.' Nick sidestepped a puddle. 'In New Orleans when it rained you needed a canoe, but the sun was out ten minutes later and that was the end of it. But here you think it's only a shower, but it soaks right through your clothes and almost right through your skin. And it's so bloody cold.' He shivered.

'A hot bath's what you need.' Susan quickened her pace. 'Come on, put a step in it, before you catch your death.'

*

He lay with the water lapping his chin. He closed his eyes and felt warmth flood through his body. And comfort and security and peace. He picked up the bar of soap from the dish. He held it to his nose. It was without scent. Plain and unadorned, like most things to do with Susan. He knew without looking that the shelves in the bathroom would not be laden with beauty products. She never wore make-up or used perfume.

'Don't you like my smell?' she had said to him when one Christmas he had bought her an expensive bottle of perfume. And she had opened her blouse and taken hold of his head and pulled his face down to her neck.

'Here, smell that. What's it like?' she had asked. And he hadn't replied. Just breathed in deeply before kissing the hollow between her collarbones.

Now he stood up and wrapped himself in a towel. She had taken his clothes to dry. Her kimono hung from a hook on the back of the door. He put it on and wrapped it around himself, knotting the belt tightly in a large bow. He looked in the mirror and smiled. He walked downstairs to the kitchen.

'What do you think?' he asked.

She turned from the stove, a wooden spoon in her hand. She giggled and handed him a glass of wine.

'It's definitely this year's look, all right. Very David Beckham, very new man.'

She had made leek and potato soup. They ate it with hunks of bread. Outside the wind was up. They sat at the kitchen table and watched the bare branches of the trees whip from side to side. The windows rattled and from somewhere further down the square a house alarm sounded.

'Susan?'

'Yes?'

'Chris. Do you not wonder about him?'

'Wonder what?'

'What is he doing with that woman and those children? Why them?'

'Why not them?'

'Why not someone of his own age, his own kind? Someone who comes without the kind of baggage that they have?'

'Well, actually, I don't wonder. He's done a good thing for Amra. He tries hard with Emir. He's kind to the little girl.'

'But how can she trust him after all she's been through? What does she really know of him?'

'Trust, now there's an interesting concept.' She put down her spoon and looked at him. 'What does she know of him? She knows he has taken her and her children into his house. She knows that he puts food on the table for them. She knows that when she goes to sleep at night he is there beside her, and when she wakes in the morning he is still there. That's what she knows. And that's what she trusts.'

He said nothing. His throat felt tight and sore.

'Susan.' He held out his hand towards her.

She turned away from him and looked out into the garden.

'Look,' she said and stood up. He moved to stand beside her. A small, dark shape was clearly visible, crossing the grass, approaching the garden wall. Susan put her hand on his arm. 'Look at her. She's a regular here now. This is her third year. She has cubs every spring. She gives birth beneath the summer house.'

THE GUILTY HEART

'Do you remember?'
'Of course, of course I do.'
She held up the bottle. It was empty.
'Will I open another?'
He nodded.
'Please,' he said. 'Please.'

Twenty-five

It would never be dramatic. It would always be painstaking and slow. Tedious, dull, systematic, routine. She had been taking part in the house-to-house questioning, handing out the questionnaires to be completed, then returning to collect them. There had been a number of sightings of Marianne as she made her way along the railway line. But so far the only positive identification of Nick Cassidy was that given by Chris Goulding. There was that statement from the woman in Glenageary that she had seen a man who resembled Nick. But it could have been any number of men. And the more they questioned her the less clear she became.

But the initial forensic evidence against him was strong. The hairs they had found on Marianne's body corresponded to his. The tissue they found under her fingernails also matched his. They were waiting for DNA analysis of the semen found in her vaginal canal. That would take a bit longer Johnny Harris had told her. But in the meantime Nick Cassidy was the only suspect in the frame.

And then there was the other business. The child pornography on his computer. She couldn't come to terms with it. And Conor Hickey had phoned her. Said she should come into the office, that he had something he was sure she would want to see. And it was an excuse, any excuse, to break the tedium of the slog.

It was the usual traffic on the Stillorgan dual carriageway into town. Bumper to bumper for miles. Surprisingly bad because it wasn't even rush hour. And then she saw the reason. A three-car pile up at the Foster Avenue junction. A BMW, a Nissan Micra and a Volkswagen Golf slewed across the middle of the road. Broken glass everywhere. An ambulance with its doors open and the paramedics tending to a woman lying on a stretcher. And two groups of people huddled together, shocked expressions on their faces, tears, anger, gestures of defiance as a motorbike guard, notebook and pencil in hand took down the details.

She saluted him as she passed. She recognized him. He'd been in Dun Laoghaire for years. He grinned and leaned in to her open window.

'Jaysus.' He wiped his brow with an exaggerated gesture. 'This lot are all right, the other guys are all wrong. And, as for the women, they're about to sue on the grounds of the equality legislation. One of them reckons she was sexually harassed by the fella in the BMW as they were waiting for the lights to change.'

He waved his notebook at her. 'This is the basis of a bloody great sitcom, do you know that?'

She laughed, 'Yeah, your ticket to ride out of this mess, is that it?'

He stepped back and beckoned her forward. She watched him in her rear-view mirror. The patience of a saint and the wisdom of Solomon was what was needed in that situation, she thought.

*

Conor was at his desk when she walked into the office. He called her over impatiently.

'Here, come here, pull up a chair. Come and have a look at what I've found.' She dumped her bag and coat and sat down beside him. She leaned over and looked.

'Who is it?' she asked. 'Do you know?'

Conor shook his head. He explained. They didn't know who the child was. But they knew the pictures well. They'd been around for a good few years. They were unusual, he said. They showed the child spreadeagled from behind. Arms out. Legs out. The lighting was different, very sophisticated. It made him glow as if he was transparent, made some kind of supernatural material, not flesh and blood. Everyone said the same thing about him. He was so perfect he didn't look real. The photographs always showed him in that same pose and with the light behind him, fanning out around the edges of his body in the same way. And there was another special point about the pictures.

'What's that?' Min tried to keep her voice neutral.

'There are never any shots of his face. Never. His body, every part of it has been seen, used, enjoyed and passed on from man to man, all around the world. But whoever it was who took the pictures made sure they were keeping his face only unto themselves.'

Conor's hand moved on his mouse and his keyboard, and she watched as picture after picture scrolled down and across the screen. In some of them the child was facing the viewer but he was masked. Sometimes he wore a knitted balaclava, sometimes a pointed cap that made him look like a wizard or a member of the Ku Klux Klan. Sometimes the masks were pretty, covered with sequins or feathers.

Occasionally there was a glimpse of eyes. Deadened, blank, almost as if they had been inked out.

'Some of the graphics experts we use to look at this stuff, think there's been a lot of morphing done to these pictures. They reckon that quite a number of them have been enhanced, embellished you could say. For example, this one.' He maximized the image. In spite of herself Min put her hand to her mouth and averted her eyes, reluctant to find herself a spectator to the act.

She turned away and gazed out the window towards the purple smear of the Dublin mountains along the horizon. The boys had asked her this morning when it was going to snow. They had some kind of a memory of tobogganing with their father. Not long before he died. She closed her eyes for a moment and felt tears press against her eyelids.

'And look here, have a look at this. Down here in the corner. See, on the wall.'

She leaned closer. Conor moved the mouse and magnified the area. There was something like a drawing, a scribble. He clicked again, and again. She saw that it looked familiar. It was a child, but with the face of a frog and a body that was covered in small perfectly formed scales. Like the scales of a fish.

'Wow.' She reached out and touched the screen. 'How amazing. I recognize it. Do you know what that is?'

He shook his head and reached for his cigarettes, then paused.

'OK, OK, in deference to you.' He opened his desk drawer and pulled out a packet of chewing gum. 'Better?' His tone was sarcastic, but he smiled as he peeled the silver foil from the stick and began to chew with vigour. 'Go on,' he said through his teeth, 'tell me.'

'Well, you tell me first of all. Where did you get this?'

He chewed noisily, his mouth open. 'Where do you think? Your friend Mr Cassidy. He has some very interesting stuff on his cute little laptop.'

She sat back in her chair. 'I can't believe it. I just can't. How did the star child end up there?'

'Star child? Is that what you call it. It's a good name for the pictures too. The star child series. That's what we'll call them.' He touched his computer screen with the tip of his biro. 'I name thee star child. Bad luck to all who seek to profit from thee.'

'No,' she said, 'you can't do that. It's a lovely story. The pictures in the book are really beautiful. It's won awards all over the world. It made Nick Cassidy's reputation as an illustrator. It's one of my kids' favourites. You can't taint it with this,' she waved her hand at the screen, 'this muck.'

'Yeah, can't I? Well, it may surprise you to know that it's not me who's tainted this story, or this book, or whatever you're going on about. It's Cassidy himself who did it.'

She pushed herself back in her chair. 'But just because the star child is in these pictures it doesn't prove that Cassidy had anything to do with them, does it? Surely anyone could scan in the image? There's nothing that complicated about it, is there?'

'Well, it's not quite as simple as that. For a start you'd only be able to access this stuff if you were a member of one of the most elite of the pornography clubs. You'd only be able to alter these pictures if you were very high up in the newsgroup where they came from. Not just any old Tom, Dick or Harry could change them. But, as I said, we got these pictures from the hard drive of Cassidy's computer. So.' He screwed up his eyes. 'It kind of adds up.'

She was silent for a moment.

'It's such a pity. It's a lovely book. My kids really like it. And I always show them where Oscar Wilde lived whenever I bring them into town.'

'Oh, it's one of his, is it? Well, that explains a lot.' He leaned back and folded his arms behind his head.

'What do you mean?'

'Well, you know what kind of a bloke Oscar Wilde was, don't you?' The tone in his voice was harsh.

'No, I don't. You tell me, you obviously do.'

'He was a paedophile. Pure and simple. He was a user of rent boys and abuser of children. He'd get fifteen years now for what he did then.'

'Oh come on.' Her voice rose. 'That's a bit harsh, isn't it? He was persecuted for his sexuality. He suffered and paid a huge price. His reputation was lost. His marriage ended. His relationship with his sons was finished.'

'Yeah and what about those kids he had sex with? Can you imagine the state of them at that time? You want to see the state of them nowadays. You want to take a trip to the casualty department in any of the city's hospitals. And it's men like Oscar Wilde, from his background, his class, his place in society, whose cars are lined up in the Phoenix Park waiting for the next available piece of meat.' Conor's face was suddenly very red. 'And it looks like we've another one here in Cassidy. Another man of culture, learning and art. And all the time he's just like the rest of them. An abuser of the weak.' He stood, picked up his coat and shrugged it on.

'I'm out of here. I'm going to get some fresh air.' As he walked away he spat the chewing gum from his mouth into a waste bin and pulled his cigarettes from his pocket. He paused and lit up. Then he was gone.

'Conor.' She got to her feet and rushed after him out in the corridor. But the lift doors had already closed. She walked back to his desk and sat down. She scrolled back through the star child pictures. She leaned forward. She began to look.

It was lunchtime. Her stomach told her, although she didn't much feel like eating. Still she needed a break. Outside it was cold but bright. She phoned Conor's mobile, but the answering machine was switched on. She left a message. 'I'm going for lunch to that place you really like, Conor,' she said. 'You know the one where the lasagne's nearly as good as the chips. Join me if you get this message.'

But it was Susan Cassidy who joined her as she sat with her bowl of soup, her salad and her thick crusty bread.

'May I?' Susan asked, but without waiting for an answer she slumped down at the small table and ordered spaghetti bolognese.

'I am so tired,' she said, and Min thought she looked it. There were dark circles under her eyes and her skin looked grey. 'It's this time of the year, I hate it. Every day less light, every day more reminders. It's the worst time for me.'

The waitress put down a bowl of pasta. Steam rose from the sauce. Susan picked up her fork and began to twist the spaghetti round it. Then put it down as if the effort of the movement was too great.

'I can't eat,' she said. 'I keep on wanting to. I feel hungry. But when it comes to it I just feel nauseous. It's worse than ever this time.'

'And is that because your husband has come home? And maybe it's just so much more real.' Min looked carefully at her, waiting for her response.

Susan sighed deeply. 'Maybe, maybe it is. I'm not sure. Maybe it's because of what's happened. Marianne dying in that way. I was with her parents when they went to identify her body. When Marianne's mother saw her she wailed out loud. It was like an animal facing its death. You know, I always wanted to be able to see Owen's body. I reasoned that because I was a doctor and had seen so many deaths that I would have been able to handle it. But I'm not sure any longer.'

Min stared at her plate. She tried not to remember.

'And I don't understand,' Susan continued, 'I don't understand what happened that night. I can't believe that Nick had anything to do with it. In all the years we were together he never ever showed any sign of being physically violent. But who else would have wanted to hurt her? She was a harmless, pathetic creature. She was incapable of hurting anyone except herself. I just don't understand.' She tried the food again, but the fork hovered in front of her mouth then dropped back into the plate.

'And do you mind if I ask you?' Min leaned towards her. 'You do know about this complaint about Nick and the little boy next door. What do you make of it?'

Susan shook her head. 'Again I don't understand any of it. I know Nick. I know he isn't like that.'

'But what about all the photographs they found in his bag? Why would he have all those pictures?'

'Because, because he was trying to find Owen. I know what he was doing. I've done it myself. I didn't take the pictures, but I looked. I've sat on beaches in Spain and Greece and stared at children. I've followed children home. I've been tempted to steal children from supermarket car parks and department stores. You've no idea, Min, what this thing does to you. You've no idea the extent to which you lose your grip on reality. Nick did what Nick has always done. He records people. He's always done it. When we were students, when we first knew each other, he always had a pad and pencil in his pocket. He would sit all afternoon in Stephen's Green drawing faces. Even when we went on dates together he had that bloody pad. I used to go crazy the way he would look at other girls. But it wasn't for the obvious reasons, well, mostly it wasn't. He just wanted to see how their faces were put together.'

'Well.' Min fiddled with the slices of tomato on her plate. 'That may be the way it looks to you, Susan, but it's not the way it looks to the guys in headquarters who deal with this stuff every day. To them it looks like a classic case of a child pornographer who gets off on collecting pictures of kids. They see it all the time. It fits the pattern.'

Susan pushed her plate away.

'Not Nick's pattern. Nick is a collector, that's true. But he's not a pornographer or paedophile. I know what they're like. I've come across them occasionally in the hospital. And not just in relation to the patients and their families. We've had staff members who are abusers. And, yes, it can be hard to distinguish between men who genuinely love children and men who only love themselves. But I would swear by everything I know that Nick is not like that.'

She wiped her fingers on a paper napkin.

'You know, after Nick left I used to go down to the basement to his studio. My excuse to myself was that I was tidying it up. I had thought I might rent it out. Purge the place of him, if you know what I mean. I'd sit there on his old sofa and drink tea, cup after cup, the way he did. He had a collection of CDs that he listened to all the time. A funny mixture. Talking Heads, Little Feat, all those seventies kind of alternative American bands. And lots of jazz. He was always mad about John Coltrane. I'd turn the music up really loudly and blast it out. And I'd go through all his notebooks and his pads. There were hundreds, literally hundreds of pictures of Owen. From his first day in the hospital up until a couple of days before he went. It helped me a lot at the time. It made me see that there are many ways of holding onto someone you love. You may not have them physically any longer. But so much of their essence still remains in the flotsam and jetsam of our lives.'

She stood up. 'I'd better go. There's a child I'm very worried about. I'm better off at work. At least there I'm distracted all the time.'

'Hold on.' Min held up her bill and gestured to the waitress. 'I'll come with you.'

Outside it was already beginning to get dark. The tall buildings around them pushed the light back from the street. Susan shivered and wrapped her scarf tightly around her neck. They turned and began to walk towards the hospital.

'It's dog and wolf time,' Min said, shoving her hands into her pockets.

'Dog and wolf?'

'It's a phrase the French have. *Entre chien et loup.* Between dog and wolf. They use it to describe this time of the day when it's between light and dark. It's one of my mother's favourites. She reckons that Irish winters are a permanent state of dog and wolf.'

'I know what she means.' Susan smiled wanly.

They stopped outside the hospital entrance. Susan turned towards Min.

'Thanks for listening to me. Of course, I know you understand. Nick told me about your husband. I remember him. I liked him actually. He was very straight with me. I appreciated it. And you've children too I hear. Boys. You're lucky.'

She held out her hand. Min took it, held it, then turned away. Flotsam and jetsam. She turned the phrase over in her mouth. What did she have of Andy's? she wondered. Not much. Most of his clothes had gone to the Oxfam shop. There were a few books, some old LPs, his car. He wasn't a great one for possessions. When they'd first met he was living in a furnished flat and when he died most of what he had gathered around him had been presents from Min. Except for his notebooks, she thought. There were a couple of hundred. He was meticulous about them. Each was dated and he kept them in strict chronological order in a box under the bed. He had used them too, referred back to them.

'You'd be amazed how much information is here,' he'd say. 'All kinds of stuff that might seem irrelevant to begin with. But give it time. It kind of ferments, bubbles away until it's ready to surface.'

She still had them all. She was going to give them to the boys when they were old enough to read Andy's scrawl. And what else was it that he used to say about them? They're a unique record. Put them together with the notebooks of every other guard in the station and you'd know every single thing that happened on a particular day in a particular location.

She got into her car. She picked up her phone. She punched in the number. She waited for the answer.

'Hi, Dave Hennigan, it's me, it's Min Sweeney. Listen, sorry to bother you. I know you've enough going on out there. But there's something I want to ask you. I know it's going back a bit, but I was wondering if you could help me track down some of the guards who were working out there ten years ago.'

She listened. She could hear the irritation in his voice. She explained what she wanted. She waited for his reply, smiled as she heard him say,

'OK, OK, if that's what you want. OK I'll do what I can. By the time you come out to me I'll have the list for you. I'll have the names, where they are now, phone numbers. Then after that it's all up to you. Got it?'

She got it. It was a long shot. But she'd known as she sat and looked at Susan Cassidy's face. There had to be an answer somewhere.

'Andy,' she said out loud, 'I know you think I'm doing the right thing, don't you? Painstaking and slow. Attention to detail. Reading between the lines. That's what you always said, didn't you? Help me now, Andy, please help me.'

Twenty-six

The child sat on the wall and looked down at Nick. It was a clear bright day. The golden leaves which drooped from the ash trees at the end of the garden shimmered in the early morning sunlight. The child was dressed in his faded pyjamas. In one hand he held a half-eaten piece of toast. The other hand clutched onto the crumbling cement which capped the wall's granite blocks. Nick walked slowly towards him and stopped. He smiled tentatively. The child looked down. His face was solemn and serious. He dropped his toast and put both index fingers into his mouth, catching the corners of his lips and pulling them away from his teeth, sticking out his tongue and waving his head from side to side with exaggerated movements. Then he stopped and held out his arms, waiting for Nick to reach up and pull him down to the ground. But Nick stepped back.

'Sorry, kiddo, but we're not playing that game today. Or any other day. You can't come in here any more. You'd better go home. It's cold to be out without your coat and your hat.'

The child's face crumpled. He continued to hold out his arms towards Nick, his small hands twisting and turning, beckoning him to come towards him. But Nick stood his ground, shook his head, then turned and walked away. He did not look back. He did not see the child begin to cry, tears silently filling his eyes and rolling down his smeared cheeks, his mouth opening wide in agonized despair. Or the hands which reached up from behind to pull him roughly down from the wall, to drag him away, twisting fingers in the child's thick hair and knocking his feet out from under him so he fell to the ground, and lay curled into a ball, as heavy punches landed on his back.

Sunshine too laying blocks of brightness across Dave Hennigan's desk as Min sat beside him and looked at the list he had written out for her.

'It's all yours, love.' He smiled sympathetically as he handed her the sheet of paper. 'You can have a grand time now doing a bit of real detective work, can't you?' And he put his arm around her shoulders and gave her a quick squeeze.

'Gee, shucks, Dave, you're all heart.' She scanned the page. 'You've excelled yourself this time. Names, addresses and phone numbers. Wow. I am impressed.'

'Yeah, yeah, go on with you.' He stood and looked down at her. 'Are you all right? You're looking a bit tired. Kids giving you a hard time?'

She shook her head. 'No it's not that. Just got a lot on. You know the way it is.'

'So you miss us, do you? You miss the cups of tea and the chats.'

'Oh yeah, nothing like your tea, Dave. No one in headquarters can quite match your brewing technique. It's the way you dunk the tea bag in the cup, the way you hold it with your fingertips, then swirl it around with the teaspoon. That's your secret isn't it?'

He laughed. 'Yeah, you're right, chicken. Now go on away with you, some of us have work to do.'

Nick waited, sitting on the sofa, listening, until he heard the sound of the front door close. He stood up and looked out the window. He saw Amra with the children, the little girl in a buggy and Emir lagging behind, as they headed down the square towards the main road. He moved away from the window and let himself out into the back garden. He walked over to the wall and put his hands up, resting them on the top. He'd climbed this wall before with ease. Retrieved Owen's football countless times. Now he transferred his weight to his arms, springing up from his feet, his toes scrabbling for purchase between the stones. He rested for a moment, looking up at the house, hoping no one was watching. Then he dropped gently down onto the grass below.

Once there had been a large vegetable plot here. Hilary Goulding had her neat rows of raspberry canes and gooseberry bushes, her lettuces and courgettes with their spreading leaves and orange flowers the shape of a French horn. And at the height of summer the dahlias she used to grow.

'Just for fun,' she had said to him, her small mousy head peeping over the wall. 'My indulgence, my gesture towards frivolity.' Turning back to admire the extravagant colours, the reds and oranges, the yellows with dashes of crimson through their furled petals.

'Lovely, aren't they?' she had said, her voice tinged with wistfulness, and he had nodded and agreed and wondered at her passion for flowers that were so out of keeping with the sobriety of the rest of the garden, with its two large

compost bins, clipped lavender edging and sober utili-
tarianism.

But now, where once vegetables had grown, there was a
scraggy lawn with a child's rope swing and beside it the
summer house. He moved towards it. Its small, glass-paned
door stood open. The bottom hinge was broken and the
door had dropped and wedged against the wooden saddle.
He stepped up onto the veranda. A deckchair was folded
against the railing, its striped canvas faded and torn. He
looked inside. Leaves lay in a drift against the back wall
and there was a smell of decay. Old newspapers had been
shredded and torn into strips. Small bones, gnawed and
chewed, were scattered across the dirty wooden floor. And
there was a variety of feathers, some black, some white and
a few the cloudy grey of the pigeons whose loft was two
streets away. A strong musky smell made Nick draw back.
He recognized it immediately. It was fox. An old tobacco
tin, dented and rusty, was lying on the window ledge. He
prised off the lid. Inside were the stub of a candle and a
box of matches. Dangerous, he thought with all these
inflammables. But fun, he was sure, for someone.

He turned away and stepped down onto the grass. He
looked towards the house. Its windows were dark and
empty. They gave nothing away. He stood on the grass and
tried to remember. That day, ten years ago. How had this
house looked then? He remembered that the basement door
had always been unlocked. That the kids went in and out
whenever they wanted to. He remembered the times he had
climbed the wall, calling Owen's name.

Teatime, Owen. Bedtime, Owen. Mummy's home, Owen.

Pushing open the door, the smell of damp and coal
smoke. The sound of music, rock, loud. The sagging

broken-down sofa covered with an Indian cotton bedspread. Chris and Marianne sitting up, turning towards him. Owen snuggled down between them. Róisín standing by the fireplace, a bucket of coal heavy in her grip. Mugs with broken handles and chipped rims. Ashtrays overflowing. And his son saying, 'I don't want to come home, Daddy. I'm having fun here. Please, Daddy.' Overcoming his resistance. Picking him up, even though he was heavier now, his body no longer malleable in that small-child way.

Now he walked quickly towards the basement door and tried the handle. It was locked. He stood back and lifted up his foot. He kicked out hard. The door shook and small splinters appeared in the jamb. He took a deep breath and kicked again. This time the lock broke and the door swung inwards. He looked around again, then stepped inside and closed the door behind him. He took a deep breath. His heart fluttered in his chest, its movement irregular and uncertain so his breath caught in his throat. He put out a hand to steady himself against the wall. It was cold and damp. He pulled his hand away quickly and wiped it down his jeans. Then he began to walk slowly down the corridor through the silent basement.

His basement had been like this when he and Susan had first moved in. A warren of small rooms, cold, wet, miserable. Servants' quarters, kitchen, scullery and wash house in the days when the occupants of these houses were served and cosseted by the less fortunate. He had broken down the interior walls, opening it up to the light. But down here it was dark and gloomy. There was a strong smell of damp and rot. He pushed open the door nearest to him. The barred windows were dirty, cobwebs spangled with dead flies draped across the glass. He moved towards the fireplace. Soot had cascaded down the chimney and lay across the floor. Small footprints had smeared it everywhere. A mattress rested against the wall. It was wet to his touch. The stench of urine filled his nostrils. A blanket was flung into a corner. He stirred it with his toe and saw beneath it a piece of paper. He bent down and picked it up. He knew what it was. A child's hand had drawn the figures that covered it. Heavy strokes that had gouged holes in the paper. He folded it and put it in his pocket. He sat down on the window sill.

What was it Marianne had said? Screaming, blood on the walls, blood on the floor. But she had been hallucinating, hadn't she? She had been almost psychotic in her reaction to the drug. She had been about to go down into the depths from whence there is no redemption. Hadn't she?

Susan had said Marianne shouldn't take him with her when she went to visit the Goulding kids.

'It's not right, Nicky,' she said. 'It's confusing. For her and for him. She's his minder not his buddy. He's a child not some half-grown teenager.'

But he had swatted away her objections. Dismissed them out of hand. Said that they'd known the Gouldings for years. The kids had babysat Owen, for God's sake. He'd been in and out of their house all the time. What was different about this? And he had won. The way he always won. But that day Owen hadn't been here. That was what they all said. All four of them. Owen had not come with Marianne that day. She had come here on her own.

He got up. Now he needed to know. Whatever this house could tell him. Now he needed to know it all.

He turned and walked out into the corridor. The second

door was closed and locked. Again he lifted his foot and kicked hard. The wood splintered and he put his shoulder to it and pushed it open. The room was dark. Heavy curtains were pulled across the window, which opened onto the small front garden. He reached for the light switch. Neon crackled and flickered then burst from the ceiling reflecting off the white-painted walls and the concrete floor, which had been painted the same bright white. This room was clean, spotless and completely empty. He stood beneath the light and looked around, then backed away.

Outside was the staircase which led to the rest of the house. He walked slowly up it, hearing the boards creak beneath his feet. He stopped in the hall and listened. Silence within. He moved from room to room, opening cupboards, pulling out drawers, looking under chairs, under beds. And found nothing. The house was neglected and dirty. Everywhere there were piles of unwashed clothes and the smell of grease and stale food filled the air and turned his stomach. At the top of the stairs was a small bedroom, like the one in which Owen had slept. But there were no toys in this room. Just a cot with a plastic sheet stretched over the mattress, and a tattered teddy bear, stuffing protruding from its head, lying abandoned on the floor. He bent down to pick it up. And heard suddenly, loud in the quiet of the house, the sound of the front door opening. Footsteps in the hall. And a voice.

'Amra, are you here? I'm home. I'm hungry. Is there food?'

He stopped still. He tried to hold his breath. He could feel his pulse race and his heart surge.

'Amra, don't tell me you're still in bed. Get up, you lazy bitch.'

Footsteps on the stairs. Running into the bedroom at the front of the house. Then turning around and walking down to the kitchen. Tap turned on, water gushing into sink. Radio. Music, loud. And the sound of whistling.

Now Nick began to move carefully, step by slow step, down from floor to floor. Ahead he could see the front door. But just as he was about to walk towards it, Chris came out from the kitchen, a steaming mug in his hand. Nick flattened himself against the wall and waited, hardly able to watch him walk past and turn into the front room. He clenched his fists and tried to still the panic in his chest. He waited for a moment then quickly took the rest of the stairs two at a time and turned to go down into the basement. Floor creaking loudly beneath his feet, so, as he reached the bottom, he heard the voice again calling after him.

'Who is it? Is someone there?'

Heard the voice getting louder all the time.

'Emir, is that you? Are you downstairs? Come up here. This minute.' Anger, impatience. He shrank back and pressed himself into the space behind the stairs. He tried to hold his breath. Footsteps now, right above his head, so close that he could see the wood giving beneath the weight of Chris's body. He pushed himself back as tightly as he could against the wall. As he heard Chris's voice, loudly, 'Is there someone there? Who is it?'

Heard him walk towards the outside door. Heard him swear as he pulled open the door and the lock fell uselessly to the floor. Heard him slam it and the sound of the bolts being drawn across, top and bottom. Heard him again, walk from room to room, quickly peering inside as Nick pulled himself away, closing his eyes. Willing him not to see him. Until at last he heard his steps on the stairs, the sound lessening as he walked up again.

Then Nick let out his breath. He bent over, his head hanging down low, dizzy, sick. Heard the front door opening, then banging shut, and the sound of voices. Moved quickly out of his hiding place, pulling back the bolts, then slipping into the garden. Flattening himself against the side of the house as he headed for the wall. Scrambling up and over, not looking back, dropping down into the safety of his own garden. Slipping back into his own basement again. Gasping for breath, light-headed with relief as he sat down. Laid his head on the kitchen table, closed his eyes, waited for his breathing to slow and his heart to stop its dreadful beating. For calm and peace to return.

It was quiet in the office. For once she was on her own. She worked her way through the list. Dave had been thorough. Of the twenty names he had given her all were at the phone numbers he had provided. Ten of them were retired now. Ardent golfers and part-time farmers. She left messages on answering machines and with wives. The men who were still working were helpful, if sceptical about her task.

'We went over all that stuff years ago, Min,' they said. 'We checked out anything that was worth checking, you know we did. Sure, weren't you part of the initial investigation? And that husband of yours. Sure, if there'd been anything to find, he of all people would have found it.'

They all wanted to talk about Andy. Tell her stories. Some of them she'd rather not have heard.

She phoned home during the afternoon. All was well. Vika's voice was unusually bright and cheerful.

'It's good here today, Minuschka. Boys happy, sun shining, Vika happy too.'

'And last night, tell me, did you have fun?'

'You said it, Minuschka, very good fun.'

'That's great, but listen, Vika, in future when you come home late make sure to put the chain on the door, won't you, and also remember to put on the alarm. OK? Just in case.'

In case of what, she wondered and answered herself. Just in case.

'Sure, sure, Min, whatever you say. Oh listen, a man call you just half an hour ago. He say his name is Paddy O'Higgins. He is friend of your husband. He say you phone his house. He say you call him back. He thinks he has something for you. He leave mobile number. You got a pen?'

Paddy O'Higgins. He'd worked in the traffic section. A motorbike cop. He'd had a bad accident a few years ago. Chasing a gang who'd robbed a post office. Child allowance day, the place full of women and kids. And a couple of guys with balaclavas and sawn off shotguns. He'd crashed at speed out on the dual carriageway. Broke both legs and his pelvis. A right mess. Running a B and B with his wife, Nancy, now. Somewhere in Wexford.

He answered her immediately. His voice was animated.

'Think I might have something for you, Min. Listen to this and, if you think it's useful, I'll Fastrack the notebook up to you.'

She listened. She made notes. 31 October 1991. 4.35 p.m. Incident at junction of Marine Road and Sea Road. Pedestrian, female, knocked over by vehicle travelling at speed. Vehicle, BMW?, failed to stop. Ambulance called at 4.40 p.m.

Victim, Mrs Annie Molloy, age 82, 16 Rollins Villas, Sallynoggin. Information about the speeding car passed on to the traffic police. Pedestrian suffered cardiac arrest. Assistance given by William Metcalfe, 28 Moorview Avenue, Bradford, Yorkshire. Victim taken to St Michael's hospital at 4.58 p.m.

'What happened, Paddy, to the driver of the car? Who was he?'

'A kid from Dolphin House flats. Mick Burke aged sixteen and the passenger was a seventeen-year-old, called Damien Smith. They were both killed about an hour later. A collision with an articulated lorry out on the Arklow Road.'

'So there was no direct connection with the Cassidys?'

'None at all, but if there had been we'd have had it checked out already. But you never know. It's something that I hadn't thought about for years. Let me know, won't you, if it turns up anything useful?'

She looked down at her pad. She sighed. She couldn't see that it would. But it was the only thing of any interest she'd come across so far. The office door swung open and closed with a bang.

She looked up. Conor was standing in front of her.

'Hey, how you doing?'

She smiled. 'Fine. And you?'

He shrugged off his jacket and sat down. There was an awkward silence for a moment. Then they both spoke together.

'Look,' she began.

'Listen,' he started. They laughed.

'Ladies first,' he said, swinging back in his chair.

'I was going to say, dirt before the brush, but seeing as

how you put it so elegantly.' She paused. 'I just wanted to say I was sorry I upset you yesterday.'

'No.' He shook his head. 'I'm sorry I was so over the top. I don't know why I reacted the way I did. You're probably right. I spend too much time here. I should get out more.'

'Yeah, well, whatever.' She looked down at her list again. 'Listen, will you do something for me? I've got to go. The kids are doing a Halloween pageant at school this evening and my presence is requested. So would you do a search of a few people? It's probably absolutely pointless, but what the hell.' She underlined the names on her pad and passed it over to him.

'You're on.' He rested his hands on the keyboard. 'My magic fingers are at your service. I'll give you a call later if I find anything interesting. Oh, and bring me a lucky bag of sweets and nuts tomorrow. OK?'

She stood, slung her bag over her shoulder.

'You got it. I'll keep you all the best.'

She turned back as she got to the door. He was hunched over his desk, his legs twisted around his swivel chair. He was humming in a low monotone. He lifted one hand and without looking in her direction he waved and dismissed her. She turned away.

It was a fine bright day, 31 October 1991. Unusually warm. Leaves dropping in a soft pattern of red, gold and orange on the footpaths. A day that was fine enough for eighty-two-year-old Annie Molloy to get the bus down the hill to Dun Laoghaire to do her shopping. Usually her grand-daughter, Stacy, came in her little red car and took her list and went to the supermarket for her. But Stacy never listened when Annie said she liked loose tea and not tea bags, and milk with full fat instead of that low-fat stuff. And Stacy always forgot to get her packets of mint hum-bugs that reminded Annie of the old days. When there were still trams in the town and the horse-drawn cabs stood in a line at the east pier waiting for the passengers from the mail boat.

Besides which, she wanted to get her pension in the post office at the bottom of Marine Road. A chance to see who was still coming in person to collect it. And she was careful that day with the crossing. She waited at the lights until the green man came up and the beeper sounded and then and only then did she step off the footpath. She didn't see the car coming. She just heard the screech of its brakes as it tried to stop and felt the impact of the glancing blow that spun her around and dumped her hip first on the road.

She wasn't sure what happened after that. But there was a guard bending over her. Wearing a motorbike helmet and a heavy leather jacket. Asking her name, her address. Using his radio. Calling for an ambulance. And a crowd standing around. And someone took off their coat and made a pillow for her head. And someone else picked up her bag and said they'd mind it. And then she began to feel very bad. A sudden, sharp pain in her left arm and in her chest. Breathless, frightened. Reaching up to grab hold of the guard's hand, seeing black spots in front of her eyes and that cruel pain splitting her chest in two.

Panic then. The guard kneels beside her. He reaches for her wrist. He takes her pulse. He tries to lift her to sitting. He looks for help to the crowd around him. Then he hears a voice. An English accent.

'Do you need a hand, mate? Is she OK?'

He looks up. A man squats down beside the old lady. He puts his index and first finger against her neck. He kneels down and presses his ear to her chest. He sits back up and holds her mouth open and pinches her nostrils closed.

'Now,' he says, 'on my count.'

The guard leans over the woman. He waits.

'One, two, three, four, five, six, seven, rest.' The guard presses hard and rhythmically down on her winter coat.

The man leans over her and breathes air into her lungs.

'Now, again, one, two, three, four, five, six, seven. Rest.'

Again he breathes and again and again, until miraculously colour comes back into her face, her eyes flicker open, she gasps for air, she lives.

Afterwards as the ambulance takes her away the guard turns to him.

'Brilliant, thanks, that was great,' he says. He takes out his notebook. 'What's your name, where are you from?'

'Metcalfe, William Metcalfe, I'm from Bradford in Yorkshire, 25 Moorview Avenue. But look, I'm about to miss my ferry, I'd better go.'

'Hold on.' The guard lifts his radio. He speaks quickly into it. 'That's OK, they'll wait for you. One good turn.' He smiles.

Metcalfe smiles too, and salutes him, the two fingers closed together against an imaginary peak of a cap. He picks up his bag.

'Nothing to it, mate. It's what comes from being in the Boy Scouts.' He turns and walks away towards the ferry terminal.

*

'Boy Scouts.' Conor's voice on the phone was sour. 'He was a Boy Scout leader. He was also a bad bastard. Six months after that he was charged and convicted on fifty-two counts of buggery, sexual assault and gross sexual indecency. He was sentenced to ten years in prison.'

It was late when he called. She was just about to go to bed. There'd been tears and tantrums when she got the boys home. She'd come very close to losing her temper. They'd fought over everything. Joe had deemed the division of the spoils unfair. It had taken all her negotiating skills to extract the extra bag of peanuts from Jim and split it between the two. Now she sat with a cup of tea by the dying fire.

'Tell me all that again, Conor. The man who gave the old lady mouth to mouth was convicted of buggery, sexual assault and gross sexual indecency. And sentenced to prison. The same man who was in Dun Laoghaire the day that Owen Cassidy went missing.'

'That's it. That's what happened.'

'And we didn't know? How could we not have known?'

'Well, why should we? We had no reason to make any connections between a minor incident in Dun Laoghaire that day and someone who, after all, wasn't accused of any crime here, wasn't charged with any crime here. There was no reason for us to know.'

'So, what do we do now? Which prison is he in? Can we see him do you think?'

'Well, that's a bit of a problem. He was in a prison just outside Manchester. High security. Lots of Category As. But he isn't any longer. He was attacked by another of the inmates. He died in June ninety-eight.'

She sipped her tea.

'So who killed him? Was it a random thing?'

'Well, they were never absolutely sure about the motive. I spoke to the deputy governor this evening. He told me they were certain who killed him. And this is interesting. It was an Irish prisoner, one Colm O Laoire, that's spelt the Irish way. The poor Brit couldn't get his tongue around it. Anyway, there were no witnesses. Well, apparently there was one lad present, but he would say nothing. So they couldn't get a charge or a conviction.'

'And this O Laoire is he still in prison?'

'You can be sure of it. He was convicted of murdering his wife. He got life. He's still got plenty of it left to serve.'

'So what should we do? Should we go over and see him?' Her voice rose with excitement.

'Yeah, I think a visit would be in order. I'll do a bit more of a trawl and see what else I can find out about Mr Metcalfe. First thing tomorrow you get on the phone to the prison and sort the details out. I'll leave all the numbers on your desk. And listen, I'll come with you if you like.' He yawned loudly. 'I'm wrecked. If you need me in the meantime you can get me on the mobile. OK?'

'Sure thing.'

'And listen, Min, well done. Goodnight.'

She sat by the fire until her teeth began to chatter. Then she walked upstairs to bed. These were the times when it really hurt. No one with whom to share her excitement.

'Andy,' she said out loud. 'What do you think? Do you think we're on to something? Do you think we're going to get somewhere? Are you proud of me? Andy, tell me.'

But the only sound was the wind in the trees outside and the plaintive cry of a car alarm two streets away.

Twenty-seven

Nick woke. It was dark. He was lying on his side, his hands tucked between his thighs. He was naked. There were words were running through his head. Once there had been music to go with them, but now there was just the words.

> Grief for sin,
> Rends the guilty heart within.

His mother had sung them. She had been in a choir when he was a teenager. A first step, so she said, towards reclaiming her life from her husband and her children. She had a record. Kathleen Ferrier singing Bach arias. St Matthew Passion, St John Passion, the B Minor Mass. She played it over and over again, and sang along. Trying to master the phrasing, the tone, the quality of the voice. Saying, 'Listen, Nicky, isn't it beautiful?' While he just grunted and turned his attention to his dinner.

He stirred and moved his legs. He reached out. The bed beside him was empty. He remembered. They had drunk the second bottle of wine. Then Susan had found a bottle of Calvados in a cupboard. They had talked and laughed. They had been happy. He had kissed her. Pulled her onto his knee. She had rested her head on his shoulder. He had felt her warmth. He had touched her breasts. She had slipped her hand beneath his shirt and stroked his stomach. She had taken hold of him and they had walked together up the stairs. They had faced each other, standing beside the bed, and he had put his hands on her shoulders. They had kissed again. She tasted the same. She felt the same. He had pulled her closer, pressing her body against his. He had felt safe at last.

And then she had drawn back. Screamed at him. How could he? Who did he think he was? Who did he think she was? That a couple of bottles of wine for old time's sake could make up for everything. And she had backed away, her fists clenched, tears pouring down her cheeks. Shouted at him to go away and leave her alone. Rushed out of the bedroom, running down the stairs, dragging open the front door and slamming it behind her.

He had stood still for a while. He couldn't move. Then he had gone down to the kitchen. Washed the dishes. Tidied them away. Wiped down the table. Swept the floor. Took some kind of comfort from the simple, routine tasks. And heard the door open. And saw her standing in the hall. Her face was white. Her hands were cold. But her voice was calm and steady.

'Stay with me tonight, Nick. I want you to. Come upstairs with me now. I want you here with me. I need you. Whatever about the past, I need you now.'

She had fallen asleep as soon as she closed her eyes. He had lain beside her and listened to her breathing. Then he too had slept. And woke sometime later. She had turned her back into his chest and they were lying curled around each other. He moved her hair away and kissed the nape of her neck. She took his hand and curved it over her breast and ran the sole of her right foot over his instep. And they slept again.

Now the bedroom door opened. Nick rolled over.

'It's early, but I have to go. I've brought you tea.' She was dressed for work. He pushed himself up and she sat down beside him. She handed him the mug. He sipped carefully.

'I'll be home around six this evening. Will you be here?'

He nodded.

'Good. We'll talk more then.' She kissed his cheek. She smelt of toothpaste. She stood. She smoothed down her skirt.

'Susan.' He looked up at her. 'I love you.'

'Do you?' She moved away. She looked back at him. She smiled. He heard her footsteps on the stairs and the front door closing.

He got out of bed and went to the window. All around the square the lights were on. Breakfasts were being eaten. Children readied for school. Parents for work. Front doors opened and slammed shut as goodbyes were said. Cars inched from the footpath in a slow stream towards the main road. He watched some of the older kids taking a short cut across the green. They stopped to look at the bonfire. He watched them light cigarettes furtively, their hands cupped around each other's mouths, as they hung around, calling to the girl who came out from the large house on the corner. She was tall, long legged, very pretty in her tartan school skirt and shapeless green raincoat. She was laughing and flirting with them, taking her belt and flicking it at them like a long whip, running away in mock fright as it made contact with the backs of their legs. As they made their way towards the gate he heard a shout and saw Chris come down the steps of his house, calling out their names as he ran along the footpath in their direction. He watched how the girl turned to greet him, how the boys deferred to him, how they stood in a huddle for a few moments, Chris's arms outstretched, resting across the shoulder of the girl and the smaller of the two boys. Until they all turned and walked away, the boys heading towards their school and Chris and the girl taking the short cut through the houses to the upper road to Laurel Park.

Once there had been woodlands which stretched across the wide valley and up the gentle foothills towards the southerly aspect of the Dublin mountains. Once there had been gracious country houses dotted among the fields and surrounded by large gardens, where men had laboured summer and winter to keep their employers supplied with cut flowers, fruit and vegetables. Once there had been tennis courts, croquet lawns and cricket pitches. Now there were streets and shopping centres, petrol stations and news-agents, bus stops and pedestrian crossings, schools and houses. And everywhere there were houses, long snaking rows spreading out, eating up every green space with their patios and sheds, their garages and washing lines. Where once had stood stands of beech and oak, ash and elm.

There was a path that ran behind the school. Few people knew it and even fewer went there now. Its entrance was partially obstructed by an electricity substation, fenced off with barbed wire and warning signs. It had been a right of way, a short cut between one small village and the next at a time when people walked and rode bicycles. Now it was blocked off at various points along its course, ugly barri-cades of concrete, decorated with graffiti and fouled with excrement and rubbish dumped carelessly over back walls.

Only behind the school did it still have some remnant of the peace and tranquillity of days gone by. A hedgerow, in summer a mass of twisted honeysuckle, wild roses and blackberries, but brown and desiccated now by the winter, separated it from the playground. Along its perimeter the remains of the woods were still to be seen. A huge copper beech spread its silver-grey branches in a wide canopy and a cluster of lime trees stood together, birds' nests clearly visible, empty now until spring.

Laurel Park once had a formal garden, with ornamental box hedges clipped and tidy and wide gravel paths that were raked regularly. Now it was all tarmacadam. The school had grown in size over the last few years and had swallowed up, amoeba-like, the houses on either side of the original building. Gone were the high walls which had separated the gardens one from the other. Nick stood on tiptoes and peered around him. What had once been out-buildings, stables probably, had been converted into small classrooms. And to one side was a long low building with big windows of frosted glass. It must be a swimming pool, Nick thought. He could hear the sound of splashing and girls' voices raised in shrieks of pleasure.

It was mid-morning and school was in full swing. Chris Goulding was clearly visible. He was standing at the head of the class. He had a book in one hand and in the other something that looked like a piece of chalk. He turned and wrote on the blackboard, then walked around the room, stopping every now and then to address one or other of the girls. He appeared animated, his thin face expressive, engaged. The class looked as if they were hanging on his every word. Hands were shooting up to offer opinions, girls were jumping to their feet. Chris was laughing, enjoying himself. His gestures were extravagant and theatrical. He moved towards the window, and stopped and looked out. And saw Nick standing in the lane beneath the trees. Nick could see the surprise on his face, the sudden look of concern, of anxiety. He could see the way in which he stepped back, far from the glass, as if somehow he was no longer sure that there was any kind of barrier between himself and the outside world. Nick could see, suddenly, that Chris was afraid. He raised his hand and waved. He watched and waited. Then he turned and walked quickly away. And was gone.

Conor and Min stood in front of the prison. It was early afternoon. An hour and a half earlier they'd been in traffic on the airport road from Dublin.

'Strange, isn't it?' Min pulled her scarf free from her neck. 'The British empire.'

'How do you mean?' Conor looked down at her.

'Well, take this, this ugly great hulk?' She gestured towards the prison's massive wooden gate and two brick watchtowers. 'It's the spit of Mountjoy in Dublin. You can just imagine all those civil servants sitting in London in the middle of the nineteenth century, with their wing collars and their pinstriped suits, drawing up the plans for the prisons and courthouses, the railway stations and the town halls. Sending them to every corner of the known world. To all those great splodges of pink that you see in the old atlases. A plan and a system. And by hook or by crook they were going to make everything from Delhi to Dublin look the same.'

'Yeah, well, I don't know about the outside, but the

inside of this one didn't survive. It's all been rebuilt in the last few years.'

'Oh yeah, that's right. They had a riot, didn't they?'

'They call it a "disturbance" on their website. It's like the way we call the Second World War the emergency.'

'Or the civil war up north, the troubles. Great things euphemisms, aren't they?' And she smiled at him.

'So.' He took a step forward. 'Are you ready?'

He'd filled her in about Metcalfe on the flight over. He had been married with two children. He'd been a carpenter. Worked for himself. Did fitted kitchens, bookshelves, small attic conversions, that sort of thing. He'd travelled a lot. He'd lived in Belgium and the Netherlands for a while. He had a record that went back to his early twenties. Started off with a bit of messing around when he was a teenager, kids younger and more vulnerable than he was. But then it got more serious. Finally, not long after he was in Dublin, he was arrested for the rape of three boys. They were just the tip of the iceberg. A whole load of others came forward too. And pictures of some of those kids had been identified on the Net. They were part of the loot seized from one of the groups prosecuted in Britain last year.

'So,' Conor said as he polished off his airline lunch, 'you can see why I'm so interested.'

They had agreed. Min would visit Colm O Laoire. Conor would question some of the other sex offenders in the prison, those whom Metcalfe had been closest to.

'OK with you?' Conor said.

'Absolutely fine,' she replied. 'Have fun.'

*

O Laoire was a small man. Wiry, weather-beaten, whippet thin. The prison officer filled her in as they walked from the reception area to the visiting rooms.

'O'Leary,' he said emphasizing the anglicization of the name. 'O'Leary, that's what we call him. Nice and straight-forward. None of your fancy Gaelic how's your father. Colm O'Leary, aged fifty. Convicted of murdering his wife twelve years ago. Received a life sentence with a recommendation that he serve no less than twenty years.'

'That's a stiff one. In Ireland it would be unusual to serve more than twelve years or so even for murder.'

'Is that right?' The officer glanced at her. 'Well, maybe O'Leary should have killed her in Ireland then, instead of in London. Or maybe he shouldn't have done what he did to her at all. Maybe when he discovered she was having it off with someone else he should have called it quits and buggered off back to whatever bog it was he came from.'

She didn't respond. But she had read the description in O Laoire's file. He had tied her up, tied her to the bed. Then set fire to her. He had untied her after she was dead, claimed it was an accident, that a cigarette had gone astray. But the post-mortem had revealed the marks of the rope on her wrists and ankles. And he had used her perfume as an accelerant.

The smell in the prison was overpowering. A mixture of boiled cabbage and urine. She could feel her gorge rising. She swallowed hard and kept her eyes fixed on the patterned linoleum beneath her feet.

'So what happened with Metcalfe?'

They paused while the officer unlocked yet another set of doors. He stepped back to let her pass. The crowd of men waiting on the other side moved reluctantly away. She could hear the comments. The usual stuff. She'd done her stint of escort duty years ago. The first couple of times the desperation was frightening, but soon it was all very routine.

'Well now. William Metcalfe. Another piece of scum. We don't know exactly what happened, but both Metcalfe and O'Leary were in the hospital wing together. It was a Sunday, skeleton staff, and they were all watching a match on the box. Manchester United playing Sunderland or some such. Anyway, suddenly there's a commotion and one of the other prisoners comes rushing into the orderlies' room to say that Metcalfe's done himself in. When they found him his throat was cut, there was a piece of glass in his hand. Blood everywhere, it was a right mess. And O'Leary was sitting up in his bed, the next bed, reading a book. Cool as a cucumber, didn't even look up, said he'd seen nothing, knew nothing, heard nothing. And that was that. And the only other witness was the guy who raised the alarm, who by now was a gibbering idiot and said he knew nothing either. But, you know, the likelihood of anyone topping themselves by slitting their own throat is something like a million to one. It just doesn't happen.'

Again the pause while he opened another barred door. 'Anyway, he's all yours. Go on in.' He gestured to the small room at the end of the corridor. 'I'll get him and bring him in to you. Not that he'll have much to say. He never does. He's a quiet sort of bloke is your O'Leary.'

Quiet, whippet thin, wiry, weather-beaten. The kind you'd see on a fishing boat hauling in nets on a blustery November day, a cigarette jammed into the corner of his mouth and his eyes screwed up against the biting wind. He stood inside the door and looked at her. He said nothing. She stood up and held out her hand. He made no move to take it. Behind him the prison officer gave him a push in the small of his back.

'Manners, O'Leary. Shake the lady's hand, there's a good boy. She's come all the way from Ireland to talk to you.'

'No really, it's OK.' Min backed off, sat down again and gestured to the chair on the other side of the Formica-topped table. 'Why don't you join me for a bit? Here.'

She took a packet of cigarettes from her bag. 'Have them. Courtesy of the Irish state.'

'*Go raibh math agat.*' He leaned over and took them from her, then sat down and peeled the cellophane from the packet.

'*Ná bach,*' she replied and watched him crush it into a small springy ball. His fingernails were ridged, yellow with nicotine. The veins stood out on the backs of his hands, pale blue.

'Oh, very smart, speaking the Gaelic.' The officer scratched his chin, a rasping sound. 'He doesn't get much chance to practise in here, do you, Paddy boy?'

O Laoire took a box of matches from his trouser pocket. His movements were slow and deliberate. He leaned forward to hold the tip of the cigarette into the flame. Min noticed the pale pink scar, puckered and twisted, which disfigured his left cheek.

'A bit of bother?' She searched for the words of Irish as she gestured towards his face.

'An argument with a razor and the bloke that was holding it. Nothing much. You should see what he looks like.' O Laoire replied quickly and fluently.

'Oh, that's nice, isn't it? Having a private conversation,

are we? Very polite.' The officer looked at her with disapproval all over his surly face.

'Ignore him and he'll go away, vanish like the morning
mist on the hillside.' O Laoire smiled at her through the
smoke of his cigarette. 'That's what I do, anyway.'

She sat back in her chair and looked at him. He was
sitting very still, his arms folded across his chest, the
cigarette drooping from his mouth. He gazed past her head
at the wall, his eyes half closed. She wondered what he
could see.

She cleared her throat. She spoke. The Irish flowed from
her mouth. There was pleasure in the words, the construction of the sentences. He replied to her fluently, easily. She
remembered what his file had said. He was from the island
of Cape Clear. A native speaker. He had spent the first
sixteen years of his life battling the wind and the sea,
drenched in the beauty of that wild place. She could see as
they talked how he carried it with him. When he closed
his eyes it was Cape he saw. The dark green of the water in
the South Harbour, the rust red of the bracken on the cliffs,
the scarlet of the fuchsia in the hedgerows in the summer
and the wide sweep of the sky, the clouds pouring in from
the Atlantic, changing constantly from one hour to the
next.

'Tell me,' she said, 'about William Metcalfe.'

He shrugged his shoulders and lit another cigarette from
the butt of the first. 'What's there to tell?'

'You didn't like him? You knew him from outside prison
and you didn't like him. You didn't know him before and
you still didn't like him. Which was it?'

'I didn't know him, I didn't want to know him. He was
scum. I had no interest in him, one way or the other.'

'And yet you killed him, so I understand. You slit his throat with a piece of glass, then sat back and watched him while he bled to death.'

Again he shrugged and closed his eyes.

'You don't want to believe everything these gobshites tell you. And anyway, if they really thought that, I'd have been charged with something. But I wasn't.'

'Only because there were no witnesses to his death, isn't that right?'

'No fingerprints, no forensic evidence that connected me to him. And yes I did sit and read my book while he died, but as far as I understand the law there's no crime in that. The burden of responsibility rests with the staff of the prison hospital, who were all watching television at the time. Why don't you go and talk to them? And anyway why are you so interested? Metcalfe was a fucking Brit.'

'A fucking Brit who happened to be in Dun Laoghaire on the afternoon of 31st October 1991, ten years ago. The afternoon of the day that an eight-year-old boy called Owen Cassidy disappeared from his home. A boy who has never been seen again. No trace of him. No body for his parents to bury. No way for them to grieve. And Metcalfe, so I understand, had a history of crimes of a sexual nature against children, boys, to be precise. A bit of a coincidence, I think. But of course you know nothing about him. You had no interest in him. You had no knowledge of him, knew nothing about him at all. Isn't that so?'

His eyes half closed and he gazed above her head. He began to hum. She listened. She knew the air, she knew the words. It was 'The Rocks of Bawn', a song of exile, of longing for home.

'Sing it,' she said. 'It's a long time since I heard it sung.'

He opened his eyes wide and stared at her for a moment, then dropped his gaze. He rocked backwards and forwards. His voice had the assurance of someone who had sung unaccompanied for years, without the support or comfort of an instrument to carry the tune.

'My shoes they are well worn now, My stockings they
   are thin,
My heart is always trembling, afraid I might give in,
My heart is always trembling from the clear daylight
   till the dawn,
I'm afraid you'll ne'er be able to plough the rocks of
   Bawn,'

He paused, looked up at her again. Kept his eyes on her as he sang.

'So rise up lovely Sweeney, and give your horse some
   hay,
And give to it some oats to eat, before you start the
   day,
Don't feed it on raw turnip, boy, take it down to my
   green lawn,
And then you'll maybe be able to plough the rocks of
   Bawn.'

She looked around her at the dirty cream walls of the room, the barred window set high up, the scuffed and scarred grey lino on the floor. And the indifferent stare of the warder. And she joined in and sang with him the final verse of the song,

'I wish the Queen of England would send for me in
   time,
And put me in some regiment all in my youth and
   prime,
I would fight for Ireland's glory from the clear daylight
   till the dawn
And I never would return again to plough the rocks of
   Bawn.'

'Come on now, lads, that's enough of all that.' The officer
stepped forward. 'We're not having a concert party here,
are we?'

'I don't know about that.' She looked up at him. 'What's
your party piece? What do you like to sing when you've
had a few?'

'Mr Walker here,' O Laoire jerked his head in his
direction, 'he's a great one for "The Birdy Song", aren't you,
Mr Walker? I've seen you down in the yard with some of
the others, when you thought no one was looking. You've
all the actions to go with it too, haven't you?'

Min took a breath, but the officer just laughed.

'Yeah, right. "The Birdy Song's" the one for me. It's
about as daft as those whiny old numbers that you Irish
blokes in here are always singing whenever you get a chance.'

'Each to their own, isn't that what we say at home?' Min
looked from one man to the other. 'Each to their own.
Look, Mr Walker, how would it be if you left us for a few
minutes? There are a couple of things I'd like to talk to
your man about, things to do with the investigation I'm
involved in back in Dublin. You understand, don't you?'
She smiled in what she hoped was a winning way. 'It'd be
appreciated.'

She waited until the door was closed and locked behind him. Then she leaned forward again.

'OK, O Laoire, enough of this pissing about. I've told you what I want to know about William Metcalfe. I think it's about time you told me what you know about him.'

He took another cigarette and lit it slowly, exhaling a plume of smoke towards the ceiling. 'What's it worth to you? What will it do for me?'

'You've put in for a transfer. You're hoping that they'll ship you back to Limerick prison. Your mother isn't well, I hear. Bad arthritis. Can't travel easily. Finds it hard enough to get on and off the ferry from Cape to the mainland, and virtually impossible to get all the way to England to see you. But if you were in Limerick, well that would make a difference, wouldn't it? You need all the help you can get, O Laoire. Time for a bit of quid pro quo, don't you think?'

There was silence. He stared down at the floor for a moment. He scraped the toe of his trainer backwards and forwards across the lino. Then he looked up at her.

'Do you know they say the worst thing about a pig is its squeal? Everything else about the pig is fine and dandy. They're intelligent, they'll eat anything and everything, they're clean if you keep them that way, and every single bit is edible. But it's the noise they make when you kill them, that's the truly bad part.' He looked down again at the floor and again scraped the toe of his shoe back and forth. 'Well, your man Metcalfe, he was the exact opposite to the pig. He was dirty, he was lazy, he was stupid. He smelt. Rotten, sour, always the stink of corruption around him. But when I slit his throat with that piece of glass he didn't make a sound. He just lay there and looked up at me and he opened his mouth, but not a whisper, not a squeal, came out of it. And, do you know, he died very quickly. It was all over in seconds. But, Jesus, there was a fierce mess. When we kill the pig at home we have him hung him up and we have a bucket to catch the blood. But here it just poured out all over the floor. And, do you know, it had began to coagulate before he'd stopped breathing.'

He began to hum again. She waited.

'But why did you do it, Colm? Did you have a reason?'

He sat back in the chair. He put his hand into his pocket. He pulled out a plastic wallet. Delicately, with the tips of his finger, he removed a small photograph. He put it down on the table between them.

'I did it for him. For the boy. Bill Metcalfe was always going on about the boy. The Irish boy. I couldn't take it any longer. And after I'd killed him, and before the bollocks in the next bed started screaming his head off, I took this from him. I didn't want the boy to go any further with Metcalfe. I didn't want him to spend any more time with that stinking piece of shit. So I took him from his pocket and I've been looking after him ever since.'

Min leaned forward and looked down. Owen Cassidy's round blue eyes stared back up at her.

'May I?'

He nodded. She picked up the photograph and turned it over. She ran her finger along the rough edges at the top and bottom.

'He was eight,' she said. 'He'd be eighteen now, if he was still alive.' She paused. 'Did he say what happened to him?' She paused again.

'No, he didn't. He didn't know. He said that he wasn't into taking it that far. That it was much better to keep them alive and keep them happy. That you got a lot more from them when they were — what was the word he used? — amenable, that was it. It was better when they were amenable.' There was shouting suddenly from the landing outside. And the sound of a heavy tread. O Laoire stood. He put the packet of cigarettes into his pocket. He turned away.

'You can keep him now. I'm done with him. Maybe you can do something for him. More than I could do.'

'Thanks, I appreciate your help. And about the other thing, the transfer, I'll do my best.'

He looked back at her.

'You will, I'm sure you will.' He smiled.

'Tell me, Colm?' She stopped.

'Tell you what?'

'Why did you kill your wife? Couldn't you have sorted out your differences some other way?'

'Some other way? What other way is there? For every crime there is a fit punishment. You know that and I know that. And she knew it too.'

'Do you think that, Conor?'

'Think what?'

She raised her glass and swirled the slice of lemon and the ice cubes around in an eddy of bubbles. It was late now. They'd had dinner in the hotel. Steak and chips and a bottle of Valpolicella. Now they were in the bar. It was half empty. The lights were low. She could see their reflections in the wall of windows that gave on to the car park and the motorway in the distance. Frank Sinatra's voice drifted softly from the speakers set into the ceiling tiles.

'That there's a fit punishment for every crime.'

He shrugged and drained the last of his pint, raising his hand to call for a refill.

'Nice here, isn't it?' He leaned back into the large leather armchair and stretched out his legs. 'Bit of a change from the office and all the usual crap.' He folded his arms behind his head and sighed with pleasure. 'Music's good too. I love all those old American standards. Irving Berlin, Rodgers and Hammerstein, Lerner and Lowe.'

'Do you really?' She sat forward for a moment. 'You amaze me. I'd have put you down as a Meatloaf, Deep Purple, heavy-metal kind of guy.'

'Not at all.' He shoved a pile of coins across the table as the lounge boy dumped down a tray of drinks. 'My granny, who reared me, was mad about Frank and Bing, Dino and Sammy. All that kind of stuff.'

'Dino?'

'Dino, you know. Dean Martin. My granny was on intimate terms with all the lads. Intimate, that's what she was. And as for Frankie, well, *High Society* was her favourite film. She dragged me along to see it I don't know many times. I was brought up singing all that stuff.' He picked up his glass and raised it towards her. 'So, how about it? Here's to romance. To moons and Junes and red lipstick and white sports coats.'

'But you haven't answered me, Conor. Do you think there's a punishment fit for every crime?'

He stared at her over the rim of his glass. Then he grinned.

'Yeah, Min, I do. Otherwise I wouldn't bother with this job. I'd have taken myself off into the computer industry. I'd be making a fortune. I'd be wearing Armani suits and driving a top-of-the-range Jag instead of a ten-year-old

Honda Civic. You know.' He paused and drank. 'You know, there are people who think being a guard is akin to being a social worker. We should be out there helping the less fortunate, the marginalized, the weak. Would you be a bit like that?'

'That's bloody typical.' She sat up straight in her chair. 'Just because I'm a woman you think I'm a softie, a push-over.'

'Well, aren't you?'

'No, I'm not. But I do believe in the criminal justice system. I believe in the rule of law. I believe in the courts and the judiciary. But I also believe in punishment. I believe that people should suffer when they hurt others. And I don't believe that to know all is to forgive all. Not by a long shot.'

She sat back in her chair. It was a long time since she had done anything like this. She realized she was enjoying herself. She smiled.

'What's the joke? Is it private or can anyone join in?'

'I was just thinking how nice it is to be out at night. To have left the kids at home. I haven't been away from them like this since Andy died. And do you know something? When I wake up in the morning I'm going to have at least half an hour all to myself. And I know what I'm going to do with it. I'm going to go for a swim. Can you imagine the luxury of that? Swimming lengths instead of splashing in the paddling pool. I can't wait.'

Conor raised his glass to her again. 'Well, here's another toast. To a good cop and a good person. Not often you get the two together.'

She woke in the night. She pushed herself up to sitting to look at her watch. It was just after four. She had forgotten to pull the curtains and an orange glow from the lights on the motorway lit up the room. It fell across the face of the boy in the small square photograph. She had left it propped up against her bag on the bedside table. And across the face of the man who lay beside her. She had sung 'The Rocks of Bawn' to him as they rode up through the building in the high-speed lift. He had sung 'True Love' to her as they walked to their rooms. And somehow it had happened. He had kissed her and she had kissed him back. And for the first time in nearly four years she had felt the warmth, the strength, the pleasure of a man's body next to her. And now she lay with her arm around him and thought of her sons at home, fast asleep beneath the photograph of their father framed on their bedroom wall. She turned over and looked at Conor and reached out and stroked his face, watching the way he smiled in his sleep and moved towards her hand, as a baby turns to the touch of the breast on its small cheek. And she thought then of Colm O Laoire and she saw him, lying on his back staring up at the ceiling, his eyes wide open, as he gazed out at the deep, dark blue of the Atlantic Ocean.

Twenty-eight

The photograph was one of a series of four. It had come from an automatic photo booth. That much was obvious. But not much else was. Min held it in her hand and looked at it as the train bumped and rattled out of Manchester Oxford Street station. Owen Cassidy again, after so long. His thick cockscomb of fair hair, his round blue eyes, but no smile on his oval face the day that the picture was taken.

It was two hours by train from Manchester to Llandudno, the small seaside town in north Wales where the prison authorities had told her that William Metcalfe's widow lived with her two children. Min tried to catch up on some sleep, leaning her head against the window, but her hangover had kicked in viciously. She felt sick and shaky. Nearly as shaky as Conor had been when he sat down beside her at breakfast. She hadn't known what to say. He had made as if to kiss her on the cheek, but she had pulled awkwardly away, knocking over a jug of milk, making a mess on the pearly white tablecloth. A right mess, she thought. Just like the rest of it.

She told him straight. She regretted what had happened between them. She shouldn't have encouraged him. She couldn't cope with a relationship. She had too much to do. And the priority right now was to visit Metcalfe's widow.

'So.' She stood up. 'I'm catching the train this morning. I might as well do it now. So I'll see you when I see you.'

She saw him again as she was checking out. He was waiting for a cab. He looked tired and miserable. A cigarette drooped from his fingers.

'Not your responsibility,' she said out loud. 'He's a big boy. Well able to make his own mistakes.'

But sitting in the train she remembered the gentleness of his touch. And the way he had fallen asleep beside her with a smile on his face.

Grey-green breakers smashed against the shelving pebble beach. A wooden pier stretched out into the Irish Sea. A headland loomed above with a cable car running up it. The Victorian seafront curved away, perspective narrowing it to a small dark dot. It was like something from a picture postcard.

She walked along the row of terraced houses. They were all small hotels, bed and breakfasts. Guest houses. Old faces, wizened and wrinkled, peered through lace curtains as she passed and elderly men and women walked at a snail's pace in front of her with sticks and walking frames. She'd heard about places like this, but she'd never seen it before. It sent a chill down her back.

The street where Jean Metcalfe lived was at right angles to the front. The B and B sign hanging over the porch was faded, its paint flaking. The name 'Jones' was printed in careful capitals above the doorbell. Min checked her notebook. This was definitely the place. She pressed the buzzer and waited. A teenage girl answered the door.

'Sorry to bother you, but I'm looking for someone called

Jean Metcalfe. I was given this address, but perhaps I've got it wrong.'

The girl stared impassively at her, then shouted loudly down the narrow corridor behind her.

'Mum, it's for you.'

'So this is right? The name is Metcalfe, is it?'

The girl shrugged and turned away. 'Ask her yourself,' she said as she walked off.

Jean Metcalfe was tall and plump. She was a formidable figure, filling the doorway. She glared at Min, her dark brows furrowing with displeasure as Min explained why she was there.

'You're wasting your time and mine,' she said eventually. 'I know nothing about the bastard. We split up years ago when the kids were small. I hadn't seen him for about six months when he went to prison and when I heard he was dead I went straight out and bought myself a nice bottle of Scotch. And I toasted his roasting in hell.'

'Please.' Min inched her way forward into the house. 'You may think you know nothing, but you were still married to him ten years ago, weren't you? Perhaps there's something, something small, something that might mean nothing to you. If I could just come in for a few minutes. It's so important. We've been trying for all this time to find out what happened to this little boy, and this is the first break we've had. I'm sure as a mother yourself you can imagine what it's been like for his parents.'

The woman's face froze. Her eyes filled with tears. She turned and walked away and Min followed her, closing the door to the street firmly behind her.

The kitchen was warm and cluttered. A kettle steamed on a gas cooker and there was a smell of baking. Jean

Metcalfe picked up a pair of padded gloves and opened the oven door. She carefully removed a tray of fruit scones. Min's mouth began to water.

'Yum, they look absolutely gorgeous.'

'Hungry eh? It's the sea air. Hold on while I turn them out.'

She buttered the scones and piled raspberry jam on top. Min ate greedily. Butter dripped over her fingers.

'Here.' Jean passed her a napkin. 'Before you get grease all over yourself. And here.' She pointed to Min's cheek. 'You've a lump of jam just under your nose.'

'God.' Min laughed. 'Can't take me anywhere, can you?'

They sat in companionable silence for a moment or two. Min drained her cup of tea. Then she spoke.

'Did you divorce Metcalfe? Is Jones your married name?'

The woman shook her head. 'No, I don't believe in divorce. I'm very strict about some things. Jones was the name of my first husband. I was a widow when I met William. The kids are from that marriage.'

'And I presume you had no idea what he was like?'

The woman looked at her with an expression of surprised contempt on her face. 'What do you think, for God's sake? I would never had got involved with a man like that. Never put my kids at risk. No, when I met him I thought he was a decent bloke. Hard-working, honest, pillar of the community. He was a carpenter, very skilled. He went to church, he was involved with the Boy Scouts. In fact that's how we first met. My lad Terry was a scout. He brought William home with him one evening.' She paused and refilled her cup. 'And before you ask, no, he didn't interfere with them. If the truth be told he was good to them and they liked him. And if the truth be told I liked him too.

In fact I loved him. I was shattered when I found out that the police were after him.' Tears dribbled down her plump cheeks. Min put her hand in her bag and produced a packet of tissues. She slid them across the table.

'Thanks.' Jean wiped her eyes and blew her nose loudly. 'Silly, isn't it, after all this time. I thought I was over it. I thought I really didn't care.'

There was the sound of footsteps on the corridor and the girl appeared again. Jean looked up at her and put out her hand to draw her close.

'You met my Jackie, didn't you? She's my pet, aren't you, love?' She pulled her close and squeezed her tightly around her waist. The girl's stare, above her mother's head, was cold.

'You've upset her,' she said. 'Why can't you coppers just leave her alone? She can't help the fact that she married him. She didn't know what he was like. And neither did we.'

'You didn't at all? There was nothing about his behaviour towards you or your brother that made you feel strange or uncomfortable?'

The girl shook her head. She dropped onto her mother's ample knees, her expression suddenly babyish.

'It wasn't Jackie, I'm afraid. It was her best friend, Carol. She was the one he picked on. But we only found that out after he'd gone to prison. When Carol heard he'd been put away she confessed everything to her mother. And that was when we had to move. We'd been living in Bradford, but we couldn't stay there any longer. I felt responsible. And Carol's family wouldn't believe that I didn't know what was going on. So we came here. My family had this house.'

'So.' Min paused. 'Can I just get the sequence of events clear? That time that we know William was in Ireland, was he still living with you? Was everything the way it always had been?'

There was silence for a moment.

'Yes it was.' Jean looked down at the table. 'But looking back afterwards I realized that he was planning to do a runner. He didn't tell me he'd been to Ireland. He often went off for a few days. He said it was to do with scouting business. And I believed him. I shouldn't have.' She began to cry again. 'I was such a stupid cow. I believed every bloody thing he said to me.'

As Min watched mother and daughter changed roles, daughter cradling her mother's head to her small bosom, stroking her hair and whispering comfort into her ear. Min stood up.

'I'll make more tea,' she said and picked up the pot.

Afterwards, after they'd all had their cry, Min asked them again.

'So that trip to Dublin, you've no idea what it was really about?'

Two heads shook.

'And do you still have any of William's things? Address book, diary, letters, bills, phone bills, notebooks. Anything like that.'

'No.' Jean looked at her, her expression cold again. 'No. I went through all his stuff after he was arrested. He had a big suitcase that he kept in the attic. It had come with him when we got married. I never asked him what was in it. I just thought it was, you know, the kind of stuff people collect through their lives and want to keep. Letters, family photographs, that sort of thing. But when I looked at it I thought I would die. It was disgusting. Filth. Pictures of children. So I burned it all.'

Jackie got up from the table. She turned and walked from the room. Her mother looked after her.

'I was terrified that she or her brother would get hold of some of it. It was bad enough having everyone talking about him, and then the trial was all over the papers, even the telly. We'd reporters hanging around the house. It was a nightmare. The kids were persecuted. And the stuff I did read, well there was nothing to do with your kiddie, no mention of anything to do with Ireland or anyone Irish. Nothing like that at all. I'm sorry I haven't been more help to you.'

'No.' Min reached across and touched her hand. 'No. Really it's fine. I'm trying to imagine what it must have been like for you. I have children too. I'm a widow as well. I'd never thought before about being careful who I brought into the house. But, I tell you, I'll be thinking about it now.'

She stood. She picked up her bag.

'I should go. I've taken up enough of your time.' She turned towards the door. Then turned back. 'But if anything should occur to you.'

'Yes, I know.' Jean stood up slowly. 'I'll be in touch.' She took the card that Min held out to her and looked at it. 'I'll say one thing for you. You're a lot nicer than the English coppers who were in and out my house during all those years. Some of them were right bastards. And don't defend them. Don't say anything like they were just doing their jobs. Because they weren't.' As she spoke her eyes moved past Min to the kitchen door. 'Where on earth did you get that from, Jackie?'

Min turned and saw the girl standing behind her. Her face was covered with a mask. It was the shape of a bird's head. Feathered, black and white, a magpie with a sharp beak. Her voice when she spoke was muffled.

'Don't you remember, Mum? He brought this for me. And another one for Terry. Terry's was some kind of an animal, a fox or something. He said a friend of his in Dublin had made them for us. Don't you remember? He said they were made for Halloween. And we could wear them for Guy Fawkes night. We could dress up for the bonfire.'

The fox and the magpie. The cat and the badger. The squirrel. She could see them all now. The drawings, the designs that Nick Cassidy had done. She remembered that they were pinned to the wall in his studio. And Marianne O'Neill had said in her statement that they had spent weeks working on them, so they would be ready to wear that night, the night of Halloween.

We were all going to dress up. We had all our costumes ready. Owen was to be the fox. His was the most elaborate. But there was a costume and a mask for each of us.

'May I?' she reached out her hand. Jackie pulled the mask from her face and handed it to her.

'I'd forgotten.' Jean stepped forward to get a better look at it. 'I remember now. I didn't like them much then and I still don't. I thought they were a bit creepy.'

Min turned the mask over in her hands. It was made of papier mâché, covered with feathers and small pieces of glass and shell which made it glint with a shimmery iridescence. Just like the sheen of the magpie's feathers, she thought. It was well observed, the beak sharp and pointed.

'Here, you try it.' Jackie put it up to Min's face, slipping the elastic band over her head. Min peered out through the small eye holes. Her view of the kitchen was narrowed. The sensation was uncomfortable. Oppressive. She felt for a moment as if she would suffocate, as if the breath would never flow into her body again. Her palms began to tingle and moisten and she could feel the pulse in her neck quicken. She snatched the mask from her face, trying to sound calm as she spoke.

'He didn't say anything more specific about where this came from? He didn't mention a name? He didn't tell you anything about how it was made or anything else? No?'

The girl shook her head. 'Nothing that I can remember. But it was a long time ago. I was only a little 'un then.'

'And you, Jean, what about you? Did he say anything to you about them?'

She shook her head. 'I don't remember. Just that he did say they were hand-made. That a friend had made them. That they were to be worn for Halloween. Something like that. But I can't be sure.'

Min took the mask with her when she left. Jackie had put it in a shoebox and strapped the lid down with Sellotape. She put it between her feet on the flight from Manchester to Dublin. She held it on her knee in the taxi from the airport. She put it carefully out of reach on the top shelf of the hall cupboard. Tomorrow she would take it to headquarters and pass it on to the forensics people. Perhaps they would be able to find something hidden beneath its feathers. But there again perhaps not. Perhaps she already knew everything there was to know about the mask. That it had been designed by Nick Cassidy. That it had been made by Nick Cassidy. That it had been given to William Metcalfe by a man he called his friend. That he had brought it with him from Dun Laoghaire to Bradford. In the same way that he had brought the photograph of Owen Cassidy. And who had given him that picture? Was it the same person who gave him the mask?

The house was dark and quiet. The boys were asleep. Vika was asleep. She put on the kettle. She poured whiskey into a glass and added brown sugar, cloves and a slice of lemon. She added the boiling water, letting it slip down over the curved back of the teaspoon. She sat down on the sofa and sipped. She closed her eyes and leaned her head against a cushion. Outside the wind rattled the branches of the trees and whispered and sighed as it funnelled through the cul de sac. It was time for bed, but she was too exhausted to move. The sitting room was untidy. The children must have undressed in front of the fire this evening. Their clothes were in a heap on the hearthrug along with the usual collection of books and pencils and discarded toys. She reached forward and began to tidy them up. Her fingers slipped over the shiny covers of the books. She looked down at them. And saw the large-format hardback, the colours of the illustration on the front bright and vivid. She pulled it onto her knee. *The Star Child and Other Stories*, the flowing script read. The author's name was garlanded with golden flowers. And below it the name of the illustrator was decorated with birds and animals. Magpies and crows, foxes and squirrels. She turned to the back and looked at the familiar photograph on the inside flap. She read the short paragraph.

Nick Cassidy, award-winning illustrator, was born in Dublin and studied art at the National College of Art and Design. His drawings and paintings and his illustrations for this and many other best-selling books have brought him acclaim worldwide. He is known internationally for his interpretations of the works of Oscar Wilde.

She lay back on the sofa. She rested the book on her chest. She drained her glass and placed it carefully on the floor. She wrapped her arms around her body. She lay with her eyes wide open staring up at the ceiling. It was dawn by the time she slept.

Twenty-nine

Róisín was back. Nick stood in Susan's kitchen and watched her. She was out in the garden with Emir. She was holding him by his hands. They were playing a game. She was twirling him around, faster and faster and faster. She was leaning back, almost to the point of falling over. Nick watched the child's face. He couldn't decide. Was it pleasure or fear he saw on his features? It was certainly anticipation, but of what?

And then the boy fell. He let go her hands, or did she let go of his? He toppled backwards. He lay on the wet grass, his legs and arms in the air. And as Nick watched she lent over him and pulled him up again, bending down, whispering in his ear, then taking him by the hand and leading him towards the summer house.

The square was full of kids today. Mid-term break. The Halloween holiday. They were standing around the bonfire. Some were adding wood to the pile. A tall thin boy with cropped dark hair dribbled a football towards them and they formed themselves into two teams and began to play. Nick stood in the front window and watched. There was pleasure to be had from their movements, their swerves and lunges, their kicks and sudden sprints. Their gaiety, their grace, their sense of fun. But as he stood and watched, he heard Conor Hickey's voice.

'We've identified some more of those boys whose pictures we found on your hard drive. They were victims of a paedophile. A man called William Metcalfe. Did you know him? He was from the north of England, but we have reason to believe that he was also operating in Dublin in the early nineties. Name ring a bell?'

'No.'

'Sure? Want to think about it?'

'I told you. I've never heard of him. Never heard of anyone called that.'

'Well, Nick, there aren't many people who have access to that kind of material. It's from a newsgroup that's heavily protected. You need a whole series of passwords to get into it. You need to be a net contributor of anything up to ten thousand new images before you'll get anything back. You need to have a very sophisticated knowledge of the Web to get anywhere near it. They're not the kind of visuals you happen across if you just put a couple of keywords into a search engine. Do you know what I mean, Nick?'

He didn't reply.

'They've also been found on a pay-per-view site in the States. You were in America for a long time, weren't you, Nick? A hell of a lot of money is being made out of all this. So we're going to want you to come in for questioning again.'

'Why? Are you arresting me? Are you going to charge me this time?'

'Well, that depends.'

'On what?'

'On how cooperative you are with us. On how much you tell us. Whether we think we can believe you or not. And whether you're going to tell us about any of the others who are also involved in this business.'

'For Christ's sake, haven't I told you before? I don't know anything about any of it. There are no others. There is no ring, isn't that what you like to call it? Haven't I made my position clear to you already?'

There was a pause and a sigh. Then Hickey spoke again.

'There you go again, Nick, making life difficult. Listen, you think about it. I'll phone you later this afternoon and we can make a date for tomorrow. How's that?'

Another pause.

'And listen, Nick, we know you're not likely to go anywhere. Because, if you did, we'd find you and we would not be pleased. And we might start making all kinds of assumptions about your guilt and your innocence. So I suggest you discuss it with your wife. She seems like a sensible woman. Look at all your options. And if you need legal advice, well, there's plenty of it about. How does that sound? Fair enough? Talk to you later. Bye for now.'

There was another boy in the square. Tall and broad. Well built, stocky. Dark blond hair tied back in a ponytail. Baggy jeans that flopped around his ankles as he trotted into the middle of the game. Nick watched him with the others. Then he closed his eyes. He could see Owen there too. Laughing as he chased the ball. Flicking it up with the side of his foot and bending his torso to get his head under-neath it. Then straining upwards, the tendons in his neck distended as he struggled to make contact.

Look at me, Dad. Look what I can do.

He opened his eyes. The game had stopped. The boys were standing around Luke Reynolds. One of them was holding a newspaper. Their heads made a neat circle above it. Luke looked up and saw him. He smiled tentatively then looked down again. Nick moved away from the window and into the hall. He opened the front door and walked out onto the front step. As he began to head down towards them, the group shuffled awkwardly and as he approached the railings he saw Luke grab hold of the paper and try to hide it behind his back.

'Hey, Luke, how are you?' he called out as he walked through the small iron gate and across the grass. 'Nice to see you again.'

A tense silence fell. The boys looked at him, then began to drift away, leaving Luke by himself.

'What is it? What's wrong?' Nick moved closer. Luke took a step backwards. Nick reached behind him. His fingers closed on the newspaper. He jerked it from Luke's grasp.

'What is it? What's in it?'

The boy squirmed. His face flushed. He looked down at his muddy shoes, then up at Nick.

'It's just, you know. It's an article about what happened. It's ten years ago, you know, you know what the papers are like, wanting to stir everything up. And you see,' he gestured around him, 'none of these kids remember Owen the way I do. They're all, you know, dead nosey about it. But I – ' he paused – 'I didn't want you to see it, because I thought it would upset you. You know what I mean?'

The paper was crumpled and creased. Nick turned away and walked back towards the house. He smoothed it out and looked down. Owen's eight-year-old face looked back at him. Beside it there was a photograph of the square. And an out-of-focus shot of himself and Susan, anguish showing clearly on their faces, standing with their arms around each other outside the Garda station.

The headline read 'Unsolved Mysteries in Quiet Dublin

Suburb.' At the bottom of the page in a separate box there was another picture. A pretty girl with long dark curling hair. And another caption. 'Winter Nights Bring Unsolved Crimes.'

He sat down on the top step and began to read. Luke sat beside him and leaned over his shoulder. The article was simple and straightforward. A clear restatement of the facts.

'It's all right, Luke. There's nothing here to hurt. But thanks for your concern.'

Luke stared down at the crumpled page. 'Did you know her?' He looked up at Nick. 'That girl who was murdered near here?'

Nick shook his head. 'No, it happened before we moved here. I don't remember hearing much about it at the time. I don't think people liked to talk about it. Why?' He looked at the boy. 'You wouldn't have known her. She was dead before you were born.'

'Yeah, I reckon so. But her face is very familiar.' A frown creased his forehead.

'It was a famous case. I hadn't thought of it that way, but she died around the same time of the year as Owen's disappearance. I've never put the two dates together before. But I'm sure others have.' He put his arm around Luke's shoulder. 'Now, what brings you out here today? Did you come to see me?'

'No, not really. It's mid-term, you know. I thought I'd chill out for a bit. Get away from the city.' He stood up. 'Get away from Da and all his crap. I'd better go.' He gestured to the kids, who had now gathered around the bonfire again. 'We're all off to the movies.'

Nick put his hand in his pocket and pulled out some notes. 'Here, the popcorn's on me.' He leaned back against the step. 'Remember where I am if you need anything? OK?'

The boy smiled. Then turned away. He took the steps two at a time, his ponytail flopping against his fleece jacket. Halfway across the square he looked back and raised his hand in a clenched-fist salute. Nick stood and waved in response. Then heard the Gouldings' front door open. Chris, Róisín and Emir came out together. He stared at them. They didn't speak. They walked down the steps, holding hands. Chris had a sports bag slung over his shoulder.

'Going somewhere?' Nick called out. Chris looked up and smiled without warmth. Emir pulled away. He peeled one hand from Róisín's and waved. Nick waved back. He watched them as they walked quickly along the square. He watched them out of sight. Then he stood up and went back into the house. He laid the newspaper on the kitchen table. He put on his coat. He opened the back door and hurried down the steps to the garden. He walked across the grass and opened the gate into the back lane. He closed it quickly behind him. He turned and walked away from the house.

Chris and Róisín and a small fair-haired boy. Hand in hand along the square. Where did they go when they reached the end of the row of houses? Did they turn towards the main road and the town? Or did they turn away from the sea, towards the mountains. He tried to imagine. He could see them in the distance. The brother and sister. One with straight dark hair falling to the collar of his coat. The other with short blonde hair. Slicked to her neat little skull. And the boy between them. Holding a right hand with his left hand, a left hand with his right hand. Swinging out of the hands, putting all his weight onto them as he leapt and danced between them.

Or was he struggling? Was he trying to free his hands from theirs, pulling down on them, rather than them pulling him up? Hanging back, trying to wrest his wrists from the grasp of their fingers. Not running backwards and forwards between the span of their arms in play? He could not tell. As they walked along these quiet streets, the trees shedding their leaves in deep piles of brown and gold and red, the houses set back from his gaze, their windows empty, their gardens neat and tidy. No sign of life anywhere as he passed by the bunches of flowers, the candles, the hand-written messages for Lizzie Anderson. They did not stop to look or comment. They kept on going, and he followed quickly, keeping his eyes on the trio ahead.

Mid-term break. The schools closed for four days. The Halloween holiday. Called *samhain* in the old language. A time when day slipped into night as gently and neatly as the grey line of the horizon slid into the grey of the sky. And what was the girl ahead saying as she bent down and spoke into the child's sea-shell ear? Were they words of comfort and love, or words that threatened and frightened? He watched how the boy pulled away from her for an instant and then gambolled sideways, cannoning into her legs so she stopped and spoke across his head to Chris. And they laughed and leaned towards each other and kissed, their lips meeting above the child's fair head. Not the kiss of a brother and sister, he thought, as they joined together in one silhouette against the low winter sun.

It was the school they were going to. He could see that now. He held back and watched them walk up its long drive. At the top they turned left towards the house that had once belonged to their grandmother. They stopped. There was a builder's lorry parked outside. The front door was open. A man in overalls came out with a paintbrush in his hand. Chris spoke briefly to him, then ushered Róisín and the boy past him into the house.

Nick turned away. He broke into a jog as he followed the high stone wall along the footpath and turned into the lane that ran behind. He began to run. When he came to the end he scrambled through the hedge into the gardens. In front of him was the swimming pool. He could see nothing through the frosted glass of its windows. But he could hear voices. He crept closer. There were shouts and screams. Were they expressions of pleasure, of fun? Was that laughter? He could hear the sound of water splashing. He pressed his face close to the cold glass. He strained to see, but there was nothing but fragments of light and patches of darkness. He stood back from the wall and slumped to the ground. He waited.

The afternoon passed slowly. It was cold now. The light began to fade from the garden. There were no more sounds from within the low concrete building. He got up and walked around the swimming pool to the house. The windows at ground level were locked and barred. A fire escape spiralled upwards. He climbed it quickly. At the top was a glass-paned door. He tried the handle and it opened. He stepped onto a wide landing. Paint-stained sheets covered the carpet. There was a strong smell of turpentine. He heard music. A radio turned on in one of the rooms on the floor below.

He began to run down the wide staircase. A man stood on scaffolding high above his head. He looked down at Nick and saluted him with a brush.

'How's it going?' Nick stopped and gazed up. 'Everything all right?'

'Grand, no problem. No worries,' the man replied.

'Great.' Nick turned away. He took the rest of the stairs two at a time. Below was the entrance hall, the front door open. He moved away from it towards the garden and the narrow staircase that led to the basement. It was cold and quiet down here. Small doors, each labelled, led off on either side. He read the names out loud. Miss Jennings, Miss Nelson, Miss Williams, Mr Benson, Mr Goulding. He tried the handle. It was locked. He did not hesitate. His foot splintered the wood and the door fell back from its hinges. He stepped inside quickly. The room was dark. He switched on the light. It was furnished with a row of bookcases, a desk and chair. There was a filing cabinet against the wall. He sat down at the desk. A small cardboard calendar rested on its scratched wooden top. The days of the month had been crossed off one by one. He picked it up and flipped to November. The date of the sixth had been circled with a heavy red marker. He put it back down. He tried the drawers. They too were locked. He tugged hard at the handles. Then stood up and lifted the desk from the floor, sending it crashing backwards. He stamped down hard on the drawers and the wood splintered. He dragged them from their slots. Inside was a laptop computer. He sat down on the floor and switched it on. He waited as the computer clicked and hummed, its tone warm and welcoming. His right hand slipped over its touch pad and soon the screen was filled with lists of files. He scrolled down through them, opening them at random. Reports, essays marked, assessments given, letters to parents and pupils. All to do with school and school work.

He pulled out the rest of the drawers. Exercise books, biros and pencils, paper clips, half a bar of chocolate, some tea bags, scattered in front of him. He stood up and tried the filing cabinet. Its drawers were unlocked and half empty. Nothing but old exam papers and files relating to pupils. He stood in the middle of the room and looked around him. He wanted to tear it all apart, rip up the floorboards, drag the plaster from the walls. He was dizzy with anger. His heart slammed against his ribcage.

'Calm down,' he said out loud. 'If there's anything here it will be easy to find.'

He walked to the bookshelf and turned his head sideways to read the titles. They were mostly classics. Jane Austen, the Brontë sisters, Fielding, Trollope, Dickens. There were also James Joyce, Beckett, Yeats and Synge. Standard material for an English teacher. And on a shelf low enough for a small child to reach, a row of children's books. He squatted to look. So this was where his books had ended up. He pulled them out in turn. *The Thirty-Nine Steps* was there and all the William books. There were *My Friend Flicka* and *Thunderhead* and *Green Grass of Wyoming* and there was his father's copy of *Treasure Island*, its buff-coloured cover with the drawing of Long John Silver just as he remembered it.

He separated it carefully from the others and held it gently. Then he opened it, flicking through the pages. And saw that half of them were missing and that in their place was a small plastic box. He put the book down on the floor and moved back towards the computer. He prised open the lid. Inside were two CDs. He picked them up carefully by their silvery edges and knelt down beside the laptop. He slotted one in. He clicked the file open icon. The computer beeped loudly and a dialogue box appeared. 'Password protected' it said. The cursor flicked slowly. He typed the word 'Owen'. The computer sang out. The message appeared. 'The password is incorrect. Word cannot open this document.' Cassidy, he tried. Again the same response. Marianne, he tried. Still the same response. He tried again and again. Chris. Róisín, Victoria. Running through every name and word he could remember. Even his own name. Nick, Nicky, Nicholas. Then Susan, Suzy, Sue. But still no response. He banged his fist against his head. He felt sick with frustration. This was a useless enterprise. The list of possible passwords was infinite.

He stared around him. And saw the book on the floor. And remembered. How Owen had loved it. Especially the parrot. He had called it the parrot book.

'Read it to me,' he had squawked. And squawked again in the voice of the bird, 'Pieces of eight, pieces of eight.'

Pieces of eight. Nick's fingers rested on the keyboard. He spelt the words out aloud as he typed them and clicked OK. And heard the whirr and hum of the CD engaging. And saw the list of contents. And the attachments with them. He double clicked on each of the little icons. And saw the photographs, the pictures of Owen. The pictures of Marianne. The pictures of them together and apart. And then the other pictures. Of a child posed and framed. The hands that probed his body. The masks that hid his face. The lights that shone so brightly that they seemed to shine right through the transparency of the child's fair skin. Until he could look no more, could see nothing more because of the tears that flooded from his eyes and blinded him in a stinging salty rush.

Thirty

Once upon a time there was a boy. He was eight years old. He had thick blond hair which stood up in a cockscomb on the top of his head. He had bright blue eyes. He had long thin legs and arms. He wasn't scared of the dark. He wasn't scared of anything, he said. Except in the middle of the night when he sat up straight and screamed for his mother to come and comfort him. And his mouth was wide open but no words came from it. No words, just sounds. Groans and grunts and short sharp shrieks. And he buried his face in his mother's warm body and cried. And she lay down beside him and held him to her until sleep claimed him again. And then she would move away slowly, so slowly, waiting until she was sure that he would not stir. And when she came back to her own bed she would say, 'There's something wrong with him, I don't understand why he has these nightmares.' And her husband would say, sleepily, 'It's his age. He'll grow out of it. He'll be fine. You'll see.'

But now Nick had seen. And he had seen other sights too. Like the pictures of Lizzie Anderson. Pretty in her school uniform. Walking through these same streets that he walked through now. Carrying her schoolbag. Laughing with her friends. Alive, happy, carefree. And dead too. Her face was bloated and blackened. The whites of her eyes were scarlet with burst blood vessels. He had covered his own eyes and peeped through his fingers at the image on the screen. And at all the other images too. Girls and boys, all ages, all shapes and sizes. All ready and waiting at the touch of the keyboard and the click of the mouse.

He had tried to delete them. To make them go away, but they wouldn't. They kept on flashing right back up at him again. Until all he could do was pick up the computer and send it crashing down onto the floor. Plastic and glass, metal and wire to be stamped on, the heel of his boot grinding them into shards and fragments. But the pictures still, untouched, still inside him.

Once there was a man with a perfect life. He had a wife and a child and a home. He had a reputation. He had made a name for himself. He was a creator of beauty. An artist. He was like the star child in the story. He had it all. But he turned his back on goodness. And he became as the creature with the face of a toad and a scaly body like that of an adder. Shunned, despised, lost.

Now he began to run, his feet scuffling through piles of wet leaves, his breath catching in his throat. Once upon a time there was a boy. But now the boy was dead. He was sure of it. He had seen the picture. The boy on the floor. His eyes were open, but his stare was fixed. And there was one more photograph. The summer house. In the garden that was now part of the school. Róisín was sitting on the low step. She was holding a bunch of flowers. She was smiling.

He burst in through the back gate. He took the steps to the kitchen two at a time. Susan was at the table. She looked pale and tired. She stood up. She shouted at him. 'Where have you been? I've been trying to find you.'

He stood in front of her. He gasped for breath.

'The summer house. Next door. Why did he move it?'

'What are you talking about?' she screamed. 'Why on earth does that matter?'

He took a step towards her. She backed away from him.

'Don't come near me,' she said. 'How could you? How could you do it? I never believed you had anything to do with Owen's disappearance. I knew other people thought it. I know there is a view that the father is always involved. But I never believed it of you. Never.'

'What? What are you saying, Susan, what's the matter? Why are you saying this?'

'You really thought you'd get away with it, didn't you? And you know you nearly did. If you hadn't come back. Why did you come back? Why?'

'Susan, tell me, tell me what's happened.' He tried to take her hands, but she pushed him away. He tried to put his arms around her, but she pulled herself free.

'Don't touch me, don't come near me. The police are waiting for you. They told me I was to phone them as soon as you got here. And I will, I promise I will.' She made a move towards the phone on the wall, but he grabbed it and flung it to the floor. She sobbed, her face grey with exhaustion.

'Susan, tell me what's happened. I don't understand why you're like this. I don't know what's wrong. Sit down. I won't hurt you. You know that. I would never hurt you. I would never hurt anyone. Please, trust me. Tell me.'

The guards had called at the house an hour ago. Susan had just got in from work. They told her they had been to

England. They had interviewed a prisoner in gaol there. The man had a photograph of Owen.

'They showed it to me. I'd never seen it before. It must have been taken in one of those automatic booths, the kind they have in the shopping centre. Apparently it was another prisoner who had the picture originally, a man who had been convicted of sexually abusing children. Anyway, he's dead now. But apparently he was here in Dublin the day that Owen disappeared and when they went to visit his wife, his former wife, she gave them something that he had brought back from Dublin with him. Something he'd been given by a friend over here. And do you know what that was, Nick?' She lifted her eyes and looked into his.

'Tell me,' he said.

'It was one of your masks. The magpie mask. And apparently he had also been given the fox mask. Owen's fox mask. You know, the one you made for him?'

He looked at her shocked, disbelief all over his face.

'But how—' The words struggled from his mouth. 'How did he get it?'

She shrugged her shoulders. 'You tell me, Nick. You tell me.'

'And his name, did they tell you his name?'

And as she said it he thought of the phone call from Hickey. Metcalfe, the abuser, and the boys whose pictures they had found on his own hard disk, and he put his head in his hands and groaned out loud with despair.

'So.' Her voice was cold, controlled now. 'What do you have to say?'

*

They sat in Conor's car outside the Cassidys' house. Min was glad it was dark. She'd avoided being alone with him for as long as she could since she got back from Llandudno. But she couldn't avoid it any longer. She could feel his tension and anger. He looked straight ahead, one hand resting on the steering wheel, a cigarette drooping from his fingers, the other rubbing the tight denim of his jeans.

She lifted the lid from the shoebox on her knees and looked down at the mask.

'What do you think?' His voice was carefully neutral. 'Do you think she knew anything about it? She was pretty clear in her denial that he had anything to do with it. Did you believe her?'

'Believe that she knew nothing, or believe that he knew nothing?'

'Either, both. Whatever.' He drew on his cigarette, his face illuminated in its red glow.

'I believe that she knows nothing, her shock seemed genuine to me. As for him? Before we went to England I would have sworn that he was innocent of any involvement. But since then my certainty has gone.'

'Really? How unusual for you.' He shifted his weight on the seat.

'You mean?'

'Well, you're usually pretty certain about everything, aren't you, Min? Certain you wanted to sleep with me. And then the next morning certain you didn't want to have any-thing more to do with me. No ifs, buts or maybes. Just your fucking certainty.'

She felt sick. She looked out of the window.

'Nothing to say, nothing more to add?' He leaned back and half turned towards her.

'I said all I have to say, Conor. It was lovely, I mean I really enjoyed it, but look at my situation. For a start I'm older than you. Secondly, I've two kids who need all of me.'

'And thirdly you don't fancy me, you don't want me, you certainly don't love me.' He spat the words in her direction.

'Oh, come on, Conor, cut me some slack here. You don't honestly mean to say that you love me, do you? After, after, just.'

'Just a boozy shag in a crap hotel, is that what you mean? Too much alcohol, too much excitement, not enough sense. Is that it?'

'Yes, OK, if that's the way you want to see it.' Anger washed through her. 'You're a great ride Conor, but not much else.'

She got out of the car and slammed the door behind her. She walked across the road to the railings. The cherry trees cast long shadows across the grass. Somewhere over on the other side of the square a firework exploded with a loud bang and a sunburst of colour lit up the sky. She heard the car door open and close. She heard his footsteps. She felt him beside her.

'Look, I'm sorry I shouldn't.' He paused.

She turned towards him. 'No, don't apologize. It's not your fault. I shouldn't have done it. You know, Conor, these past weeks, they've really been decision time for me. I've been treading water for long enough. I've got to decide. Do I want to be a real guard again? Or do I want to be a housewife and a mother and a part-timer. And do you know something? Being with you, seeing how you operate, how you work, how you love your job, it's shown me the way forward. And I can't let go of that. I've got to stay with it. Do you understand?'

He nodded.

She turned around and leaned against the railings. 'You know what I think? I think we should pay Susan Cassidy another visit. It's getting late. She must have heard from him by now.'

She moved away.

'Are you with me?' she asked.

He nodded. He stretched his arms up above his head, catching one elbow with the other hand.

'You're on,' he said.

Nick pulled himself up onto the wall and hesitated for a moment. Then he dropped to the grass below. The door to the summer house was open. He turned and looked back. Susan was standing at the kitchen door. He lifted his hand to her. She did not move.

He had begged her.

'Listen to me, please. Listen to me. You've got to believe me. The last time I saw the masks was that morning. I went into Marianne's room and she and Owen were sitting up on her bed. They were glueing the feathers onto them, finishing them off. I did not see them again. Ever. I have no idea what happened to them. Absolutely none. Susan, you have to believe me. Please just give me an hour. And I promise you it will all be over then.'

She didn't reply.

'An hour is all I ask. Then you can call the police. Then I will do whatever they want. Please.'

It had come to him that afternoon when he saw the photograph of Lizzie Anderson. Something Róisín had said. *We watched you and that slag from up the road. We watched you.* The window to Gina's studio was huge. She and her husband had knocked out the original rectangular sash and put in a large plate-glass square. *You need curtains*, he'd said to her. But she'd laughed. *Me*, she said, *curtains, the idea of it.* They'd watched Lizzie too. Beautiful, young, naked. Offered up to their gaze. He was sure of it.

He moved towards the summer house. He stepped inside. The floor creaked beneath his weight. He squatted and rummaged through the litter of dead leaves and torn paper. His fingers found the tobacco tin. He prised open the lid. He took out the candle. He lit it. He cupped his hands around the flame until it gained strength. Then he turned the candle on its side and let the wax drip down onto the window sill until there was a soft malleable heap. He turned it upright again and pressed it down firmly. Then he sat down on the floor, his back to the wall. He closed his eyes. And he waited.

'How much longer are we going to have to wait for your husband to come home, Dr Cassidy?' Conor's tone was cold.

'I've told you already. I tried his mobile but it seems he has it switched off.' Her voice was equally cold. 'I'm not his keeper. I don't clock him in and out. Perhaps, if you've something to say, you might say, it to me.'

'Susan.' Min moved closer towards her. 'I'm not sure you realize how serious this is. Do you know that among the material that Conor found on Nick's laptop were pictures of a number of boys who have been identified as victims of William Metcalfe? The same William Metcalfe whose wife gave me the magpie mask.'

Susan didn't reply.

'So, if you don't mind, I think we'll wait.'

She nodded. She stepped aside and showed them into the sitting room.

'You'll join us.' Conor's tone was friendly but firm. She nodded again. She put more coal on the fire, then sat down, her back to the square. The house was silent. Outside more and more fireworks began to explode across the night sky.

'It's a bad time of year, this, for cats and dogs.' Conor stood up and looked out the window. 'My granny's poodle used to go bananas at Halloween.'

Min smiled. 'Not a very appealing idea, is it, a poodle that's bananas?'

Susan didn't respond. She looked exhausted, tense, terrified. Min leaned towards her.

'Look,' she said, 'I'm sure there's some kind of an explanation for all this. And I'm sure when we find Nick he'll be able to tell us what it all means.'

'When you find him?' Susan's voice was querulous.

'When we find him.' Conor sat down again. 'We are looking for him. His description has been circulated. There's nowhere he can go. You do know that, don't you?'

Nick opened his eyes. He looked towards the house. The light was on in the kitchen. Chris and Róisín were standing at the door. He watched them walk down the steps to the garden. He felt inside his coat. His fingers slipped across the CDs. He laid them on the floor. The light from the candle glanced across their shiny surfaces. Rainbows danced and bands of colour flicked and flitted from edge to gleaming edge. He leaned over and looked down. His own face looked back up at him. And the faces of all the others whose images were trapped within those discs of polished metal.

'You found them.' Chris stood at the door. 'I wondered if you would.' He stepped into the summer house, his sister behind him. They sat down, cross-legged, side by side and faced Nick.

'And now.' Chris put his arm around her and pulled her head to his shoulder. Her green eyes stared. They were like stones, Nick thought. The kind you'd find at the bottom of a rock pool. Lustrous when wet. But dull and lifeless when the water dried from their surface.

'And now.' Nick repeated the words.

'And now you'll want to know. Why and what and how and where. Isn't that right?'

Nick nodded.

Chris turned to his sister. She lifted her face towards him. He kissed her gently on the mouth.

'Will we tell him, sweetness? Will we tell him all the clever things we've done?'

'Let's start with where.' Nick shifted his weight. 'Where did you put my son? Is he here somewhere? Is he underneath us? You had to move him didn't you? When the swimming pool was built in your grandmother's garden. You had to shift him from there. That was it, wasn't it?'

Chris smiled and pulled Róisín closer. He smoothed her long dark skirt down over her legs. She was wearing boots, laced up the instep.

'Clever boy, aren't you? Very clever. Clever like Owen.

He was such a clever boy. But he wasn't smart. He didn't know when to leave well alone. Did he, Róisín? That was his problem, clever but not smart.'

Róisín did not answer. She picked up Chris's hand and held it over her face. She pressed his fingers to her jaw, then moved them down so they were around her throat. Her dull green eyes stared at Nick.

'We'll tell him. We'll put him out of his misery. Shall we?'

She closed her eyes.

'Close your eyes, Nick, and open your imagination. I'm going to tell you a story. And you can provide the pictures. Are you ready? Are you paying attention? Once upon a time.

'Once upon a time there was a boy. He was eight years old. He had thick blond hair which stood up in a cockscomb on the top of his head. He had bright blue eyes. He had long thin legs and arms. He lived in a big house with his father and his mother and his minder. But she wasn't just his minder. She was his love. He would do anything she wanted him to do. But she didn't love him the way he loved her. She loved another. And she would do anything for him that he wanted her to do. It was a triangle really. Each dependent on the other behaving in a certain way.

'And then the boy became jealous of the other two. And that day, 31st October 1991, he saw them together. And he didn't like it. He was a clever boy. He could read very well, too well for his age. That day he read a newspaper. There was a picture of a girl and an article about her death. And the boy knew suddenly what to do. He knew he had seen her picture somewhere else. And he knew who had taken it.

'He arrived in the basement. He shouldn't have been there. He had been told not to come. But he was there. And he said to me that he was going to tell the police about the pictures I had taken of Lizzie. He had seen them. Not all of them. But enough. He was angry. He was crying and shouting. I couldn't get him to shut up.'

'So you killed him.'

'No, he didn't. I did.' Róisín moved Chris's hand from her throat. Her gaze was calm and cold. 'I killed him. I couldn't let him do anything that would hurt Chris. I couldn't. So I grabbed him round the throat. And I squeezed and squeezed and squeezed. Just the way I'd seen Chris kill Lizzie. And that was that. He was dead. And Chris was safe. It was all so easy.'

She sighed. She leaned against Chris and took hold of his hand again. She kissed his palm. Nick swallowed. He tried to speak, but his mouth was dry. His tongue refused to move. His lips refused to open.

'Chris killed Lizzie.' The words came out in a sudden rush.

'That's right. The day she laughed at me when I came to her in the shed. The day she said she didn't want me. That she was doing OK.' He mimicked her voice. 'She was fine, she said, she didn't want any kid around her. I was too young for her. I was only thirteen, and she was fifteen and she had a real man, she said. And she told me to get lost. To leave her alone.'

'But you didn't.'

'No, I didn't. She couldn't get away with that. I'd been watching her for weeks posing for her picture. She knew I was there. She'd seen me. She'd seen me follow her when she went to meet him, her real man.' Again he mimicked her voice. 'So I did what had to be done.'

'And I saw him. I had gone to meet him. I saw it all. And we were both so surprised, weren't we, how easy it was.' Róisín's eyes shone now. Sea-water green again.

The wind shook the summer house's wooden frame. The flame of the candle flickered.

'It was the surprise that made it so easy. The last thing she expected.' Chris smiled.

'The last thing she expected,' Róisín repeated. 'She was laughing at Chris. And I pushed her. And she fell over.'

'She was drunk, wasn't she? She'd been drinking vodka with the real man. And when Róisín pushed her—'

'Just a little push, not a big one.'

'Just a little push, not a big one, she toppled right over, just like one of those dolls that babies have, the kind that can't stay upright.'

'And then Chris jumped on her, didn't you, Chris?'

'Yes I jumped on her and I grabbed her. It was the surprise. The last thing she was expecting.'

'And she just kept on laughing until she couldn't laugh any more.'

'And we got away with it, didn't we, Róisín. No one ever knew it was us. No one ever suspected that we had anything to do with her death. We kept on thinking someone would suspect us. But they didn't. And after that we realized that we could do anything with anyone. Anything at all.'

'But Owen found out and he was going to tell.' Nick's voice was level.

'Owen found out. Owen was going to tell. Owen was

dead. Owen was wrapped in a blanket and hidden in the cupboard under the stairs.'

'But not—' Nick swallowed again. 'But not before you photographed him. I saw the picture.'

'Yes, we did that. There's money in those pictures. They're rare, they're precious. I knew. And when Mr Metcalfe came I told him I'd have something special for him in a few days. I gave him a couple of the masks to take with him and I gave him a little picture of Owen that I found in his pocket. And he was well pleased.'

'Metcalfe. The man the guards want to talk to me about. You knew him?'

'Oh yes, I knew him well. I'd known him for a while. He was a friend of my father's. Oh.' Chris looked amused. 'You didn't know about my father, did you? He was the expert. He taught me what to do. Isn't that right, Róisín? This was all Daddy's idea.'

She smiled at him and nodded. A sudden gust of wind shook the summer house. The candle flickered. Nick cleared his throat. He felt cold and sick. He felt set apart as if the words that came from his mouth were not his words. He opened his mouth and spoke again.

'So, you killed him. You took the pictures of him. You wrapped him in a blanket. You hid him in a cupboard. And then? What did you do then?'

'What did I do then, Róisín? Do you remember?'

She nodded. 'I remember. You hid him until it was dark. And then there was such a fuss because he was missing. You said you'd go and see if you could find him. You didn't lie. You just didn't say that you knew where he was. So I carried him out to the car, which was parked in the back lane. Then when you came back you drove him to granny's house. You hid him in the compost bin. Then the next day we went to help her with her garden. She always liked you to dig it for her in the autumn. I stayed inside with her and made her tea and showed her the dance I was learning for my ballet recital. And you dug over her vegetable patch and buried him. And that was that.'

'But I thought—' Chris's voice chimed with hers. 'I thought that when our granny died she would leave the house to us. But she didn't. She left it to the school. And they decided to put in a swimming pool. So I think you can imagine what I had to do then.'

He sighed again.

'Why are you telling me this, Chris?' Nick sat up straight. 'It was you who killed Marianne, wasn't it?'

'Ah, you're wrong there. You're wrong about that one. It was an accident. A genuine accident. Well.' He paused and looked away for a moment. 'Perhaps not quite. She didn't want to have sex with me. She tried to stop me, but I wasn't having any of that. So I pushed her up against the wall and to keep her quiet I banged her head, just a couple of times, just enough so she wouldn't struggle. And then afterwards, well she couldn't stand, so I laid her down on the track. And, then, and then . . .'

'But my watch? How did my watch end up there?'

'Your watch. Now that was a master stroke.' He leaned forward and picked up the CDs. He handed them to Róisín.

'You're much too trusting, you know. You let your little friend, Emir, poor little voiceless Emir, rummage around in all your things. And he found your watch and he stole it. And I took it from him. I was actually going to give it back to you. But then I found another use for it. Didn't I, Róisín?'

She nodded. She picked up the candle from the window sill. She held the CDs over its flame in turn until they were blackened and scorched and twisted out of shape. She laid them on the floor again.

'And did you teach him what to do with the computer? Did you do that too? What did you do to him to make him show me the pictures? Did you hurt him?'

He smiled. 'Hurt Emir? Not at all. I bribed him that was all. A few sweets here. A bit of kiss and a cuddle there. Emir wants to be loved. He doesn't have a father of his own. So he's always looking for one. The social workers and the shrinks and the police call it grooming. I call it having fun. It's what our daddy did with us. Oh, don't get me wrong. Not the computer part. That was a bit after his time, you understand. But before computers there were books and magazines and films and then there were video cameras. You get the picture, I'm sure. There are generations of people like me and my father. There was his father before him and probably his father before him too. But it's why we've decided to tell you all this. Isn't it, sister of mine?'

She nodded.

'Tell him now, why are we doing this and what are we going to do next?'

She turned her head. She looked at Nick.

'We're shedding our burdens. That's what we're doing. We've made our decision. We've had enough. We're going away. And we're going to do one good thing before we leave.'

'And what's that, sister?'

'We're giving him back his lost boy.'

'And in return?' Nick leaned forward. 'What do you want of me?'

'In return you will give us time.' Chris stood up and pulled the girl to her feet. 'We're going now.' He swayed gently from side to side. 'I have one last thing for you.' He stepped out into the garden. 'Come with me.'

Nick hesitated.

'Come on.' Chris giggled. 'I won't hurt you, if that's what you're thinking. I have no interest in hurting you.' He beckoned to him and Nick slowly followed him out into the darkness.

'Here.' Chris walked around the summer house. A long-handled spade was propped against the wall. He lifted it above his head and brought it down hard.

'Here,' he repeated, 'dig here. Dig deep. And you will find him.'

Min stood in the Cassidys' kitchen in the darkness. She had offered to make tea.

'I know where everything is,' she said. 'I'll do it.'

She put her hand on the light switch. Then she stopped. She moved to the window. A small flame flickered in the Gouldings' garden. She opened the door and walked out onto the top step. She could see a figure moving below and hear the sound of a spade. It made a steady rhythmic thud. She hurried down the stairs and across the grass to the wall. She jumped up at it, digging her fingers into the spaces between the granite stones, her toes struggling to find purchase. She pulled herself on top, then dropped gently down the other side. A candle was propped against the low step into the summer house. In its light she could see a man's body lying on the ground. Its face was covered in blood and more blood was seeping onto the grass in a spreading dark pool. Sods of earth were piled beside it in a haphazard mound. And Nick was kneeling, scrabbling in the hole he had dug.

'Nick,' she said quietly, 'what have you done? What are you doing?'

He looked up at her. He was crying. He was holding something small and round cupped in his hands.

'Don't come any closer,' he said. 'You have children too. I don't want you to see this.'

She made as if to jump down beside him.

'Please.' He looked up at her. 'Please get Susan. He needs his mother now.'

Thirty-one

It was a strange thing to find, those shoes lined up neatly on the shore of the upper lake at Glendalough. The forest ranger bent down to have a closer look. They were women's boots, the kind that lace snugly up the instep. Size five, black, with a neat Cuban heel.

Suicides by drowning, they always take off their shoes. Sometimes they leave their clothes behind too. But not in this case. The lake at Glendalough is deep and cold. It doesn't easily give up its secrets. The search was abandoned after a week. One day, Min thought, as she watched the bright orange inflatable and its crew of Garda divers return across the choppy grey water, the body of Róisín Goulding, the tormentor of Lizzie Anderson, the killer of Owen Cassidy would surface. One day. And she would join her brother, Chris, and they would be inseparable at last.

They buried Owen for a second time next to Nick's mother and father. Nick designed a simple headstone. Smooth limestone with his son's name carved into it and the year of his birth and the year of his death. Nick and Susan were constant visitors to his grave. They brought flowers in spring and summer. They were a couple again now. It had taken a while. But they both knew that whatever they had gone through in the past their future was with each other. They usually came together to see Owen. Hand in hand. Arm in arm. But as Susan's pregnancy became more advanced Nick would come on his own. He didn't stay long. Just long enough to tell his son the latest news. How his mother was getting on. How they were longing for the day when their baby would be born. How they knew it would never replace him. But it would give them hope for the future.

'The fox has left the garden now,' he told his son. 'There were too many strange people disturbing the quiet, threatening her safety and that of her cubs. And the summer house is gone too. But not to worry. She'll find another den for next year's litter. You can be sure of that.'

Sometimes Min drives along the square and past the house. She slows down but doesn't stop. She doesn't go in. She saw the birth notice in the paper. She was pleased for them both. Her boys don't read the star child story any longer. They've moved on. And so has she.

She will be a witness at the trial of Nick Cassidy for the manslaughter of Chris Goulding. Opinion is divided as to what the outcome will be. A custodial sentence she thinks. And she thinks that he will cope well. He will behave himself. He will volunteer his sevices for the prison's school. And he will be released within a few short years. And it will all be over. Although sometimes at the time of dog and wolf she thinks she sees out of the corner of her eye, a familiar figure. A girl with a slight body, white blonde hair and dull green eyes. And she wonders about the shoes on the lakeshore. Watch out, she thinks, watch out.